VENGEANCE FROM THE DEEP
BOOK 1
PLIOSAUR

RUSS ELLIOTT

~~~~~

*This book is dedicated to the memory
of the greatest man I've ever known,
Bob Elliott, my dad.*

**T-Rex Skull
3·5 Feet**

**Pliosaur Lower Jaw
9·8 Feet**

No Genetic Engineering Necessary . . .
IT'S ALREADY HERE.

On June 12, 1985, renowned wildlife enthusiast, Owen Burnham, in the presence of family members, discovered an incredible wash-up on South Africa's Bungalow Beach. The carcass was sixteen feet long, had a long pair of jaws containing eighty teeth, a pair of nostrils, and two pairs of paddle fins. . . paddle fins that could have only come from a prehistoric monster thought extinct for sixty-five million years.

Also startling was the fact that, other than a torn rear flipper, the carcass showed no signs of decomposition—*it was entirely intact!* Sadly, when Owen returned with his instruments to fully document the apparent juvenile pliosaur carcass, he found the locals had already disposed of it.

It is this and other sightings that have led many to believe pliosaurs still exist somewhere in the deep, dark reaches of our contemporary seas.

~~~

In the last century, thousands of plesiosaur and pliosaur sightings have been reported throughout the world's lakes and oceans.

www.vengeancefromthedeep.com

Chapter 1
KUTA KEB-LA

Three years earlier

A loud clap of thunder brought fifty-five-year-old Captain Frank Addelson back to consciousness. A hazy darkness flashed before him until he drifted out. He inhaled the salty air, and that's when the pain came. His shoulder joints ached deeply, and his wrists were on fire. "Aaagh!" he grimaced, feeling like he was being pulled in half. As his vision cleared, it was easy to see why. He was stretched out in an X shape, bound between two huge posts by wrists and ankles—and as naked as the day he was born.

"What the—?"

He had once awakened buck naked in a Durban pig's trough, but the lads at Murphy's Law Saloon weren't capable of this. The roughly hewn poles were spaced about fifteen feet apart. A glance down showed the pilings leading into the misty, black sea. Lapping waves transformed into froth against the wood.

What kind of madness is this? Squinting his eyes, he glanced all around him, only to discover that he was inside a massive underground lagoon. Twinkling in the pitch, a series of small fires outlined the hazy shoreline. Their dancing flames reflected eerily along the water's edge. The air was foul. Every time the wind calmed, a vile stench rose from the pilings.

Maybe that's it. He gazed into the flames. *Maybe I died at sea, and this is hell.*

His vision blurred. He almost blacked out until the pain once again awakened him. He groaned, throwing his head straight back. Looking up, he saw the poles reaching high above toward the roof of the cavern. A fiery torch atop each piling illuminated dagger-like stalactites. He felt the heat radiating from the lapping flames, yet an icy chill crept over his bare skin.

No, this isn't hell. At least not yet.

Above the poles, and strung beneath the roof of the cave were a series of ropes and pulleys. Best he could tell, it looked like rigging from an old sailing ship. The ropes led to a towering cliff off to his left that hung eerily in the darkness. Its rocky ledge was illuminated by a single torch.

"WHO PUT ME IN HERE?" The captain's voice roared through the cavern.

The pounding in his head made it difficult to think. Vaguely, he recalled piloting a fishing trawler off Port Elizabeth, South Africa. Images of a hostile storm flashed before him—the forty-foot swell off port side, clinging to a lifejacket while rolling over huge waves in the pounding rain. Lastly, he remembered waking on a dark shoreline.

Like a fly snared in a spider's web, Frank squirmed helplessly between the ropes. A loud crack of thunder resonated through the cave. As the deafening rumble faded into the distance, it seemed to take on a rhythm—or was it something else . . . a drumbeat? Slowly, the tribal drums grew louder, echoing impressively throughout the vast cavern. Squinting into the pitch, Frank inhaled a deep breath of salty sea air. The mist cleared further, and then he could see them.

Like demons in hell, countless dark figures glistened in the flames along the banks. Every face wore a strange white stripe. Spears in hands, their shimmering bodies writhed like serpents to the drumbeat.

The cave fell darker. The wind swirled around Frank's bare flesh, growing cooler.

KABOOM! A flash of lightning illuminated the cavern, and for a split second he could see his captors clearly. With half-painted faces, their blue-black bodies seemed frozen in the light. And then darkness returned, leaving only the silhouetted figures writhing in the hellish flames.

Frank twisted, screaming between the ropes, "Take me down from here, you black devils!" he snarled. "Cut me down!"

There was a squeak from above.

Peering up, he saw a small tribesman dangling by one of the ropes. The little man scurried across the rope like a monkey, muscles glistening in the torchlight until he disappeared behind the ledge of the nearby cliff. Beyond the ledge, Frank saw more shadowy faces peering down at him, their eyes shining in the pitch.

A loud squeak from one of the pulleys.

Another squeak. And then another. The ropes above the captain grew taut and came to life, twisting and turning beneath the stalactites of the cave.

SWOOOOSH.

Frank struggled to look upward as a large, brown object glided down a rope and squeaked to a stop, swaying ominously above his head. It was a four-foot round sack, constructed of animal hide. The stench was undeniable . . . and unbearable.

"What are you doing?" Frank screamed. "What have I done?" His pleas echoed through the huge cavern, unanswered.

This is madness. What kind of nightmare have I awakened in? Straining against the ropes, Frank's eyes darted back down to the hazy shoreline. One of the tribesmen appeared to be some kind of chief. Bathed in firelight, the portly man stood and raised his arms as though in worship. The drumbeat ceased. Spears and torches stopped waving, and the banks fell quiet. The crashing sea could once again be heard. The chief pointed toward the posts that held Frank's body. Thunder cracked. Lightning flickered off every half-painted face as they all turned and looked Frank's way.

If this is a nightmare, now would be a good time to wake up. But Frank's aching shoulders and the ropes burning into his wrists were all too real.

"KUTA KEB-LA!" bellowed the chief.

The surrounding tribesmen roared with delight, "T'lay, t'lay!"

Thunder rumbled. Lightning flared.

Upon signal from the chief, a tall tribesman took off along the bank, spear in hand.

WHOOOOSH!

Frank's eyes widened as the spear arced over the lagoon, flashing through the darkness, plummeting toward the posts. He screamed, thinking the spear would go right through his chest. But it didn't. It struck the sack above his head.

SWOOOOSH!

A gushing warmth cascaded over his naked skin and splashed down into the black water. Chunks of flesh pelted him. He writhed in the warm blood, as he screamed, strung up like a pig between the poles. Out of the periphery of his vision, he could see a length of intestine dangling from his right arm like a snake. He shook the ropes violently until the intestine slid off and plopped into the black sea, coiling beneath the waves.

Twisting frantically, Frank looked down at the blood spilling from his body and into the water below. A scarlet cloud swelled between the poles.

The drumming intensified.

A shout went up from one of the tribesmen. He pointed to the far side of the lagoon.

A shark fin broke the surface.

Panic surged through Frank's body. Another glance down showed small metallic blurs—a shoal of fish—shooting by the pilings, fleeing the area.

A trail of urine splattered against the sea—Frank's bladder contracting from sheer terror.

The men along the banks roared with fury. Rhythmically pounding the blunt end of their spears against the rocks, they began to shout, "T'lay, t'lay! Kuta Keb-la." The chant grew louder and louder, echoing madly through the cavern.

The drinking, the divorce, his daughter's tears—every mistake of

Frank's life flashed before him. "God, no," he shook his head. "Not now. Not like this."

The tall fin emerged from the pitch in unison with a crack of thunder. Then a flash of lightning illuminated the giant, torpedo-shaped body beneath the fin. The great white circled below, attracted to the blood still draining into the lagoon. A former army sergeant, Frank had seen action on the front line, but he'd never known fear like this. Had the drumming increased in tempo . . . or was it his pounding heart? His breathing was rapid and shallow.

The ropes tore into his flesh as he twisted more violently in an attempt to pull his hands free.

Below, the giant shark glided between the pilings. The crimson waters divided in the wake of the passing fin. Frank's heart was about to burst. He didn't know how much longer he could survive the enormous foreboding in his heart. He knew that with just one leap from the water, the creature could easily reach him, devour him.

His tormented screams echoed in the darkness.

"You'll burn in hell for this, you bloody savages. Burn in hell," he shouted. "BURN IN HEELLLLL!"

~~~

On the rocky shoreline, one of the chief's guards watched eagerly from behind the flames. Thirty yards out in the center of the lagoon, the sacrificial offering twisted hideously between the poles. His painted-red flesh shimmered; his screams muted by the thundering drums.

~~~

Frank's eyes were riveted to the approaching great white. His body quivered uncontrollably.

Then, in an instant, he stopped moving. His terror and pain was diverted completely by what he saw beyond the great white's fin.

Again, the surface of the lagoon rose and dropped as if something of immense proportion had stirred beneath it. A swell sent out from the movement slapped the posts, sending a cool mist around his bare thighs.

~~~

Along the banks, the drumming increased in tempo. Anticipation swelled. Shouts and cheers rose from the tribesmen as the fin arced through the darkness and turned toward the posts. The great white lunged from the lagoon. The shark's hyper-extended jaws soared above the surface, zeroing in on the bound man.

As it did, a new set of colossal jaws burst from the water. Machete-sized, spiked teeth surrounded the great white shark *and* the sacrifice, engulfing them both in a single split second.

The mammoth creature had elicited such a splash that it was

impossible to make out its lines. All the men could see were jaws—massive, indomitable, twelve feet or more in circumference—closing around its prey, ripping the man from the wooden poles, leaving only his hands and feet still tied to them.

"Kuta Keb-la! Kuta Keb-la!" The tribesmen went wild with religious fervor as the body of Captain Frank Addelson disappeared beneath the waves, into the jaws of . . . the beast.

A clap of thunder echoed through the cave.

A flicker of lightning, and a huge swell sent out from the plunging head crashed into the rocks, sending a spray over the cheering crowd. In the center of the lagoon, the water boiled beneath the empty pilings, while smoke from the extinguished torches curled and drifted upward to the stalactites.

Chapter 2
SEARCHING FOR "OLD FOUR LEGS"
Present Day

It was quarter past eleven by the time John Paxton wheeled his rented Jeep onto the Port Elizabeth College campus. It was late November, and on this side of the globe, the middle of summer. *But was it always this hot?* He gasped as he crossed the sunbaked parking lot. Raking moist hair from his eyes, he hurried along a sidewalk, dodging students who were obviously more acclimated to the heat.

Having attended the school two decades ago and returning just last year, he assumed he could find the professor's office. But now that he was here, every one of the ivy-covered buildings looked the same. *Nice move . . . forgot to write down the building number again.*

After canceling another expedition and paying an exorbitant airfare to get to South Africa on such short notice, he didn't want to be late for the appointment. Besides, this expedition was different. This wasn't just another one of the professor's witch-hunts or expeditions based on a hunch or hearsay. No, that much he could sense in her voice the moment she had called. As the professor had pointed out over the phone, this one could prove to be the crowning jewel in an otherwise stale career. *She always did know how to push my buttons,* John thought. But the old girl was right about one thing: on a find this significant, other archeologists would be waiting in the wings to take his place. Being late wasn't an option.

John stopped and peered up at one of the old buildings. "Computer Center," he muttered. "Not this one." He glanced at his watch then picked up his pace while his thoughts raced ahead. Why the professor had selected him for this particular expedition was still a mystery. John was more accustomed to excavations on dry land, like the fossilized eggs of the prehistoric elephant bird of Madagascar he had helped the professor unearth eight months ago. Ichthyology was hardly his field.

Two young coeds carrying tennis rackets were heading along the sidewalk. In passing, one of the girls flashed him a shy smile. John wondered briefly if she thought he was a teacher or maybe a student. *Yeah right.* He glanced back. *They're practically children.* At forty-two, John didn't consider himself old. Other than a scar on his left eyebrow, he knew his smooth complexion seemed to contradict his years of excavating in the hot sun. But every time he visited this campus, the students appeared to get younger. Now he felt like he was visiting a middle school.

He turned onto another winding sidewalk, and it was more of the same. Rows of ivy-leafed geraniums, striking pink flowers common to South Africa, cascaded down ivory-colored walls. He passed two more identical buildings. Two more lady coeds. He looked at one of the buildings again. *Was that the one?* No.

"I'll never find her office." Then he sensed a familiarity to the building at the end of the sidewalk. Walking closer, he saw the bronze imprint of a prehistoric fish above the double doors. "Figures . . . the last building."

Opening the door, a burst of air conditioning brought welcome relief from the blazing heat. *Okay, right building, now which room?* He squinted his eyes as he thought. *Wait a minute . . . three oh two, second room on the right!* John opened the door to the sound of creaking hinges. As his eyes adjusted to the dark, he saw a striking, silver-haired Englishwoman in her early sixties. She was seated behind a desk in front of a large aquarium. Beneath the faint aroma of cigar smoke, the room held a strange, ancient scent, matching the surroundings.

"Well, tally along, take a seat. I haven't got all day." The professor waved him closer.

John smiled. "Professor Atkins. Crotchety as always."

"John Paxton, I presume," countered the professor. "Discourteous as always. And late."

John walked deeper into the professor's lair. Various skulls of prehistoric creatures, including a velociraptor, stared out from illuminated nooks in the wall to his right. Anchored to the wall to his left was a six-foot-long mammoth tusk recovered from the Bering Sea. Past it was a series of flat sheets of rock containing the fossilized indentations of fish from the Devonian period. John passed all these interesting items without a second glance.

The professor stood behind her desk and extended a hand. "Welcome back to Port Elizabeth. Seriously, I appreciate you coming out here on such short notice."

Up close, her square-rimmed glasses magnified piercing gray eyes. As always, John imagined how stunning she must have been in her youth. Her coarse fingers and battered nails contrasted with her beauty, attesting that she was still doing her own excavating.

"I see you're still not acclimated to our weather?"

John nodded without a word. He pulled out an antique chair in front of the desk and sat down. He could almost feel the professor's anticipation of his questions. He didn't disappoint. "Okay, what exactly did you see that night?" he asked. "Repeat what you told me over the phone. Start with the village . . . and exactly where was this island?"

"Eager to get on with it, are you? That's what I always liked about you, John. Not one for, as the Americans call it, chitchat."

The professor picked up a lit cigar from an ashtray, drew on it, and spewed the smoke from the side of her mouth. "Handelsgold," she said, withdrawing the stogie from her lips and holding it delicately between her fingers as only an Englishwoman could. She eyed the cigar in her hand. "Dreadful habit, I thought at first. My second husband, Randall, got me hooked on these bloody things. I've acquired quite a taste for them over the years ... too bad I can't say the same about his lazy carcass."

She took another drag from the cigar and paused as if intentionally drawing out the moment. A tendril of smoke curled from the side of her mouth and rose beside her square-rimmed glasses. An excited look appeared in her eyes that seemed to brighten the room.

"Okay, I was on a little island off South Africa. It's about three hundred miles southeast of Port Elizabeth and was completely off the charts until only three years ago. Seems the Navy discovered it while searching for a fishing trawler that went missing in the vicinity. Oddly, the Navy found the capsized trawler less than a mile from this tiny island, but not a trace of her eight-man crew. They assumed that the sharks got to them before they could make the short swim to shore."

The professor leaned closer. Bubbles from the aquarium's regulator rose behind her head. "Anyway, our expedition involved studying a remote fishing village on the island's southern tip. After a quick gander at the village, Chief Omad led us into a large hut, where we were seated at a table. The chief stood, clapped his hands, and shouted, 'Unda-Kuta-Legway.' Then someone leaned over to me and said, 'That mean let's eat.'

"That someone was Kota. As a youth, a visiting missionary took Kota back with him to South Africa where he was educated in Cape Town. I'm not sure how many years of schooling the lad received, but he spoke Afrikaans and some English. Later he returned to the island and became the villagers' link to the outside world. He was like a shadow ... never far from the chief's side."

John listened eagerly as the professor spoke, perched on the edge of her chair. "Anyway, they served us these exceptionally large fish. I thought nothing of it at first because good-sized fish are not uncommon in those waters—especially that far out. I must say it tasted horrible in spite of all the seasoning, and it was extremely bony for its size. I continued to eat this foul-tasting fish because I didn't want to risk offending Chief Omad. He was seated right next to me and watched my every move. I mean, I wanted to spit the fish into my napkin, but there were no napkins. It nearly made me ill."

"Yes, yes, I get the picture," John cut in with a laugh. "They weren't very tasty." He impatiently motioned for her to continue.

"Yes, anyway, as I was eating this fish, I noticed an odd fin configuration along its pectoral region, and asked myself, *where have I seen this structure before?* It just seemed so bloody familiar. Then it hit me. I was eating a coelacanth! A prehistoric fish that was, until recently, thought to have been extinct since the Cretaceous period, nearly seventy million years ago."

John's brows raised. Only the low hum of the aquarium disturbed the long silence. The professor pulled a drawing of a fish from her desk drawer and set it in front of him. She pointed to the fin structure along its underside.

"*Old Four Legs*, that's what Professor J.L.B. Smith, a South African ichthyologist, nicknamed it when the first specimen was discovered off the tip of South Africa in 1938."

"I'm familiar with the coelacanth discovery," John said, looking up from the drawing. The professor seemed not to hear and tapped the illustration. "He called it that because the pectoral and pelvic fins looked very much like legs. These fins even move in opposite directions of one another when the fish swims, the same way animals move their limbs as they walk.

"Catching a living coelacanth was smashing news back in '38— practically the marine equivalent of running across a living dinosaur."

John nodded. "I didn't realize there were any colonies that far off the coast. Why didn't you bring a specimen back with you?"

The professor leaned back in her chair and folded her arms. "That's just it! When I asked where they got the fish, Kota told me they've been catching them all around the island for generations and that the waters are full of them. Then he smiled and said, 'Very tasty, yes?'

"I guess the bloke thought I was trying to pay him a compliment. But when I tried to explain the scientific significance of a new colony of these fish ... well, let's just say the lads became considerably less cordial. They became extremely agitated. Kota said, 'There no more fish. You must go now.' He practically pulled me from the table.

"I tried to explain that I was sorry if I offended him or his people in any way. But he didn't seem to hear a word I said. Then they literally forced us from the village and escorted us all the way back to our helicopter." She paused, remembering the moment, then sighed. She waved her hands in the air—*empty*. "So, there you have it. That's all I know."

John rubbed the bottom of his chin. "That's an interesting story, but I don't see what all the excitement's about concerning another coelacanth sighting. Pardon me for saying it, but it's not like you discovered the first one. You just said local fishermen have been catching them off the South African coast since '38."

The professor leaned forward and peered over her glasses. "Yes, that's true. But they've never appeared in such abundance. Take a look at this." The professor pulled out a map of South Africa and the surrounding waters of the Indian Ocean. John stood in order to see the map clearly. The point of her pen rested on an area east of the southern tip of Africa. "The Chalumna River near East London. This is where the first coelacanth was caught in 1938."

Her pen made a red X on the area, then moved around the coastline until it stopped in the Mozambique Channel. She made another X on a series of small islands and said, "Fourteen years later, a second coelacanth was caught near the Comoro Islands." The professor then moved her pen straight out and drew a circle in the Indian Ocean. "The island is located here. Notice anything interesting about its location?"

John studied the red circle and its reference to the other marked areas. The professor nodded at the map. "See? It's right between the first and second sighting. This island also has many deep caves and volcanic drop-offs similar to the Comoro Islands. So it's really no surprise that it harbors undiscovered coelacanth colonies. Kota said that they've been catching these fish in abundance for generations, for as long as their ancestors can remember. So, chances are, and remember this is only a theory, that we can trace the coelacanth back to this island for at least one hundred years, maybe even back to the beginning of the Cretaceous period or whenever the earth's shifting plates collided and first created this tiny little island."

John looked up from the map. "I suppose it's possible."

The professor thumped her pen on the red circle in the Indian Ocean. "If this is true, it would be safe to conclude that coelacanths inhabited this island coast long before the first and second sightings off the coast of South Africa. This would then lead me to believe that the coastal area of this island is, and has always been, a primary breeding ground for coelacanths, possibly for millions of years. And that the first and second sightings off South Africa were merely misplaced residents from this island."

John nodded and began to speak, but the enthusiastic little woman raised a finger. "In other words, I believe that all the coelacanth colonies along South Africa today originated from this island."

The professor paused, and her eyes grew brighter. The chair made a long squeak as she leaned closer to the map. "There was also something else I noticed that night," she whispered excitedly. "Something truly extraordinary if it turns out to be what I think it is."

John sat back down and pulled his chair closer to the desk as the little silver-haired woman continued. "The coelacanth is one of the groups from the Sarcopterygian subclass of bony fishes. From this subclass, three very significant groups emerged with paired fins containing bones and muscles. More importantly, they were the only fish that possessed functional lungs."

"The fleshy-finned fishes. Weren't they from the Devonian period?" asked John.

"Yes, precisely. I guess you paid some attention in class after all," she said with a light chuckle, then back to her serious tone. "They all first appeared during the Devonian, in which three groups emerged. First, you have the coelacanths, with their fleshy fins and lungs that became swim bladders to regulate the fish's buoyancy. Then, you have the lungfish, which have lobe fins and crude lungs that allow the creature to burrow into the mud during times of drought and survive on atmospheric air."

The professor pulled out another illustration. As she slid it closer, John stared at a fish like none he had ever seen.

"The third grouping of these lobe-finned creatures is the Rhipidistians. They were long-bodied, flesh-eaters that lived in the shallows. They, too, had lobe fins and lungs that could breathe air. Another characteristic of this fish was its distinctive three-pronged tail." The professor smiled widely. "However, what makes this group of lobe-finned fish so extraordinary is the simple fact that, unlike the coelacanth and lungfish, a living specimen has never been discovered."

She thumped her finger on the illustration's tail. "That night, I thought I saw a long slender fish like this. It was about two feet long and had this, the three-pronged tail. It was difficult to tell for certain because it was cooked and a family of four had already eaten half of it. I hope the bloody thing tasted better than the coelacanth I was eating." She slapped a hand on her knee. "Just imagine how brilliant it would be to come back with a Rhipidistian . . . a 'true' living fossil from 390 million years ago." She looked John square in the eye. "I want you to go catch me one!"

John leaned back in his chair with a grin. "You want to make a name for yourself?"

The professor smiled sweetly. "While I'm still young."

Eyes wide, she tauntingly pushed the illustration closer to him. "But not just me. Can't think of a better way to impress your colleagues, not to mention raise an eyebrow of those two brothers of yours . . . renowned surgeons, right? As I recall, they never had much regard for your chosen profession."

John squinted, thinking, *she's really working all the angles. She must really want me to go.* The professor was still looking at him as if knowing the answer already but only awaiting confirmation.

John still had one question. "Why me?"

"Come now, John." The professor gave a sly wink. "You know you're the only one I can really trust. On previous expeditions, you've handled yourself well in these types of situations. Like the Minui we encountered in Ethiopia last year. You have a sense of gaining trust in people, a quality I rarely see."

"You're not gonna fall for that line of rubbish, are you?" bellowed a female voice from a doorway adjacent to the office. In walked Kate Atkins. If John ever wondered what the professor looked like in her youth, the answer was standing in front of him. She was the spitting image of her mother at twenty-eight years old ... stunning without a touch of makeup. She casually held onto a towel draped over her shoulders as her form-fitting workout clothes displayed every curve of her long, lean body.

The professor smirked. "John, this is my soft-spoken daughter, Kate."

John perked up. The expedition was looking even more promising. It had been years since he'd seen the professor's daughter. *My, how she's matured.* He'd heard Kate was quite the adventurer, not to mention an excellent chopper pilot. "So, I guess you'll be my pilot and guide?"

Kate scoffed as the professor answered for her. "No, I'm afraid she has another engagement. But I've arranged another pilot for you."

"Yeah ... Brad." Kate arced her eyebrows. "He's a real charmer. I still can't believe this. She's actually onto something big this time and won't let me go."

John did his best not to show his disappointment. The professor seemed annoyed by the untimely interruption. "Don't you have a spin class or something?"

"Mother." Kate said. "I'm not your sickly little girl anymore. Don't you think it's time to stop treating me as such?"

The professor nodded toward the doorway.

Before excusing herself, Kate gave John a long, warm smile that nearly knocked him off his chair. "It was really nice to meet you ... John." With that, she disappeared through the doorway. For a long moment, John found himself staring blankly at the doorway, wondering if Kate really meant anything by the suggestive smile, or was it just a childish ploy to annoy her mother?

His eyes dropped to a business card holder on the desk. In it, the remaining card read: Alexander Aviation, Kate Alexander, Helicopter Pilot. He discreetly slid the card into his pocket. "Sickly little girl? Is your daughter ... ?"

"Kate was born with a congenital heart defect. Spent most of her childhood in and out hospitals, all while waiting to see if the hole in her heart would mend itself as she aged. If not, she would need surgery."

The professor's gray eyes softened. "Then on her fourteenth birthday when Kate heard that the hole had closed, she practically made up for her sickly childhood in one week. She got a dirt bike, signed up for every sport . . . even joined the boy's bloody soccer team." She paused. "But I guess to me she'll always be my little china doll."

"So she's okay now?" John said.

"Oh, yes." The professor scoffed. "And there isn't a day that goes by that she doesn't let me know it." She cleared her throat. "Now back to business." She tapped her finger on the illustration of the Rhipidistian. "I just know we'll find this in the waters around this island."

John refocused on the professor. "We?"

"Merely a figure of speech, my boy. Maybe you'll have better luck with the chief than I did. Perhaps you'll be able to haggle with him or work out some type of trade."

The room brightened at the sound of creaking door hinges. John turned around and saw a figure silhouetted against the blinding light of the corridor. As the dark figure entered the room, John saw a powerfully built blond, late thirties with a three-day growth of beard. The man stepped into the light. His thick neck rose to a wide, square jaw and a nose that was a little off kilter—a nose that had obviously been broken and reset one too many times, but not quite enough to distract from his rugged allure.

The man patted the holster on his hip. "Yeah, I got something to trade if they don't cooperate."

"I don't think that will be necessary," replied the professor. "John, this is Brad Anderson, a transplant here from Australia. He's quite a helo pilot and a splendid diver. He'll be escorting you on the expedition. If that's okay with you?"

There's a catch, thought John looking at the burly man standing in front of him. *The professor doesn't want to go herself, but wanted to send him with this poster boy for Soldier of Fortune magazine.*

John hesitated, "Well, my regular pilot is booked up for the next couple of weeks . . . I guess so."

The professor slowly smiled. "Then, it's a deal?"

"An undiscovered species of fish? Okay, I'll go." He looked at Brad. "But no funny stuff. We're going there to offer them a trade and to reason with them, and I don't want—"

Before John could finish, Professor Atkins stood victoriously. "SPLENDID! You leave tomorrow morning." She motioned for Brad to come closer to her desk where the map and illustrations were splayed. She leaned over her desk. "All right. Now listen carefully. This is vital to the survival of the specimen. On board the helicopter, you'll be using a temperature-controlled aquarium to transport the fish back. The water temperature is critical. For the coelacanth, which is a deep-water fish, you'll need to take the temperature reading at the same depth where you find the fish. Otherwise, due to the creature's delicate metabolism, it won't have a chance of making it back alive."

"Now, with the Rhipidistians, just the opposite is true. They're shallow-water fish, so again . . . be sure to set the aquarium's thermostat to match the surface temperature." She sat down, clearly content. "Well then, if everything's clear, that's all I have for now. Get a good night's sleep, and I'll talk to you both tomorrow morning before you leave."

John nodded and reached for the door handle just as the professor spoke again. "Oh yes, one more thing. Bloody glad I remembered this!" she gasped, hand placed dramatically over her heart. "Don't fly over the southeastern side of the island. It's some sort of sacred ground. I saw the area from a distance. It had huge pilings set out in the water to keep unwelcome boats from entering that side of the island. Apparently, they take their sacred ground very seriously. Just avoid that area to be safe. We don't want them refusing to see you." Brad turned to follow John to the door when the professor suddenly called him back. "Brad, wait. I have one more thing for you."

John turned to go back to the desk as well, but the professor looked at him curiously. "That's okay, John. You're free to go."

As he left the office, John looked back at the little woman smiling from behind the desk. He wondered if there were any other important bits of information that the professor failed to mention. Or for that matter, what part of the expedition was relevant to Brad but didn't apply to him? John was curious as the door closed behind him.

~~~

From a window in the small airport office, John could see Brad loading the last of the cases into the helicopter. He turned his attention to the phone at his ear.

A deep voice sighed, "No can do, I'm booked."

"Come on, Charley. Are you sure you can't fly me to the island? This could be really big. You owe it to science—could even get your name in the history books."

"Pax," Charley laughed, using his nickname for John. "You give me that line every time I take you up. So, this time it's a prehistoric fish? What'll she have you looking for next, Jimmy Hoffa? Besides, I thought the old lady usually hooks you up with a pilot, chopper, the works?"

"Yeah, she did, but I'm not so sure about this guy." John glanced at Brad through the window. "He's worse than the last one. I don't know where the professor finds these people. I'm starting to wonder if she has some sort of deal worked out with the local prison."

"Well, I'm sorry, old buddy, but like I said, I'm booked. If you could wait a couple of weeks, I could do it, but not now."

"No, if I don't go now, she'll get someone else."

"Sorry, but I just can't cancel my regular clients like that. Besides, if I were you, I'd be more worried about those natives out there. Your skin might be a few shades too light for their liking."

"Why? Do you know something about these people?" asked John, suddenly anxious.

"Nah, I'm just kidding. I'm sure they like white people just fine . . . if seasoned properly."

"Thanks a lot. You always know how to ease my nerves."

"Don't mention it." Charley's deep chuckle reverberated through the phone. "Relax. You always get a little jumpy before a long flight."

Through the window, John saw Brad frantically waving for him then pointing at his watch.

"I've got to go. We're already four hours behind schedule because of a malfunction with the aquarium's thermostat. I'll call you when I get back."

"Bring back an extra one of those fish, and I'll put some of my special sauce on it. We'll have us some *gooood* eatin'!" replied Charley with a laugh.

"I'll keep that in mind, but I've heard the taste of these fish might be a little not-so-good, even with your special sauce."

~~~

John gazed through the side window, watching the passing waters of the Indian Ocean. The sound of the helicopter blades had long since faded into a muffled hum in the back of his mind. He glanced at Brad, who continued to tap his thumb on the joystick. He had barely spoken a word since they lifted off nearly four hours ago.

Moments after flying clear of the coast, Brad traded his communication headset for a MP3 player and had been bobbing his head to a heavy-metal beat ever since.

Brad's demeanor was almost unnerving with his fatigue pants and sleeveless shirt that emphasized the size of his arms. He appeared more like a crazed commando psyching himself up for battle rather than someone escorting an archeologist on a peaceful expedition. John turned his attention to the drawing in his lap. For the hundredth time, his eyes wandered over the fish's three-pronged tail. He could only imagine how it would feel to bring one back alive.

Yes, the professor was right. Bringing back one of these would certainly impress his colleagues—all those moderately renowned archeologists who stared down their noses at him at fundraisers. News of this magnitude would also reach his family, raising an eyebrow or two from his stuffy older brothers. Heck, such a discovery would have the entire world talking.

It had always been John's dream to follow in his father's footsteps and become a surgeon, a career path both of his brothers had taken. But for the youngest of the Paxtons, it seemed fate had other plans. John studied diligently, made better grades than either of his siblings. But to be a surgeon, it took something else—something John learned early on that he didn't have.

And how his brothers had scoffed at him . . . the laughs the day he announced his chosen profession. "Archeology is a career not worthy of a sound mind. Little more than menial labor," they'd said. In the early going, those very words fueled John's passion on every expedition. Redemption was always one great find away.

Now, after two decades of unearthing bones and fragments of creatures already discovered a hundred times over, his enthusiasm had stalled. In the back of John's mind, he wondered if maybe his brothers were right; he certainly had little to show for his efforts.

He ran his finger along the illustration, tracing the three-pronged tail. He felt a thrill that rumbled in his bones. *Everything is about to change.*

John's thoughts were disrupted by a thunderous belch from Brad, so loud that it drowned out the sound of the chopping blades.

"Ooww, mate! I've needed to do that ever since we flew over Skoen!" Brad finally clicked off the MP3 player and looked away from the windshield. He glanced at the drawing in John's hand. "I can't wait to get one of those in my cooler," he shouted. "Just imagine, by this time tomorrow we could both be famous, ay?"

John smiled and asked, "How far are we now?"

"About fifteen minutes away. If you check straight ahead, you can see the island."

John looked at the approaching small green patch amid the endless blue sea, and said, "Remember what the professor said about flying over the southeastern side."

"Oh yeah, their sacred ground. It's a little late in the day to be dodging spears. I'll find a clearing about a mile from the village so we can land without spookin' 'em."

"I hope we have better luck than the professor did," John said absentmindedly as he looked at the lush tropical coastline. He then felt a tingling sensation deep in his stomach—a biological warning signal that, over the years, had never been wrong.

~~~

Finding the professor's office empty, Kate crept in and took a seat behind the desk. She studied the desk calendar. Again, she ran her finger along every date. "I knew it!" she gasped.

Just then, Professor Atkins appeared in the doorway, surprised to see her daughter rummaging around on her desk.

"I know you mark everything on your calendar," said Kate, not hiding the anger in her voice. "For the next two weeks, there's nothing marked in for me. So where is this important booking that kept me from flying John Paxton to the island? This is huge. You knew how much I wanted to be a part of it."

"It was canceled!" The professor's tone was as firm as her expression.

"Who canceled, Mom? Who?"

The professor didn't say a word. Kate recognized the look on her mother's face and knew not to ask again.

Chapter 3
THE CRIMSON POOL

John Paxton stared through the side window as the helicopter slowly descended into a small clearing. He saw nothing but branchless trunks and darkness. The tall trunks continued to rise above them until there was an explosion of vibrant, green foliage. The surrounding leaves danced violently from the wind generated by the powerful blades as the helicopter softly touched down. The engine shut off with a high-pitched whine, and the blades began to slow. He popped open the passenger-side door.

Placing his well-worn brown hat on his head, he grabbed his canteen, a small black sack which he put in his hip pocket, and stepped down onto the soft jungle floor. The air was moist, a welcome relief from the stale cockpit. An occasional birdcall echoed through the trees.

Slowly, he looked around the perimeter of the clearing but saw only a thick, green wall of plant life, some of the largest leaves he'd ever seen. Above the dense vegetation, long vines draped between tall trees, like a green spider web laced through the jungle.

Crack! A stick snapped somewhere behind him. He turned around and saw the top of a spear gliding above a fast-moving trail of rustling leaves. The spear tip headed further north until it vanished into the thick. *So much for surprises. It looks like they'll be expecting us,* thought John.

Crouching slightly, he walked beneath the slow-moving blades and made his way to the opposite side of the helicopter. Brad was unloading two large cases from the cargo bay. John said, "Well, looks like someone knows we're here. I just caught a glimpse of one of the locals heading toward the village."

"If I'd known they were gonna see us anyway, I would have parked closer," grumbled Brad, reaching into the helicopter. "Considering how thick this jungle is, we've got quite a trek ahead of us."

As the big man pulled out another cooler, John looked at him curiously. "Do you think we really need all of that? They're gonna think we're moving in."

Brad threw the three-and-a-half-foot plastic chest to the ground, looking frustrated. "I need the cooler to carry the fish back to the aquarium. Unless you'd rather strap it across your back?"

"Yeah, I know we need that, but what about those cases? Do you have to take them both?"

Brad wiped the sweat from his brow then pointed to the first case. "What's your pluck, mate? That one has the diving equipment and your backpack. The other case has the underwater lighting rig. So, you tell me, which one should we chuck?"

"Okay, okay," said John as he looked at the two cases, trying to determine which one would be the lightest to carry.

Brad pulled out an automatic machine gun from under the pilot's seat and threw the strap over his shoulder.

"You're not taking that," insisted John, staring at Brad. Every inch of this guy reeked of violence, from his wide, chiseled deltoids protruding from his sleeveless shirt, to the camouflage fatigue pants, to the AK-47 dangling at his waist.

"I never leave home without it, mate." Brad smirked. "Besides, the jungle can be a dangerous place. It might come in handy." He patted the ammunition clip. "Or it could be a good bargaining tool, eh."

John took the black sack from his hip pocket and slid out several thick gold chains. "This is what we came here to bargain with. Remember the professor said they spook easily, and if anything's going to spook them, it's going to be you showing up looking like Rambo."

Brad frowned. "Okay, have it your way. But I feel kinda naked."

John picked up the cases and walked to the edge of the jungle. Waiting at the perimeter of the clearing, he wondered what was taking Brad so long. He looked back and saw Brad carefully pulling down the back of his shirt as he jogged to catch up.

Why is he so worried about his appearance? We're in the middle of nowhere, thought John as Brad reached the edge of the clearing. After stepping in front of John with a confident smile, Brad unsheathed his machete and began to slice into the thick jungle. On the third swipe of the blade, John noticed something drop from under Brad's shirt. John set down the cases, reached between several leaves, and felt the warm metal handle of a German Luger pistol.

"Oh thanks, mate. You found my good luck charm." Brad plucked the pistol from John's hand and slipped it into the back of his pants. He looked back. "What? You can't expect me to go trekking through the jungle completely naked."

"All right. But make sure you keep it covered."

Brad proceeded to slice through the vines as John picked up the cases, almost afraid to imagine what Brad may have packed inside them.

~~~

From a towering perch of a takamaka tree, a slender, black figure stared at the strangers below. The larger one in front carved his way through the dense jungle, while the other man struggled to carry two awkward objects. He continued to watch as the two men stopped for a moment, as if questioning the accuracy of their course, then headed in the same direction.

The native looked off to his right and motioned toward the village. A final glance at the two strangers, and he shimmied down the tree, picked up his spear, and vanished into the jungle.

~~~

"Ah, we must be getting close. I can feel the breeze coming from the ocean," John said, struggling with the cases. As they neared the edge of the jungle, the leaves and palm fronds came to life in the wind.

Soon they'd be at the village. John felt a growing sense of unease about what Brad might do. By now, he thought that he would've gotten to know him better, but even after the long flight, he still couldn't quite figure him out. Looking ahead to the muscular man swiping the machete, John tried to think of topics to spark up a conversation.

"So, Brad, did the professor mention anything more to you about the villagers? Like anything that might be helpful in our negotiations?"

"Yeah," Brad grunted with another sweep of the blade. "Did she tell you about the mate they call Kota . . . how he can kill you with his eyes?"

"Kill with his eyes." John said. "No, the professor did not share that with me."

"The villagers believe that if he stares into your eyes for more than six seconds, you'll die," explained Brad, hacking through the thick. "The legend started one day when Kota got a little stroppy with one of the elders. He stared at the old man with such hatred that he gave him a heart attack. Later that night the man died. Since then, other than the chief, no one in the tribe will look Kota in the eye."

Brad turned around and smiled. "I can't wait until we get there. In front of the entire village, I'm gonna give that Kota character a stare that'll loosen his bowels." He squeezed the machete handle, making a fist. "One wrong look from that monger, and it'll be lights out for sure, ay."

Not feeling comfortable with the direction of the conversation, John decided to change the subject. "So, do you have any hobbies? Play football, anything like that. You look like you stay in shape."

"Naaah, mate. Been taking it easy. Haven't done much more than pump iron and watch telly for the last few months."

Good one, John thought. *He's starting to open up.* "So, what happened? Did you have a little time between expeditions, take some time off to work out and relax?"

"Guess ya could say that. I was three months into a one-year stint in a Durban jail when the professor bailed me out for this expedition. Relax, mate. I wasn't in for nothing serious. Just opened up some military skeef at a local dive . . . he lived." Brad winked. "But no doubt he thinks of me every time he checks his belly, ay."

Well, at least I've got him talking, thought John, although getting to know Brad better didn't bring him much comfort. As Brad continued his assault on the thick leaves, John tried another question. "So, what do you think set them off that night when the professor asked them about the fish?"

"Not sure," Brad said. "Could have something to do with their slavery background."

"Slavery background?"

Brad glanced back. "You mean the old lady didn't mention that either?"

"Mention what?"

"Some of the tribe's ancestors were slaves. It was when the first American ships started coming to Africa searching for slaves. Good ole Yanks, ay." Brad laughed and continued to clear the thick. "After leaving South Africa, one of the ships wasn't satisfied with the size of its cargo and stopped at this island to capture additional slaves, bump up the inventory. But when the mates reached the island, they weren't prepared for the deadly welcome they received. Every one of those mates were butchered. Then the natives returned to the ship wearing the slave traders' clothes while pretending to be escorting slaves. Once they boarded the ship, that was it, mate. The ship was torched. Every white man was slaughtered, and the remaining slaves swam ashore and inhabited the island. They even placed the charred remains of the ship's main mast in the center of the village where it still stands today as a type of monument. So, considering that the last whites that came to this island tried to capture them, I'd say that might have had something to do with their lack of cooperation, ay."

"No. She didn't tell me that," John said. "She just told me about the part where they escorted her back to the helicopter."

"Escort!" Brad laughed aloud. "Some escort. They chased her all the way to the chopper. At the banquet that night, when the professor first saw the fish, she realized how agitated the natives were. The old larnie was smart. She told them she and her pilot needed to go water the lily—you know, take a wee—but instead, they legged it back to the chopper. If she hadn't got that jump on them, she said they would have never made it back. Should have seen her chopper, had at least a dozen spear holes in the fuselage." He laughed again. "Why do ya think she needed me? Her pilot at the time said she couldn't pay him enough to come back here."

"You . . . you're serious?" asked John in a stammer.

After a long moment, Brad winked, "Nah. I'm just foolin', mate." He turned and continued his assault on the draping vines.

"What about that eye thing with Kota?"

"That's weird," said Brad.

"You mean that part is true? John asked. "The part where he looked at—"

Brad cut him off. "No . . . that over there." He lifted his machete blade in the direction of a tidal pool near the edge of the jungle.

They walked over to examine the small body of water. In the distance, the jungle wall began to thin out, and bits of the sandy coastline slowly appeared through the tall takamaka trees. Brad squinted. He stooped down at the edge of the tidal pool. "It must have been the way the setting sun was reflecting off the surface, because when I first saw it, the water looked like blood. I can still see some spots of red in it. Must be the sunlight."

"What's that?" John set down the cases and approached a small, dark object lying beside the tidal pool. "Look, it's some type of hoof or at least part of one." John picked it up and examined the clean, smooth edge where it had been severed. He glanced around the bank to see if there were any hoof prints in the moist sand. "It looks like it came from a horse or some other large mammal, but I can't imagine what animal native to this island would have a hoof this size."

"Got me." Brad couldn't have cared less.

Dropping the hoof into a hip pocket, John picked up the cases and walked past the tidal pool. Brad stepped ahead of John and continued to lead the way, hacking through the brush.

After a few minutes, John's shoulders began to ache. *Hope we're getting close,* he thought. *These cases aren't getting any lighter.* Brad sliced through a thick cluster of vines, and they entered a vast clearing. In it were forty or so evenly spaced stones, each capped with a large conch shell. East of the clearing, the jungle seemed to spill over the rocks, offering a spectacular view of the Indian Ocean.

Breathtaking, thought John, marveling at how the multicolored shells stood out against the turquoise waters.

John set down the case and cooler. "What are all those shells?"

"The professor mentioned something about that." Brad stopped and lowered his blade. "About ten years ago, one-third of the tribe died from a mysterious disease. Most of the victims were children. Those are the gravesites."

All at once, the vibrant scene faded beneath a dark cloud. The jungle grew cooler, and a clap of thunder rumbled overhead.

"Disease," muttered John. "I wonder what kind."

"I guess we'll have to wait and ask them." John followed Brad's gaze. About fifty yards beyond the clearing, he saw the front wall of the village.

Chapter 4
THE VILLAGE

Stepping clear of the jungle, John could now see the small village in plain view. East of the village was a series of caves. Starting at the caves, a roughly hewn wall made up of vertical logs stretched around the village and gradually tapered back to the blue-green sea. "I guess they do like their privacy," muttered John. He looked up at the pointed tops of the logs as the strong ocean breeze tousled his hair. "Must be at least twelve feet high." They continued to walk beside the massive wall until they came to a large, gate-like structure.

A pair of dark eyes appeared behind a small opening beside the gate. John leaned toward the opening. He spoke loud and slow, "We're friends of Professor Atkins from Africa. We'd like to talk to your chief."

The eyes disappeared from the small hole. A few seconds later, a different pair appeared, and John repeated himself.

Nothing happened for a moment. Then there was a clank, followed by a loud squeak of wood. The large gate slowly opened revealing a row of dark figures. John's stomach tightened. Behind them, he saw a tall ship's mast protruding from the center of the village.

Brad looked at John with a smirk. "Whatta ya know, mate?"

One black man stood a head taller than the others. He wore a loincloth made from an animal hide and a necklace with multicolored stones. His demeanor alone told them he was the man in charge. This demeanor was reinforced when he spoke. "My name is Kota-leg-way. I remember professor." The dark figure glanced at Brad. "Why you come here?"

Brad locked eyes with Kota and smiled like a madman, refusing to break his gaze. Kota's brow deepened. The men around him grew agitated. They pointed at Brad and put their hands to their eyes, motioning him to look away. Several seconds into the stare, John threw himself in front of Brad. He waved his hands, breaking the stare. "We came to speak to your chief. We'd like to offer him a trade."

Kota's eyes remained narrow. He looked them over for a long moment then motioned them to step inside the gate.

The huge gate slowly closed behind them.

John looked at the eight men who stood around Kota with their intimidating spears in hand. Behind them, off to the right, he noticed a large, dark statue of a figure seated on a throne. Kota said abruptly, "Stay here." A final glance at Brad, and he left the others and disappeared into the village.

"Nice going," John whispered to Brad. "You're a regular ambassador of goodwill."

"You gotta let these savages know who's the boss right up front, ay."

"In case you haven't noticed, those are spears in their hands. Just leave the talking to me. And keep your eyes to yourself."

John gazed past the eight imposing figures. Beneath a beautiful sunset was a village of simple huts made of bamboo and straw. Various villagers, mostly women and children, were preparing for nightfall. To his right, behind the large statue, several women gathered up tools around an enormous fishing net. Nearby, a group of young boys played what appeared to be a mock game of spear fishing. He watched as the youngsters threw long sticks at a rock carved in the shape of a fish that sat in a large circle of stones. Taking it in turns, they hurled their spears at the object, careful not to step within the circle.

John's attention turned to the large ebony statue he had noticed earlier. It rested on an island in the center of a manmade pond about thirty feet wide. While the guards watched, John picked up the cooler and slowly walked to the edge of the pond in front of the sculpture. Brad picked up the cases and followed.

John looked up at the towering figure as it boldly sat on a throne with a staff in its right hand. A lit torch was on either side of the throne. John marveled at how the flames illuminated the enormous black head with flickering light. His eyes were drawn to the only color on the statue, a long, white triangle that covered the right side of its face.

Wow, you can't even see a chisel mark, thought John, admiring the detail of the smooth, black face. He studied how the mysterious white spike started on the forehead just below the hairline and gradually tapered down to a point beside the figure's mouth, completely covering the right eye. *Very interesting,* he thought. *Must be of great significance to the tribe.*

An elbow in the ribs snatched John's attention. "You still with me, mate? I think the chief's here."

John turned to face a man in his early fifties, about five feet nine inches tall, with a waistline that nearly matched his height in inches. His long, braided hair was pulled straight back. He wore several layers of pearl necklaces around his neck and a bright-red animal skin around his generous waistline.

"This is Chief Omad," announced Kota.

John nodded in a gesture of respect. "I'm John Paxton, and this is Brad Anderson."

"I see you like statue?" said Kota, translating for the chief.

"Yes, the craftsmanship's excellent." John pointed to the carved inscription at the base of the sculpture. "What does that say?"

"TAO-EB-DOLI," replied Kota.

"What does it mean?"

Kota slowly looked at John and said, "Keeper to the Door of Death."

Brad whispered over John's shoulder, "Isn't that sweet. Ask him about the fish already."

The chief glanced at the cases beside John and Brad then spoke to Kota. Kota said, "Chief want to know what kind of trade you here for?"

"Yes. A friend of ours, Professor Atkins, was here about a week ago," replied John. "She mentioned that your people had been catching a type of fish that we find very interesting. We were hoping to work out some sort of trade for one of them."

"I knew this about fish!" The words exploded from Kota's mouth. He was clearly agitated.

Sensing hostility, the chief raised a hand in a gesture for Kota to stop speaking. They spoke among themselves for a moment. A submissive nod to the chief, and Kota again turned to John. "Yes, we caught few fish the professor eat that night, but those only ones. There no more fish you speak of." Kota looked again at the chief then back at John. "It dark soon. Chief say tonight, you sleep in village. Tomorrow, he find bones of fish you speak, then talk trade."

The chief motioned them to follow him. "Come," Kota said. "Chief want to show you village before dark."

Brad whispered to John, "You're not buying that crap?"

"Sssssshhh, I'll do the talking. For now, we'll take whatever they offer and try to negotiate with them in the morning."

Brad gave him an impatient stare as they picked up the cases and followed the chief. He muttered just loud enough for John to hear, "I didn't come all the way out here for a couple of stinking bones."

The chief clapped his hands. "Phata, phata!" Two tribesmen came up to John and Brad to take their equipment. Brad hesitated, holding onto his case. "I can handle this one, mate." He pulled it back.

"Don't worry. They take to hut where you sleep," assured Kota.

John glared at Brad. "Just let them take it. Lighten up!"

Brad loosened his grip on the handle as if releasing the hand of a loved one, and reluctantly fell in behind John. Flanked by Kota and the chief, they were led through a maze of tiny huts. The guards stayed close behind them. Curious villagers watched as they passed, murmurs spreading through the crowd. As far as John could tell, it was an unknown dialect mixed with fragments of Zulu, including one word he heard repeatedly—indoda, meaning white man.

From shadowy doorways and windows, anxious eyes peered at them. A small boy, about three years old, emerged from one of the huts and toddled toward John. His mother frantically ran out and picked him up, quickly returning to the shadows of her hut.

The beautiful orange sunset slowly gave way to darkness. Still, no one in the group said a word. They passed several villagers gathering their tools from around an unfinished canoe. A few yards farther, John noticed a shapely native girl as she and two other young women went about lighting the large torches placed throughout the village. She glanced at John with a shy smile.

Wiping his brow, John discretely glanced back. He was quick to notice that the men held their spears loosely with the tips pointed upward and not at his and Brad's backs. *A good sign,* he thought, *no early signs of hostility.*

Along the way, he tried to read the chief, but his expression left him little to go on. He just stared forward, occasionally glancing at Kota. In an attempt to ease the tension, John looked over at Kota and said, "I've heard that you were educated in Africa?"

"Yes, for eight years," said Kota. He then translated the question for the chief.

Judging from the chief's grin, John could tell that he was quite proud of Kota's scholastic achievements. He continued with his questions. "What university did you attend? What was your field of study?" *Oceanography or perhaps marine biology,* John guessed.

The tall native stood up straight, heaved his chest and bellowed, "Cape Town Elementary, sixth grade!" he smiled proudly, as did the chief.

Brad leaned close to John's ear, and in his best hillbilly accent, muttered, "Gee, Uncle Jed, now I know we're in some fast company, especially with Jethro here and all."

John bit his lip to keep from laughing aloud and whispered, "Maybe he's just big for his age."

The chief continued to guide them through the labyrinth of huts until they found themselves confronted by a massive wooden wall. John felt the breeze growing stronger and could hear the waves crashing against the shore behind the towering structure.

He looked up at the vertical logs. They had the same pointed tops as the perimeter wall of village, except these were much higher. The wall seemed to slowly arc around toward the water. *It was clearly designed to separate the interior of the village from the coastline*, he thought. *But why?*

Having apparently achieved the full tour, they were now led back to the center of the village. Ahead, John saw the ship's mast protruding from the ground and quickly looked away from it. He hoped the topic wouldn't come up in conversation.

Brad kept looking back over his shoulder at the wall. He was staring at a pair of large gated doors flanked by two enormous torches. "What's on the other side of those doors?"

Kota replied simply, "Sacred ground."

The chief raised his hand. "Ni-lamba?"

"You hungry?" asked Kota, translating.

"I'm starved," replied Brad.

"Yeah, sure," John gave a forced smile. He looked at the chief, all the while doubting he could swallow a bite of food, so nervous was he about the entire trip, mostly that they might return without the Rhipidistian. He also knew that he couldn't risk offending the chief, so he smiled and followed the chief and Kota. He glanced at Brad to check his demeanor. *If I'm starting to get agitated, I'm afraid to imagine what thoughts must be racing through his mind by now.*

~~~

They entered a large hut in the center of the village, where John and Brad were seated at a long banquet table. The chief walked around in front of them, Kota ever near his side. The chief clapped his hands. An attractive girl placed two large wooden bowls before them. John looked down to what appeared to be a mixture of chopped fish and brown rice smothered in a thick, white seasoning. He whispered to Brad, "Can't tell the type of fish it is the way they serve it. Interesting."

His mouth already full, Brad nodded and continued his meal.

After nervously taking his first bite, John looked at the chief and said honestly, "Very tasty." Within seconds, he heard Brad's wooden spoon scraping aggressively against the bottom of his bowl. John glanced over. *If he's nervous, his appetite doesn't show it. He's acting like he hasn't eaten in a week.*

John discretely looked up from his bowl to study his surroundings. The walls were bamboo. The ceiling was made of multiple layers of large leaves held together with some type of black sap that looked like tar. At the room's focal point, he saw a dark stone sculpture. It was a seated figure similar to the one in the village entryway, but much smaller. He recognized the same white spike covering the right side of the ebony face.

On a wooden table ten feet away, he saw something that made him do a double take. What appeared to be a *National Geographic* magazine was sticking out from beneath a wooden box.

John elbowed Brad, interrupting his feeding frenzy, and motioned to the table with his eyes. Brad looked over, sauce running from the side of his mouth, and said, "I wonder if they have a subscription or pick it up at the local 7-Eleven every week, ay?"

The chief saw them looking toward the *National Geographic*. "Neowenta!"

"The magazines." Kota said. "Chief thinks you wonder where come from? When I was at school in Africa, I bring back to island."

The chief walked over to the table, opened the wooden box, and pulled out three more copies. He dropped the other copies on the table and brought one back over with him. Kota followed. The chief thumbed through the pages until he stopped on one with its corner folded. "Iapha–udalla!" He turned the magazine around and pulled it wide open for John and Brad to see. Kota translated in a somber tone. "These show me all the evil white man done to ocean!"

John stared at a double-page spread of a huge drain emptying waste into the sea.

The chief turned the page, "Iapha!" He pointed to a photo of a pile of rusty drums on the ocean floor, leaking streams of toxic waste into the blue water.

John stopped chewing and laid down his spoon.

The chief picked up a second magazine. Jerking it open, he held it in front of them, his words translated. "Look what come from white man's ships." John stared at a photo of an oil tanker in the middle of a massive black stain. The chief quickly turned the page, his tone more aggravated. "And look what it do to fish!" He pointed to a sea lion carcass and hundreds of dead fish on an oil-stained coastline.

John's eyes widened in recognition of the tragedies.

Suddenly, the chief slapped the magazine down on the table in front of John, his eyes smoldering in rage. When he blinked, tears streaked his rugged cheeks. "Ten year ago . . . when my son, Peekay Little," said Kota echoing the chief's words in English. "Big ship like in picture, hit rocks . . . turn water black as night. We later eat fish caught in lagoon this same color. Next day many get sick. After many moon, men and women get better. But not little ones. Many sleep and not wake up . . . forty children die, including my son."

His lips tightened, and his fist came down hard against the table. "The white man learn so much, make life easier. But he only destroy—bring death to sea. Sea is our life. Sea is all life!" He leaned closer, staring straight at John. "And soon, sea will take back all life. Very soon!"

John's jaw dropped, unchewed fish in his mouth. He watched in disbelief as the chief stormed out of the hut.

Brad, scraping the last drop of juice from his bowl, glanced over at John, "I don't think he's going to cooperate, mate. When he comes back, ask him again about the fish. Maybe it's about time to break out the gold chains. Unless you'd rather I try other tactics, ay."

"Now's not the time," John said in a hard whisper. "Let's let him cool off for a while; I'll talk to him in the morning. And wipe your face."

As the native girl who served them backed away with a disturbed look, Kota approached the table. "That's touchy subject with Chief. He be in better mood in morning. Come, I show you to your hut."

~~~

Entering the small hut, John sat on the corner of one of two straw beds. He was nearly sick with disappointment at the events of the day as he slipped off his vest without a word. He looked at the empty cooler beside his bed and slowly began to accept the possibility of the entire trip being a waste.

On the opposite side of the hut, Brad was on his knees rambling frantically through his case. The rambling then stopped, and Brad closed the case with a sigh of relief.

"What are you so relieved about?" asked John. "Worried they were gonna steal the lighting equipment?"

Brad sat down on top of the case with a confident smile. "Nah, mate. Everything's in there just as I left it."

"Well, a lot of good the light head's gonna do us as long as the chief has a bug up his—" John stopped when he saw Kota standing in the doorway. Beside the tall tribesman was the girl he had noticed earlier lighting the village torches.

Kota smiled and led the girl forward. "Chief apologize for his behavior and send gift. This is Lana, one of his wives. She keep you warm for the night."

John stared back, his mind racing to find an excuse that wouldn't offend the chief. After a few awkward moments, he broke his silence. "No ... no thank you. I don't think my wife back home would appreciate it too much." John thought wryly, *that sociopath I used to be married to would be the last person on earth I'd want to please.* But it did make for a convincing excuse.

Kota turned his attention to Brad, who was already looking her up and down. John watched nervously as Brad studied her shapely body, small grass skirt, and tight animal-skin top that hid very little. He could see his eyes slowly working their way up her body as torchlight danced off her perfect dark skin.

She is gorgeous, thought John. *Come on Brad. Be strong ... don't do it.*

Then the girl smiled, revealing the teeth of a badly carved jack-o-lantern.

After giving her another long look, Brad finally answered, "Not a bad-looking goose you got there, mate. Afraid my old lady wouldn't think too much of it either. But thanks for asking."

Kota just shook his head. "Okay, have it your way," muttered the powerful native, releasing the frail shoulder. "Hope you don't get too cold tonight!" The stern look in his eyes spoke louder than his words.

After Kota disappeared from the doorway, John rolled up his vest to use as a pillow and eased back on the bed. "What do you make of that? The chief is willing to give us his wife for the night but won't let us take a look at a prehistoric fish?"

Brad laughed as he crawled onto his bed. "I guess a man's got to draw the line somewhere, ay?" After slipping the pistol from the back of his pants, he laid it beside his hip. He leaned over on one elbow and looked at John. "You know the chief only sent his bokkie over here to keep an eye on us tonight."

"Yeah," replied John, tilting his hat down over his eyes. "I knew that, but I was starting to wonder if you did? For a minute, I thought your eyes were going to light her skirt on fire."

"She wasn't half bad. But I don't think the tribe has much of a dental plan, ay?"

John heard Brad lie back down, but he could tell by the rustling straw his frustration wouldn't let him sleep. He knew both of their thoughts were rehashing the day, thinking of the chief's obvious lies about the fish and the mysterious doors that led to the lagoon. The thought of going back empty-handed was more than John could bear. Redemption for his career—everything—was about to slip through his fingers.

"Hey," John whispered from under his hat. "I'll bet what we want is on the other side of that wall . . . I can feel it."

Brad sprang up on the side of his bed. "You read my mind, mate. You know they have those fish, but the chief doesn't want to give us any because he thinks we might've whizzed in the ocean or something. You heard his whole spiel. All that environmental crap." He swung his feet onto the sand floor. "Well, what are we sitting in here for?"

John adjusted the vest under his neck, "Relax, we'll wait until morning. After what happened at dinner, we'd better not press our luck. I still have the gold. There's a chance he'll change his mind . . . if they really have those fish."

A rebellious grumble from Brad, and he eased back onto the bed.

John released a slow breath. He tried to allow his surroundings to ease his tension. Palm fronds rustled gently outside the window. The doorway and walls shimmered in a golden glow of torchlight while a salty breeze swept beneath his hat and across his face. The hut was relaxing enough, but the tension of the expedition refused to let him sleep. He thought about previous encounters with unfamiliar tribes and how he'd never broken the first basic rule—always leave at the first sign of hostility. Never risk it. The chief had definitely shown hostility. And they were still there.

His mind went back to the dinner. He retraced every word he'd said to the chief and still didn't have the slightest clue what had set him off. And the part about the ocean taking revenge—it made him wonder . . .

Before making a final attempt at sleep, John lifted the front of his hat. "Hey," he whispered. "What do you make of what the chief said earlier?"

"Don't know. Guess he's a little wacko about losing his kid, ay."

"That's not the part I was talking about. It was when he said the ocean will take it all back . . . I guess, like reclaiming the life that was taken from it, avenging itself. Bizarre, huh? Any ideas on that one?"

"I don't know, mate, but he sure was excited about it," replied Brad as he stared at the ceiling, left hand resting on his pistol.

"Maybe he meant that if man continues to destroy all of the life in the ocean that he'll eventually starve from depleting one of earth's most valuable food sources?"

"Or maybe the old guy is just wound too tight!" suggested Brad as he pressed a button on his watch, as if setting the time.

John dropped his hat back down over his eyes. "I guess you've got a point."

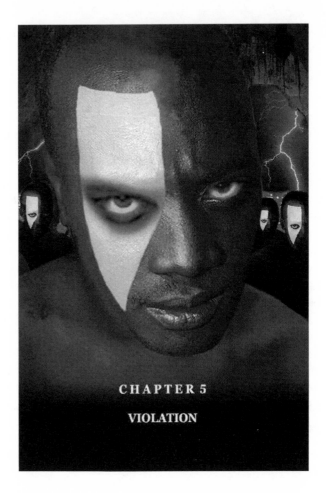

CHAPTER 5

VIOLATION

Brad woke abruptly when he felt a vibration on his left wrist. He turned off the silent alarm on his watch and looked at the glowing numbers. *Three fifteen a.m. Been asleep for nearly five hours.* Brad looked over at the bed across from him and heard a faint snore coming from beneath John's hat.

Quietly, he slid to the side of his bed, trying not to rustle the straw. Another glance at John, and he reached back, grabbed his pistol, and slid it into his waistband.

He picked up the cooler and the case containing the lighting equipment and tiptoed toward the door. Brad looked from side to side before stepping outside the hut. He searched for the darkest unlit areas of the village while mentally plotting his course.

Carefully, he followed a series of shadows that led him through a maze of tiny huts. The night air was invigorating. The damp mist felt good against the tight skin of his bare shoulders and arms. Adrenaline raced through his veins. Muscles coiled beneath his skin like springs begging for release. Moments like these were what he lived for, to feel the adrenaline, the juices flowing. And the juices were definitely flowing now.

He ran across a lit walkway and disappeared into another series of shadows. His mind raced. No more talking, no more bending over backward trying not to offend these savages. Time to cut through the crap and get what we came here for.

At any moment he could be discovered, and that excited him even more. He took pride in his raw nerve, daring himself to press forward into situations where few would follow. *Just let one of those savages step from the shadows and try to stop me.* He laughed, stepping past another hut. *We'll see what happens then, ay.*

He passed a fishing net strung between two palm trees and found himself in front of the massive wooden wall. To his far left, he saw the light from the torches illuminating the enormous doors. He glanced over his shoulder and saw no one. Quickly, he approached the wall and set the case and cooler within its shadow.

He looked up the eighteen-foot structure and thought of how difficult it was going to be to get over. Then he recalled the hundred-thousand-dollar incentive the professor had offered him for the return of a new species, and the wall didn't seem nearly as high.

He unlocked the case and removed a rope with knots spaced two feet apart. He uncoiled the rope until he reached the grappling hook at its end. Twirling it around, he released it toward the top of the wall. The silver hook flashed in the night sky, and with a light clank, landed between the pointed tops of the logs. Brad pulled back on the rope until he felt the hook's claws bite deep into the wood.

He reached back into the case and extracted another rope. After tying one end of the rope to the handle of the case and cooler, he tied a large knot at the opposite end. With an overhand toss, the heavy knot flew over the wall beside the grappling hook.

He again reached into the case. "Oh, now we wouldn't want to leave you behind," he whispered as he pulled out a MAC-10 machine gun. He tossed the strap over his shoulder. "Okay. Time to get down to business," he muttered. He grabbed the knotted rope and began to scale the wall.

Within seconds, he reached the pointed tops of the logs. Carefully, he pulled his leg to the inside of the wall and braced himself at the top. Looking down inside the wall, there was total darkness. About thirty yards out from the wall was a dark stretch of sand that led to the shimmering water of the lagoon. Beyond the dark shoreline, he could see evenly spaced torches that went out deep into the water, outlining the lagoon in a series of illuminated red dots.

Brad reached over and grabbed the rope attached to the case and cooler. He pulled them up beside him. He slid the awkward bundle over the pointed tips and slowly lowered it down until he felt the rope go slack in his hand.

"My turn," he muttered. He turned the hook and put it on the outside of the wall, allowing the knotted rope to drop to the inside. He looked down to make sure it wasn't tangled, but could see only a few yards of knotted rope leading into blackness. Descending the wall, he misjudged the location of one of the knots. He lost his grip.

Helplessly, he plummeted through darkness for what seemed like forever, until he hit the ground with his back, emitting a loud, squishy sound.

To his relief, the landing was soft and almost painless. He took a moment to catch his breath, staring up at the night sky. "What's that smell?" He looked around in total darkness. He struggled to sit up in the soft mud.

He reached down and wiped a thick substance from the side of his pants, and before his fingertips reached his nose, he stopped. *Manure! How in the—?* His thought was interrupted as he felt a huge, wet tongue slide across his face. He kicked back in horror, falling flat into the excrement. His right hand fumbled through his pants pocket for his flashlight.

The beam shot in all directions, searching the darkness. It fell across two huge eyes peering back at him from behind flared nostrils. He pushed backward, sliding through the muck. His shoulder hit something large and furry. A loud "*mmmoooo*" echoed around him, and a long tail brushed across his face.

"A cow? A cow!" Brad swung the light around and found that he was sitting in the middle of a cow pasture. He jumped to his feet. "I can't believe it. An eighteen-foot pointed fence for a bunch of cows? This is whacked. Must be one of those cow-worshipping tribes." He began to calm down, still not believing that a cow had spooked him like that. The best he could tell, they looked like the Braunvieh cows he'd seen in South Africa's Northern Cape. He turned his flashlight toward the base of the wall and spotted the case and cooler. He untied the rope from the handles. Holding the flashlight in his mouth, he picked up the case and cooler and made his way through the muddy pasture.

Ahead, behind the silhouettes of the cows, he saw water shimmering in the moonlight. He approached the edge of the mushy grass. He climbed over a short, wooden fence, and crossed a sandy area about twenty-five feet wide that separated the pasture from the lagoon.

Finally, Brad reached a wooden dock. It was about eight feet wide and arced around the lagoon as far as the darkness would allow him to see. Quietly, he set the case and cooler on the dock and took the flashlight from his mouth. He glanced left then right. Still no sign of anyone.

Brad turned off the flashlight. The darkness was even greater until his eyes slowly adjusted. The clouds inched past the moon, and he could now see the immense size of the lagoon. He walked closer to the edge of the dock. In the distance, he could see the dock's support pilings silhouetted against the shimmering waters. Although the dock and the pilings were only shadows, he could still see how they surrounded the lagoon and seemed to separate it from the outside ocean.

Exactly as the professor described it.

Brad noticed how the pilings were evenly spaced. A lit torch was on top of every fourth piling. He estimated that the distance between pilings was around six to eight feet—a gap narrow enough to prevent larger boats from entering, yet wide enough to accommodate the natives' canoes. To his far left, the east side of the lagoon disappeared into a vast cavern as if being swallowed by a giant mouth.

He turned and looked back toward the wall. Just to the right of the fenced pasture—the one he had just mucked his way through—were the enormous wooden doors. Torchlight flickered across their pointed tops. Inside the doorway was a twenty-foot-wide sand walkway that led to the base of the lagoon. Where the sand met the shallows, he saw some type of tall, rounded sculpture, but couldn't make it out.

He looked back at the fenced-in cow pasture that ran along the inside of the wall for about two hundred feet. From the silhouetted humped backs, he estimated that there were at least sixty head of cattle. He laughed.

"The whole tribe is nothing but a bunch of nuts worshipping cows. Unbelievable! They're eating those stinking fish when they could be having steak every night. Now I know they're whacked!" He said this aloud, and the words became the darkness too. Nothing.

Brad turned his attention to the dock once again. It rose about six feet above the water and followed the pilings out into the lagoon and beyond to obscurity. Picking up the case and cooler, he walked around the west side of the dock where it extended farther over the water. The strong ocean wind whistled between the planks. Five yards in the distance, he saw three wooden barrels—each about the size of an oil drum.

The deep mooing sounds faded as Brad pressed on. Passing a torch, he entered a dimly lit section of the dock. His foot slipped and he almost fell, catching himself on the case. "Ahg!" he snorted, looking down. "What's this slop?" He set down the case and cooler and took out his flashlight to inspect the slippery surface. The light reflected a shiny, red liquid. Brad stooped down and touched it, smelled it, confirming his suspicion.

Blood. It was fresh, not yet coagulated, and it hadn't been there long. Playing the light around the area, he discovered the substance covered the entire section of the dock where he stood. Waving his flashlight around the perimeter of the stain, he searched for the source of the blood. He spotted a red trail leading to one of the barrels. Leaving the case and cooler behind, Brad walked closer. The light followed a red streak that ran up the side of the first barrel. The coppery smell of blood was thick in the air.

The sound of swarming flies grew louder with each step. He looked over the side of the barrel. The beam of his flashlight found a pair of brown eyes looking back at him from the severed head of a cow floating in the dark-red liquid. Brad jumped back and almost slipped again. Swatting an onslaught of flies, he looked over at the second barrel. Floating in a pool of blood was a long section of intestine coiled in the barrel like a snake. "These people are sick!" Brad gasped, stepping back in disgust.

Shaking his head, he eased back to the case and cooler, picked them up, and continued to head farther along the shadowy dock. The wooden planks creaked beneath his every step.

As he walked over the water, he could feel the dock beginning to sway from the strong waves and ocean wind. He refocused on his agenda. He murmured to himself, "Okay, the coelacanth is a deep-water fish, but the other one is a shallow-water fish. The one with the long body and three-pronged tail, the Rhipidian . . . or Rhapidis . . . Radipis . . . who names these doff fishes anyway?" He gazed over the lagoon as moonlight danced off its black surface.

Suddenly, something flew out of the water and landed on the dock about three yards in front of him. Startled, he dropped the case and cooler and shined his flashlight toward the fluttering sound. The beam reflected off the rainbow-colored scales of the strange creature as it desperately flapped its large wing-like fins against the dock.

Brad looked closer at the bizarre fish. "Jislaaik! You're like no flying fish I've ever seen. I don't know what you are, but I'll bet you're prehistoric!"

The fluttering sound intensified as the fish drew itself closer to the edge of the dock then flopped back into the lagoon. Brad walked to the edge of the dock and stared across the water. Suddenly, toward the middle of the lagoon, dozens of what looked like these same creatures burst from the surface. Moonlight reflected from their multicolored scales as the fish soared through the air like birds then simultaneously plunged back into the water on the far side of the lagoon.

Brad's face lit up. "I . . . I've got to get one of those in my cooler!" He stepped back to his case and opened it. "Oowee yes, it's payday, mate! Forget the other two fishes—whatever. That's yesterday's news. I'm bringing me back one of these guys!"

He slipped the machine gun from his shoulder and quietly laid it on the dock. He reached into the case and pulled out a three-foot fishing net. Quickly, he slipped a long extension into the handle, making sure it would be long enough to drop the net deep beneath the surface. Reaching back into the case for the underwater light, he mentally rehearsed his plan:

After I net the fish, I'll put a little water in the cooler from the shallow area of the lagoon. The fish should be okay in the cooler for at least thirty-five minutes. That should give me plenty of time to get to the aquarium in the chopper. Then I'll come back for John.

He glanced back to the wall.

But I'm not going to be leaving the same way I came, not with the cooler partially filled with water. I gotta use those doors. But if anyone sees me . . . let 'em try to stop me.

Satisfied with his plan, Brad set the net on the dock. He then reached back into the case and extracted the underwater light along with an extension for its handle. He imagined himself sneaking back into the hut after dropping off the fish in the helicopter's aquarium. He nearly laughed aloud as he thought how John would probably crap himself after hearing what he'd done.

After slipping in the extension, Brad laid the underwater light beside the net. Quickly, he walked to the cooler and slid it close to the edge of the dock. He opened the top, making sure it was ready for the catch. Then he angled the flashlight so that its beam glared off the side of the cooler, illuminating it in the darkness.

"Just one of you little guys, that's all I need." He crept to the edge of the dock. Dropping to his knees, he picked up the light head and slowly lowered it down to the cold, black surface. A glance over his shoulder showed the glowing cooler with its mouth open wide. He lay down flat on the dock with his head and arms extended over the edge. The moist planks cooled his chest.

Brad lowered the light about ten feet beneath the surface.

"Okay, who's the lucky winner?" he whispered. "Which one of you little guys wants to take a trip . . . be famous? Just one of you for my cooler . . . that's all I need!"

With the click of a switch, a yellow hue illuminated the shape before—the massive shape before him—not a flying fish but a creature that virtually filled the lagoon before him and beyond. An enormous reptilian head. A thick neck that tapered back into a pair of sprawling paddle fins. The tip of its nose just beneath his face.

"That . . . that's . . . not going to fit in the cooler!" stammered Brad, recoiling from the edge of the dock and onto his knees. Without a word, he switched off the light and slowly slid it from the water. He stepped back, staring at the lagoon in disbelief.

"Wooow! What've they got in there? That's got to be at least," he did rapid mental calculations, "at least eighty feet long."

A plank creaked behind him. He stood, whipping around to see a black face, a long, white spike covering its right side—a perfect match to the statue at the village entryway, except this time the ebony figure was real.

Behind the imposing native, dozens of other white spikes appeared in the darkness. They drew closer. In his frozen state, Brad randomly noted the white spikes bore a strong resemblance to a long dinosaur tooth. Another plank creaked behind him and he heard the underwater light being smashed as glass scattered across the dock. He whirled around again.

A crushing sound, and everything went black.

~~~

Brad awakened to a language he didn't understand. He had no idea how long he had been out, but darkness still surrounded him. His stomach was nauseous. The stars overhead were blurry as he felt himself being pulled along the dock by his feet. The motion suddenly stopped. He tried to get up, but his strength was gone. The back of his head throbbed in pain.

Shadowy figures held him down, one man on each leg and arm. Kota was now standing over him, taunting him with Brad's own machete. Kota held it sideways, tilting it until torchlight shone across the metal, revealing the blade's full breadth. Beside the long painted spike, a row of white teeth appeared and widened into a smile.

"I'll break you in half," growled Brad through clenched teeth, straining to lift his arms. But he couldn't budge. Only the back of his head lifted from the dock.

The machete playfully leapt from Kota's left hand, then back to his right. Each time the blade passed above Brad's chest he heard the laughter increasing, knowing that if Kota missed the catch, the blade would slice his chest in half. The blade paused and slowly lowered to

Brad's throat. It moved lower, to the left, and he felt the metal tip press the shirt to his chest. A little deeper, and the blade slowly pushed the skin into his pectoral muscle until he felt the pressure release as his flesh swallowed the tip of the blade. A searing pain shot down to his ribs.

The laughter grew. And the blade rose, its shiny tip now moist and red. Brad felt another slash across his chest. He clenched his teeth, refusing to cry out in pain. No way would he give them that pleasure.

He saw Kota nod and step away. Half-painted faces flashed before him, and he was brutally flipped to his stomach. Out of the corner of his eye, he saw a flicker of light reflecting from the blade. "What are you—?" A foot on the back of his neck pressed his face into the dock, muting his words.

This time the pain was unbearable as something sank into the back of his thighs. They now flipped him over on his back again. His buttocks and lower back turned warm from his own blood. He was moving faster along the dock, again being pulled by his legs. They paused. He felt the slippery warmth spreading beneath him. *No, that can't be my own blood.*

They grabbed his left arm, sliding him sideways. "No . . . what are you doing?" His free hand clawed at the planks trying to stop. He lifted his head finding his destination. "NO! NOT . . . NOT THE WATER!"

Chapter 6
THE SIGN

On the third ring, John answered the phone in his office and heard a perky voice. "Hi, it's Jenny. Jenny Heartfield."

"Jenny!" said John, feeling a lump form in his throat. This was a voice that hadn't made his heart race since college. Jenny was a nursing major, and the first girl he'd ever truly cared for. They had dated for eight glorious months his freshmen year until she dumped him for a pre-med student.

"Yeah, it's me, I heard the great news. I still can't believe it—an entire new species—and you're responsible! A Rhidiphis . . . tian, I can't even pronounce it. But they say you practically discovered a living dinosaur. I'm so proud of you."

John leaned back against the corner of his desk. His mouth dropped open in disbelief, "Jenny, it's been years. How are you? How did you know where to reach me?"

"Are you kidding?" The familiar soft voice laughed. "You're famous! It's big news everywhere. I first saw it on *Fox News*. So how've you been? What have you been up to . . . I mean, besides making headlines?"

John answered slowly, "I thought you got married, and lived in—"

Jenny quickly interrupted, "Oh no. We were divorced after two months. It was a mistake." There was an awkward silence. "After everything that happened with you, I was confused, didn't know what I wanted anymore. I tried to look you up when I got back, but couldn't find a trace of you. That is, until now." After a short pause, the female voice continued in a shyer tone, "You've been on my mind long before I saw your face on TV, John. *I have never stopped. . .*"

Suddenly, the phone dissolved in John's hand as a crashing noise awakened him from his dream. Two tribesmen burst into the hut. The blinding morning sun shone through the doorway. Someone raised the straw bed, violently tossing him onto the floor. John looked up through sleepy eyes. Two more men shot through the doorway, spears pointed toward him. His mind clearing, he looked at Brad's empty bed, then beside it, and saw that the case and cooler were missing.

What's Brad done now?

He felt himself being pulled across the bed. He reached for his vest, but it was ripped from his hand and thrown across the hut. "What's happening? What's wrong?" He looked around for Kota or the chief. Once he was pushed through the doorway, they were joined by six more armed men. Two of them grabbed him by the arms and forced him toward the tall walls along the coast.

As he passed, women and children glared at him with a sort of eagerness from the dark doorways of their huts. The anticipation he saw there turned his mouth dry. Approaching the large wall, John could hear the rumble of distant thunder. Moving closer, he realized it was the dull thud of a drumbeat coming from behind the wall. They paused in front of the massive wooden doors. Dozens of armed tribesmen appeared from out of nowhere and forced him forward as the doors opened inward as if by magic. The pulsating drumbeat grew louder and clearer.

Before he knew what was happening, John found himself on a long, sandy path leading to the lagoon. Natives, spears in hand, formed walls on either side of him. Their angry faces all bore the strange white spike.

They forced John farther along the walkway. He glimpsed cattle rustling behind the men off to his right. Straight ahead in front of the shallows of the lagoon, he saw what he guessed was his destination: two guards holding torches in front of a large rounded stone. To the right of the guards was an enormous dock that extended from the shoreline and formed a half circle around the lagoon. This isn't looking so good. John tried to slow down but felt the hateful shoves from behind him. The powerful drumbeat surrounded him with its hypnotic rhythm.

At the end of the path, he saw Brad's cooler and net at the guards' feet. *This isn't looking good at all.* If Brad were still alive, he would have seen him by now. The thought made John feel faint. His stomach tightened. A surge of sweat rose through his pores and turned cold against his skin.

Someone grabbed him, then another pair of hands. Powerful fingers sank deep into his arms. Helplessly, he floated toward the end of the walkway, his boots barely skimming the sand.

His captors dropped him in front of the dark figures bearing torches in front of the rounded stone. He didn't move. The torches divided, and Kota appeared between the flames like the Devil himself. John looked up into his smoldering eyes. The white spike on Kota's face wrinkled with his smile.

Then his black eyes flared with delight. "Now you will see!"

Kota stepped aside and allowed John to see a rod standing in front of the large stone. It was a perfect match for the staff held by the statue at the village entryway. John's eyes followed the four-foot-long, wooden shaft that projected up from the sand. At its top were three sticks tied together to form a long triangle. But the triangle of sticks appeared to be a support structure for a long white object in its center.

John came to his feet and stepped closer. He stared at the curious, white object inside the triangle. Then his eyes widened in disbelief as he recognized the largest prehistoric tooth he'd ever seen. In that instant, he realized the significance of the white spike when he saw Kota's face beside the tooth. A chill ran up John's spine. He looked behind the staff at the large, rounded stone and realized it was carved in the shape of a prehistoric paddle fin—only it was fifteen feet tall.

John's fear gave way to awe as he held his hand in front of the enormous tooth to give it scale. *That's got to be twenty inches long,* thought John as he stared at a tooth longer than his forearm. "It's white," he muttered. He started to ask Kota if it was real, then noticed gum tissue speckled along the root.

He couldn't believe what his eyes were forcing him to accept. He was certain that no one had discovered a tooth in this condition. For a tooth to be in this condition could only mean one frightening thing. Its owner was still alive.

"Where?" John demanded, "Do you know where this came from?"

Kota glanced at the chief with a smile. "We have good idea."

"But no one has ever discovered a tooth like this. They've always been black or at least dark, in the form of fossils—never white like this. Where'd you find it? Are there more?"

"Yes," replied Kota, nodding with a knowing grin. "Many more . . . and we take you to them soon."

The group led John along the shoreline toward the dock. The chief stepped onto the wooden structure first, followed by Kota.

John felt the powerful hands return to his arms and lift him onto the dock. "But when did you find the tooth? On what part of the island?" In all of his dismay, he was oblivious to the men pulling his arms behind his back. He finally felt a tug when they tightened the knot. He tried to pull his hands apart, but it was too late.

"KUTA KEB-LA!" announced the chief in a bold tone.

Kota stepped closer. "We call him Kuta Keb-la. In our tongue it means 'Great Mouth of Death.' Or as you people call it in your books, pliosaur . . . prehistoric marine reptile."

John looked at Kota in disbelief. "A pliosaur . . . but how? They've been extinct for millions of years. Where? When did you see it?"

Kota interpreted the question for the chief.

The chief turned and gazed out at the sea as Kota translated the chief's response. John hung on every word. All the while, they headed farther along the dock. "Kuta Keb-la came in time when white man spilled blood of whales with his spears. They kill whales all around island. Much blood. Blood lure Kuta Keb-la from deep water. Then, maybe thirty year ago, white man stop killing whales. I don't know why. Maybe there no more left to kill or they go somewhere else to kill. That when Kuta Keb-la come to island for food. Many of our fishermen go out, but not come back. Twenty men missing before we see giant shadow outside lagoon."

The chief pointed to the waters south of the lagoon. Kota continued translating, "That where reef opens that surround most of lagoon. One day Kuta Keb-la come into lagoon between opening. He hide in deep water of lagoon in daytime. Then come into shallow water at night and kill more people when they fish and bathe."

John looked at the huge, wooden posts surrounding the lagoon, "So, then you put pilings around the lagoon to keep it out, giving your people a safe place to fish and bathe?"

Kota shook his head, "No, to keep him in."

"In! How long was it able to survive in the lagoon?"

Kota stepped forward and pointed to the pilings. "The lagoon is surrounded by a reef with many large openings. The main opening is about thirty-five feet wide where we put a large gate-like structure that runs deep beneath the surface. We used pilings to block off the other openings that were wider than thirty feet. See all those pilings that appear to go deep into the water? Most of them are actually embedded into the top of the reef to prevent the creature from going over at high tide."

He pointed east where the lagoon entered a dark cavern, becoming more animated the more he spoke. "Also, there's a series of underwater caverns that run beneath the island and connect to small tidal pools. The island has a strong current that flows through this lagoon and exits on the other side of the island. We learned this from the feedings. Sometimes parts of cows that we fed to Kuta Keb-la in this lagoon have been found on the banks of tidal pools on the other side of the island."

I guess that explains the hoof.

Kota continued. "So what we have with the lagoon and underwater caverns is a very large, contained area that has a constant flow of outside water passing through it."

John paused, no longer looking out at the lagoon but instead staring at Kota. Throughout this incredible history lesson, he was slow to realize that Kota no longer spoke in pigeon English. His speech was fluent. "You . . . your speech?"

"Aha!" Kota laughed. "What's the matter? I no longer sound like the ignorant savage you took me for? Let's just say, my education in Africa well exceeded the sixth grade. That's just a game I like to play. You had another question?"

John paused, trying to focus. He heard deep mooing sounds behind him and looked back at the pasture. Kota followed his gaze. "Guess you wonder how they got here? They were a donation from your ancestors.

Generations ago when the white devils—the slave traders—came to this island to steal our people, their ships were also loaded with cattle from Africa. After we destroyed their ship, the cattle swam to the island. They have flourished for generations."

"So, you use the cows to feed it?"

"Yes," said Kota, "among other things. We started feeding Kuta Keb-la in the daytime by putting slaughtered cows on small canoes. Other times, we would leave the carcass in the shallows, sometimes during the day and other times at night."

"Why the change up in methods?"

"We wanted to expand its feeding habits," replied Kota. "We wanted Kuta Keb-la to look to the surface for food, and if it's not there, to come into the shallows—day or night."

"But what difference did its feeding habits make when you had it in captivity anyway?"

Kota smiled. "So that upon release, it will not return to—"

John, his eyes open in horror, cut him off. "Upon release? You mean, it's still here? You still have it?"

Kota continued in a somber tone, "So that upon release, it would not return to the depths of the ocean in search of food, but instead, look to the coastal areas to feed."

"What are you, insane?" John locked eyes with Kota. "Do you have any idea what kind of effect that thing would have on populated areas?"

Kota's lips widened into a malicious grin. "Exactly!"

"But why? I thought you only trapped it to protect your people?"

The towering native stepped back, raised his arms grandly. "At first that was true . . . until the chief's prophecy revealed all. For Kuta Keb-la is no mortal creature, but a spirit of vengeance risen from the depths!" He glared at John, eyes ablaze. "I've seen your world, and it's evil, the white man's ships raping the sea with great nets—pollution, oil spills like the one that killed our people. You've used your technology to make your lives easier, but you've only destroyed, brought death to the sea. The sea is our life. The sea is *all life.* And now the sea will reclaim all life that has been taken from it!"

John gasped. "This is insane!"

"No. All will know the prophecy is true when they see the first sign." Kota looked up into the sky, "It is foretold, by the first full moon, the blood of the necala will be shed, and then innocent blood will fill the sea." Kota paused, again with a wicked smile. "But you will see none of this."

With that, he pushed John, sending him stumbling along the dock. Ahead, John saw the sun reflecting from the broken glass of Brad's underwater light. A few steps closer and he saw a puddle of blood beside the glass. His eyes followed the red smear to the edge of the dock. "What did you do with Brad?"

"For thirty years we've slowly increased Kuta Keb-la's appetite for warm blood while awaiting the sign. The sign to let Kuta Keb-la fulfill the prophecy and drive man back onto land where he belongs."

Kota turned and pointed to the wall behind the cow pasture. "All this time no white man has ever entered our sacred ground." John looked to the top of the wall and saw the rope dangling from the grappling hook. "Last night, your friend violated our sacred ground. This we take to be the sign!"

In that instant, John's astonishment faded, and his stomach churned in fear. "What've you done with Brad?" he demanded, fearing he knew the answer.

Kota's mouth stretched once again into that unsettling smile. "Last night Kuta Keb-la had his second taste of white meat. Today he'll have, as you people say, one more for the road."

John looked to an area of the dock about thirty yards ahead where several men poured blood into the lagoon from a barrel. Behind them were the tops of the large gated doors that separated the lagoon from the open sea.

John turned to the chief. He looked into his smoldering eyes, searching for the slightest trace of reason. But he saw nothing; the eyes were dead, vacant, as if the chief were under a hypnotic spell. Again, John looked at the tribesmen as they poured blood in front of the gated doors, "Why—why are they doing that?"

"To make sure he sees you!" replied Kota.

Kota pointed to the east side of the lagoon where it emptied into an enormous cavern. Inside, two parallel poles reached up from the water toward the roof of the cave. "Normally, our criminals are tied between those. But today we have something different for you."

The sickening feeling in John's stomach rose in his throat. His mouth tasted bile as his body's danger signals went into full alert.

He looked ahead where two men picked up a large, bamboo ring about the size of a hula- hoop, threaded with disks cut from coconut shells. They used a long wooden handle to submerge the hoop-like rattle halfway into the water, then vigorously shook it. John's heart pounded louder in his throat. He recognized this practice similar to the one used by shark-worshiping tribes of the Pacific. He recalled how the shark callers would use their hoop rattles to make strange vibrations beneath the surface. Vibrations that attracted sharks to their boat like an underwater dinner bell.

John tried in vain to twist his wrist inside the rope, knowing with each step he drew closer to certain death. He was now on an area of dock about forty yards from shore. His eyes searched for options. But there were none. Ahead were the backs of Kota, the chief, and two armed guards. A glance over his shoulder showed dozens of half-painted faces following closely. To his right, past the edge of the dock, was the outside ocean. Had his hands not been bound, that might have been an option. But even if he was free and able to swim at full speed, he knew the natives could run back across the dock and reach the shoreline ahead of him. He looked to his left, to the waters of the lagoon. He knew what was in there.

As they reached a dark-stained section of the dock, John felt his boots sticking to what he knew was coagulated blood. He glanced over the top of one of the barrels. The sight of a section of intestines floating in blood combined with the rancid smell made him stop and hunch over. He gagged as the taste of last night's supper came to the back of his throat.

Whaaack! A tribesman jabbed him from behind with the blunt end of his spear. John lunged forward, stumbling down onto one knee. He slowly rose from the dock, his pant leg sticking to the blood. Regaining his balance, he looked up and saw bits of glass glittering in the distance. His eyes fixed on Brad's broken underwater light near the edge of the dock about five yards ahead. As they continued to walk, he glanced back and saw one native following closely. Again, he looked to the broken light head, now only ten feet away.

There's no more time, this is it.

John slowed his pace and looked down at his feet. As the first set of bare toes came into view from behind him, he lifted his left boot high and stomped down with all his weight. The tribesman howled in agony and jabbed the blunt end of his spear between John's shoulder blades with his full strength. John flew forward, twisting in midair, and landed back first on the broken glass. It sank deep into his forearms and back as he writhed in pain on the dock.

Two guards violently grabbed John by the arms and yanked him to his feet. They followed more cautiously, the points of their spears aimed at his back.

Kota looked at the free-flowing blood on John's forearm and laughed. "No need to help. We have plenty of blood in the water already." Although the surrounding natives didn't understand a word of English, they saw Kota laughing and quickly joined in.

The group was now about halfway around the lagoon where the dock was farthest from the shoreline. Just ahead, the dock passed in front of the tops of the large gate-like doors—doors that dropped deep beneath the surface and closed off the widest section of the reef from the outside ocean.

John's thoughts reeled wildly as he tried to maintain a modicum of calm. *Come on. Don't let your face give it away.* Teeth clenched, he tried to keep the pain from his face as his fingers extracted a small piece of glass from the palm of his left hand. Streams of warm blood flowed across his fingers as he discretely slid the glass back and forth across the rope.

To hopefully draw attention away from his busy fingers, he asked Kota, "Just out of curiosity, do you really have any of those fish we came here for?"

"I had two small ones for breakfast this morning." Kota translated his comment to the guards, and they all burst into laughter.

The chief raised a hand, bringing the group to a stop. They were now on the section of dock that crossed in front of the giant gated doors. The chief turned to the others. Thrusting his fist into the air, he shouted, "Usuku-osa-dedela-Kuta Keb-la!"

The men responded in a chant while pounding their spears against the dock in rhythm. "Tala, tala, Kuta Keb-la! Tala, tala, Kuta Keb-la!"

A primal roar erupted from the cavern and echoed across the lagoon. It was absolutely horrific. It was like nothing John had ever heard before.

The men around him jumped and howled with delight.

The chief turned and shouted, "Kolegwa!" He pointed to a thick rope connected to a wooden latch across the doors. A tall, muscular native ran over to the rope and picked up a crude ax.

John watched the two men continue to shake the hoop rattle. The others stopped pouring blood from the barrel and slid it back onto the dock. The chief walked over in front of John, his chin held high, eyes cold, dead.

Kota interpreted, "Today is day we have waited . . . day of release! The day death come to all who enter sea!" John gazed behind the chief as the hoop rattle was pulled from the water, and the guards cautiously stepped back on the dock, staring into the lagoon.

An enormous, black shadow slowly emerged beneath the bloodstained waters. Although John had seen the nineteen-inch tooth, it did little to prepare him for what was rising before him. The black silhouette became more distinct as it ascended to the top of the crimson cloud. More than twice the size he'd imagined.

John stood hypnotized by the sheer width of the shadowy head. The long, jagged frill along its back broke the surface. The frill rose higher until a stretch of slate-gray skin glittered beneath the water.

"Tala, tala, Kuta Keb-la!" The chanting grew louder.

The chief turned his attention to John and spoke. Again, Kota interpreted, "I not dislike you, but you are sign. It not my choice. It not your choice. It meant to be. Destiny. Today you must die!"

"Sorry you feel that way," replied John. With that, he rammed his now free hands into the chief's chest with all his strength. The chief flew backward, two bloody handprints on his chest, and plunged into the lagoon.

The chanting stopped, replaced first by a chilling silence, then by screams.

Stunned, the two guards in front of John slapped at the water with the blunt end of their spears trying to give the chief something to grab onto. The water came to life. The chief's head rose above the surface, his hair matted back with bloody water. He looked up toward the dock, his previously cold, somber expression replaced by a mask of horror. Frantically, he lunged for the end of one of the spears but missed, dipping again beneath the surface.

John raced past the two guards as they tried to save their chief. He heard the chief's screams above those of his guardsmen. Screams like he had never heard before. He looked briefly over his shoulder as the guards went silent, staring at the hand that reached from the water, a red cloud forming around it.

Like a switch turned to "on," John's fear turned to adrenaline. He had about a twenty-yard head start.

Kota yelled, "Dedela Kuta Keb-la!" and a chopping sound echoed throughout the lagoon. It was a word John recognized: in Zulu, *dedela* meant *release*. A second glance back, and he saw about 40 men in pursuit while Kota pointed towards him.

He felt a supercharged rush of adrenaline that kept him running at a speed he couldn't believe. John could now see dozens of men approaching from the dock on the opposite side of the lagoon. He heard a flurry of spears thudding into the planks behind him. He felt the dock beginning to sway from the charging natives in front of him. Their screams of hatred filled the air.

John saw the first tribesman from the approaching group stop and draw back his spear. He was well in range. Still, John kept running forward at full speed. The native hesitated, not knowing whether to throw or get out of the way. Two more strides and John propelled himself from the dock just in front of the approaching natives. The screams disappeared as he plunged beneath the surface. Saltwater burned deep into his numerous cuts and wounds.

Beneath the water, he glanced back to check his distance from the creature still within the gates. He saw the dark shadow thrashing amid the red cloud and felt its thunderous vibration from forty yards away. Looking upward, he saw the shimmering figures above the edge of the dock as they followed his trail of bubbles.

John tried to go as far as he could on a single breath of air, but his racing heart quickly consumed his oxygen. When he reached the surface, he twisted his body so that only his face came out of the water. The tranquil underwater sounds transformed into the screams of frenzied natives as he took a deep, desperate breath.

A spear plunged into the water, barely missing his shoulder. John quickly dove deeper to avoid the flurry as dozens of spears pierced the surface. Around him, trails of bubbles flowed from the wooden shafts that streaked toward the bottom of the lagoon.

John looked ahead to where the pilings went deep beneath the surface. He hoped he could make it to the outside ocean on this same breath of air. The minute and a half since his last breath felt more like five. He concentrated on trying to relax and conserve the precious oxygen in his lungs. If he could make it to the open ocean, he'd have a chance of reaching the coastline before the natives got to him.

Swimming toward the pilings, he noticed a faint flash of light. He dropped his gaze to the bottom of the lagoon. *No . . . no, it can't be!* His eyes locked on something more frightening than the monstrosity behind him. The light he saw was reflecting from a long piece of metal—a helicopter blade lying beneath the murky depths. He tried to determine if the rotor had two blades or four, but didn't dare take time for a second glance.

As John glided between the eight-foot gap, he noticed something white embedded in the piling to his left. Lungs burning, he reached along the thick wooden post and pulled out a nineteen-inch tooth. He looked at the huge white object in his hand.

If I ever make it back . . . A spear streaked between the pilings. John slid the tooth under his belt like a sword, and made for the surface, keeping the piling at his back. Breaking the waterline, he drew a desperate breath. Behind him, the dock shook, screams growing closer. He looked out to the open ocean and realized that his plan was doomed. East of the cavern, where he had hoped to make his escape, was nothing but a rocky cliff—a fifty-foot vertical embankment impossible to climb.

There was only one option: the cavern back inside the lagoon. He recalled that the dock stopped about thirty yards before the mouth of the cave. If he could swim past the end of the dock, the tribesmen couldn't follow without going into the water.

John dove beneath the dock and back into the lagoon. Staying as deep as possible, he followed the row of pilings toward the cavern. Every time he surfaced for a breath, he could hear the stampede of natives above, searching madly.

He reached the end of the dock. Drawing a deep breath, he pushed off from the last piling and glided beneath the waves. He kept swimming farther and farther, his oxygen-starved lungs burning, but he didn't dare to go up. Finally the water grew dark and cool.

He was inside the cave.

After a few more strokes, John came to the surface. The underwater serenity again transformed into deafening screams and the pulsating drumbeat. He looked back. He could see tribesmen crowded along the edge of the dock. A flurry of spears arced over the water splashing just behind him, reminding him that he was still within deadly range. John plunged beneath the surface.

Through the dark waters, he could see the lagoon floor rising toward the shallows of the cavern. Drawing closer to the shoreline, he felt something nip his right forearm. Quickly, he pulled his arm back. The slender fish was about three feet long. While it swam beside him, he noticed its distinctive three-pronged tail. The Rhipidistian darted away when John angrily swung at it with his fist.

Finally, he felt the sandy bottom beneath his boots. He sloshed onto the bank, gasping. He glanced around, catching his breath for a moment. The cavern was enormous. He glanced up at the two bloody poles projecting from the water. Ropes dangled from them where countless victims had been tied. Above the posts, a series of ropes hung down from the cave ceiling. "This place looks like fun," he muttered. But there was something else, something strange. It was quiet. He looked back outside the cavern and realized the dock was completely empty, not a tribesman in sight.

He slid the giant tooth from his belt. He gripped it tightly around its middle so he could run, and that's when he heard it. The horrible screams. The cries grew louder, echoing through the cavern, making it impossible to tell from which direction they were coming.

His eyes darted around. "Looks like the party's not over."

John hurried along the bank, looking for a way out. He came to three tunnels. The natives' cries grew impossibly louder.

"Crap! Which one?"

He started for the first tunnel, then stopped, second-guessing himself. "No! What are you nuts?—the prize is never behind door number one." After only a brief hesitation, he entered the center opening.

Enveloped in darkness, he ran, stumbling and scraping the walls. Feeling his way around a corner, he saw a speck of light in the distance. He picked up the pace. The light grew closer until he shot from the cave like a bullet from a gun. He squinted in the sunlight, realizing that the cave had spat him out somewhere east of the perimeter wall of the village. "Maybe my luck's starting to change," he muttered. "There isn't a soul in sight . . . uh, maybe not." A glance back showed tribesmen emerging from a different tunnel. Others swarmed through the front door of the village only sixty yards away.

John broke into full stride as he crossed the beach. His waterlogged boots felt like lead in the soft sand. Still they did little to slow him down as he entered the thick of the jungle, cold, moist leaves beating against his chest.

~~~

The underwater gate slowly swung open to the pulsating drumbeat. A rope trailed behind the gate loosely on the surface. The vast gap between the reef filled with darkness as a massive shadow slowly passed through it.

Just outside the entrance, the eighty-foot-long silhouette paused. A long, gray frill broke the surface, barely visible in the endless blue sea. On the dock, two muscular natives pulled with all their strength. The rope became taut, springing from the water until the doors slowly closed. Several villagers watched from atop the interior wall of the village, adjusting their positions to keep the creature in view. The ghostly black shadow streaked across the surface heading north, away from the lagoon. A splash from a huge paddle fin, and the frill rolled, vanishing beneath the waves.

Chapter 7
THE HUNT

The jungle was silent, with the exception of a drizzling sound that echoed across the leaves as a tribesman relieved himself on the local fauna. His spear leaned against a nearby tree. Gazing blankly through the draping vines, he heard something. The villagers' cries grew louder— closer. A sudden rustling of leaves snatched his attention. He looked over his shoulder, trying to discern what was crashing through the jungle.

~~~

John ducked as he continued his rapid pace, keeping branches from hitting his eyes. Long leaves and vines slashed cruelly at his chest and arms. Bursting through another thick cluster of leaves, he looked up and saw a tribesman's back. He couldn't stop. He was going too fast to change direction.

The moment seemed suspended in time. The native grabbed his spear. His surprised expression twisted into hatred. The blurred image of the spear swung out beside the native's waist, poised for the kill. Before the razor-sharp stone found its mark, John twisted his body. He swung the giant tooth over the spear, and its blunt side collided with the native's forehead with a loud, crushing *pop.* . John didn't miss a stride, though he did glance at the tooth to make sure it wasn't broken.

Without looking back, he continued to run pell-mell through the jungle. Flickers of sunlight flashed before him from breaks in the palm fronds overhead. His mind flashed to a haunting image—not the creature, but the helicopter blade at the bottom of the lagoon. *Please don't let it be ours.* His thoughts raced as fast as his feet. He tried to remember if there was more than one blade. *What did I see?* His mind was a blur. Brad's helicopter had four blades. Did he see four blades? He tried to reason with himself, that surely whatever it was belonged to some other unlucky explorer who wandered here years ago. *Who knows? . . . By now, it probably looks like the bottom of the Bermuda Triangle down there,* he thought.

John began to slow as his adrenaline high started to fade. His thoughts switched to Brad. Why? Why did he have to climb over the wall? If only he'd waited until morning.

A spear streaking through some nearby leaves caught John's attention. He looked out the corner of his eye. *I'd better find our 'copter soon or I'll be discussing the issue with Brad face-to-face.*

As he tried to glean his general whereabouts, another thought occurred to him. Had he passed the clearing already? He tried to recall the path he had taken to get him this far. When he first entered the jungle after coming out of the cave, he was east of the lagoon. Along the way, he had adjusted his course west in hope of picking up the trail. *But I haven't found it.* He hadn't seen a single sliced leaf or broken branch since he had been in the jungle. *Have I cut too far west and completely missed the clearing? Have I run a mile already?* He tried to think how long he had been running. Had it been ten minutes, fifteen, or only five? He had no perception of time.

Still he kept his running, losing steam but ever determined to keep moving. Why couldn't he hear the natives? Were their cries muted by the sound of his own body crashing through the leaves, the roar of thoughts in his head? Or were they gone? They could be right on his tail and he not realize it. He imagined them running behind him, matching his pace with little effort. They could probably run at this pace all day.

They're probably just playing with me, waiting for me to give out.

He was tempted to stop just long enough to see if he could hear them. A second to rest. *No way. I can't risk it.* Even if he had run past the clearing, he knew he had to keep moving.

His body involuntarily started to slow the pace as he questioned the accuracy of his course. *Maybe that's why I can't hear them. They know I passed the clearing. They know I'm running in the wrong direction, so they went back to the helicopter.*

Again he resisted the temptation to backtrack, certain that if he had indeed missed the clearing, by the time he came back to it, the natives would already be there waiting for him.

He continued to argue with himself—one possibility versus another. "I know I didn't pass it!" he muttered. "It's around here somewhere." He did his best to force the self-doubt from his mind.

Another sixty yards and he could hear his heart pounding louder than the crashing leaves beneath his feet. The front of his t-shirt was torn to ribbons. His chest stung as sweat entered the cuts. He felt the tooth in his right hand and instinctively pulled it closer to his side as if to keep it from being stripped away. For a moment, the surreal scene reminded him of his college football days. The rushing adrenaline, his burning quadriceps, the large waving leaves that silently cheered him on from the sidelines. *What I wouldn't give for the endurance I had back then!*

He remembered how he could feel Jenny's eyes on him every time he touched the ball. His mind drifted to when they first met one day after practice. He recalled her warm embrace and their first kiss. The image of the Christmas he spent with her passed before his eyes.

I can't believe my mind is drifting at a time like this. He shouted at himself, "Oh no you don't! That better not be my life starting to flash before my eyes. I know I didn't pass that chopper!"

As quickly as he began to motivate himself, he felt his heart sink—if he hadn't passed the chopper, then either he hadn't gotten to it yet . . . or it was at the bottom of the lagoon. All at once, his legs turned to lead. John slowed to barely a walk, trying to catch his breath. *Just for a few seconds, and then I'll pick it back up.* But when he tried to get back up to speed, the muscles in his legs screamed in protest. They were completely cramped up with nothing left. He then realized his mistake. The brief pause had allowed lactic acid to set in.

Out of the corner of his watering eye, he saw a reflection. He adjusted his course and jogged west, his heavy boots barely leaving the jungle floor. Another flicker of light. Pressing through a thick cluster of leaves, John saw the sun shining from the tail rotor of the helicopter. He stepped into the clearing, not believing that amidst the panic and madness, his calculations had been correct after all. A glance upward gave him a renewed jolt of adrenaline when he saw the four long blades of the main rotor perched above the cockpit.

John jogged toward the helicopter. He reached the landing gear and realized it was quiet. Too quiet, not a rustling leaf. Then, on the opposite side of the helicopter, he saw several dark figures creep into the clearing without a sound. Realizing they'd been discovered, the tribesmen sprang to life.

John threw open the door to the chopper. A pinging noise echoed overhead from a spear hitting the main rotor. Another crashed through the windshield.

John leaped into the cockpit and saw the key in the ignition. He'd never been so grateful for Brad's carelessness. He threw the tooth onto the passenger seat and reached under the pilot's seat. He grabbed Brad's machine gun while twisting the key in the ignition.

"Come on, come on!"

Another spear crashed through the windshield and jabbed into the passenger seat. Through the broken windshield, John saw dozens of natives pouring into the clearing. He knew he'd never make it off the ground.

In one desperate sweep, he grabbed the strap of the machine gun and fell backward from the pilot's side door. Landing hard on his side beneath the helicopter, John took aim at the dozens of legs that quickly came into view. The screams from his attack were muted by the sound of the kicking weapon as John slowly moved it from side to side, firing in short, controlled bursts.

Masses of natives and spears fell to the ground. John jumped back into the cockpit. He turned the ignition key as he threw his body across both seats in an attempt to stay below the windshield.

The spears were back. Pinging sounds echoed around him from spears hitting the fuselage. Another spear came through the windshield and plunged into the passenger seat six inches above his ear.

"Wooooh! Too Close!"

The engine whined and finally fired up. The sound of the engine gave way to the thumping rotor as John felt the downdraft blowing through the holes in the windshield. Glass scattered across his face. Yet another spear pierced the windshield. Sitting up, he pulled one spear out of the seat and backed it through the glass, then slid the smoking machine gun barrel into the entry hole. Squeezing the trigger, fire erupted from the windshield. Spent shells spewed through the cockpit, bouncing from the passenger seat and onto the floor.

He tossed the machine gun into the passenger seat. A cloud of smoke rose and curled from the hot barrel. He grabbed the throttle, twisting it all the way open to reach operational RPM. He pulled up on the collective. Simultaneously, his feet found the pedals, depressing the left pedal until he felt the aircraft lighten on its skids. All this John did almost out of instinct, not having piloted in years.

Slowly, the helicopter lifted off the ground. The pinging noises of the spears subsided like a rainstorm transforming into a drizzle. Through the pilot's side window, he saw the dark figures in the clearing growing smaller and smaller, while the helicopter's shadow swept across the tops of the coconut palms. He turned the helicopter north and headed away from the village. His heart rate slowly returned to normal.

Okay, it's been a few years. Just hold her steady. You're doing just fine.

Chapter 8
WILLIE'S SOUVENIR

John gazed below at the passing coconut palms, knowing that they would soon disappear, and he would be over the water. He eased back in his seat and prepared for the long flight ahead. Spear holes in the fuselage let in a constant smell of fuel and exhaust. But that was of little concern. All that mattered was that he had enough fuel, and the craft was still functional.

He glanced around the cockpit. Everything seemed to be in working order. He looked at a spear protruding from the passenger's side window. His eyes followed the long, wooden shaft to the stone head imbedded in the radio on the console. "Well, almost everything," he said.

He realized he wouldn't be able to call ahead to the South Africa Coast Guard and warn them about the pliosaur. He pulled up a little more on the collective pitch control and laughed. *Like they'd believe me anyway.*

An explosion of white light appeared in front of the helicopter. John looked up at a blinding streak of lightning as the roaring thunder shook the small craft.

A curtain of rain fell from a darkening sky.

Whoa, that was close. John looked at the instrument panel, thankful that the lightning hadn't hit the chopper. "I've got to get out from under this," he muttered, looking up. But the sky was black for as far as he could see. It wasn't long until rain started pouring into the cockpit through numerous spear holes in the windshield.

The engine sputtered. John looked at the fuel gauge, fearing that a spear had severed the fuel line, but the fuel level read half full. He glanced behind the seat. Streams of water were flowing down the inside walls from spear holes near the engine. He realized that water must be leaking onto some of the wiring.

The engine sputtered again and the helicopter dipped. John looked below to the treetops, thankful that he was still over the island. He saw the trees start to thin out as he neared the northern shoreline and decided to bring it down while he still had a choice. He safely touched down on the beach about fifty yards from the waterline.

While the engine whined down, John peered back into the jungle. The tall trees were barely visible through the driving sheets of rain. Only one question haunted him now. *Have the natives given up the chase and assumed I've already left the island?* Estimating that there were at least eight or ten miles separating him from the tribesmen, he felt confident that he had time to wait out the storm.

After positioning himself away from the water pouring through the holes in the windshield, he tried to make himself comfortable. The rain thickened until he couldn't see the shoreline ahead. *Kaboom!* The beach lit up as thunder shook his seat. He knew he was going to be there for a while.

He glanced over at the passenger seat. A flash of lightening illuminated the wet enamel of the giant tooth. *At least when I do make it back, I'll have proof,* he thought. *Otherwise, who knows how many lives would be lost before they'd start taking my story seriously?* He reached over and picked it up. In all of the madness, it was the first time he'd had a chance to look at it up close.

The sheer size of the tooth was unbelievable, longer than his forearm. Holding its blunt end even with his elbow, the pointed crown extended well beyond his fingertips. He lifted it up and down trying to guess its weight. *Now the big question,* he thought. *Who do I show this to first, once I get back?* He recalled an old friend from college and smiled. "What would Willie make of this?"

In his mind's eye, John went back two decades to a quiet afternoon in the UCLA college library. He was sitting at a table, engrossed in his studies when a thick book plopped down in front of him. It was open to a page titled: *"Largest Predators of the Sea."*

John looked up at the curly-haired student. "What have you got now, Willie?"

"This is the prehistoric marine reptile I was telling you about—pliosaur!" replied the lanky young man, barely able to contain himself.

"Pliosaur?"

"Yeah, they were short-necked plesiosaurs with huge heads and massive jaws. And their teeth were enormous; some of them were about the size of a machete."

John had looked at the drawings and pointed to a tiny silhouette one quarter the size of the pliosaur. "What's that small one?"

Willie grinned, "That's a twenty-one-foot great white—looks like a sardine compared to pliosaur, huh?"

John looked at the silhouette of a whale at the top of the page. "It's the size of an adult sperm whale."

"Could sure kick the crap out of Jaws, huh?" Willie laughed.

"No doubt," muttered John. "How long since it's been around?"

"Most paleontologists agree that it died out in the late Jurassic."

"Guess that's why old T-rex was afraid of the water," replied John.

"Yeah, who wouldn't be? They say it was longer than a greyhound bus and had jaws big and powerful enough to pick up a truck and tear it in half. It was the largest carnivore of all time . . . on land or sea!"

Another clap of thunder snatched John from his daydream. Staring at the giant tooth, he noticed what appeared to be gum tissue on the root. "Late Jurassic," he snickered. "Well, Willie old buddy, we'll see what the experts make of this."

~~~

Beneath the dark churning sky, the Indian Ocean grew violent. Slowly, amid the rolling swells, the tip of the jagged frill began to rise— growing longer as more of it broke the surface. The waterline appeared before widely spaced eyes. The roaring thunder and crackling lightning overhead were of no concern.

The giant maw remained slightly agape, forcing the flow of water up into a pair of orifices in the roof of the creature's mouth. The left fore paddle fin tilted, keeping the long, slit-like nostrils on track with the scent just ahead. Armor-plated skin slid silently through the water. Then all four paddle fins pumped in unison—thrusting the colossal beast forward with blinding speed. Every sensory device locked in. A sudden explosion caused the ocean to rumble. The impact drove shock waves through the water as the pliosaur's field of view turned red. The juvenile sperm whale never saw it coming.

Chapter 9
THE STORM

Two hundred miles off the coast of Durban, a small commercial fishing boat struggled to navigate the hostile sea. Standing alone at the helm, a sturdy man in his mid-fifties gripped the wheel firmly. A familiar bottle of Johnny Walker Black was harnessed to the instrument cluster, well within reach.

For thirty-eight years, Captain Sam Buitendach had seen the worst storms these waters could dish out and felt little concern; however, tonight's thirty-foot swells were an exception. With every passing minute, the mountains of water seemed to grow higher.

He glanced at the clock above the instrument cluster. "Ten forty-five. Are we ever gonna find the end of this blasted thing?" he snorted. He peered through the windshield, barely able to see the face of each wave through the wind-driven rain. Again, the bow rose, lifting his view nearly straight up into the black sky, the wheel feeling weightless in his hands. Then the bow dropped over the giant swell, and the windshield washed white with foam as the boat slammed the sea.

Rolling toward another swell, one of his patrons emerged from the lower level. The young man hugging a life jacket grabbed the captain's shoulder. "What's going on, bro? This weather ain't getting any better! You . . . you sure you're going in the right direction to get us out o' this?" He noticed the bottle of whisky on the instrument cluster. "Hey! With weather like this, you think it's a good time to be drinking?"

The captain nodded toward the windshield. "Looking into the face of a thirty-foot swell is as good a time as any . . . boy!"

The young man followed the captain's gaze to the windshield. "I . . . I gotta go back below . . . I can't look at this!" With that, he disappeared into the stairwell.

"Left your sea legs at home, did ya?" bellowed the captain. "That's okay, honey. You just go back to bed, and I'll rock ya to sleep!"

He took another swig and laughed.

For several minutes Buitendach continued to stare at the windshield, unable to see the approaching swells until they were practically on him. The bow repeatedly tilted, looking into the black sky, until the vessel rolled forward and filled the windshield with white foam. The captain lifted the bottle from the harness for another sip. But the bottle stopped short of his lips.

His eyes widened.

The water pounding the windshield was suddenly blood red! The rain washed the substance from the windshield, flowing back across the side windows in disturbing pink streaks. He looked closer at the windshield.

Something white, twice the length of his boat appeared in the face of the approaching wave. At first, it looked like the hull of an overturned boat. Then, *crash!* More bloody seawater smashed against the windshield, obscuring his view. Climbing the next swell, it was clear that what looked like the hull of a boat was actually the white flesh of a whale.

The bow continued to rise straight toward the enormous underbelly, when suddenly the mountain of flesh rolled, revealing a gaping wound in its side. Its giant fluke burst from the sea, rising high into the night. The bottle of Johnny Walker dropped to the deck. Captain Buitendach ducked as the colossal tail swept over the wheelhouse, spewing water against the windshield as the creature was pulled beneath the waves by an unseen force.

The captain fought the wheel, turning against the undertow from the descending whale. He rolled up another swell. A glance back showed an enormous upwelling of white froth in the creature's absence until another swell blocked his view.

A primal roar rose from the waves, echoing across the sea.

He slowly turned back to the windshield. Gripping the wheel with both hands, he stared straight ahead into the torrential rain. His position never changed until they were clear of the storm.

~~~

Lightning reflected from a small tribesman's back as he raced through the jungle hurdling leaves and branches. It was the middle of the night, and the rain continued to pour. His mind raced, thinking about the great discovery he'd made, the white man's machine sitting in front of the coastline. He couldn't believe his hunch had paid off after trekking through the rain all night to the opposite side of the island. He imagined being treated like a hero once he returned. Kota would be proud. He leaped from the thick and stepped onto the wet sand. Finally, Onue could see the torchlight from the village.

~~~

Inside a large hut in the center of the village, Kota wiped the white triangle from his face. Around him dozens of tribesmen drew sharp shells across their chests, mourning the chief's death—a painful tradition to be endured throughout the night with no food or rest. Kota sloshed a rag in a wooden bowl and brought it to his face, and then he heard shouting outside the hut. The sound drew nearer.

The men gathered protectively around Kota and turned their attention toward the entryway.

"White man can't fly in rain! He's here! He's here!" shouted Onue in their native tongue. He ran up to Kota, pointing to the rain outside. "White man still here. He can't fly in rain. I see him. I show you! I show you!"

Kota looked outside the window. Every flash of lightning revealed rain falling at a sharp angle in front of the waving coconut palms. He had the evil one now; Kota knew destiny had delivered the white man into his hands to pay for what he'd done. Kota smiled at Onue. He grabbed the small man's left hand and thrust it into the air for all to see. Onue stood on his tiptoes to increase his height. It was the proudest moment of his life.

The surrounding tribesmen screamed in assumed victory, and Kota pointed to the tiny tribesman with the ear-to-ear smile. "Follow him to the white man!" he commanded in their native tongue. "Do not let the murderer leave the island." Kota reached down to his hip and unsheathed a knife. Multicolored stones sparkled in its handle as he thrust it overhead. "This is for the one who returns with the white man's head."

Kota turned his attention to a large man by his side and said, "Kolegwa, make sure the murderer does not leave the island alive."

Kolegwa replied in their native tongue, "I bring his head in honor of Chief, this I take oath." He took his knife and cut an "X" on the left side of his chest, just deep enough to draw blood.

Kota looked at Kolegwa's chest. "I'm not asking you to do that."

Kolegwa sheathed his knife and said, "I take oath in Chief honor. I not fail," knowing full well that if he returned without killing the white man, he must force his own knife through the "X" on his chest to make up for the life of his enemy with his own.

Kota turned and pointed to the sky. "Now go get the white man while the rain still falls." Through a window, Kota watched as the small native grabbed a torch in each hand and raced through the double doors of the village, the others falling in behind. The points of flickering light slowly disappeared into the pitch-black jungle.

~~~

John woke as cold water hit his face. Looking up, he saw that he was lying beneath one of the numerous spear holes in the windshield. Groggily he sat up and absorbed his surroundings. Beneath several inches of water in the floorboard lighting reflected off dozens of spent shells. To his right, streams of rainwater flowed down, spattering against the machine gun in the passenger's seat. In front of the machine gun he saw the enormous white tooth. "Yeah . . . guess this nightmare is for real."

John leaned back as far away from the broken windshield as possible. It did little good. There wasn't a dry spot in the cockpit. No matter how he positioned himself, an occasional gust of wind would push the rain sideways through the spear holes and splatter his face.

He looked back toward the jungle and then straight ahead to the ocean. But they both remained hidden behind the pouring rain. He looked down and wiped the water from the face of his wristwatch. Four fifteen a.m. It had been over twenty-four hours since they'd arrived on the island. He recalled how Brad had glanced at the drawing in his lap and jokingly said that by now they both might be famous. John leaned his head back and closed his eyes. "I don't think this is quite what Brad had in mind."

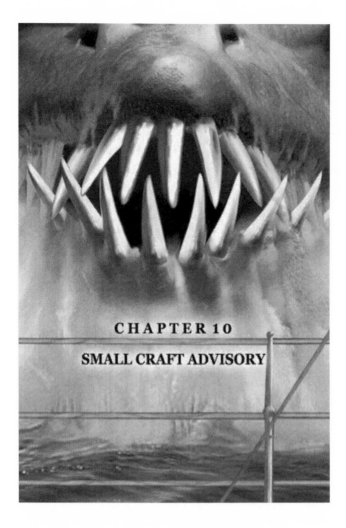

CHAPTER 10

SMALL CRAFT ADVISORY

Carl Jennings stood proudly at the rail of his forty-two-foot yacht, staring across the water. Several miles away, the sandy coast of Mazeppa Bay brightened with the rising sun. The sky bathed in a beautiful reddish-orange hue. He took a deep breath and released it slowly. The early morning air was exceptionally crisp from the remnants of a storm that had passed through during the night.

To Jennings, a marine biologist based in East London, the last few days of snorkeling along Mazeppa Bay had hardly seemed like a vacation. It just felt like another day in the field. But to his new bride, Angela, who had never experienced diving, the ocean was a magical new world she couldn't get enough of. Still Carl had to admit that doing so from the comfort of their new Catalina 42, an anniversary present from

Angela's well-to-do father, did put a fresh spin on things. *I guess there could be worse vacations*, he thought with a smile.

Carl continued to stare into the distance. Although Angela now considered herself an expert and was only snorkeling near the boat, he still liked to keep her in sight. Twenty yards out, a geyser of water shot up from her snorkel. He spotted her long, blond hair and watched her swim closer to an enormous shadow. A tall fin rose behind her. She turned, catching onto the fin. Bubbles streamed from her snorkel as the massive creature pulled her beneath the waves.

Carl's hands tightened on the rail. It was unnerving watching the figure of his wife fade into the depths. But what could he do? It had always been Angela's dream to dive with a whale shark.

Carl's eyes followed her shapely form while she playfully swam with the immense, spotted shark. Holding the fin with one hand, she looked up and waved. Carl waved back without a worry. In spite of the creature's size, he knew that it was completely harmless. Still it never failed to amaze him how a shark so large and intimidating could exist solely on a diet of microscopic plankton. His attention was suddenly drawn to the waters past the bow. He excitedly waved to his wife while holding up two fingers.

Another massive figure slowly moved up behind her.

Angela glanced over her shoulder toward the second whale shark. She broke the surface and pulled out her snorkel. Eyes wide, she pointed to the new arrival. "I've never swam with one whale shark, let alone two! Carl, this is great. You should come in. He wants some attention too."

"No thanks, hon, I'm still a little tired. I was up most of the night watching the weather reports. I'll just watch from here."

"Okay ... but you don't get a chance like this every day." She returned the snorkel to her mouth and dropped beneath the water.

Minutes passed as Carl watched the shimmering figure of his wife swim playfully around the gentle giant. The tip of its nose was just beneath the ship's bow. Angela slowly swam forward and ran her hand along the creature's tall dorsal fin.

Carl looked off port side and into the distance. He raised his hand above his forehead and squinted. In front of the distant Maputo coastline, he saw a third large shadow heading in their direction. "Looks like someone else wants some attention," he muttered.

As the shadow moved closer, Carl realized it was significantly larger than the others. At first, he thought it was a shadow cast from a cloud because of its size. Then, the way it methodically turned toward the boat suggested otherwise.

The huge form glided closer then faded into the sea.

Carl leaned against the rail, searching. Had it left, or was it somewhere on the bottom?

"Angela." Carl called out to his wife.

At the sound of his voice she broke the surface, on her back, holding onto the fin of the whale shark. She looked back at him then squinted in the direction he was pointing. "Where? I don't see anything."

At that same moment, the whale shark she was holding onto registered the newcomer, breaking away in an effort to escape. It bumped the yacht, which yawed violently, knocking Carl from his feet. When he pulled himself back up on the rail, he found Angela looking down, all around her.

She swung her gaze in panic. "The seafloor . . . it's all moving!"

The blood rushed from Carl's face. All he could make out was a gray blur as the pliosaur rose at an angle . . . and barreled its open mouth into the whale shark, catching Angela at the waistline.

In an explosion of whitewater, the colossal jaws lunged from the sea, lifting Angela and the whale shark twenty feet above the surface and then slammed them back beneath the waves.

A curtain of water washed Carl back from the rail. On all fours, staring between the rails, he screamed for his wife. "Angela! Noooooooooo!"

A plume of froth rushed to the surface. Beneath the haze, he saw his wife's lower half buried in the depths of the monster's giant maw. Her arms reached out to him, mouth open in a silent scream, bubbles escaping in a foamy, red cascade.

Pulling himself up on the rail, Carl then got a clear view of the pliosaur in all of its terrifying glory. He realized the creature's dizzying size as it deepened its grip on the whale. Amidst the froth, he saw the jagged frill atop its armor-plated back, the dinosaur-shaped head twisting, a huge front paddle fin pumping.

The second whale shark swam away, escaping the thrashing waters.

Carl couldn't move. It was as if his body had turned to lead. He stared down at the gray, zebra-striped back of the behemoth—wider than his yacht. His mind scrambled to focus, to understand the horror that was happening before him. It wouldn't register. He saw the creature's head even with the bow, yet the tip of its sweeping tail extended forty feet past the stern. Carl's confusion gave way to sheer terror.

The monster rolled. The surface filled with gray, striped flesh as it tried to bite off a large section of the whale. A spiraling paddle fin sent a wave over the rail, pounding Carl. But he managed to hang on.

Carl shook his eyes clear of bloody seawater just in time to wish he hadn't. The horrible, sixteen-foot-long head rose above the waves. His wife's torso hung lifelessly from the side of its jaw. The head arced to swallow a huge chunk of the whale shark. Carl could only watch as his wife's torso fell hideously from the jaws—a disregarded scrap, tumbling, blond hair waving, until it flopped into the sea.

Carl gripped the rail, screaming his wife's name. And in his horror, he realized his mistake. A slit in the gray flesh widened, revealing a red, glowing eye. The colossal head turned toward the boat. Bloody seawater and shards of whale-shark meat flowed from its jaws.

The huge snout paused above the rail, and Carl stared from point-blank range at the most hideous display of teeth he'd ever seen. Gray, pebbled lips did little to contain the nineteen-inch sabers curling out toward him.

Carl stood frozen. A guttural growl made the rail, indeed the entire boat, tremble. Even his shirt shook against his skin. The jaws cracked open, revealing a huge, writhing serpentine tongue. Like a two-headed snake, the forked appendage rose, slithering between machete-sized teeth.

A hot stench of death swept over him.

The jaws opened wider, blotting out the sun.

The head cocked back, releasing a deafening, primal roar. Wind from its breath caught the sail, making the yacht yaw. Carl ducked as the boom swung around and hit the creature's lower jaw.

The colossal head thrashed.

Snap! The towering mast, sail, lines, and all flew clear from the deck and plunged into the sea.

~~~

One mile away, an elderly black man and boy on a small boat stopped hoisting in a net. Eyes bugging, they looked out to sea in the direction of the horrific sound.

~~~

Carl struggled to find his feet. He scrambled across the deck, trying to get out from beneath the creature's shadow. The jaws swept down behind him. A glance back showed planks spraying everywhere as the huge teeth of the lower jaw raked across the deck, collecting lounge chairs and anything in the way.

They grew closer.

He could feel its breath on his back.

Ahead, he saw the stairwell leading to the yacht's lower level. The deck dropped from beneath his feet. He flew into the stairwell face first, sliding to the bottom of the stairs on his chest. But he felt no pain; he was completely numb with fear.

Then . . . a grotesque ripping sound as the top of the stairwell was completely torn away, revealing clouds.

A deafening roar shook the stairs. Carl rolled to his knees. He steadied himself against the wall and scrambled down the hallway in a half-crawling motion. The vessel rocked so violently, he didn't dare try to stand.

His mind was a blur. *Marine crocs aren't a fraction of that size. They don't have paddle fins. And the markings. . . they're all wrong. That was a dinosaur!* His years of marine research and teaching provided no answer for what he'd just witnessed.

He pressed farther along the swaying hallway. The narrow passageway tilted crazily—right, then left. The door to the head swung open in front of him. Grabbing the door for balance, he looked through the doorway to his right. Above a towel rack, he saw a small round window filled with gray skin. Releasing the door, he struggled toward the end of the hallway.

Carl finally reached the cabin containing the radio. His vision was blurring. *Come on, keep it together.* He steadied himself in the doorway, trying to control his breathing in an attempt to fight off shock. The cabin was barely recognizable. His desk that had been anchored to the floor was now lying beside the closet. The closet door hung from one hinge and waved with the room's movement. Its contents were strewn everywhere. On the verge of hysteria, he walked over books, papers, and clothing that littered the floor. Just when he reached the radio, the ship stopped moving.

His trembling hand queued the microphone. "Mayday! Mayday!" His mind swirled. *Try to focus. Come on, think.* He took a deep breath and looked down at the floor. His eyes locked on a picture he'd stepped on. The distorted face of his wife stared back at him from beneath the broken glass. The sudden thought of Angela in the massive jaws buckled his knees. Was the cabin still moving? He couldn't tell—everything was spinning. He leaned back against the wall in a crouched position. His left hand braced on his knee.

Carl continued transmitting, when a dull thud caught him off balance. The boat was moving again. A loud creaking noise. Suddenly, the floor rose, hurling him into the wall. After another tumble and crash, he found himself lying on the light fixture on the ceiling. The entire cabin was upside down. Books, papers and clothing rained down upon him.

A sharp jolt, and the momentum changed. He fell against the wall, then back down to the floor as the boat seemed to right itself. He could picture the creature turning the vessel every which way to get to the prize inside.

A crease formed near the ceiling. A line shot down from the crease, and the walls buckled as the enormous snout plowed into the cabin.

The ship lunged from the impact. The wall in front of Carl crashed in, throwing him across the cabin. Smashing his head against a table, he dropped to the floor like a rag doll.

He could not move or feel anything, but he could see it all. Nineteen-inch teeth sliced through the cabin only a few feet from his body. Overhead, the jagged skin from the great nose scraped across the ceiling, ripping lights from their fixtures. Sparks danced off cold, gray skin.

Beside a dangling light fixture, a red reptilian eye opened. A black, diamond-shaped pupil turned and locked on him. Then the upper jaw slammed down against the floor. A wooden table disintegrated as the massive mouth closed and disappeared, taking with it a large section of the floor and hull. Water gushed in through the immense opening. Carl's left shoulder lifted from the carpet and rose with the flooding waters.

The cabin quickly filled to the ceiling. Carl held what he knew was his last breath. Bed sheets, papers, and clothing swirled around him. Then, with a gurgling roar, the hyperextended jaws crashed back into the cabin, and everything disappeared.

Chapter 11
FIRST FLIGHT OUT

The early morning sun glittered through the broken windshield and into the cockpit. John lay motionless in the pilot's seat, his mouth half open, his head leaning to one side. The damp beach remained completely silent with the exception of an occasional tropical birdcall. Nearby at the edge of the jungle large leaves and palm fronds drooped from the weight of the night's rain.

"KOOOWWWAAAAA!" A loud scream echoed through the cockpit. Reaching immediately for the passenger seat, John grabbed the machine gun. He pointed the barrel at a hole in the windshield and squeezed the trigger. Nothing. The gun only made a clicking sound. *Out of ammo.* As the sleep left John's eyes, he saw the face of a chimpanzee staring at him through a plate-sized hole in the windshield. John sighed with relief. "All that come out of you?" grumbled John with a yawn. He slowly leaned back in his seat and shut his eyes. Even through closed eyes, he had to squint from the bright morning sun. He slowly lifted his hands and rubbed his face. Then he realized something was different. *No rain.*

Sitting up, he grimaced as he felt the tightness of the dried cuts on his chest and left arm. He looked down at the blood on his torn shirt and then at the white tooth in the passenger seat, reminding him that the lingering images in his mind were from more than some strange, twisted dream.

He looked again at the smiling chimp. "Some set of lungs you've got there. You're the first friendly face I've seen around here. So, what's your name? I know," he grinned, thinking about his ex-wife, "with a voice like that, there's only one name for you—I'll call you Crystal."

John looked to the side of the chimp's face at the numerous holes in the windshield and suddenly remembered the urgency of his departure. "Hey, you better get down from there. I've gotta go!" He made a shooing gesture with his hand. Then he reached down to the ignition key.

To John's relief, the engine started without any problem and sounded okay. "Just needed to dry off a little—didn't you?" Preparing for liftoff, he paused. *Maybe I should try to patch the leak from the spear hole while it's still dry. Don't want to run into any rain over the open ocean . . . it would be a long swim back to Durban.*

John turned off the engine. "Let's see if we can find that leak." After sliding between the seats, he stepped into the cargo area. His boots sloshed across the floor. He examined the numerous streaks of light shining through spear holes on the side of the helicopter. With a glance back at the cockpit, he saw the little chimp swing through the shattered passenger-side window and drop into the seat. "Oh, want to help, do you?" John said with a laugh.

He slid open the cargo door. Streams of water cascaded down from the doorway and splattered onto the beach until the cargo floor was exposed. He stepped outside the helicopter and felt his boots sink deep into the moist sand. He looked up at the top of the craft. Just below the main rotor, he spotted a spear hole in the crowning. "That's gotta be the one."

John climbed back into the helicopter through the cargo door. He saw the chimp looking over the back of the seat. "You're just in time. I could use a good navigator." John looked around the floor, "But what I really need is some duct tape—wouldn't happen to have any of that on ya, would you?"

He spotted a large toolbox. "Aha!" Kneeling down, he clicked it open and began rustling through its contents, "Oooh yeah. I can use that too!" John pulled out a Baby Ruth candy bar and laid it by his side.

After rambling through the entire contents of the toolbox, he leaned back on his knees. "A toolbox with no duct tape. What kinda toolbox is this?" The chimp just stared at him. *Wait a minute . . . maybe that'll work.* He pulled out an old 3" x 8" Champion spark plug sticker. Quickly, John opened the candy bar and stepped outside the craft. He put the candy bar in his mouth and thought about the chimp sitting in the cockpit. Then he walked back to the pilot's side door, reached in front of the chimp and pulled out the ignition key. "Nothing personal." The chimp gave him a toothy grin.

After climbing up to the top of the helicopter, John pulled his leg to the opposite side and straddled the craft. He looked down at the five-inch-long spear hole in the crowning. "Should be just big enough to cover it." With his head sticking up between the blades, he peeled the sticker off its backing and realized oil had seeped into part of it. He did his best to stick the unsoiled part of the sticker over the hole. "That's gonna have to do it," he muttered, pressing the sticker down tightly with the palm of his hand.

Suddenly, he heard movement in the nearby foliage. Off to his right, he saw a line of rustling leaves heading in his direction. He quickly realized it wasn't the wind.

John slid down the side of the helicopter like it was a sliding board. He landed in front of the pilot's door and dove to the floorboard beneath the startled chimp. He grabbed the machine gun, ripped the empty clip from its bottom, and thrust his hand under the passenger seat. His hand desperately searched until he felt a cold metal rectangular object and quickly pulled it out. With a crisp "click," the new clip found its way into the bottom of the automatic weapon.

The rustling grew closer.

John dove back out through the pilot's side door, landed on his back, and pointed the barrel in the direction of the rustling leaves, the Baby Ruth bar still protruding from his mouth. Squinting, he looked down the barrel to where the thick foliage of the jungle met the beach. The pilot's door slowly swung shut above him. The sound of the thrashing leaves drew closer when suddenly a wild boar burst from the thick foliage and ran across the beach.

John let out a sigh of relief and laid his head back on the damp sand. Eventually, he came to his feet and reached to open the pilot's side door. Pulling the door open, a thought crossed his mind. *What scared the boar?*

A spear shot through the passenger side window. At the last second, John ducked, feeling the wind brush his cheek as the weapon barely missed his head. He looked back up and saw a tribesman on the opposite side of the helicopter. He was soon joined by his fellow warriors. Aware that John had seen them, the natives screamed in unison as they burst into full stride. John jumped back into the cockpit. From the pilot's seat, he fired his machine gun through the passenger-side window at the oncoming natives. The startled chimp jumped into the floorboard and put her hands over her ears.

Machine gun fire ripped through the passenger-side door, tearing most of it from its hinges. The ebony figures dove to the side, avoiding fragments from the exploding door and the flurry of bullets. John started the helicopter. The chimp raced across the back of John's seat toward the open pilot's side window. John glanced at the black streak behind him. *She's got the right idea.*

He twisted the throttle to maximum RPM. He pulled up on the collective to lift the helicopter, then he pulled to the left, letting the bottom of the helicopter come between him and the wall of natives. A series of dull thuds and pinging sounds echoed from the craft's underbelly. A spear flew past the windshield and was disintegrated by the chopping blades. Fragments of wood sprayed the windshield. Below, buffeted by the wash from the main rotor, John saw half-painted faces shouting up at the sky. One large man stood out among the others. There was no mistaking the burning eyes of Kota glaring up at him. John gave him a final salute and increased his altitude. The surrounding tribesmen ran past Kota and continued pursuit in the shadow of the helicopter. Waving their spears, they crossed the beach and never slowed until they were waist high in the ocean.

The dark figures on the distant shoreline shrank as the chopper pulled farther away. The shoreline eventually disappeared. Soon, the island was only a small green speck in endless blue water . . . and then it was gone.

John turned his attention back to the windshield. He squinted into the distance, carefully scanning for storm clouds. The sunny sky and long white clouds brought him a little piece of mind. He leaned back in his seat and tried to relax. A few deep breaths and his pulse rate lowered closer to normal. Slowly he turned his head from side to side to ease the tension in his neck. His gaze stopped on the giant tooth in the passenger seat. The image of the screaming natives faded and left only one thought on his mind. *The creature's already been free for more than a day!*

~~~

Kate sat at her computer desk in her small Cape St. Francis airport office. The monitor displayed a weather map while she listened to her cell phone. "You still haven't heard from them?" Her face showed genuine concern. "Mom, you know something's not right . . . they're more than a day late. And you said Paxton's always been meticulous about his flight schedule."

Kate listened while looking at the monitor. "I suppose you could be right. I'm looking at a weather map now . . . looks like it's been a bit nasty out there, it could have been a weather delay."

She paused while a plane taxied past the window. "When I get back from my next flight, if you still haven't heard from them, I'll start calling around . . . see if any choppers have been reported down or anything of the sort. And if they don't turn up by tomorrow morning, I was considering flying out there and having a look around—"

Kate paused. Her nose wrinkled, "You can't forbid me from doing anything! If I want to go out there, you can't—"

Kate listened for a moment. "Okay, okay. I promise. I won't go without calling you first. We'll wait . . . see what happens in the next couple hours."

Although she didn't necessarily agree, she decided to humor her mother. "Yeah, I'm sure you're right . . . probably just a weather delay."

Kate closed the phone and stared blankly at the screen. Why did her mother practically forbid her from going to the island? Now she was certain that John and Brad's delay was due to more than just the weather.

~~~

After hours of flying under ideal conditions, the sky began to grow more ominous. The waters flashing below faded to dark gray. The wind whipping through the cockpit grew cooler.

About two miles ahead, John saw an enormous storm cloud in his path. He wondered how the sticker on the crowning was holding out, or if it was even still there. "Better not risk it," he muttered. He pulled the stick to the left, adjusting his course to avoid the dark cloud. He glanced down to the fuel gauge. "Yow. It's going to be close." He knew there was only so far he could alter his course and still make it to the African coast.

Easing off the stick, he noticed a piece of broken windscreen lying on the instrument cluster. In it he saw his reflection. In spite of all the scratches crusted on his face, his eye went to an old scar that had left a slight separation in his left eyebrow. Over the years he'd told everyone it was from a playground mishap. *If only I'd been that lucky*, he thought.

In his mind's eye, John went back twenty-four years to the morning after the accident, when he saw his picture in the local newspaper. Above it, the headline read: "Medical Student Fails Major Test." Those five words had changed the course of his life. He glanced at the giant tooth in the passenger's seat, and like a long-lost friend, a familiar sense of guilt began to swell inside. He was afraid to imagine what the headlines would say this time.

Chapter 12
MOTANZA

Three miles off the coast of Mazeppa Bay, Mike Boland stood at the bow of a *Coastal Eight News* boat, adjusting his camera. Through the lens, he watched an attractive young newscaster receive a final touch of makeup. In the glistening waters behind her, a flotilla of small boats formed a circle around an enormous fishing net.

The newscaster turned her microphone to make sure the red number eight on its front was in proper alignment.

The makeup girl stepped out of frame.

"Five seconds, Susan." Mike called out from behind the camera. He counted down with his fingers ... three ... two ... one, and signaled that she was on the air. "Okay, baby. Let's see that million-dollar smile," he whispered.

The young woman's eyes came to life. "Susan Sherman, Coastal Eight News, reporting to you live. We're just a few miles off Mazeppa Bay on this warm, sunny day to bring you the Mazeppa Motanza." She had to speak above a nearby boat of environmentalists who were shouting and waving signs.

"What's a Motanza, you ask? Well, that's Italian for Bloody Festival—not for the squeamish, I might add. This tradition was adapted from the original Motanza held annually in Italy off the coast of Sicily."

Susan brushed a strand of hair from her face. "Now the way this works, as you can see behind me, is that the local fishermen circle their boats around an enormous net dropped deep beneath the surface. Then the fishermen in each boat pull in the net until it rises to the surface, trapping everything within the circle. The goal is to trap some forty or fifty yellow fin tuna, each weighing in at around two hundred pounds. Although not quite as large as the blue fin variety caught off Sicily, these fish can still put up quite a struggle.

"Now this is where the Motanza lives up to its name. The fishermen use large hooks in an attempt to bring these massive fish on board their dinghies where it all turns into a bloody struggle between man and fish."

Mike gave Susan her queue. She stepped aside, allowing the camera to close in on the action. Dredged up from the depths and pulled taut by the fishermen, the giant net was filled with thrashing tuna. Mike closed on one of the two-hundred-pounders as it slipped off a fisherman's hook and thrashed back down to the center of the net, blood spewing from its side. He panned to another group of fishermen. Several hooks ripped into a giant tuna, hauling it on board. Beneath the thrashing tail, blood gushed down the side of the boat and flowed into the rising net.

The camera panned back to Susan. "Oftentimes, dolphins, sharks, and other forms of sea life fall victim to the indiscriminate net. And, as you may have noticed from the signs around me, not everyone is happy about this newly adapted form of fishing."

The camera zoomed in on a group of eight, standing at the rail of a yacht. They all held a banner that spelled MURDERERS in smeared red letters. Waving the banner, they chanted, "No more Motanza! No more Motanza!"

As the protests grew louder, Susan moved back into the shot. "Whether you're a spectator or participant, one thing is for sure—the Motanza festival is certainly not for the faint-hearted." She gave a winning smile. "This is Susan Sherman for Coastal Eight News, Mazeppa." As per tradition, she held her smile for a few moments. Then it turned to a grimace. "Yuk! Get what you need, and then let's get out of here before I lose my lunch."

Susan clicked off her mike with a sigh of relief. Then in the background a huge, gray shape burst out of the waters below the net, pushing the net upward. Mike stood up from behind the camera, not believing his eyes.

Ten feet . . .

Twenty feet . . .

The net continued to rise while taking on the form of a massive head.

Susan turned around and dropped the microphone, her facial expression one of horror. She tried to speak, but her words were muted by the cries of the fishermen.

The net rose higher. With nearly half its body towering above the surface, the veiled monstrosity thrashed in midair. Dozens of yellow fin tuna were propelled upward, flopping and twisting forty feet above the sea.

Fishermen in the creature's shadow dove from their boats. The towering body began to fall. In an explosion of whitewater, the tangled giant crashed down on the boats on the west side of the circle, splintering them throughout the sea. Simultaneously boats on the opposite side were capsized from the violent pull of the net. A swell shot out and slapped the news boat's hull, rocking the deck. Mike and Susan struggled to maintain her balance. Screams battered the air. In disbelief, Mike quickly ducked back down behind his camera, fighting to cover the scene. Before the swaying lens were shoulders ripped from their sockets and fingers torn from hands still clinging to the net.

The tangled beast dove and rolled beneath the waves, taking with it several fishermen who couldn't free themselves in time.

Splash! A plume of water shot up in front of the camera. Another splash . . . the tuna sent skyward were dropping like bombs. Another fish slapped the water near the bow. Without warning, a gigantic tuna landed on a girl holding part of the banner on the protestors' boat. To Mike's left, another tuna had landed on another boat, catapulting a man into the water. Tuna continued to fall at random, water spewing into the air like exploding depth charges.

Mike frantically panned the camera, trying to get the bizarre scene into frame. He searched for the netted creature, but found only the damage left in its wake. On the protestors' boat, he saw a woman's leg protruding from beneath one of the tuna. Three men struggled to move the huge fish while the woman's heel slid from side to side on the deck.

In front of the protestors' boat were many capsized fishing boats. Men in the water struggled to crawl on top of their overturned hulls. Other fishermen swam for the spectators' boats where they were eagerly pulled aboard. Mike panned left and saw two men lying on the deck of a fishing boat. Their faces grimaced in pain while several men around them ripped off parts of their shirts to wrap their bleeding hands.

Mike scanned the water searching for the creature. He tried to lower the camera to where several spectators were pointing, but the bow of his boat blocked his view. Stepping in front of the camera, he walked to the edge of the bow. Susan backed away. Beneath the rippling surface, Mike saw the huge shadow still under the swirling net while several tangled figures trailed behind. With another thrash, two of the men were thrown clear of the net. They quickly paddled upward and broke surface, blood streaming from their hands.

Mike watched the remaining fisherman trying to free his hand from the metal hook tangled in the net. He was trying to undo the strap that secured the hook to his wrist. Every time he had it loose, the net pulled, causing the strap to tighten. Again the net jerked. The shimmering figure went limp, his now lifeless body tossed about with the creature's every move. Mike wanted to jump in and help, but he hesitated. He had no idea what was under the net.

He stood on the edge of the bow, struggling to get up his nerve. Adrenaline pounded in his veins. Then the trail of bubbles flowing from the fisherman's nose stopped. Before Mike knew what he was doing, he was already in the water. Susan's screams disappeared when he dropped below the waves. He swam toward the tangled creature. The enormous net billowed, reaching for him as if it had a mind of its own.

He reached the unconscious man and felt his way through a blood cloud around the strapped wrist. The net went slack. Mike carefully looked to make sure the massive head was still pointed in the opposite direction.

He jiggled the hook, trying to get it to release. Blood swooshed around his hands. He almost had it free when a sudden thrash from the beast tossed the net over them. Mike felt his way through the swirling maze until he found the edge of the net. Pushing the bundled net aside, the hook released from the extra slack.

He grabbed the limp body around the neck and swam clear of the net. He looked back. The massive tail thrust, throwing the net clear of the creature's body. From Mike's angle, he caught a glimpse of an enormous paddle fin until the swirling net again blocked his view.

A few more strokes, and Mike finally reached the surface. He gasped for air, again hearing the cries and moans. Men on a nearby fishing boat quickly pulled the injured fisherman from his arms. Mike swam back to the news boat where Susan was waiting for him behind the ladder.

"Are you okay?" Susan had tears streaming down her face.

"Yeah, yeah. Where is it? Is it still tangled?"

"I . . . I don't know."

Mike ran to the camera and searched for the rising net. Water from his drenched clothes poured onto the deck while he jockeyed the large TV camera.

The creature suddenly burst from the surface, thrashing wildly to free itself from the net. Water spewed over the bow of Mike's boat and onto the camera lens.

After finding her microphone, Susan, crouching low, poked her head in front of the camera. "Are you getting this?"

"You better believe it!" Mike said. "I don't know what it is—but we're looking at worldwide news. And to think you didn't want to come out here and cover a lousy protest!"

The camera followed the choppy water until the bundled net submerged. Little remained of the circular formation of boats as Mike searched the debris and overturned hulls, looking for the slightest trace of whitewater.

"Well, what are you waiting for, Susan?" yelled Mike. "Say something!"

Susan, her makeup streaked with tears, gathered her composure. She searched for words to describe what was unfolding before her.

As she began to speak, there was a loud splash behind her, and then the boat jarred abruptly as the deck rose from the water. The camera continued to roll, filming only white clouds while Susan's commentary was reduced to a scream.

Moments later, Mike opened his eyes to find Susan lying on the deck beside him, frantically crying. Mike rolled over on his side. "Are you okay?"

"I . . . I think so," Susan got up and ran back behind the helm.

He looked back and saw the camera protruding from the boat's windshield. "Yeah, I'm okay too. Thanks for asking!" Mike slowly stood, his eyes scanning the water. The entangled bulk glided away from the scene. Mike pressed his hand to his heart.

~~~

Due west, just beyond the tattered circle of boats, a couple in their sixties watched from the starboard rail of their yacht. They held hands and silently witnessed the horror unfold, unsure what had happened. That's when they saw a bundled net heading their way, bumping smaller boats out of its path.

The bundle drew closer.

Thud!

The net rose before their eyes, piling up against the starboard rail. They ran to the opposite side of the ship and looked over the port rail. Their eyes grew wide. Freed from its netted veil, a mass of gray, zebra-striped flesh emerged from beneath the boat, the jagged tips of the frill just breaking the water. The stunned couple backed away as the sea creature slowly faded into the depths, leaving a bloody haze that pointed north, toward the African coast.

Chapter 13
THE SIX O'CLOCK NEWS

Lieutenant Vic Greeman unbuttoned the shirt of his Navy uniform while he walked along the hallway of his East London beachfront home. After a full day's work, the lush carpet felt soothing beneath his bare feet. He entered the family room to a familiar sight. His eight-year-old son Timmy sat in the center of the couch watching TV. The child didn't acknowledge his presence. He just stared at the screen, the shield to his familiar space helmet flipped up. A plastic ray gun was by his side.

This isn't getting any better. Unbuttoning his cuff, he glanced at the program that had Timmy on the edge of his seat. He saw an immense, netted creature burst from the sea while scattered fishermen clung to the hulls of their overturned boats. Then the screen turned blue, showing the sky, while a woman screamed in the background. He looked at the back of the eight-year-old's space helmet.

"That's it. I've had it. All you do is sit around here all day long watching that science fiction channel."

"But Dad!" Timmy protested.

"No, it's not healthy. You should be out playing ball with your friends. That is if you still have any since all you do is watch this rubbish all day!"

"But Dad!"

"When I was your age, I was always out playing ball, climbing trees, or riding my bike."

A female voice yelled out from the kitchen, "I don't want him climbing any trees."

Vic glanced toward the kitchen and continued, "Too much of that science fiction stuff will warp your mind. I want you to turn that TV off right now. Go get your soccer ball and go outside and practice kicking goals like you used to!"

"But Dad!" pleaded Timmy.

"No. I'll hear no more of it."

"But Dad . . . it's not the *Sci Fi Channel*. It's the six o'clock news!"

Vic looked back at the TV. The footage stopped and an anchorwoman appeared on screen. "And that was the scene earlier today just off the coast of Mazeppa Bay, South Africa, where apparently a whale attacked the net during the Mazeppa Motanza, a traditional fishing festival. As of now, there are no known fatalities. But the thrashing whale was responsible for dozens of injuries, some of which were quite serious."

She glanced down at a paper on her desk and continued. "Seventeen fishermen had injuries ranging from dislocated shoulders to missing fingers and hands from the tremendous pull of the net. Several other men nearly drowned after they became entangled in the net and were pulled beneath the surface. An unsuspecting bystander suffered a broken leg and a dislocated hip when a tuna in excess of two hundred pounds landed on her after being thrown from the net.

"Also damaged were eleven fishing boats and one pleasure boat which sank after being capsized from what marine biologists are calling an extremely aggressive humpback whale. They claim that the creature must have been attracted to the net by the thrashing tuna, then became disoriented when the net tangled around its head.

"On a final note, our own Mike Boland who covered the event claimed that the creature he saw had a strange paddle-like fin unlike any found on a whale. Amid all the confusion, one thing's for certain; this year's festival truly lived up to its name. We'll have more on this bizarre incident tonight at eleven."

Vic finished unbuttoning his shirt and walked back to his bedroom, sensing that tomorrow was going to be more than just another day at the office.

~~~

"No. I'm sorry, Mr. Patterson, but moving your flight back two hours won't help. I'm afraid I have to cancel," said Kate into the speakerphone in her Cape St. Francis office. She raised her voice while another plane taxied to the runway. "I know you have been a client for years, but I must cancel all of my flights for tomorrow. I'm afraid there's been an emergency. I have to leave first thing in the morning.

"Okay, thanks for understanding . . . and if the photo shoot can wait a few days, I'll be glad to take you when I get back. Thanks again. Sorry for the inconvenience."

Kate clicked off the speakerphone. "Well, that was the last of the cancellations, at least for tomorrow." She reached back across her desk and pressed the button to play the messages on her answering machine. The tape revealed nothing new. *Mom still hasn't heard from them. Come on, John. Where are you?* She glanced up at the clock on the wall. "Quarter after seven," she muttered. "Nearly two days late, now it's official. Something's definitely wrong."

~~~

Like an entity with a mind of its own, the enormous storm cloud seemed to sense John's every move. No matter how far he altered his course, the darkness lingered above. The wind whipping through the cockpit grew moist.

He looked at his fuel gauge. *I just don't have enough fuel to keep trying to fly around this thing. I've got to get back on course, or I'm not going to make it. That's it! If it won't let me fly around it, I'll fly through it.* Adjusting his course, he noticed the pressure on his bladder, a constant reminder that he hadn't had time to relieve himself before leaving the island. He looked around the cockpit wondering how to alleviate the situation. Then a glance back up at the sky made him change his priorities. *I'll worry about that after I reach the other side of the cloud.*

Flying below the swelling cloud, a few raindrops began hitting the windshield. A chill shot up John's spine, but the hint of clear sky on the other side of the cloud calmed his nerves. The scattered drops of rain transformed into a steady drizzle. John held his breath, listening to the engine. The engine sounded okay. He watched the clear sky inch its way closer. He glanced down at the fuel gauge. *That should be enough. I knew I could make it—I can't believe I wasted all of that fuel trying to fly around this thing.* Still, he wondered how the sticker on the crowning was holding out. He knew it was on there pretty good, but just the same, he felt behind his seat to make sure the bundled life raft was well within reach.

"Lighten up," he whispered, staring into the dark cloud, "you're gonna give yourself a heart attack." He let out a slow breath and tried to relax. He leaned back in his seat and closed his eyes for a moment to relieve the tension.

The engine sputtered.

It sputtered again.

John's eyes flew open and he saw the blue waters racing up to meet the windshield. He pulled back on the stick shouting, "I knew it—how could I've been so stupid? I can't believe I tried to fly through this thing!"

The engine stopped sputtering, giving the helicopter a sudden burst of power. John pulled back on the stick, raising the nose as the landing gear scraped across the white caps. The engine ran smoothly for a few seconds allowing the helicopter to regain proper altitude. John squinted, trying to see if there was any trace of the South African coastline through the drizzling rain. He had to be close.

Again the engine sputtered and then completely shut off. As the helicopter dropped, he fought to keep it steady, trying to let the spinning main rotor act as a wing to slow his descent. It didn't work—the helicopter dropped faster than expected.

John braced for impact.

Suddenly, the engine fired once and started. John pulled back on the stick. The engine whined, trying to turn the rotor fast enough to slow the rapid descent. He twisted the throttle to full power, but the landing gear was already touching the waves.

John struggled to keep the main rotor flat, hoping to lift the helicopter straight up from the water. Then the loss of control of the foot pedals told him it was too late. The tail rotor was slapping the sea. In a last-ditch effort to lift the tail rotor from the water, he pushed the stick forward, allowing the main rotor to dip forward. He overcorrected. Through the windshield, he saw the blades of the main rotor scraping the surface. He pulled back, trying to level it off. The blades only slapped louder. Whitewater flew into the windshield as the stick jerked violently from his hands.

When the water level reached the cockpit, John realized he had no chance. Instinctively, he grabbed the tooth and slid it behind his belt. There was a screech of metal as the blades snapped. The cockpit dipped violently. He reached behind his seat and grabbed a life vest and an orange plastic bag.

The rolling cockpit flooded with cool ocean water, quickly reaching John's throat. He took a deep breath just before it shot above his head. Shoving the plastic bag through the door, John pushed off from the seat with his feet. He glided away from the sinking craft, his arms wrapped around the lifejacket until its buoyancy pulled him toward the surface.

His face burst above the waves and was met by sprinkling rain. He looked across the water. The plastic bag popped up about fifteen feet away. A head broke the surface, just in front of the bag.

"Crystal! I thought you skipped out on me back at the island." John laughed and swam toward the chimp. He slipped on the lifejacket then reached over and yanked the cord on the thick plastic bag. Crystal screamed when an orange raft suddenly inflated beside her.

John tossed the chimp in first then rolled in behind her, careful not to let the tip of the pliosaur tooth touch the fabric. Pulling his boots into the raft, he noticed the pressure in his bladder was gone. Apparently, the problem of relieving himself took care of itself upon impact. He looked across the choppy waters through the drizzling rain, searching for the slightest hint of coastline. In every direction, the view was the same. Water.

He lay back in total exhaustion and felt the raft following the contours of the waves. Cool rain sprinkled lightly onto his face. He looked over at the shivering chimp. "Pretty rough flight, huh?" The chimp nodded her head up and down, making John laugh out loud for the first time in two days.

As he lay gazing into the dark clouds, he couldn't help but think of the obvious. He tried to convince himself that the pliosaur should be at least a hundred miles away. But how could he be sure? He took the tooth from his waistband and slid it a couple feet away, suddenly finding it unsettling to have the giant fang touching his skin.

Chapter 14
DEADLY DISCOVERY

Sandy Winston jumped the wake of the silver speedboat and glided through another turn, her blond hair pulled back in a ponytail. Her lime-green ski vest and swimsuit glowed against her tan skin as she skimmed across the water at top speed. A glance over the teen's shoulder showed the Mazeppa Bay coastline flashing by.

Sandy eased up on the handle, setting up for the next turn. She leaned sharp. The surface glided below her left elbow as a twenty-foot wall of whitewater sprayed up from the edges of her skis. Her ponytail then shot straight back as she pulled from the turn with a burst of speed. The momentum brought her even with the side of the boat. She glanced over to wink at her father, but he was taking a sip from his water bottle and didn't see her.

At that moment, her left ski stopped dead in the water. Sandy flew forward, skimming and rolling across the surface in a lime-green flash. She finally bounced to a stop and pulled her head above the waves. Slowly regaining her senses, she watched the abandoned ski handle skim across the surface as the boat pulled farther away.

Her left ankle began to throb. She reached down to the pain. "At least my foot's still there," she muttered. She reached for her heel but couldn't feel the touch through the throbbing numbness. Slightly disoriented, she looked around for her skis. She swam back until she found her right ski, then spotted the second one about ten yards behind it.

With each slow kick, Sandy gave a whimper from the pain in her ankle. She reached her left ski and picked it up. The front of the ski was completely missing from about six inches in front of the boot. She stared at the splintered edge. "Oh no!" she screamed. "There's something down there!"

She dropped the ski and slowly swam backward, away from it. Every shark attack movie she'd ever seen rushed through her mind. Something rammed her in the back, and her blood-curdling scream echoed across the water. She lunged forward, slapping at the surface.

~~~

Eventually, Val looked back to check on his daughter and found the empty handle bouncing in his wake. He cut the throttle and circled back around. That was when he heard the screams above the boat's idling engine. Fifty yards in the distance, he saw the horrible splashing. "God no, not that!" He slammed the throttle wide open and raced toward the whitewater, already blaming himself for what he knew he'd find.

~~~

Sandy twisted on the surface. Her eyes squeezed shut as she pulled her legs up, waiting in horror for the next hit. But it didn't come. She slowly opened her eyes. Turning around, she saw a round, white object protruding six inches above the surface. Waving just below the water was something white, like a parachute. She put her hand on top of the pole-like object and dipped her head below the clear water. Her eyes followed the long mast all the way down to where its splintered end met the seafloor. It was being held up by air trapped in the tangled sail. Not far from the mast was a sunken yacht. Beside the yacht, she noticed another large shape. It looked like some kind of whale lying on its side a few yards from the yacht's hull.

Sandy pulled her face from the water when she heard the boat's engine. She turned as the wake from the ski boat rolled over her vest. "It's a ship! There's a ship down here and a dead whale. Get your mask, you gotta see this."

Val frantically reached down from the side of the boat, "Sandy, are you all right? That scream . . . I thought you were—"

Sandy waved. "I'm okay. It was the mast from the ship." She pointed to the white object protruding from the surface. "I must have hit it. You should see my left ski, it's totally trashed." She again felt the pulsating pain in her ankle. "I think my left ankle is broken or at least sprained."

Val pulled his fourteen-year-old from the water and lifted her over the gunwale. Sandy released a moan when her left foot touched the deck. Her father quickly scooped his arm under her legs and carried her to a long seat at the stern where he carefully set her down. "That doesn't look so good. It's already starting to swell. Can you move your toes?"

Sandy bit down on her lip, straining, but her toes barely wiggled, "Yeah, but I can't feel 'em."

"Sit tight. I'll go get some ice from the chest. I don't think it's all melted yet."

"No! First drop the anchor," Sandy pleaded. "We don't want to lose the spot, and it'll be dark soon."

"Okay, but don't you stand up."

"You should see it . . . it's really spooky! The ship is down there at the bottom, and the whale is right beside it with its belly almost touching the bottom of the ship. It's a huge whale, at least as big as the ship. Maybe bigger."

"Well, right now I'm more worried about that ankle," replied Val, banging the bag against the deck to break the ice into more manageable pieces.

"But Dad, we've got the diving gear on board, and we just had the tanks filled yesterday. Come on. Don't be a moffie."

Val looked up from the ice bag. "What's a moffie?"

"It's South African surf slang. It means like a pansy or a wimp. But I'm just kidding, Dad. I know you're not a moffie. But you gotta take a look."

"Surf slang, huh? Does your mother know you've been hanging around with surfers?"

"Yeah. They're always around us. They always try to leave their towels near our chairs. Yesterday, one of them called Mom a bokkie."

"Bokkie."

"Yeah, it means young pretty lady."

Val's eyebrows arched. "Well, we'll see if you two go to the beach alone anymore."

He stood back up and glanced at the water. "I guess I better take a look."

"All right!" Sandy shouted victoriously.

Val slid the ice chest to the stern and carefully placed his daughter's foot on top of it. "What are you so excited about? You're not going anywhere."

"Come on, Dad, I'll never get another chance to make a dive like this. Look, I can move my toes. It's not broken; it's not that bad."

Val walked starboard and strapped on his tank. "No, just hold that ice right where it is, and don't take your foot off the chest. The Durban slalom finals are just a month away. We want you healthy for that, don't we? I'll take a quick look, and then we're going to get you back and have someone take a look at that ankle."

Sandy continued to plead. "Come on, Dad, my ankle will be okay. Besides, you know it's dangerous to dive alone."

"Good point, it could be dangerous—that's why you're staying on the boat." Val placed the regulator in his mouth and dropped backward from starboard.

The passing minutes seemed more like hours as Sandy sat with the ice bag balanced on her left foot. Her gaze drifted toward starboard deck, where she saw the sun twinkling on her dive mask. The pull of her curiosity was too strong. "Okay, time for a break."

After hopping on her right foot, she picked up her mask and snorkel. She leaned over the side of the boat as far as possible, straining to reach the surface with her mask. The throbbing pain in her ankle intensified. Still, she had to see what was going on. The moment her dive mask touched the water, her father broke the surface and shot up the ladder in a single motion.

He ripped off his mask and gasped. "It looks like Sea World's Shark Encounter down there. There are sharks everywhere! The whale carcass must have attracted every bull shark for miles." Sandy's eyes widened beneath her mask, and she quickly leaned over the gunwale to take another look.

Val grabbed her by her ski vest and pulled her up. "Get your face away from there! Didn't you hear me? There are about a dozen sharks down there. Hey. You shouldn't even be standing up. Get back over there and sit down. And put that ice pack on your ankle before it gets to be the size of an elephant's."

With a rebellious sneer, Sandy hopped back to the stern, took a seat, and slid the ice chest beneath her foot. "So what else did you see down there? Were there any dead bodies?"

"No . . . I don't know," replied Val, pulling off his fins, still shaken. "I didn't really get a chance to look inside the ship."

Placing the ice bag on her ankle, Sandy looked up. "But Dad, don't you think we should call someone, like the Coast Guard?"

Val slid the tank off his back, "Yeah, I'll call it in right now. But I don't think South Africa has a Coast Guard. I think those duties are handled by some special branch of the Navy. You just sit tight, and we'll wait until they get here."

~~~

John pressed his elbow over the side of the raft and stared across the open sea. His visibility was limited in the drizzling rain. He squinted, then rubbed his eyes and again it was gone. What appeared to be lights from a boat turned out to be only another wave twinkling in the distance.

Boat, John thought almost with a laugh. He tried to tell himself he was searching for boats to rescue him, but knew he was on the lookout for something else. He looked at the giant tooth beside his boots and then at the chimp who was staring out across the open sea. "Yeah, you know there's something out there too. Don't you, girl?"

John slowly lay back down, and the tension in his neck released. Knowing what was out there made it impossible to sleep, though. The best he could manage was to pass out for brief intervals. It was difficult to determine how long he was out because every time he woke, it was to the same sky and light rain.

Earlier he saw a row of lights from what appeared to be a cruise ship passing from a few miles away. To the best of his calculations, the ship was northeast of the raft. Maybe he was close to a shipping lane. There was a chance that by morning the current would bring him close enough to be seen in the daylight. John didn't get his hopes up, though—as far as he could tell, the current was pulling him westward.

His head throbbed from dehydration. His mind had started playing tricks on him, making time and distance almost impossible to calculate.

John noticed movement out of the corner of his eye. He froze. At first he thought it was his over-stimulated imagination, but he knew better as an obscure shape grew closer, rippling the smooth black waters.

The chimp sensed John's alarm and scooted to his side.

Drawing closer, a dorsal fin broke the surface. As the shimmering gray back glided past, John realized it was a great white about fourteen feet long. He lay back down on one elbow and rubbed the chimp's head. "Relax, Crystal, it's practically a minnow."

He watched as the fin made another pass, and in spite of his predicament, he couldn't help laughing. Who would have ever thought that watching a large great white from a six-foot raft would bring a sense of relief? As the fin continued to circle, John gazed at the passing clouds. With a bizarre sense of safety, he knew that if this great white was still in the area, the eighty-foot monstrosity was not.

He shook his head and stared blankly into the drizzling rain. "How did I ever let the professor talk me into this?"

~~~

"Just a few more minutes, and we'll take it off," said Val, carefully holding the bag of ice on his daughter's ankle.

"But it's so cold . . . can't we take it off now?"

Val slowly lifted the bag. "Well, let's see how it looks." He rubbed two fingers across her tight, cool skin. "Not bad," he said. "The swelling doesn't seem to have gotten any worse."

Sandy began to fidget in her seat and excitedly pointed from the stern. "Look, they're here! I can see them!"

Val looked back toward the approaching boat. "It's about time. It's been over an hour. Another twenty minutes and it'll be dark."

The thirty-eight-foot Naval Patrol vessel pulled alongside the ski boat. A black man in a wet suit tossed Val a line. Val pulled the rope taut as the diver put his hand on the speedboat's starboard, easing the vessels closer together. Another man dressed in a naval uniform stepped across and boarded the ski boat. He was a stocky blonde in his late forties. His gray eyes were filled with curiosity.

"Sorry it took us so long. We were only a couple miles away when we received your call. We were helping with cleanup at the Motanza. We would have been here sooner, but on the way we ran into someone with engine trouble. I'm Captain Longland." He extended his hand.

"Val Winston, and the one over there with her foot up is my daughter Sandy."

"So we hear you've come across something quite interesting out here."

"Actually, my daughter was the one who came across it, and come across it she did! The impact nearly broke her ankle." Val glanced at his watch and called back to Sandy. "Time to put the ice back on." Sandy frowned but reached for the ice bag.

Val pointed to an area about ten yards off port. "We were going at a pretty good pace when, right over there, she apparently hit the tip of the mast. You can barely see it. It broke her ski in half, but fortunately the ski took most of the force. I grabbed my tank and went down to take a look.

"It was really strange. A yacht, maybe a thirty-five- or forty-footer on its side, and parallel to its hull was a dead whale shark. I was going to take a closer look until I nearly butted heads with a good-sized bull. I decided that was a good time to get back to the boat. There are at least a dozen sharks around the carcass. Better tell your guys to keep their eyes open down there."

The captain stepped closer to Val and lowered his voice. "Did you run across any bodies or human remains?" Sandy craned her neck, trying to listen.

"No. But like I said, I wasn't down that long."

The captain looked toward the Mazeppa Bay coastline. "That's peculiar. We didn't receive any distress calls from this area." He turned his attention to the patrol boat. He looked at the two divers gearing up at the stern. One man looked Italian, and the other was black, but they both had regulation crew cuts and sleek athletic builds. "Angelo, Marty, apparently there are a number of sharks down there feeding from the carcass. Make sure to take your spear guns."

The captain pointed to a spot about twenty yards past the patrol boat. "See? There's the tip of the mast." The divers looked toward the white tip. "Try dropping down from there straight to the bottom then approach the ship from the west side. That way you may be able to use the ship to keep you out of view of the sharks. Good luck and be careful." The two divers gave him the thumbs-up then slipped into the water, being careful not to make a splash.

As the two figures faded into the depths, Captain Longland approached Sandy. "Now let's have a look at that ankle, shall we?"

~~~

Beneath the surface, the divers followed the mast until they reached the huge air bubble trapped in the sail, then slowly descended straight down to the ocean floor. Staying close to the bottom, they left the severed mast and swam toward the ship while carefully looking in all directions. They took the yacht's ID number, then swam over the side rail and reached the tilted deck. Angelo pointed up. There was a long section of the deck where the planks had been torn up. It led to the stairwell, where the top had been completely ripped away. Marty shook his head in disbelief.

The two divers swam farther up the deck. They examined the jagged shards of wood around the cavity that once was the stairwell, then descended into the ship's lower level. Angelo entered the hallway. The light from behind suddenly disappeared. He looked back and caught a glimpse of something passing over the stairwell. Judging from the shadow, it looked very large. Quickly he spun around in the hallway and decided to investigate. Marty followed just behind Angelo's fins.

After gliding through the stairwell, Angelo looked across the deck and saw nothing. Staying close to the tilted deck, they swam farther up toward the portside rail. Angelo reached the rail first and looked through. At point-blank range, he found a pair of cold black eyes staring back at him. He pushed back from the rail in terror, bumping into Marty. Their eyes never left the twelve-foot bull shark as it continued its gaze from behind the rail. The shark slowly lifted its nose above the rail curiously, watching the fleeing divers. Then with a sudden lateral movement the creature turned and swam in the opposite direction, joining the feast below.

From the higher angle, Angelo could see the entire body of the dead whale shark. Its white underbelly ran parallel with the bow of the ship. Just past the flopped-over pectoral fin he saw where the creature's head had been nearly severed. The massive carcass rocked while dozens of gray tails thrashed in front of the gaping wound.

Beneath Angelo a large torpedo-shaped shadow crossed the deck. He looked up and ducked. The white underbelly of another bull shark flashed over him and disappeared behind the side rail. Angelo made a pounding gesture over his heart then pointed back to the stairwell.

Marty quickly nodded.

The divers descended to the deck. Silver clouds of bubbles rose above the leaning rail and raced toward the surface. Dropping into the dark stairwell, Angelo turned on his dive light. The beam shined through the hallway illuminating the open doors that swung with the flow of the current—a current that seemed mysteriously strong to be flowing through an enclosed ship.

Marty fell behind Angelo and entered a cabin on their left. Angelo ventured forward and shined his light into a restroom on the right. Inside, a terrycloth robe reached out from a towel rack, waving with the current from a nearby open window. He opened a closet door beside the shower. A stack of white towels dropped out, unfolding as they glided through the water. Pushing the towels aside, he swam back through the doorway. Again he felt the current surge through the hall. Angelo continued to make his way around hovering articles of clothing until he reached a partially opened door at the end of the hall.

When he reached for the handle, the door blew open from the passing current. Oddly, the cabin was slightly illuminated. A glance to the right revealed why. There was an immense jagged opening which allowed dim light reflecting from the seafloor to enter the room. Swimming closer to the hole, the white underbelly of the whale shark came into view.

Marty entered the doorway with his spear gun in hand. Through his dive mask Angelo could see the surprise in his eyes when he saw the massive jagged opening.

Angelo pointed the beam of light toward the ceiling. Light reflected from a long splintered indentation that ran the width of the cabin. Broken light bulbs dangled from wires and swayed with the current. A bull shark poked its head into the opening and turned toward the dive light. The beam fell across the widely spaced black eyes. Angelo backed toward the doorway.

Marty moved aside, allowing Angelo to exit the cabin first. Once outside the cabin, Marty quickly closed the door behind them and swam back through the hallway, his spear gun trained on the door. Marty turned around, and a flannel shirt wrapped around his face. Pushing the shirt away, he caught his mask and slid it off, his spear gun dropping to the hallway floor. Angelo swam back to Marty and grabbed the shirt. Just as he tossed it aside, the massive head of the bull shark crashed through the cabin door. The shirt rolled across the shark's back, catching on the speeding dorsal fin.

Tossing the dive light, Angelo scooped up the spear gun from the floor. He took aim at the fast-approaching head. Click. The spear streaked through the hallway and plunged into the bathroom door, just as it swung open in front of the shark's head. The door split in half, falling from its hinges as the bull shark burst through it. Angelo reached the stairwell and saw the back of Marty's fins fluttering above the steps. Marty looked back, motioning for them to surface.

With an eager thumbs-up, Angelo followed.

Leaving the stairwell, Angelo saw another large shadow cross the deck—another bull shark passing overhead. Looking down, he saw the thick, gray head of their aggressor rise from the shadowy stairwell. While ascending, Angelo reloaded the spear gun and pointed it toward the stairwell. The shark soared over the deck, adjusting its course to continue the hunt. The thirty-yard gap between the shark and divers was quickly reduced to ten.

Angelo nervously took aim. He knew that if he missed a second time, there would never be a third. Slowly, he squinted. His finger tightened on the trigger. The spear streaked through the water, glazing the bull's gills. The creature thrashed for a moment, then arced back around and headed toward the whale carcass. As the fluttering tail sped toward the seafloor, Angelo made for the surface.

~~~

At the waterline Captain Longland helped the divers up the ladder of the patrol boat. Angelo pulled up his mask first. "Sir, he wasn't exaggerating about the number of sharks down there. They're everywhere, even inside the ship. We had a couple of close ones!"

Marty nodded and looked at the captain. "Yeah, it's just like the gentleman described, Sir. A yacht lying beside a forty-foot whale shark. We didn't run across any human remains, but if there were any, I'm certain the sharks would've finished them off by now."

The captain looked at Angelo. "Were you able to find any evidence that might suggest why the ship went down?"

The two divers looked at each other and chorused, "Oh yeah!"

Angelo set down his mask. "There was an enormous section of the hull missing. Apparently, something came through the outside wall and floor of the main cabin. It was the strangest thing I'd ever seen."

"So what do you think happened?" asked Val from the stern of his speedboat.

The captain spoke up. "My guess is the whale shark was feeding too close to the surface, and the yacht ran into it, doing enough damage for the vessel to take on water. The whale shark apparently sustained an injury, which drew the sharks in to finish it off. Collisions with whale sharks are quite common in these waters, especially this time of the year."

Angelo sat down at the stern. "I don't know, Captain. That would have to have been some kind of bump. The damage extended all the way up to the ceiling of the cabin ... and even topside, like something plowed across the deck, and took off the top of the stairwell. But as far as the whale's concerned, it was difficult to determine the exact wound placement because its head was nearly torn off from the scavenger sharks."

Marty slipped off his tank. "He's right, Captain. The hole in the cabin was massive. It had to be fifteen feet wide. It looked more like it was hit by a torpedo than bumped by a whale. Also, the placement of the damage seemed odd. It was more toward the middle of the hull rather than in the bow where you would expect it to be in a ramming situation. Seemed more like the whale shark ran into the ship rather than vice versa."

Val returned to the driver's seat of the speedboat. He glanced back at his daughter's swollen ankle and said, "Well, if you gentlemen are finished with us, I'm gonna head in and get Sandy's ankle looked at."

The captain turned and caught the bowline as Val tossed it over. "Appreciate you calling this in and waiting for us to arrive."

"Don't mention it." Val accelerated the boat and pulled away while Sandy waved enthusiastically.

The captain turned his attention to the water and contemplated what to do next. Concerned about the divers' safety, he looked at Angelo and shook his head. "There are too many sharks to go back down tonight. You already checked for survivors. We'll just mark the spot for now and come back to finish the investigation in the morning."

Chapter 15
AT THE MERCY OF THE SEA

John sat tattered and dehydrated in the life raft, floating aimlessly beneath a moonlit sky. He reached up and felt the dried blood and scratches crusted on his face. His feet and hands were numb. The knot in the back of his neck burned from the endless hours of holding up his head. But he pushed back the pain. Only the vast expanse of open sea held his attention. Still not a trace of a boat, nothing but blackness divided by a faint horizon line. Was he still in the middle of the ocean or was land less than a mile away, hidden by the night?

He thought he heard a splash, turned quickly, but saw nothing. He could no longer distinguish reality from his imagination. Every white cap brought a rush of panic until further scrutiny proved it was only the wind. Although John rarely attended church, something deep within his inner being insisted that he pray. And he complied as best he could. His whispers carried off to the heavens on an ocean breeze—a last line of defense against an unseen terror.

A twinkle of light caught his eye. He turned his gaze to the giant tooth at his feet, moonlight dancing off the white enamel with every wave. "A priceless find." The words rolled bitterly off cracked lips. The initial magnificence the tooth held when he'd discovered it on the island was long gone. Now it served only as a grim reminder of the prehistoric monstrosity he knew was out there somewhere. Daylight was terrifying enough when he could at least see across the dark waters. But the night was more than his frazzled nerves could stand.

As the moon drifted behind a cloud, dimming the light, his attention turned inward. The expedition had gone wrong on every level. After narrowly escaping from the island with his life, only to end up crashing at sea, he felt as if he'd been hurled from one nightmare into another. And in this one the odds were definitely not on his side. He reached over and rubbed the head of his sole companion. The small chimpanzee was still staring out into the darkness. *Yes, she senses something's out there,* he thought.

For hours John had stared at the glimmering surface, as if his constant vigil would somehow keep the colossal creature away. The damp air grew cooler. With each gust of wind, the perspiration felt like ice against his skin. Cool, foul liquid swirled around his legs. John dared not to relieve himself overboard, knowing that even the scent of his urine could be detected from below.

A deep bellowing sound resonated across the ocean and made his hair stand on end. The haunting call of a sperm whale. But it wasn't the eeriness of the sound that unnerved him. The call meant that whales were in the area . . . and whales were among pliosaurs' choicest prey.

A towering spray of moist air shot into the night sky. A shiny gray hump slid above the waves. A pair of enormous horizontal flukes slapped the surface, and the breaching whale dove. "They're closer than they sounded," John whispered.

Staring into the pitch, the mistakes of his life became painfully clear. Every expedition, every so-called quest for science, had been nothing more than a failed attempt at redemption. He could never bring back the young life that was lost that fateful night—he understood this. Still, if he could somehow benefit humanity, he just might be able to live with his mistake.

His eyes again swept the water. The cold, dark sea was certainly bleak enough: a fitting arena for the final round. Was this where fate, after twenty four-years, would finally catch up with him and even the score?

Although John's mind stayed alert with fear, his body was starting to fail. "Looks like you're gonna have to take over for a while," he muttered to the chimp. John lay back in the raft and studied the night sky. Black smoke-like clouds drifted past the moon, and a light rain began to fall again.

He let his heavy eyelids close. *Just five minutes. Then I'll sit back up and continue the watch.* But the rhythmic sound of the waves brushing the raft lulled him into a deep sleep.

The chimp's cry shattered his respite.

He bolted awoke and rose to sitting, looking desperately at the waters around him. A shoal of fish shot through the waves and vanished into the night. He looked over the side of the raft and froze. A shadow passed beneath them. *A reef?* As the dark object rose closer to the surface, moonlight revealed craggy, gray skin. *Not a reef.* A sliver of whitewater divided before a tall, jagged frill. John felt the mist falling from the passing frill wash over him—horrifying proof that what he was seeing was really there.

The raft swirled in the wake created by the passing leviathan as the giant frill slowly submerged. John searched the water in disbelief. "No . . . how could it have found me?"

He continued to watch the surface, hearing only his racing heart. His fingers sank deep into the moist, orange fabric of the raft. The rolling wake slowly dispersed, and the raft stopped moving. *How long has it been since it passed?* He had no idea; time stood still . . . a vacuum of silence.

Did I really see that? Or did my frazzled nerves play on my imagination?

"A whale?" John whispered as if seeking confirmation from the chimp. "No. Not with a frill on its back." *Wait! A humpback maybe.* He stared into the dark water. He knew they had strange ridges along their backs and could reach fifty feet or better.

Suddenly, there was a great swoosh of air followed by splattering water as if the sea had opened up behind him. It was a sound like a breaching whale exhaling through its blowhole to ventilate its lungs. It could have been . . . but John knew it wasn't.

The moonlight disappeared. Fighting a crippling rush of fear, he turned toward the sound. Before him was an enormous black tunnel behind a curtain of falling water. Water splattered his face, distorting his vision. He looked higher, and his blood ran cold as he–stared into the horrifying source of the downpour.

An upper jaw rose as water continued to cascade from the tips of enormous, spiked teeth.

The next few seconds seemed to last an eternity.

The chimp shrieked in terror. John fell back on his knees. The raft dropped as the ocean tore open beneath them.

Noooooo!

In a cavern of darkness, the raft buckled, tearing around pearly white tips. Unseen daggers ripped into John's back. At first, it was with blunt force. Then like a bolt of lightning, an intense pain shot through his lungs. He opened his mouth to scream, but there was no sound.

The chimp's squeals dropped below him. John rose higher from the surface, snared on the lower row of teeth. He glimpsed the full moon beside the gray underside of the creature's nose, and then everything spun crazily.

There was a moment of weightlessness; he was dropping. With a tremendous crash, water spewed around John's back and through his hair when he slammed beneath the waves. Water churned in his ears. Plunging farther beneath the surface, he drew a panicked breath. But instead of lifesaving air, cold seawater invaded his lungs. In overwhelming pain, he struggled to move, free himself. The rush of water started to lift him from the lower jaw until the upper jaw moved closer. Rows of glistening white scalpels swept down out of the darkness.

His palms pressed against pink gums, straining to keep them away, but offered no resistance to the closing jaws. The upper row of teeth came down to meet his chest, forcing the air from his lungs. The pressure intensified; his last breath exploded from his mouth. Through a curtain of bubbles he saw his fists pounding against pink skin. Then, the creature's gums turned black as they plummeted to the depths of the sea.

John screamed. He awoke to find himself beating his hands against the raft in the drizzling rain. His heart was pounding like a drum. At his feet, he saw the frightened chimp staring at him as if he were crazy.

Quickly, John sat up and scanned the surface for the giant frill, but saw only the dark horizon in all directions. Releasing a deep breath, he looked down at himself. The dried blood on his shredded t-shirt and the raw skin on his rope-burned wrists were all too real. He knew he had to be hundreds of miles from the island, yet he could still feel the creature's eyes on him, watching, waiting.

John scanned the surface one more time then eased back against the raft. His heartbeat barely slowed, and he took deep breaths to regain his waning composure. He stared up at the crescent moon, unnerved by the realistic images of his nightmare.

"Will we make it back to land before it finds us?"

The chimp, now quietly gazing at John, gave no answer.

Chapter 16
PRIZED POSSESSION

Little Kevin Addelson curled up in the back seat of the minivan. He pressed his nose into the corner of the seat to keep the beach ball from hitting him in the face. But it didn't help. Even though it was seven a.m., there was no way Billy was going to let him sleep. He turned around and used his hands to cover his face. Between his fingers he saw his eleven-year-old brother taking aim for one more shot. The morning sun shone through the windows as the ball again bounced off his sandy-blond hair.

"Wake up, squirt," said the freckle-faced older brother, retrieving the bouncing ball from the floorboard. After one more shot, Kevin finally gave up on his sleep. He looked up, squinting, and moaned, "M-o-o-o-m-m. Tell him to stop."

"Billy! Stop tormenting your little brother. His head's not a basketball hoop. Seven in the morning is way too early for this." Margaret Bergh said from the driver's seat without turning around.

Kevin closed his eyes and turned his face back toward the corner of the seat. "Why do we have to go so early anyway?"

Margaret said, "You remember how it was last time when we left at nine? It was so packed we had to drive around for forty-five minutes just to find a parking place. Not this time."

Through the corner of his eye, Kevin saw his older brother drawing the ball back for another toss.

Kevin shouted, "Stop it, butt-breath!"

"Butt-breath. Did you call me butt-breath?"

Kevin turned to face his older brother. "Yeah, and that's what Tammy called you in school yesterday."

"Did not."

"That's what Johnny told me."

Billy dropped the beach ball, then self-consciously cupped his hand beneath his mouth. He exhaled several times, carefully sniffing after each breath. He looked back at Kevin. "My breath doesn't stink."

"Does too. You're just used to it."

Billy's chubby cheeks widened into a smile. "Okay. Let's see if you can tell the difference?" He leaned close to Kevin's face, exhaled, and said, "This a breath . . ." Then, he turned around and put his rear end within point-blank range of his little brother's face and . . . PEEEERRrrrrrrt! "Tell the difference?"

"*Mo-o-o-m-m-m. . . .* Billy farted on me!"

The young brunette yelled back again without turning around, "Billy, what have I told you about that?"

Billy scooted up to the edge of the seat. "No, Mom. I was just letting some air out of the beach ball. It was just the air coming out of the ball."

Kevin looked over the driver's seat, "Nuh-uh, Mom. It was the air coming out of him!"

Margaret's tone became more aggravated. "Billy. For the last time, leave him alone, or I'm going to turn around and go back home."

Margaret reached over and turned on the radio, hoping a little early morning jazz would calm her nerves. She paused a moment to listen to the news: "And the search continues this morning for three fishermen who are still missing after a bizarre whale attack at yesterday's Motanza fishing festival. The mysteries surrounding the attack continue. Scientists now question why a harmless plankton feeder would lunge into a net filled with huge tuna. Considering that the throat diameter of a humpback whale is only eight inches, sources insist that a two-hundred-pound tuna would not be on the menu. We'll have more on this controversial attack on the news at ten. Now here's Ed with Sports Rap." She reached over and turned off the radio, having lost interest in jazz, concerned by what she'd just heard.

Their van crested a small hill, and through the windshield the sprawling Paradise Beach appeared beneath a multicolored sunrise. Billy scooted up to the edge of the seat. "Cool, there's no one here. Not a single car in the parking lot!"

Margaret grinned as she slowed the minivan into a parking space. "How do you like that, boys? The whole beach to ourselves. No trouble finding a spot today."

After unloading everything they needed from the van, the family headed across the beach. Even though it was seven fifteen a.m., the beige sand was already hot to the touch. Eventually, they stopped at a spot about twenty yards from the shoreline and began to set up camp. Farther to their right, a long pile of rocks formed a jetty that separated the west side of the beach.

Setting up her lounge chair, Margaret noticed the boys eyeing the rocks. "Don't even think about it. No climbing on the rocks; it's way too dangerous. And no one goes into the water until I'm ready to go with you."

The duo reluctantly sat down on a large beach towel while their mother lathered up with suntan lotion. She set the bottle in the sand and eased back in her chair.

~~~

Fifteen minutes later, a shadow crossed the young woman's face. Billy waved his hand back and forth just above his mother's sunglasses.

"Is she already asleep?" whispered Kevin.

Billy smiled. "Told you she wouldn't last long at this hour."

The two boys looked at each other with a silent laugh, then tiptoed across the beach towel. Once they reached the sand, Billy looked over at Kevin . . . and it was on. "Race ya to the rocks!"

Billy's longer strides got him there ahead of his younger brother, and he scurried up the eight-foot-tall pile of stones. Several seconds later, little Kevin reached the first large gray rock and followed his older brother up. As Kevin neared the top of the pile, he heard his brother's voice from above. "*Woooo*! Check it out!"

Kevin looked over the top of the rocks and saw Billy pointing toward the beach on the opposite side. He stood up beside his brother and saw a huge beached whale sprawled along the shoreline. They quickly climbed down the other side of the rocks and raced across the sand toward the massive gray body.

Kevin yelled ahead to his brother, "Do you think it's still alive?"

"I don't think so!" shouted Billy without looking back.

They walked the length of the enormous creature while it lay halfway on its side with its massive underbelly parallel with the water. They stopped behind its head and faced the water. Kevin stepped closer and touched the cold, gray flesh. "Look how big it is. I wonder what it died from?"

Billy waded into the water and disappeared behind the whale. "Well, I think we can rule out natural causes."

Kevin walked around the massive head and into the water beside his brother. Then he saw the ten-foot bite mark behind the whale's head. "Wow! What a big mouth that shark must have had!"

"Yeah! You could park a car in that opening!" added Billy. Kevin stepped past his brother and waded closer to the whale. He walked into the center of the enormous wound that surrounded him like a tunnel. He stared in awe at the surrounding wall of flesh. Large chunks of blubber wobbled beside his feet with each breaking wave.

Kevin looked down at the water just in front of his feet, "Hey look. What's that?" A wave rolled back from the beach revealing an enormous white spike-like object half buried in the sand.

"Is that a tooth?" Kevin asked excitedly, and leaned over to inspect it more closely. Just then, he heard the whining sound of a boat's engine coming up behind them. A loud voice echoed across the water. "Hey, you kids get away from there!" Kevin looked up and saw a naval patrol boat just off shore.

"Kevin, let's book!" yelled Billy running, splashing through the water.

Kevin started to follow his older brother, glanced back at the tooth, and then at the approaching boat. He weighed his options, then quickly ran back to the tooth. He dug his fingers into the wet sand just above the blunt end of the tooth's root. Straining every muscle in his small body, he pulled until he felt the tooth release from the suction of the wet sand.

Billy looked back at his younger brother. "Come on. You're gonna get us busted."

Holding the tooth close to his body with both hands, little Kevin raced to his older brother who was waving him on. Billy looked at the huge tooth in Kevin's hands. "Hey, cool! Want me to carry it for you?"

"No way . . . it's mine."

"Okay, okay. Let's just get out of here."

After the two boys reached the rocks, Billy looked at Kevin. "You better not show that to anyone, or they'll take it from you."

For once, Kevin didn't doubt his brother. He carefully climbed up to the top of the rocks, never letting go of the giant tooth with either hand— not even to balance himself.

~~~

The patrol boat slowly slid into the shallows. Lieutenant Vic Greeman jumped over the gunwale and pulled the boat onto the shore beside the whale. A female in uniform leaped into the water behind him. As the two approached the massive carcass, the woman laughed with relief. "Wow. I was a bit worried there for a moment. From the water, it first looked like one big bite mark. But now that we're closer, you can see that the wound looks more like the result of several scavenger sharks feeding from the same area."

"Sharks wielding chainsaws," added Vic. "It's sloppy, even for a feeding frenzy. See the deep puncture marks around the perimeter; how they appear to pull through the flesh toward the wound?" He sloshed closer. "No doubt some of this is the work of scavengers, but not all of it."

"And the wound's long triangular shape is quite odd." added the lean, attractive black woman. Kelly Willingham waded through the water beside the wound. "It's also strange how the rest of the carcass appears to be unmarked, except for these." She stopped where there were four deep gashes across the whale's flank. She ran her fingers along the evenly spaced slashes. "Maybe it's time to give Hong Kong a call."

"Hong Kong?"

Kelly grinned. "To see if Godzilla's gotten loose again."

Vic didn't share her sense of humor.

Kelly was quick to regain her seriousness. "So what do you think? Three beachings in two days, all within eight miles of each other."

Vic looked out over the water. "Yeah there's something going on out there all right. There's a theory that when whales beach themselves like this, they're running from something. Something's scaring them in." He recalled his son watching the Motanza footage on the news the previous evening . . . and all of the damage created by a supposed humpback whale. "Yeah, there's something strange going on out there. It's like the local sea life is going berserk."

"But this is the first one with any damage," said Kelly, stepping toward the larger wound. "All the other whales apparently just beached themselves and couldn't make it back out in time."

Vic waded up beside Kelly. A wave rolled into the wound, washing over the lower layers of white blubber and retreated between their ankles. "Three beachings in the same general area within such a short time period? It does seem to strengthen the theory of the whales trying to get away from something. Already the local fishermen are spreading rumors about an increase in the shark population. Maybe, for once, they have a point."

Vic stepped closer to the immense opening in the whale, "I don't know. We've been protecting the great white for several decades now. Maybe it's starting to catch up with us. Maybe there's a price to pay for being the first nation to declare the great white as an endangered species. When we get back in, maybe I'll give the boys at Dyer Island a call to see if they've noticed an increase in shark activity."

Vic turned to a thumping in the sky—a news helicopter with a huge red number eight on its underbelly. Descending, the chopper swung sideways so the cameraman filming from the cargo bay had a clear view of the carcass.

Vic shook his head. "Great. That's all we need."

~~~

Little Kevin couldn't resist taking one more look at his prized possession. Ignoring his mother's call from downstairs telling him it was time for lunch, he again opened his second dresser drawer. He marveled at the eighteen-inch white object—he'd measured it himself—as it lay on the blue towel, dwarfing his collection of shark teeth lined up beside it.

Billy poked his head in the doorway. "Come on already. It's time for lunch. You've been staring into that drawer for two hours. It's not going anywhere, now come on. Mom won't let me eat until you're at the table." Billy started to run back down the stairs but paused in the doorway. "Remember, you'd better not show that to anyone, or they'll take it from you."

Kevin slowly slid the drawer closed. He felt like he was going to explode—he couldn't tell anyone, not even his best friend Tommy.

~~~

The midday sun glared into Kate's office at Cape St. Francis Airport while she anxiously listened to the voice on the other end of telephone. She glanced through a window at her baby: a vintage South African Air Force Atlas Oryx utility helicopter perched on a heliport. The craft was camouflage-green, complete with a toothsome grimace painted on the nose like warplanes of yore. It was a big hit with tourists, but more importantly, it reminded her of her late husband.

Beside the vintage craft was her workhorse, an electric blue Arabus H135 that she used for her daily charters. The burnt orange South African sky reflected in the craft's ample windscreen.

"Nothing reported down in your area, huh?" replied Kate. "Yes, John Paxton. No, he wasn't in a plane. It was a chopper. No, I wouldn't say he's missing, just a couple days late from a trip. I'm starting to worry a bit; he's usually quite prompt."

She switched the receiver to her other ear.

"Yes, I'm quite sure he would be coming back in your direction. Please, if you do hear anything, let me know. You have my number? Thanks again. Yes, I'll try not to worry."

After hanging up the phone, Kate swiveled back around in her chair to finish off a half-eaten baguette. She knew the sandwich would have to hold her for a while. It was going to be a long flight to the island. She looked past her desk at the computer monitor to take one last look at the weather.

~~~

The hunter glided silently. Like wings propelling a bird in flight, each thrust of its enormous paddle fins pushed the colossal beast through the ocean. Its massive shadow followed below, rippling across the seafloor. After eight hours of prowling the depths, the pliosaur had merged with a warm south-flowing current that led it between Madagascar and Mozambique and then farther along the coast of South Africa. Now, veering off from the swift current, the creature discovered a narrow band of water, rich with scents and activity.

Tilting its right forefin, adrenaline surged through the pliosaur. One hundred yards in front of the enormous reptilian eyes lay the crowded beach of Oyster Bay. Although the creature could not yet see this, the olfactory receptors inside its nasal capsule were fully alerted. The waters slowly became shallow, and it slowed its pace. The sandy seafloor rose to meet its underbelly.

A splash.

A few yards closer and the surface light revealed a floating object. Another splash. A fleshy thigh swooshed through the water beside the raft.

The creature locked in on the activity. All four paddle fins pumped in unison. Suddenly, something raked across the side of the monster's nose, and the giant head jerked back, twisting sideways. Through the shark barrier net its lantern eyes continued to watch the girl floating on the surface. For several seconds the creature glided alongside the net as if searching for an in. All the while, one enormous eye remained fixed on the raft.

The head lunged toward the beach. Again, the net brushed the side of the beast's nose. Then, recalling its last run-in with the frustrating net of the fishermen, the pliosaur rolled back, swept its powerful paddle fins, and soared in the opposite direction. Just behind the creature, the net bowed back. The great swell kicked up by the beast knocked the girl off the raft.

~~~

Surfacing, Lesley grabbed her raft and wiped her hair from her eyes. While the teenager curiously looked around the surface, the pliosaur headed out to deeper water, unaware that just a few yards farther along the net was a forty-foot gap through which its body could have easily passed.

Chapter 17
THE MAN WHO CRIED WOLF

John took his gaze off the horizon and rubbed his eyes. He looked again. "No, it's not my imagination. It's really there!" He nudged Crystal, who nudged him back. The small dot grew bigger. Its blurry outside edges slowly transformed into the shape of a boat. He quickly rose to his knees and tried to balance himself on the raft while frantically waving. The minutes seemed like hours as he watched the boat pass at a distance. Then, at the last moment of hope, the vessel slowly altered its course.

John tried to whistle but the sound never made it past his dry mouth. *That's okay. It sees me.* The craft drew nearer, a small fishing boat.

John slid the tooth through the waistband of his pants. As the vessel approached, he lifted his knee to the side of the raft and prepared to board. But his dehydrated muscles suddenly cramped, causing him to lose his balance and fall overboard, capsizing the raft.

He swam toward the boat, pained, the sting of the salt water reminding John of his numerous cuts and abrasions. A small, weathered man wearing a yellow, hooded raincoat placed a ladder over the gunwale. John climbed on board and shook his hand. The old man appeared to be in his late sixties with white hair and a long, white beard. He squinted and said, "What you doing all the way out here in that tiny little raft? Good thing I got to you before the Blue Pointers did."

"The what?" asked John, staring back at the man who now stared at him through the thickest lenses he'd ever seen on a pair of glasses. "The sharks, the great whites. A lot of tigers out here too! They'll gobble you up. I seen some big 'uns out here too. Some bigger than my boat."

John glanced across the length of the sixteen-foot vessel and muttered, "I've seen dolphins bigger than this boat." John reached into the upper left side of his pants, "You ain't seen nothing. Wait until you get a look at this!" He quickly realized the tooth was gone and desperately reached down deeper.

The little man squinted, watching as John reached around inside his pants. He stepped back, "You ain't some kind of pervo, are ya?"

"Oh no no no. I couldn't have lost it! It's the only proof I have. They're gonna think I'm nuts!" replied John, still searching frantically for the tooth.

The old man turned his attention to the water behind John. "I've seen some strange things in these waters, but never one of those."

John turned around, and saw the little chimp swimming to the side of the boat. "Crystal!" he cried. "I almost forgot about you."

"That your monkey, boy?" asked the old man.

As John reached over the gunwale and pulled the chimp from the water, he felt something drop beside his boot. After carefully pulling Crystal into the boat and trying to pry her arms off him, he reached down and pulled the prized tooth from the bottom of his left pant leg.

"Yes!" John gasped. "I still have it. Look," he shoved it toward the man, "at this."

Taking the tooth from John, the old man felt the weight of the enormous white object. He brought it to within five inches of his thick glasses. After carefully looking at the tooth from the root to the tip, he asked, "What is it?"

"What do you mean 'what is it?' It's a tooth!" replied John, thinking how it was a miracle that the old man ever saw him in the water.

"Well, if this is a tooth, boy, it came from one dandy of a beast." His eyes narrowed. "Probably came from one of those sea serpents I seen. Ya sure it's a tooth?"

"Pretty sure," replied John with a grin.

The old man handed John the tooth. "Sorry, young feller. I forgot to introduce myself." He paused for a couple seconds then said, "Libby Watson at your service."

Sensing a trace of senility, John extended a hand. "John Paxton. Pleasure to meet you, and thanks again for pulling me from the drink."

"Don't mention it, young feller. Guess you're pretty lucky old Libby decided to go fishing today." He reached into a cooler and handed John a bottle of water.

After a few long sips, John felt the tightness in his head subside a bit. He noticed the chimp watching him. "Guess you're a little parched too." John filled a plastic cup he found on the seat and raised it to Crystal's lips. He looked at Libby. "Thanks again. By the way, you wouldn't happen to have a radio on board, would you?"

"Never leave shore without it." Libby opened a compartment and handed John a small transistor radio that looked at least thirty years old.

"No, I mean a radio I can call in on. I need to call the Coast Guard." John held his left hand up to his cheek as if talking into it.

"Yeah, got one of those too. Used it a couple of weeks ago. Reckon it still works. But you ain't gonna be able to get the Coast Guard. South Africa ain't got one. They use some special branch of the Navy to handle all that."

Out of the corner of his eye, John saw a crate moving suspiciously. "What's that?" "That's me Snappy," said Libby. "Snappy, come out here and say hello to our guest." A small Chihuahua padded out from behind the crate, barking and baring its teeth. John looked down while the little dog snapped at his ankle, then latched onto his pant leg.

"Don't mind him none," Libby said. "He's just trying to get acquainted."

"Nice name," said John, kicking around, trying to free his pant leg. "You said you had a radio?"

"Oh yeah, to call in on . . . right over here."

Stepping to the driver's seat, Libby picked up the microphone while looking at the sky. "Sometimes it don't work so good in this kind of weather."

As Snappy continued to try for a clear shot at his ankle, John took the microphone and pressed the button. Static. Libby looked back up at the sky. "Give it a couple minutes, and we'll be out from under this storm cloud."

John looked to the horizon and still couldn't see a trace of land. "You always come out this far to go fishing?"

"No, it's just that sometimes I come out and drop a line and forget to drop anchor. My memory ain't quite what it used to be. But I usually don't lose sight of land . . . unless, that is, I catch a nap. But I always bring extra gas just in case."

John laid the tooth on the passenger's seat.

Libby glanced at it and said, "So what belongs to that tooth?"

"A type of prehistoric marine reptile." John finally wrestled his pant leg away from the Chihuahua.

"Ain't never seen one of those around here. But once I saw a hundred-foot sea serpent in these waters. Sucker had to be at least twenty feet around."

John looked at him, frowning slightly. He sighed. "I think I'll give the radio another try." The chimp sat beside the tooth in the passenger seat, fixated on the growling little dog. While John fiddled with the microphone, the faint outline of the mountainous South African coastline appeared in the distance.

Finally a voice came on the radio, catching John by surprise. He quickly answered, "This is John Paxton. My chopper went down about twenty miles offshore yesterday, and I was just picked up by a small fishing boat."

Libby leaned over and said, "The *Sea Hawk*."

More like the Sea Snail *judging from the pace of this thing*, thought John. He returned his attention to the microphone. "I'm a little dehydrated and sunburned, but overall I'm okay. But what I'm really calling about is . . ." John paused and glanced at the tooth in the passenger seat. He tried to think of a way to make his story sound believable. "I . . . I need to report a very large and dangerous marine reptile that could be in this area. Have there been any attacks or strange sightings reported anywhere along the southern coast in the last two days?"

The radio crackled, and the static voice answered, "No, there have been several beached whales but other than that, nothing out of the ordinary." There was a pause. "When you say 'marine reptile,' do you mean like a croc?"

"Not exactly. Considerably larger."

"How much larger?"

There's no way I can try to tell him what this thing really is, not without showing him the tooth. Against his better judgment, John decided to go for it and said, "It's enormous, better than sixty feet!"

"Did you say sixty or *sixteen*?"

"*Sixty*," John clarified, emphasizing the word.

"Sixty feet long? Sir, how, can you expect——"

"Listen, I know how it sounds. But I have proof and can show it to you as soon as I get in. For now, please trust me on this. You need to alert all the coastal authorities and have them get some eyes in the air. We've got to find this thing."

"What . . . well, what's it look like? What are we looking for?"

"Don't worry," John said. "You'll know it when you see it."

After a long pause, the dispatcher replied in a guarded tone, "Okay. I'll check around."

John wondered if the dispatcher was just pretending to believe him. "Good, but hurry. There's no time to waste."

"Yeah, okay. I said I'll check around. Out!"

John racked the mike and leaned back against the passenger's seat. "That's all I can do for now. It sounded like he believed me. Maybe." He replayed the call in his mind, wondering if he sounded remotely credible. "I guess it's a good thing I didn't try to tell him the thing was a pliosaur."

"Pli-o-who?" asked Libby.

"Pliosaur. A prehistoric marine reptile thought to have died out sixty-five million years ago with the dinosaurs. That's what belongs to this tooth, Libby." The old fisherman looked at his passenger and squinted his eyes. "You seem like an honest feller. I believe your big dinosaur story. If you say it's a dinosaur tooth, I believe it's a dinosaur tooth."

"Thanks, Libby," John said, relieved that the old man believed him. One down . . .

"How long until we reach the coast?"

"About an hour or so."

John again kicked his ankle sideways to escape the jaws of Snappy. "Uh, do you think we could put this piranha under that crate for a while?"

Libby didn't answer. He just continued to stare straight ahead at the distant coastline while the boat maintained its painfully slow pace. John slid Crystal out of her seat and sat down. Laying the tooth in his lap, he leaned back and chuckled lightly to himself. *Maybe I would have made it to the coast faster in the raft.*

~~~

After a long sip from his cup of water, naval dispatcher Sal Peterson turned to make another call. Admiral Henderson walked up behind him and said, "That sounded like a rather interesting call."

"Yeah, you could say that." Sal turned to face the Admiral. "Sir, what's the largest marine croc on record?"

"I believe it's around nineteen, twenty feet, somewhere in that area," said the admiral. "Why?"

"Someone just called in from a fishing boat. Said he saw something in the sixty-foot range, some type of marine creature, reptilian. I'm sure his size must be off a little, but the funny thing was he seemed so sincere . . . and concerned! He wants us to alert the authorities and get an eye in the sky looking for this thing. I was thinking about checking with our East London unit near the Morgan's Bay area where they've had all the beachings. Ask if they've seen anything out of the ordinary."

Admiral Henderson's tone sounded doubtful. "You said he was calling from a small fishing boat?"

"Yes, sir. I believe it was the *Sea Bird*, or maybe it was the *Sea*—"

"*Sea Hawk*."

"Yeah. That's it! How did you know?"

The admiral smiled. "That's Libby's boat. So now he's switched to dinosaurs, eh? He reported two sightings of sea serpents last month alone. He's getting on in years, and I think he's more than a little senile. The last time we investigated one of his sea serpents, it turned out to be several basking sharks lined up feeding together. I wouldn't worry about it!"

The dispatcher replied, "The caller didn't give me that impression, and this wasn't the old man. Said his name was John. Was picked up by the old man after being stranded. Do you think I should make the call anyway?"

"Still, he's calling from Libby's boat," replied the admiral. "We don't want to wave anything under the nose of the media. With all the shark attacks we've had, I don't want them to see our choppers searching the waters. That's all those vultures need to start making up headlines again. Don't worry. If there's really anything unusual out there, the Sharks Board will be on top of it."

"Okay," replied the dispatcher in an uncertain tone. He shrugged then swiveled back around to the switchboard to take another call.

Chapter 18
SHREDDING THE WAVES

With their surfboards tucked under their arms, two young men walked toward the Keurboom shoreline, eagerly watching the breaking waves. Strap-like leashes trailed behind the surfboards, dancing across the sand.

The taller of the two paused. Planting the rear of his surfboard in the sand, Dorian pulled his long, blond hair back into a ponytail and wrapped a rubber band around it. A glance across the empty beach, he pulled his surfboard up, and headed toward the surf.

Nearing the shoreline, Ron, the smaller of the two, looked at Dorian. His short, brown hair tousled in the wind. "So, where did you meet this chick?"

"About two weeks ago when I was surfing off Jay Bay," replied Dorian. "You know, right after that cold front came through. The waves were awesome. Some of the sweetest right-hand point breaks ever. Really pumping! Should have been there, bro. I had just come out of yet another one of my solid backdoor barrels when I noticed this chick checking me out from the beach with a pair of binocs. So I continued to hypnotize her with a series of floaters, three-sixties, and a couple more *sweeeet,* completely covered tube rides. Then I decided to do the noble thing. Go in and see what's up."

Ron listened intently.

"Soon as I got to the beach, she came up to me. Bro, she is hot. Wait until you see her. She was one of the finalists in the Miss Hawaiian Tropic or one of those national bikini contests. So she walks up to me and says she's gonna be in a commercial for a suntan lotion company."

"Which one?"

"African Gold or something like that. It's a new company. I think a china of hers is coming out with his own line of suntan lotions, and the commercial is for his startup campaign. Anyway, so then she starts telling me about how they want to use surfers in it. You know, real surfers really shredding, not just a bunch of doff models lying around the beach."

Ron laughed. "Real surfers, so why did she ask you?"

Dorian jokingly shoved him with his board. "She said they wanted to use surfers who could pull off some good tricks on the waves in the background; you know . . . really shredding! So she gave me the number of the guy shooting the video, and I gave her mine. Then she asked me if I knew of anyone else. They need two, one guy closer up in the foreground and one riding a wave in the background. After that, she walked with me back to the car, and I showed her one of the shots that *Surfer Magazine* photographer took of you last month at Jay Bay."

"Which one?" asked Ron excitedly.

"The one where you were doing that huge aerial."

"*Goooood* choice!"

Dorian zipped up the front of his sleeveless wetsuit. "Bro, you owe me for this one."

"Yeah, yeah. What exactly will we be doing?"

"I think she said she'll be lying on the beach at the tide line, and I'll be walking out of the water toward her with my board. And you'll be ripping a wave in the background, doing an aerial or something really rad."

They stopped at the shoreline and planted the backs of their boards in the sand. "Yeah, I see why they picked this spot," said Dorian, looking across the waves in awe.

Keurboom was right out of a surfer's dream. The sun hung above the horizon while long, white clouds scudded across the sky. Offshore, a stiff southwesterly breeze was feathering the waves into perfect form. Mounds of water as clear as liquid glass rolled into tubes that bound toward the shore.

After a minute of staring into the roaring surf, Ron spoke up. "So how come I'm the one in the background, and you're the one in the foreground up close with the chick?"

"Hey, you're the one with the great aerial, and I'm the one with the six-pack," replied Dorian, bouncing his knuckles off his lean abdomen.

"Yeah, yeah, you and your abs," Ron said. "If I spent half my life in the gym, I'd have abs like that too."

Dorian glanced at Ron's soft stomach. "I doubt it. How long has it been since you've even seen a gym, bro?"

"I go by the gym at least four times a week. Have to pass by one on the way to Jay Bay every time I go surf." He laughed theatrically at his own joke, then returned his attention to the waves. "So, how much are we getting paid for this gig anyway?"

"I think we each get about a hundred fifty rand."

"Is that a good price for something like this?"

"I don't know. How much you normally get paid to come out here and surf all day?" replied Dorian.

"Good point. What time are we supposed to hook up?"

Dorian glanced at his dive watch. "I wanted to get here a little early and catch a few waves before they arrived, but we're about an hour early." He looked out at the perfectly breaking waves and tossed his gym bag onto the beach. "Bro, check it. That front that came through left a serious groundswell. The surf is jacking up!"

"Think we've stared at those waves long enough?"

Dorian smiled. "Looks like we'll have to start without them, ay." After fastening their surfboard leashes around their ankles, the duo raced through the shallows and paddled out to deeper water.

~~~

Libby Watson continued to steer the small boat in the direction of the South African coastline. Beside him, John's hair blew in the wind while his unshaven chin gave a slight bounce off his chest with each passing wave. Despite the noise of the boat's whining engine, John continued his nap. Beneath his resting feet the little Chihuahua peered out from between the holes of the overturned milk crate.

There was a thumping in the sky. Libby looked up and saw a helicopter approaching from the northwest. The radio crackled and a voice came through, "Do you read? This is Kate Atkins. I'm looking for a John Paxton. Do you have him on board? Over."

Libby quickly picked up the mike. "Yeah, I got him. Just fished him out of the water a few hours ago. He had a little trouble with his chopper . . . oh yeah, he's fine. He's just catching a few winks right now."

~~~

John awakened to the sound of chopping blades and saw a helicopter hovering above the boat. He was quick to notice the silver Alexander Aviation logo on the electric blue craft's fuselage. He looked over and saw Libby holding out the radio mike. "It's for you. Some girly named Kate. He winked. "Sounds kinda cute."

John snatched the mike. "Kate, is that you?" He looked up and saw her waving to him from the pilot's seat. A familiar voice crackled over the mike. "Sorry to interrupt your nap. But I was wondering if you might need a lift?"

"How did you find me?" asked John as he could now make out Kate's gorgeous face peering down at him—like an angel from heaven.

"I was making a few calls on the way out. One of the dispatchers at the Cape Town Naval Station remembered your name. He said you called in, something about a marine reptile. Where have you been? Mom and I've been calling everywhere looking for you."

"You're not gonna believe it!" replied John. He picked up the tooth from the passenger seat and slid it through his belt.

"Okay. I'm dropping the ladder. Come on up."

Libby held on to the top of his hood while water blew all around the small boat from the descending helicopter. The nylon ladder dropped down to the deck and landed just behind the passenger seat. John grabbed the ladder with one hand. Before climbing up, he looked back at

Libby. "Thanks again for all your help. And promise me you'll keep it docked until we find this thing. The waters won't be safe for a boat this size while it's on the loose. Okay?"

Libby gave a slight nod.

"Promise me, Libby," John demanded. "I'm not leaving until you do."

Libby threw his hands up. "Yeah, yeah, I promise." Then he pointed beside the passenger seat. "Ain't you forgettin' somethin'? Can't leave without your monkey, boy."

The chimp looked up at him adoringly. John reached down and grabbed her, allowing her to wrap her arms and legs around his torso. After a few steps up the ladder, he stopped and looked down at Libby. "You can let Snappy out from under the crate now."

John carefully climbed up the swaying ladder and into the helicopter's cargo bay with the chimp still clinging tightly to his chest. Kate looked back at John, shaking her head with a grin as she watched the chimp hug him around the neck and nuzzle up to his cheek. "What did you do . . . run off and get married?"

"Here. Take the monkey, will you?"

As he stepped closer, Kate gasped. "Your face . . . all the scratches! Your shirt . . . what happened?"

John smiled sarcastically. "Remind me to thank your mother for the lovely field trip she sent us on." He looked down through the passenger side window and gave Libby one final wave. While John sat down and buckled in, Kate held on to the chimp's arm. "So, who's your new friend here?"

"That's Crystal—the only thing on the island that didn't try to kill me."

"Crystal, huh?" replied Kate. "What do you mean *try to kill you*? And where's the other bloke, Brad, the pilot? Is he still on the boat?"

"I'm afraid he didn't make it," replied John, feeling his slight sense of joy fade.

"What do you mean, he's dead? How did it happen? In the crash, when your helicopter came down?"

John reached into his belt and pulled out the enormous tooth. Although he'd gone over the story a hundred times in his mind, he struggled to find a place to start.

~~~

Several minutes passed while Dorian and Ron sat motionless on their boards waiting for the next swell. Ron gazed down into the water. Watching the shimmering image of his left foot, he asked, "Does it ever bother you, surfing off these un-netted beaches?"

Dorian gave a sly grin. "What's the matter, bro? Worried about the man in the gray suit—the great whites?" Dorian paused and looked out across the water. "Nah. Not really. You know, even when we surf the netted beaches, most of the time we have to paddle out past the nets anyway. Besides, most people would throw a wobbly if they realized the nets aren't continuous. Sharks can swim over them, under them, and around them." He laughed. "I've even heard that one-third of the sharks caught in the nets are caught on the inside, meaning they were already in there swimming around and got caught on the way out."

"That's comforting," said Ron. "Still, you can't argue that since they put the nets up, the attacks in those areas dropped off to nearly nothing, while the attacks on the un-netted beaches continued."

"Yeah, guess you can't deny that," agreed Dorian, glancing over his shoulder for the next swell. "Did you ever see Jerry Dunigan's board? The one he was on when a blue pointer hit him off East London? Gave him quite a skirk. Knocked him off his board and came right at him. Luckily, he was able to put the board between him and the mouth. It took a fourteen-inch bite out of the center of the board. He has it hanging in his living room. You should go check it out some time."

Ron again looked down at his legs dangling in the dark water. "Do you think we could talk about something else? Like school ... you're almost done, huh?"

"Got that right, bro! One more semester at Port Liz, and you'll be surfing with a marine biologist. So what about you, figure out your major yet?"

Ron sighed and shook his head. "That's a depressing subject, bro. Tell me more about this chick. Like ... what's her name?"

Dorian leaned his head back and closed his eyes. His wet ponytail arced with the wind. "Samantha, she's awesome, incredibly beautiful, and way cool. She even has an old-school ankle tat like mine, except on the opposite ankle. Even got it at the same place—Zowie's in Port Liz. That's gotta be destiny or something." He pulled his right foot on top of his board, exposing a tribal chain-like tattoo that wrapped around his ankle.

With his hand resting on his ankle, Dorian stared blankly toward the shore, a faraway look in his eyes. "As I was walking her to her car, the sun was starting to go down, so we decided to chill for a while and check out the sunset. Then there was this awesome moment ... it was like some kind of magical vibe. I'm sitting right beside her in the warm sand, beautiful sunset ... the wind was blowing her hair lightly around her shoulders. Neither of us had spoken for a couple minutes, then she looked down at our ankles with our matching chain tattoos almost touching and said, 'Look, it's almost like we're chained together.' I don't know what it was, but when she said it, or maybe it was the way she said it, I thought my heart was gonna jump out of my chest. Bro, you know, I really think it's destiny. She really seems to have it for me. We really connected, you know, mentally."

Ron looked back at an upcoming wave. "Don't get all worked up. She hasn't met *me* yet." Then he plopped down on his chest and started to paddle. Dorian shook his head and looked back for the next swell.

~~~

Ron dropped down into the face of the wave. He tucked low on his board. Whitewater spewed over his left shoulder as he soared through the circle of churning water. After disappearing for several seconds, completely hidden within the wave, suddenly he burst forward. The tunnel of water collapsed behind him, and he soared high on the wave, gliding across the whitecap with perfect balance. Then, after executing a perfect barrel ride, Ron pumped his fist with a victorious cry and rolled out of the wave.

Not one to be upstaged, Dorian looked back and saw an enormous swell moving up behind him. He quickly layed down and paddled with all his strength, knowing the wave had great potential. "Nice ride, Ron, but check this out," he muttered.

He paddled faster and then stood up as he dropped in position on the face of the wave. Crouching low, Dorian prepared for the tube ride of his life. His hand brushed against the rumbling wall of water to his left.

He glanced at his left hand and noticed a rough, gray object about the size of his torso gliding just beneath the surface. *Sea turtle*, he thought, then turned his attention back to the falling whitewater atop the wave. A second glance, and he realized the curious object was matching his pace.

No way that's a sea turtle, he thought. A sense of unease forced him to look more closely.

Keeping one eye on his wave position, Dorian looked at the coarse, gray object. The pebbled covering then divided, revealing a red, glowing orb. He glanced behind it and saw a wall of gray, tiger-striped skin, rippling behind the wave.

It's a flippin' eye!

Horrified, he looked ahead to check his wave position. Then he glanced back, and the mysterious red disk was gone. As the wave began to break, the blond surfer tucked lower on his board, and thought, *I knew I should have had breakfast this morning. I'm seeing things.*

Whitewater began to soar over his head. He thrust his right hand forward and dropped deeper into the tunnel. His full concentration shifted toward another perfect barrel ride. Fully surrounded by whitewater, Dorian soared through the churning tube, rapidly approaching the circle of daylight at its end.

Then it was gone. *What the–?*

Without warning, the tunnel of whitewater transformed into a cavern of giant, spiked teeth. Dorian kicked the tail of the board out sideways. *Pa–pa–pa–pop–pop!* The surfboard popped like the sound of machine-gun fire as it skimmed across pointed white teeth. Dorian fell back, his screams muffled by the terrifying walls of cartilage and flesh and bone. His vision filled with the roof of the upper jaw crashing down. In a final effort to escape the closing jaws, Dorian dove toward the outside light—but it vanished before him.

~~~

Finished paddling back out, Ron turned his board in the direction of the beach while waiting for the next swell. After looking around the surface for Dorian, he thought he must have taken the last wave all the way in. He squinted at the distant beach and spotted Dorian's yellow gym bag, but there was no trace of his friend.

Moments later, Ron dropped down on his board and started to paddle for the next wave. Dropping in, he thought, *Not quite big enough for a good tube ride, but I'll see what I can make of it!* He continued to ride the wave, doing a series of tricks and turns, then glided to the top and kick-turned off the whitecap, sending a circular spray of water over the top of the wave. *Hope Dorian saw that one.*

He dropped back into the face of the wave and slotted in, crouched low. After regaining his speed, he shot back up to the top and glided his board sideways across the whitewater, then returned to the face of the wave to set up for the next trick. *That was pretty sweet*, he thought. *But let's see if we can catch some air off this one!*

Reaching full speed, he approached the whitecap and soared over the top of the wave. In midair, he twisted his board sideways, preparing to land back onto the wave, when suddenly the water below turned pitch black.

Baffled by the black void beneath him, he didn't have much time to process exactly what he was looking at . . .

And then the horrific truth revealed itself. An immense creature burst through the surface! The huge, rising mouth opened wider, revealing an enormous black tunnel surrounded by glistening, spiked teeth. A crimson trail flowing from the side of its jaw.

Ron could feel the scrape of his surfboard as he kick-turned off the jagged flesh of the creature's jaw. The rising mouth lifted Ron higher into the air while his well-honed sense of balance kept him over the board. Completing his turn in midair, Ron miraculously landed back on the face of the wave with the board still under his feet.

With half of its enormous body out of the water, the thrashing monster crashed down behind Ron—showering him with whitewater. Desperately, Ron tried to turn his board and ride in on the huge wave. But the rear fins had been severed by the creature's rough skin. He fell into the water in a half-dive and started to bodysurf in a last-ditch effort to get away.

The shoreline approached. His speed increased with the pull of the wave. *It's a strong wave,* he thought. *It should be enough to bring me all the way in.* Then he felt something come up beneath his chest. He knew he was still too far out for it to be sand.

The massive nose lifted higher from the water as the desperate surfer tried to grip the armor-like skin. Blood streamed down his forearms. The monster continued to carry him above, then below the surface, thrashing its head to throw him forward—closer to its mouth. Sensing what the creature was trying to do, Ron tried to maintain his grip and push away from the tip of the nose, but his strength quickly failed. The beast slowed, then dove, and the water lifted Ron from its skin.

Below the waterline, Ron felt himself slipping forward on the massive head. Resurfacing, he found his chest pressed halfway over the creature's snout—his hands less than two feet away from the teeth of the upper jaw. From point-blank range, he stared into a mouth larger than a garage door. He felt his body slipping. His hands inched toward the long, spiked teeth.

Suddenly, the monster ground to a stop; it's massive bulk crashing into the sand. The momentum tore Ron from the jagged skin, hurling him over the nose—through the air until he landed in the shallow water ten feet in front of the creature's mouth.

Disoriented, Ron slowly crawled back in the shallows, his hands holding his stinging stomach. He looked up at the massive head. The enormous mouth twisted sideways and slammed shut in the shallows. Water sprayed out between huge, spiked teeth.

Then the giant head rose and rolled back into the waves. A red eye peered up from the sea. Ron crab-walked farther back to the safety of the beach. He glanced across the beach in both directions, expecting to see screaming, pointing onlookers offering confirmation that the horror before him was real. But the beach was empty. Only the sound of thrashing water filled the air. Ron stepped back onto dry sand, his eyes glued to the monstrous sight before him. In disbelief, he continued to watch the enormous beast thrash its way back into deeper water. Ron felt the cuts in his forearms, undeniable proof that this was all too real. He looked down to the stinging in his stomach, unable to discern the pieces of shredded wetsuit from his torn flesh. Still, he trembled with the realization that he shouldn't really be there, except he was. Still alive. *Miraculously still alive,* he thought as he watched the tremendous creature head back out to sea.

Gripping his stomach, Ron walked over and picked up the yellow gym bag. He staggered across the beach and through the parking lot until he reached a cream-colored station wagon with surfboard racks. Leaning against the driver's side door, he gazed over the hood, and back toward the beach. In the distance, he saw the long frill and back slowly drop below the surface, but he still couldn't comprehend what had just happened. Even at this longer distance, the creature still looked enormous.

Opening the door, Ron collapsed onto the driver's seat and pulled the car keys from the bag. The key, feeling like it was covered in oil, slipped in his bloody fingertips as he started the car and slowly pulled the old station wagon out of the dusty parking lot. Ron did his best to fight off the shock and concentrate on his driving. The steering wheel was slippery in his bloody hands.

He tried to keep his eyes on the road, resisting the temptation to look down at the expanding bloodstain on the seat. The light traffic allowed him to drive slowly in the middle of the road until a loud honking horn from behind caused him to pull onto the shoulder. A truck shot past him, and the blaring horn disappeared. Fighting dizziness and nausea, Ron proceeded, doing his best to stay in the center of the road.

He felt his strength diminishing. He was cold. His vision turned white. The car swerved, and he heard gravel hitting the side of the door. There was a sudden drop and a feeling of weightlessness. His vision cleared long enough for him to see the bottom of the ditch coming up to meet the windshield. A loud crash, and the horn blared around him as he slipped into unconsciousness.

~~~

Kate's eyes widened in astonishment, hanging on to John's every word. John adjusted his headset and continued to explain how he narrowly escaped from the lagoon. "After pushing the chief into the lagoon to create a diversion, I dove from the dock and swam—"

"Wait a minute." Kate glanced at the helicopter's windshield then back at John. "You mean you dove into the same lagoon . . . with that thing?"

"Yeah, it was preoccupied with the chief for the moment. Then I swam between the pilings and into a cavern. But the tribesmen were everywhere. I barely made it to the shoreline."

Kate glanced down at the enormous tooth in John's lap. "So, when did you get your souvenir?"

John held it up for her. "Yeah, I saw this as I swam out of the lagoon. It was sticking out of one of the pilings. Anyway, after reaching the shoreline, I blazed through the jungle and never looked back. It was really close. At first I thought I ran past the clearing, but I was still able to make it back to the chopper before the tribesmen."

"Wow, that's unbelievable!" Kate shook her head in amazement.

"Yeah, I know. An eighty-foot prehistoric marine reptile is a lot to swallow," John said.

"Oh, I believe the part about the pliosaur," Kate said. "It's the part where you outran all of those tribesmen chasing you through the jungle that I have trouble with."

"What do you mean?"

"You know . . . for someone your age."

"My age!" John scoffed. "I'm only—" His eyes wandered over Kate's young, lean figure, and he decided not to press the issue.

"So what, then you lifted off and left the island?" asked Kate.

"Well, almost. I had to spend one more night there, due to a perfectly placed spear hole in the chopper's crowning."

Kate reached over and took the tooth from John's hand. "Unbelievable . . . a living pliosaur. Glad I came to pick you up in a chopper instead of a boat."

"A prehistoric marine reptile thought to have been extinct for millions of years," added John. "That tooth you're holding is the first white pliosaur tooth ever discovered."

"No doubt!" Kate flipped a switch on the instrument cluster. "Up until now, all of the other teeth discovered have always been dark-colored in the form of fossils. Never white and fresh like this." She grinned. "I'm calling Mom now . . . she's gonna freak when she hears about this. Just wish I could see her expression."

"Let me speak to her first," John was somber. "I need to tell her about Brad."

Kate slowly nodded, her smile fading as the reality of the situation began to sink in.

Chapter 19
THE SHOOT

The side door of the minivan slid open revealing clouds of dust settling in the dirt parking lot. The rolling surf echoed in the distance. The glassy waters and white sand of Keurboom slowly appeared through the haze.

"Well, it looks like we beat them here," photographer Paul Ansel announced, stepping from the van. He was a thin man in his mid-forties with long, black hair streaked with gray. After getting out, he slid the door all the way open. "Samantha, are you sure this is the right spot?"

A young woman with shoulder-length, brown hair stepped down from the side door. Her shapely body was apparent through the contours of her long, white spa robe. She looked out across the beach and saw only a long stretch of undisturbed sand. The breakers just off shore also revealed nothing. No bodies adorning surfboards stood out amid the whitecaps and endless, blue-green waters. "Yes, this is the spot. I'm sure of it. Dorian said they would meet us right in front of the west entrance of the parking lot."

Joe Barrison, the photographer's assistant, stepped out of the van behind Samantha. "What time did you tell them to meet us here?"

Samantha glanced at her wristwatch. "They should have been here an hour ago. Dorian even mentioned getting here earlier to catch a few waves before the shoot. I don't get it. He followed me here to this exact spot so he would be sure where to meet us. He was so stoked about being in a commercial."

The driver's side door slammed shut, harder than necessary. "I knew it! Knew I should have paid the extra money and hired models. Everyone knows you can't rely on surfers!" barked Doug Evans, a heavyset man in his early forties with short, bleached-blond hair. As he stepped around the van, a gust of wind blew open the front of his Hawaiian print shirt. A white tank beneath it read "African Gold" in bamboo letters above a golden sun.

Samantha replied, "Remember your original concept, Doug. You wanted to use real surfers riding the waves. Not just a group of models. These guys are really good, and they look the part—especially Dorian!"

"Well, a lot of good they're doing me now!" Doug looked over at the photographer. "So what do you think, Paul? Is the whole shoot a bust or what?"

Paul glanced up at the sun. "Relax, Doug, the sky looks great. We can still shoot the footage of Samantha on the beach, then shoot the surfers later today, or even tomorrow, and drop them in later."

"How's that supposed to work?" asked Doug, squinting up at the clear sky.

"Hey, we're living in the digital age—a little editing is all it takes. And no one will ever know the difference."

"Well, if you say so," said Doug, a trace of concern in his voice. "But how much more is all that digital magic gonna cost me?"

Paul threw the strap to his camera case over his shoulder. "Don't worry about it. You're a friend of Samantha's . . . we'll work something out. Or if you'd like to save a little extra, I think I might have a wetsuit that will fit you and a surfboard back at the studio."

"I don't think we're that desperate," replied Doug.

Samantha gave him a smile that hid her disappointment. She couldn't believe Dorian completely blew off the shoot, or even worse, her. Still she didn't give up hope. *He'll probably show up a little later,* she thought. *He did seem like a partier; he's probably still asleep . . . hopefully alone.* She was surprised at her jealous feelings after meeting him just once.

"Okay then, if everyone's ready, let's do it," said Paul, picking up the rest of his equipment. He looked at his portly assistant who was in his early twenties with long, red hair. "Joe, could you grab the reflector and the makeup case from behind the back seat?"

Samantha followed the others across the wide beach while Paul searched for the perfect location for shooting. Finally, he sat down his lens case and pointed to an area just ahead. "There, that looks like a good spot. See how the sand's all nice and even?"

He looked over at Joe who had suddenly dropped the reflector and started to run across the beach toward an area west of their destination.

"Joe! Where are you going?" shouted Paul.

"I'll be right back," yelled Joe, as he continued to run in the direction of something he'd spotted in the shallows. Slightly out of breath, he waded toward a surfboard while it bobbled in the frothy water. "Sweeeeet! A Gordon Smith! I could use one of these." Joe quickly looked down the beach in both directions and across the water, glancing for its owner. He picked the board up and turned it over. Long, jagged gashes covered the rear section of the board where the fins used to be. "Maybe not," he frowned. "Looks like a bad case of coral rash." After dropping the board back in the water, he paused. "Maybe Brian can fix it back at his shop." He tucked it under his arm and raced back to the shoot.

"What have you got there?" asked Paul, adjusting the height of the camera's tripod.

Joe tossed the board to an area clear of the shoot. "It's an abandoned surfboard; a good brand, but the back of it's trashed. I've got a friend who owns a surf shop just down the road. Maybe he can fix it—refinish the bottom and put some new fins on it."

Paul ignored Joe's discovery and waved to Samantha to get her attention. "Samantha. We're just about ready for you."

After checking her lipstick one more time in a small mirror, Samantha took off her robe, revealing a metallic-gold bikini that glistened against her golden skin. Doug walked toward Samantha carrying a white sack. His approval was evident in his eyes. "The suit looks great! And the tan is just right, not too dark . . . just the right tone. He pulled out a gold necklace from the sack and held it up to her neckline. "Try this on for size."

Samantha looked at the large, gold sun centered between two gold palm fronds. "Awesome!" She ran her finger around the edge of the carved sun. "It's really cool how it matches your logo. Is it real gold?"

"Kinda. A friend of mine made it out of wood and covered it in gold leaf. He said it would look great on camera. Here, let's see how it looks on you."

"Oooww . . . that looks great," said Doug, stepping back. "Really works well with the suit!"

Joe looked over with his eyebrows held high. "Yeah bro, no doubt."

Several yards away, Paul started motioning to everyone. "Come on. Let's go. This light won't stay perfect forever."

Samantha walked to the water's edge and sat down slowly. After being positioned by Paul, she lay back with her elbows in the sand. The ocean breeze swept her hair back gently from her shoulders. Cool waves glided up the sand beneath her calves. The atmosphere, the camera—all of it was invigorating. Although she didn't consider herself vain, she loved the attention she received from modeling.

She stared straight ahead and into the shallows. Her abdominal muscles slightly tensed. She could almost feel Paul scrutinizing every inch of her body through the camera's lens, checking for anything that wasn't just right. *Uh, oh. Almost forgot about that*, thought Samantha as she pushed her right heel deeper into the moist sand. *I meant to cover it up with makeup this morning before I left. Maybe he can't see it.*

She glanced at Paul through the corner of her eye. He stopped and stood up behind the camera. "That's not gonna work. Samantha. What did you do to your ankle?"

Samantha raised her left foot from the sand. She rotated it, revealing a deep-green tattoo that wrapped completely around her ankle. "It's not that bad, Paul. Practically all of the top models and actresses have one on them somewhere."

"What difference does it make?" grumbled Doug, looking over the photographer's shoulder. "Aren't her feet gonna be in the water?"

The photographer paused for a moment and studied the sky. "Suppose we could let it go. Besides, there's a storm cloud moving in." He dropped back behind the camera. Adjusting the lens, he said, "Okay, everyone, we're back in business. Joe, could you grab the reflector and bring it to my left? That's it . . . now tilt it a little more. Yes, that's it, magnificent . . . just the perfect glow."

Samantha looked straight ahead and resumed her position. Paul shouted above the crashing waves, "Okay now, Samantha, keep your eyes closed and pull your head back. Feel the warm sun caress your body . . . that's it. Be careful not to knock over the bottle of suntan lotion beside your elbow. Slowly . . . slowly, that's it. Okay, now the surfer is about to approach you from the water. A bronze Adonis. At first you don't even notice him. You're just enjoying the warm sun, acting as if he isn't there."

Doug yelled from behind Paul, "That's not hard to do!" Then he muttered, "Surfer bums. I should have known better."

Paul continued his instructions. "Okay, now you can slowly tilt your head down and open your eyes. That's it. Good! Stare straight out into the water. You see his glistening body slowly approaching you from the surf. Wait a minute . . . Joe, could you get that? There's a piece of wood or something out there floating into frame."

Joe walked past Samantha and waded into the shallows up to his knees. As he neared the floating piece of debris, it slowly drifted farther out of reach. He leaned forward against the incoming waves, lifting his elbows while the water level rose to his waistline. The illusive object was only a few yards away, seemingly taunting him to go deeper into the water.

"Is that what I think it is?" he muttered as the small section of surfboard flipped up from a passing wave. The board turned over exposing a set of undamaged fins protruding from its underside. "Cool! Maybe I could use these fins for the other board."

Samantha remained in position, watching patiently while Joe waded deeper into the water.

Paul shouted, "Joe, that's okay. It's well out of frame now. Don't worry about it."

Joe yelled back without turning around, "That's okay, I've almost got—" Then, he was gone, disappearing beneath the surface with barely a splash.

Samantha started to laugh, thinking he was kidding around. Paul stood up from behind the camera and flipped off his sandals. He apparently was taking the situation more seriously. Then, just as Paul started heading for the water, Joe popped up from the surface spitting and coughing. His red hair was streaked in front of his eyes with the neckline of his wet shirt hanging low on his chest.

Wiping his hair back from his face, Joe looked at the crew. "I stepped in some kind of a ditch. It's really strange. The sand's all nice and level until you get to about right here. Then it drops off into this enormous ditch. It almost looks like someone tried to beach a submarine."

He turned and grabbed the small section of board and made his way back to the shallows. Joe stepped out of the water, studying the board's splintered edge. "It's the rear section of a surfboard." Then he stopped and took a closer look at the fins.

Paul impatiently yelled from behind the camera, "You don't have to examine it! Just get it out of frame!" Joe quickly tucked the piece of board under his arm and ran back onto the beach.

"Be careful," Paul yelled, "not in front of the model—you're disrupting the sand."

As Joe took another step, he felt the piece of surfboard being tugged from under his arm. He looked back and saw the leash taut as if caught on something in the water. He grabbed the cord and gave it a hard tug.

Something burst from the water like a flying fish. Samantha jumped back as the ghostly white object flew from the leash and landed beside her, knocking over the bottle of lotion. Her mouth dropped open in horror as she looked down at the pale foot lying in the damp sand. Before she could turn away, her eyes locked on something else. Something familiar that drew the blood from her face. Just below the red ring of flesh and smooth, milky-white edge of the bone, was a chain-like tattoo that perfectly matched her own.

~~~

The helicopter glided above the water, heading for the coast. After a few moments of silence, Kate gasped while staring through the windshield. "The Motanza!"

"What?"

Kate glanced at John. "This might be nothing. I spent the better part of yesterday canceling flights, didn't see much of the news. But I remember something. Yesterday there was an attack at the Motanza, an annual fishing festival off Mazeppa Bay. It's where the local fishermen form a circle with their boats around this enormous net and slowly bring it up. Have you heard of it?"

"I know of it, sure," John said.

"Anyway, as they were bringing up the net, something enormous attacked it and got all tangled up. It thrashed so violently almost all of the boats were capsized. On the news they said it was an aggressive humpback whale because of its size. But I only caught the tail end of it. I'm sure you'll see it tonight when we get back."

John sat silent, his mind reeling. *It's already here.* He dared to ask the next question, "Was anyone killed?"

"I think two fishermen were reported missing, but I know there were a lot of injuries. The creature just thrashed about trying to untangle itself, then swam off. Who knows? Maybe they're right; it could have been a whale. Like I said, I just caught part of it."

John was silent for a long moment. "Have there been any other attacks or anything else unusual in the news."

"The beachings. During the last couple of days, there have been several whales beached along the southern coast, just west of Natal. But I haven't heard of any attacks on humans. I guess it's a good thing we have those shark barrier nets along the more popular beaches."

John felt a new sense of urgency. "That might help the swimmers, but it's not going to do much for the boaters. There's not much time. We've got to get to the Navy ASAP, and then try to talk to that Sharks Bureau they have out here.

"You mean the Natal Sharks Board?" Kate asked.

"Yeah, that's the organization that monitors the shark barrier nets and tries to protect the beaches, right?"

Kate nodded. "Did you notify anyone from the boat on your way in?"

"Just the Navy, but I'm not sure how much they believed me."

Kate thought for a moment. "Chances are, no one in their right mind will believe a word we say until they see the tooth. And even then, who knows? I mean *I've* seen it, and I barely believe you. The Navy could say that it just looks fresh. I mean, just because it's white doesn't prove it's organic. There are plenty of ancient fossils that have been permineralized in white stone."

John nodded. "We need to prove its authenticity. But carbon testing could take weeks."

"There may be another option. If we could have someone well respected in the field examine the tooth, that just might be enough." Kate glanced at the instrument cluster. "Before heading to the Navy, there's one stop we need to make." She smiled and glanced at the tooth. "Steven . . . I sure hope you're sitting down when you sees this."

But how would they find it? The creature could truly be anywhere, thought John. He looked down through the window and wondered what new evidence he would hear about once they landed. Worse yet, what gruesome images would he see when he flipped on the news? He tried to relax and eased back in his seat.

The flight seemed to last forever.

Chapter 20
MISDIAGNOSIS

Doug wrapped his arm around Samantha while doing his best to console her in the Keurboom beach parking lot. Trembling, she leaned back against the side of the ambulance, her makeup streaked from tears. Across from them, Officer Marimba continued to take her statement. He was an exceptionally thin black man. His cheeks were hollow, and his face was weathered in a way that made it difficult to determine his age. Samantha's eyes kept going to a thick vein that protruded from beneath his officer's hat and trailed down the side of his forehead. He looked up from his pen and pad. "So it was just the two of them that were supposed to meet you here today?"

"Yes," she sniffled.

"And you're sure about the . . . tattoo?"

Samantha nodded and wiped her eyes. She glanced down at her ankle then looked up at the water. A police boat slowly idled across the surface, a cable trailing from its stern. "How long are they gonna keep doing that?"

"They'll probably keep dredging into the night or until they find something," said Officer Marimba, folding up his pad. Now that the questioning was over, his voice held compassion. "You don't have to wait around. We'll call you if anything happens. You've been through a lot. You should go home and try to get some rest."

Samantha's gaze at the boat on the water never wavered. She watched Joe walk to a section of beach and point to the water where he found the first surfboard. Dozens of people surrounded him, taking pictures, hanging on his every word. She looked away. *How pathetic. He seems to be enjoying the attention.*

She felt the ambulance rumble as its engine started. The side door popped open. The driver looked back at Officer Marimba and waved him over. The officer excused himself from Samantha and Doug and walked to the driver's side door. After glancing back at Samantha, he nodded at the driver. "Okay, I'll follow you."

Officer Marimba jogged back to Samantha and Doug. "You go on home like I told you, try to relax. We'll handle this. I have to go check out an accident just down the road, then I'm going to come back. I promise I'll call you if there's any news."

Samantha nodded, and Doug took her by the shoulder and led her back to the van.

Doug waved over to Joe with a shout, "I'm gonna take Samantha home. Are you staying?"

Joe looked back through the crowd of anxious bystanders. "Yeah, I'm gonna stick around for a while!"

"I'll be back later to pick you up then." Doug looked over at Paul who was standing beside a police car. "What about you?"

They watched another news van pull into the parking lot. Paul said, "I'll stay too!"

"Looks like nobody wants to miss any of the action," muttered Doug, closing the door of the van. Through his rearview mirror he saw the flashing lights of the ambulance and police car winding along the road until they disappeared in the distance. The gold van pulled out of the dusty parking lot and headed in the same direction.

Keeping one eye on the road, Doug took a box of tissues from the glove compartment and handed them to Samantha. "Here you go, hon. It's going to be okay."

Samantha pulled a tissue from the box and wiped her eyes. As the van came around a corner, she looked up and saw the flashing lights of the ambulance in the distance. The van slowed, keeping to the opposite side of the road while they passed the accident scene. Samantha tried not to look, but in the glow of the ambulance lights, she saw the top of a cream-colored station wagon with surfboard racks protruding from the ditch.

"Stop!" Samantha screamed. "That's Dorian's car. Stop, stop!"

"How can it be? Are you sure?" Doug slammed on the brakes.

"Yes, it even has the surfboard racks on it. Stop!"

Doug pulled the van over on the shoulder of the road, careful to stop far enough ahead of the ambulance so he didn't block its exit path. Samantha sprang from the door and ran toward the man on the stretcher. Her white robe waved in the breeze.

Officer Marimba stopped her just short of reaching the paramedics and grasped her by the shoulders. "Samantha, what are you doing here? You should be going home."

She craned her neck to look over the officer's shoulder. In the flashing light, she saw a dark-haired man, blood streaming from the front of his wetsuit. The paramedics were bringing him up from the ditch. "It's Ron, Dorian's friend," she cried. "The one who was supposed to be with him at the shoot today."

"Are you sure?" asked Officer Marimba.

Doug walked up and placed an arm around Samantha's waist, helping to hold her back. "Yes, I'm sure!" said Samantha. "Dorian showed me pictures of him. That's him in Dorian's car! He's wearing a wetsuit!" Her teeth began to chatter, and Doug and Officer Marimba tried to steer her back to the van. Still, she asked questions. "It looks serious. What happened to his chest? Is he going to live?"

"He's lost a lot of blood. Miss, you have to stay back." Officer Marimba reassured her, "They're doing all that they can."

"But what happened to his chest? Was it from the steering wheel, the impact?"

The officer looked troubled. "That's the strange part. He claims it was from some enormous sea creature."

~~~

Beneath the rhythmic sound of the helicopter's chopping blades, John mentally rehearsed his impending conversation with the Navy. *Would the tooth be enough evidence to win them over?* Although John's eyes had been closed for nearly twenty minutes, he hadn't slept a wink. He slowly opened his eyes, feeling them relax while he gazed into the distance. The faint mountaintops slowly became clearer, revealing their jagged crevices.

He peered down through the side window. The dark aquamarine water lightened into a beautiful shade of green as it met the shore. A stretch of beach flashed by, and tall sandstone cliffs reached up toward the helicopter. Finally, he was over land.

John's earphones crackled.

Kate looked over. "Feel any better?"

"Definitely," John said, looking down through the side window. "Yesterday I didn't think I'd ever see land again." He reached down and rubbed the chimp's head. Even she seemed more relaxed. "So where are we?"

"Cape St. Francis, about fifty miles east of Port Elizabeth. I need to stop for fuel first, don't have quite enough to make it back. I must warn you, though . . . this isn't the nicest place to stop for petrol. But it's the closest."

As long as they have a TV to check the news, John thought. His mind kept going back to the Motanza. If the creature was already here, he knew that attack was only the tip of the iceberg.

The helicopter flashed over another mountain and a small patch of asphalt appeared in a distant clearing. John looked down through the ample windscreen. Drawing closer, it looked like an abandoned gas station beside the shortest landing strip he'd ever seen. "Is that where we're stopping?"

"That's it," Kate said, adjusting the collective. They slowly descended before the midday sun. As the landing gear touched ground on the small runway, Kate turned off the engine. "Like I said, this isn't the nicest place to stop for fuel."

John rubbed the back of his neck. "As long as they have a TV. I'd like to check the news; see if anything has turned up. So now, how far are we from the naval station?"

"Including time to refuel, we're about forty minutes away, tops," said Kate, popping open the side door.

Leaving the tooth on the seat, John stepped from the helicopter and felt the firm asphalt beneath his boots. "Finally, back to civilization," he announced and released a deep breath. After he closed the door, a high-pitched shriek came from the cockpit.

"Uh oh," said Kate. "Sounds like we're forgetting someone, and she doesn't appreciate it."

John leaned back into the cockpit and picked up the chimp. "Okay, I guess you need to stretch your legs too." After setting Crystal gently on the ground, he walked around the helicopter, and past an old rusted Buick that hadn't seen a speck of paint in twenty years, laying on its side. He saw a small shack-like building beside the runway. Someone emerged from the doorway and ran up to greet them. The small black man wore only a pair of dark-green pants cut off just below the knees.

Kate waved. "That's Ebo."

"Ebo," John muttered, "Interesting name."

"Yeah, it means born on Tuesday. He has a brother named Ekow . . . that means born on Thursday."

Kate reached out to shake the smiling man's hand. "Ebo, how've you been? How's the family?" Leading them toward the building, Ebo glanced at John and said something to Kate in Afrikaans.

Kate laughed aloud. "No, no, he's just been doing a bit of exploring."

"What did he say?" asked John.

"He said, 'What happened to your friend; look like he try to swim with piranha?'"

John looked down at the dozens of scratches evident through his shredded shirt. He lifted his forearm and examined the dried blood covering the numerous gashes. "I guess I could use some cleaning up. But that'll have to wait. Do you have a TV?"

"Ebo and I will refuel. There's a TV in there." Kate pointed to the dilapidated building.

John stepped through the doorway holding one of Crystal's long fingers and was greeted by a black woman sitting in a chair, nursing a baby. Around her feet, several chickens pecked at crumbs on the floor of the makeshift lobby. From out of nowhere, a goat rushed by, nearly knocking him over as it ran through the doorway. Catching himself on the doorknob, John looked over at Kate who was standing by the fuel pump. Kate smiled and shouted, "Hey, welcome back to civilization!"

John looked down at the slow-moving chimp. "Come on, Crystal." He reached down and picked her up. After a glance around the room, he asked the woman, "Do you have a TV . . . a television?"

With her free hand, the woman pointed to a dirty glass partition in the back of the building. John nodded. He headed through the lobby, choosing his steps carefully among a myriad of chicken droppings. The broken tile floor turned into dirt when he entered the next room.

It was an office. A little black boy about four years old sat on a milk crate. Oblivious to the intruders, his eyes never moved from a small TV on a bookshelf. The best John could tell, it was playing *Scooby-Doo* in Spanish. John sat the chimp on the corner of an old wooden desk. The moment he reached up to change the channel, the boy's face contorted like it was ready for a major eruption.

"Okay, okay!" John said. "I just need to check something, okay? Then I'll turn it back."

No sooner than John changed the channel, an ear-splitting scream rang through the office. The little boy sprang from the crate and ran out of the room like he was on fire.

"Oh well . . . I gave it a shot."

John refocused on the TV. *Okay, this is it.* He took a breath and braced himself for what he might see when he flipped the channel. A fuzzy soccer game. Another cartoon. *Not much on this TV.* Two more channels showed only snow. He flipped to another station, and there it was: the enormous net twisted through the sea.

John turned up the volume. He crouched, eye level with the screen. Behind a weary reporter, overturned hulls flashed red and blue in the ambient light of rescue vessels. The water was speckled with divers searching the tangled maze. Thumping rotors echoed above from news helicopters.

Kate entered the room, with a glance back through the doorway. "I see you have a way with children. Come on. Chopper's ready to go."

John motioned her. "Look, this is it."

Kate stepped closer to the TV as the reporter summed it up. "As of now, two fishermen are confirmed to have drowned, and at least eighteen others have sustained injuries ranging from dislocated shoulders to missing fingers and hands from the violent pull of the net." She glanced down at her desk, "Although divers are searching, there are still several fishermen unaccounted for . . . from what marine biologists are calling an extremely rare humpback whale attack."

"Okay," John muttered. "Just maybe . . ."

The reporter spoke up. "But the attack is not without speculation. Mike Boland, who covered the event, still insists that the creature he saw was no whale, and that it had a strange paddle-like fin, something no humpback whale has."

John felt a rush of dizziness, and his mouth went dry. Although his gut told him the truth, he hoped that by some miracle the culprit really was only a whale.

"Whale!" John turned to Kate. "On top of it all, they don't even know what it is?"

"You didn't see the footage. The way it was tangled in the net, they never got a clear shot of the creature." Kate perked up. "But you could look at that as a lucky break—if the public really knew what was under that net . . ."

"Every yahoo with a boat will be out there trying to find it," John said, nodding in agreement. He glanced at an old, faded Coca-Cola clock on the wall. "Later than I thought. Come on. We'd better get moving." He swung the chimp onto his shoulders and headed through the doorway. The trio exited the building with a final wave to Ebo and the little boy.

Heading toward the chopper, John sighed with a glance back. "It's a shame he has to live like that, under those conditions, especially with kids."

Kate laughed aloud. "Who? Ebo? He's loaded! Just past that clearing behind the runway, he has a house three times the size of mine. He just thinks people are more inclined to tip him better if he leaves the place the way it is."

~~~

The Knysna General Hospital emergency entrance doors crashed open. The two paramedics released the stretcher to a doctor and a nurse. One paramedic followed, helping with the IV.

"What do we have here?" asked the doctor while guiding the front of the stretcher along the bright hallway.

"A car accident," replied the paramedic. "He ran into a deep ditch a few miles west of Keurboom. He's lost a lot of blood."

"No airbags, huh?" replied the doctor.

"No, it was an early model." The paramedic lowered his voice. "But that's the strange part. The injury doesn't look like an impact wound. It looks more like a deep scrape, like something was raked across it. You should have seen the front of his wetsuit before we cut it off. It looked like it had been through a shredder."

"Maybe it was from the broken glass from the windshield," said the nurse.

"Couldn't have been," replied the paramedic. "The windshield was only cracked. It didn't break all the way through. The passenger's side window was shattered from the side of the ditch, but the glass didn't go anywhere near his chest."

With a moan, the young man regained consciousness. He was pale.

He brought his right hand to the moist gauze on his stomach, and a nurse moved it away gently. His eyes squinted open. Slowly he rolled his head from side to side while repeating in a faint moan, "Where's Dorian? Did it get Dorian?"

~~~

Officer Marimba stepped through the emergency entrance doors. Down the long brightly lit hallway, he saw Ron moving his arms like he was trying to say something to the doctor. The officer quickly caught up with the stretcher and put his hand on the doctor's arm. "What did he say?"

"He keeps asking about Dorian. Was there a second person in the car?" asked the doctor.

"No, he was alone."

Ron repeated, in a faint moan, "Did it get Dorian? Did it get Dorian?"

Officer Marimba grabbed the side of the stretcher and asked Ron urgently, "Did *what* get Dorian?"

"The thing . . . in the water." The words faded into a whisper.

"Were you with Dorian this morning at the beach? Did you see what attacked him—what kind of shark?"

"We were there. Then I couldn't find Dorian. It . . . was . . . more than a shark," Ron said, struggling with the memory. "It was . . . the biggest thing I've ever seen."

"Your chest," demanded Officer Marimba. "What happened to your chest?"

"From . . . from its skin . . . underneath me when I was trying to swim back . . . to the beach." Ron was fading fast.

As they reached the operating room doors, the doctor put a hand on the officer's shoulder. "That's as far as you go, officer. We'll take it from here."

A nurse approached. "I'll show you to the waiting room. We'll get you as soon as we know something."

~~~

Guiding the chopper east, Kate reached down and took the chimp's hand off the cyclic control. "No thanks. I'll do the piloting if you don't mind." She glanced over at John, who was asleep. A small puddle of blood had trailed from his left forearm—a cut had come open again—and onto a folded map that was in the seat.

As she watched him, he slowly awakened, rubbing his eyes.

"You feeling okay?"

"I was just resting my eyes for a minute." He reached over, and with a slight wince, peeled the map from his bloody forearm.

Kate gave him the once-over, the torn shirt, cuts across his chest, the deep gashes in his forearms, and the tears on his pants. "Ebo was right. You're a mess. We'd better get you cleaned up before all that gets infected. And I don't believe a shower would hurt either. I don't know who smells worse—you or the chimp." She reached down and scratched the chimp's head. "No offense Crystal."

"We've got to take the tooth over to the Navy first," John insisted. "How far are we now?"

"We're only about twenty minutes from the airport," Kate adjusted the cyclic control, "Before we head for the Navy, we need to take a quick drive into Port Liz." She gave a warm wink. "I think I know someone who can help us out."

Exhausted but determined, John nodded his approval. He picked up the tooth from beside his hip. His eyes drifted across the dried blood on his shredded shirt, the cuts along his arms, and rope-burned wrists, and stopped on the giant tooth. In spite of all he'd been through, he knew the real battle was about to begin.

Chapter 21
INDISPUTABLE EVIDENCE

Kate's silver and blue Jeep skidded to a stop in the Port Elizabeth World Museum parking lot. John finished sliding on one of Kate's workout t-shirts he'd found in the back seat. It wasn't the best fit, but was more presentable than the bloodstained rag he was wearing. Leaping out, he grabbed the towel-bundled tooth and followed Kate up the stairs to the sprawling building.

Kate bounded two steps at a time as John tried to catch up. She glanced at her watch. "We made pretty good time . . . should still be able to make it to the Navy before dark. I just hope that bloody monkey of yours behaves herself in my office."

"I don't see any lights on. Sure they're open?"

"No. It's closed. But the curator's in. Mom called ahead and told him we were bringing over a tooth. His name is Steven Jensen, one of her former paleontology students. If anyone knows all there is to know about giant pliosaurs, she said it's this bloke."

"Just a tooth? You mean he doesn't know it's not a fossil . . . that it's fresh?"

Kate grinned. "I sure hope he has a change of trousers at the office."

Reaching the top step, John's smile faded. He focused on a black vintage BSA that was parked on the sidewalk. The sight of the bike took him somewhere else. He couldn't look away.

Kate glanced back. "Hey, come on!" She did a double take of his face. "What is it? You look like you've seen a ghost?" she grinned. "I know . . . guess you rode one of those back in the day, huh?"

John snapped out of it. "Hardly," he muttered with a final look back at the bike. Picking up the pace, he caught up to Kate as someone appeared behind the glass double doors. The door cracked open, and John grabbed the handle, allowing Kate to enter first. Stepping through, she eyed him as if such chivalry wasn't necessary.

Inside, they were met by a man in his late forties. His hair and beard were peppered with gray, his face flushed with anticipation. Steven introduced himself, unable to take his eyes from the towel in John's hand. "So, Professor Atkins tells me you've run across a rather unusual pliosaur tooth. Let's have a look, shall we?"

John unwrapped the towel.

Steven's eyes grew wide. He picked up the giant tooth as if he were raising the Holy Grail. "Yes indeed, an excellent specimen. It's enormous. And its unusual white coloring . . . obviously it's fossilized from some kind of shell or white stone."

"No," John said. "It's fresh."

Steven laughed it off. "No, really, where did you find it?"

"It's no joke." John's eyes were somber.

Steven looked at Kate, as if expecting a smile, a laugh. But it never came. There was a long moment of silence. "Wha—? What do you mean *fresh?*" Steven stammered. He looked closer at the tooth, running his thumb across something collected on the root. His face went white. "Where exactly did you find this? Are there more?"

"Yeah. Lots more," John said. "Probably about a hundred or so, and I'm afraid they're all fresher than this one."

"That's enough for a complete set of jaws! How . . . where did you find them? Do you have them all in your possession?"

Kate remained silent, giving John the floor.

John brought his hand to his brow, wondering where to begin.

Steven was beside himself. "We finally have proof, a white tooth! I knew it! I always knew someone would eventually find indisputable evidence of pliosaurs' survival."

"Hold on," replied John. "Speaking of indisputable evidence, there's a bit more to the story, but I'll have to fill you in later."

Steven gasped. "No! Don't tell me you found part of a carcass still intact. What?"

John let fly. "It's swimming off the coast of South Africa right now. Man, it's alive."

He grabbed Steven's shoulder as he stumbled back. Seconds later, Steven found his voice. "It's alive?" he whispered. Then his eyes grew stern. "You better not be toying with me. This isn't some kind of sick joke, is it?"

"Steven, I wish it was a joke." John's tone was solemn. "At least two people are dead."

Kate's eyes confirmed this was the truth.

After a pause, Steven shook his head as if to rid himself of shock. "You're not kidding, are you? But where? How big is it? Have you seen it? What color is its skin? Did you get a picture of it?"

"No, I was a little pressed for time when I first saw it. Like I said, I'll fill you in on all the details later. My immediate concern is far from scientific. Right now we need to find a way to stop this thing."

Steven tried to take it all in. "Have you told anyone, like the Navy or the Sharks Board? The media hasn't gotten wind of this yet, have they?"

"No. I just got back to the mainland," replied John. "I've informed the Navy, but I don't think they halfway believe me."

"This is incredible," Steven said. "I've heard about all of the beachings they've had along the southern coast for the last few days."

His jaw dropped. "The Motanza!"

"Yes," Kate said. "We think it was the pliosaur."

Steven continued, "If the media figures out what's really responsible . . ."

"I know, I've got to get to the Navy and convince them before the media gets wind of it," said John.

Kate added, "That's why we came here first. Thought you'd be able to give us a little more info on what we're up against. It would also help the credibility of our story if you could authenticate the tooth."

"Yes, of course. And it's a good thing you have this and not just your story, whatever it is." Steven raised the tooth. "Even though they'll probably want to carbon test it first, it'll certainly get their attention . . . force them to take you seriously."

Kate spoke up. "So what can you tell us about it?"

Steven clicked on the lights. The enormous room with its posed prehistoric skeletons seemed to come to life around them. Steven motioned. "Follow me. You'll want to see this."

Steven led them up a stairwell that wound around a posed Mosasaur skeleton. When they reached the top step, John and Kate stopped cold. They were confronted by a set of seven-foot-tall pliosaur jaws suspended from the ceiling."

"Unbelievable!" John was awestruck.

Kate looked like she was about to pass out. "You were in the water with *that*?"

John nodded. "And a lot of other people are gonna be, too, unless we do something." He stepped closer. Staring into the colossal jaws at this range unnerved him. Rows of twelve-inch-long teeth projected out from the cavernous mouth. As hideous as they were, at least these were various shades of brown—fossilized. *The way they are supposed to be.*

~~~

Forty-five anxious minutes later, Officer Marimba tossed a fishing magazine onto an end table. He rose from an uncomfortable vinyl couch and headed toward the operating room. "This is ridiculous. I don't have all day to sit around in a hospital." He stepped around the last corner and saw the doctor coming through the shiny stainless steel doors.

"He's a lucky guy. We got him just in time," said the doctor, lowering his mask. "Another fifteen minutes, and he would have lost too much blood. For now, he's stabilized. We're still giving him blood, but he should be okay."

"Were there any injuries other than his chest?" asked the officer.

"No, not at all. No broken bones or any type of internal damage. Just a few scrapes on his forearms and hands, similar to the ones on his chest, but not as deep."

"Did he say anything else?" asked the officer. "Anything about his whereabouts this morning?"

"Yes, he keeps asking for his friend, and talking about a big creature that knocked him off his board. He's obviously still in shock."

"What do you mean?"

"He said the thing that hit him had a mouth as big as a garage door and teeth the length of his arm. He said it looked like a dinosaur."

"Bizarre description for a shark," muttered the officer. "Any idea what really happened to his chest? A shark scrape?"

The doctor shook his head while pulling his mask back up. "I've seen quite a few shark scrapes, but they've never looked anything like this. Sharks have these fine, tooth-like prickles on their skin called denticles. That's what makes their skin feel coarse when you run your hand across it a certain way. These denticles are very small, so small they're practically invisible to the naked eye. Usually, shark scrapes are more like coarse sandpaper scrapes, not nearly this deep—especially to go through a neoprene wetsuit and still cause this much tissue damage."

The officer's brow deepened. "So if it wasn't the shark's skin, what was it?"

"Maybe a large shark did knock him off his board and caused him to land on some coral. The injury seems to be more consistent with coral abrasions than anything else I've seen."

Officer Marimba breathed a sigh of relief, happy for a reasonable explanation. "Yeah, that seems to make sense."

"However, coral doesn't usually leave such a consistent pattern."

"What do you mean?"

"The scrape marks, or points of entry, were very uniform and evenly spaced from one another. The abrasions sustained from coral are usually not this consistent. Now, if you'll excuse me, I need to get back in there."

"When can I talk to him?"

The doctor backed into the door. "Maybe tomorrow when he's stronger, more stabilized."

Officer Marimba shook his head as he walked away from the emergency room, frustrated that the answers would have to wait until the morning.

~~~

John and Kate hung onto Steven's every word as he raised the giant tooth against the enormous pliosaur jaws. "You're right. This is a plesiosaur, or pliosaur, tooth from the short-necked variety, quite possibly a Liopleurodon. You can tell by your tooth's unique shape." Steven ran his finger along the long indentions that tapered down to the tooth's tip. "See these flutes?" He turned the tooth. "And the way the crown has three distinct sides that are flat? Liopleurodon is from the Greek dialect, meaning smooth-sided tooth. The full name is Liopleurodon ferox. Ferox means fear."

John's eyebrows arched. "I get that part."

"Indeed," Steven nodded. "But interestingly, Liopleurodon wasn't believed to be one of the larger pliosaurs. I mean, the larger, or mega-pliosaurs, were enormous–prehistoric marine reptiles that made T-rex look like a gecko. The greatest predators that ever lived, land or sea. A clade of beast that made its debut during the Jurassic and should have died out at the end of the Cretaceous period sixty-five million years ago."

John spoke up. "So that tooth . . . do you think it'll be enough evidence to convince anyone? Can we prove that it's not a fossil?"

Steven ran his thumb across the tooth's root. "See these rough, moist areas along the root, that's fresh gum tissue." He grinned. "No one can dispute this." He picked up a yardstick from a nearby table. He lined it up with the tooth, still awestruck. "But its size!" Steven then looked up at the set of jaws. "The lower jaw from this set measures seven feet. And see those two giant holes in the back of the skull? Those were to accommodate jaw muscles thicker than a grown man. The owner of these jaws would have been nearly fifty feet long and weigh thirty-five tons— the combined weight of eight full-grown elephants."

He held up the fresh tooth. "The largest tooth from this set measures twelve inches . . . your tooth measures *nineteen*."

Kate gasped. "A marine reptile larger than a herd of elephants!"

"Oh yes!" He focused on John. "I'd say your jaws would dwarf this set in every dimension." Steven's eyes lit up as he envisioned such a beast. "Your creature would be about eighty feet long, maybe more. We're talking about a monster whose paddle fins would span thirty-five feet from fin tip to fin tip, propelling a fifteen-foot-long head. Not to mention twelve-foot jaws powerful enough to lift a truck and tear it in half." His eyes narrowed on John. "For you see, your creature possessed a bite force in excess of sixteen tons—the most powerful in history."

John muttered to Kate, "I wish he wouldn't call it my creature." He hesitated for a moment. "Then a beast this size would obviously be a slow swimmer because of its bulk, right? Like a whale?"

"Quite the contrary, I'm afraid. Pliosaur was, or should I say, *is* a swift ambush predator. After taking a huge gulp of air at the surface, the creature would dive down to the seafloor. There it could lay in wait up to two hours on a single breath. Then, spotting its prey, it would thrust all four of its paddle fins in unison and attack with blinding speed."

Steven paused. "This brings up another point. Considering its attack strategy, the beast could be quite difficult to spot. In other words, if it's lying in wait on the seabed and only comes up every hour or so for a breath, your chances of spotting it from a chopper could be slim. Your only hope will be to catch it en route, moving from one feeding ground to another."

"That's reassuring," Kate muttered. "The largest predator in history, and almost impossible to find."

"You said eighty feet, maybe more," John added. "How big could these things get?"

Steven rolled his eyes. "As with most presumed extinct species, scientists don't all agree on pliosaur's maximum size. However, there are a few bones from London's Oxford and Cambridge Clay mines that suggest it was enormous. A giant vertebra, and a lower jaw nearly ten feet long have been unearthed. Because the jaw is a partial find, the so-called experts can't stop reclassifying them. Initially, they said the jaw belonged to Liopleurodon macromerus; later they changed it to Pliosaurus macromerus." Steven winked. "But after looking at the size and shape of your tooth, maybe the lads had it right the first time. The bottom line is that if that colossal lower mandible didn't come from Liopleurodon . . . then he has a cousin that's even bigger!" He stroked his chin thoughtfully. "Then there's the twenty-percent factor to consider."

"Twenty-percent factor?" John and Kate said in unison.

"Yes. Unlike the dinosaurs, very few complete skeletons of giant pliosaurs have been discovered. So it would be absurd to believe the ten-foot mandible unearthed is from the largest specimen. Therefore, many scientists agree that you can safely increase the largest remains discovered by twenty percent of its size to estimate the maximum size of the species. In other words—"

Kate finished for him. "God only knows how large these things really got."

"Precisely." Steven glanced up at the jaws, still wide-eyed, then continued. "And let's not forget the Monster of Aramberri; a massive fifty-foot skeleton unearthed in Mexico in 2002. Its teeth were nearly sixteen inches long. Although scientists keep adjusting the actual length of this partial find, it was initially believed to be a Liopleurodon, then later, of course, it was reclassified. But soon after the excavation they were shocked to discover that the creature was only a juvenile. And that in its skull, which was the size of a car, there was a death wound . . . a hole that came from a much larger adult. But naturally this, too, is being debated. Many now believe that the remains are not from a juvenile."

He continued, "Then you have the infamous remains unearthed in Svalbard, Norway, in 2009 of a giant pliosaur thought to rival the Monster of Aramberri. After tentatively calling it Predator X, they settled on the name Pliosaurus funkei. Pitiful name for such a beast."

John rubbed his chin. "And I always thought the prehistoric shark megalodon was the undisputed champ of all time."

Steven gasped as if John had insulted his mother. "Please! That mere fish!" Clearly, these were fighting words to Steven. "First off, what isn't commonly known is that many of the reconstructed megalodon jaws you see have proven to be inaccurately done. They simply contain too many teeth, or they consisted of larger teeth from multiple specimens. Appropriately scaled, the largest set of megalodon jaws would be around seven feet wide. A formidable bite indeed, until you compare it to a creature with a ten-foot lower jaw—a mandible that is three feet longer than megalodon's entire bite radius. Now take pliosaur's ten-foot lower jaw and place its matching ten-foot upper jaw on top of it. Then open the mouth." Steven nodded with glee. "That's right. You're looking at a maximum bite radius of around twelve feet—nearly twice that of megalodon!"

John and Kate stood in stunned silence as Steven finished his rapid-fire lesson. "And let's not forget the teeth. The largest megalodon teeth are about seven and a half inches, whereas pliosaurs stretch the tape to eighteen inches—a full ten inches longer. And when it comes to bite force, the comparison is not even close. Scaling up the bite force of a great white shark, scientists have concluded that megalodon had a maximum bite force of twenty thousand pounds per square inch. As I mentioned earlier, pliosaur had a bite force in excess of sixteen tons. Clearly, this beast could rip a megalodon in half!"

John held up his hands. "Sorry, I didn't mean to offend you!"

Kate whistled in disbelief. She looked up at the suspended jaws. "I still can't believe it . . . a creature like this out there all these years, and no one's seen it."

"Oh, but they have." Steven grinned wide. "It's been *seen* . . . it's just that no one's been able to *find* it!"

"You mean like the creature in Loch Ness?" asked Kate.

Steven laughed. "Hardly! Everyone knows there's nothing in Loch Ness, no food supply. However, the ocean is an entirely different story." He stuck his finger high in the air and bellowed, "July 30, 1915. Off the coast of Ireland, the German submarine U-28 had just torpedoed the British ship *Iberian*. As the ship sank, there was an enormous explosion that sent debris a hundred feet into the air. Then, amidst the boiling debris, rolling up to the surface appeared a colossal prehistoric marine reptile over sixty feet long. The submarine crew witnessed the living creature writhe on the surface for about fifteen seconds until it slowly sank into the sea."

Kate's eyes grew wide. "Are you serious?"

"Every word of it's true. But that sighting pales to this one." Steven's voice grew ominous. "It involves another sub at the end of World War I. The German submarine UB-85 was caught on the surface in broad daylight and sunk by a British patrol boat. The German crew was captured. Once onboard, Captain Krech, the sub's commander, was asked why he didn't submerge when he saw the British ship . . . well, he had some story to tell."

John found himself leaning forward slightly in anticipation. He looked over at Kate; she was doing the same.

Steven's eyes glowed with fervor as he continued the story. "They had been recharging their batteries the previous night on the surface, when all of a sudden, a huge beast climbed aboard from the sea. All they could see was its enormous eyes and teeth. It was so massive it listed the sub to the point where the captain feared an open hatch would drop below the waterline. Every man on watch fired at the creature, but its teeth were latched onto the forward gun mount and wouldn't let go. Ultimately, the beast let go and slid back into the sea. But in the struggle, the forward plating had been damaged so severely the sub could no longer submerge. 'That's why you were able to catch us on the surface,' Captain Krech had concluded."

"Wow," John said, "I've never heard this."

Kate just shook her head.

"The Monongahela Monster, the Pensacola Bay Incident of '62 . . . the list goes on. In the last century there have been thousands of plesiosaur and pliosaur sightings throughout the world's oceans," assured Steven. "And in 1983 something incredible washed up in our own backyard."

John eased back against the stairwell as Steven continued. "On June 12, renowned wildlife enthusiast Owen Burnham, in the presence of family members, ran across a bizarre carcass on Bungalow Beach. It was sixteen feet long, had a long pair of jaws containing eighty teeth each . . . *and two pairs of paddle fins.*"

John's eyes lit up.

"That's right," said Steven, "paddle fins that prove it was a pliosaur. At sixteen feet it was most likely a juvenile. But what was also amazing about the carcass . . . it had not begun to decompose, other than a torn rear flipper. It was entirely intact!"

Steven grinned wide and said, "So much for it being a decomposed basking shark, which has been the case in some of the other assumed pliosaur carcasses. Not this time."

"So where is the carcass now?" asked Kate. "Lying about in formaldehyde at the Smithsonian?"

Steven's smile faded. That's just it. Burnham had left the carcass briefly to retrieve his instruments to document the find, and by the time he returned, it was gone. Apparently the locals disposed of it." Steven raised a finger. "But I assure you, Owen Burnham is an extremely reliable, knowledgeable eyewitness and was in the presence of others when he examined the carcass. And many well-respected paleontologists regard this as significant evidence of pliosaurs' existence in today's oceans. But that's not the only one. In 1922, on another beach in South Africa, a farmer—"

John cut in. "Steven, this is all riveting. But trust me, I'm the last person you need to convince that these things still exist. What we want to know is *where* this creature is likely to turn up next? What does it feed on? Territory?"

Steven squinted for a moment, realigning his thoughts. "As far as diet and territory, I would say anywhere along the coast where upwelling occurs, places producing plankton-rich waters that attract whales . . . a top item on pliosaur's diet. Keep an eye out for unusual carcasses washing—"

Kate's ringing cell phone cut Steven short.

"Sorry," she said. She listened for a moment, and her jaw went slack. She looked up at Steven. "Do you have a TV?"

~~~

Steven sat on the corner of an ornate wooden desk in his office. Kate and John were perched on chairs beside him, all eyes riveted to a small TV on a bookshelf.

"Mom said she just saw this on the news," said Kate. "But apparently it's been going on for hours."

The image on screen showed several tourists struggling to cut a beached whale from a shark barrier net. A female reporter was at the tide line. "This is the second beaching in Plettenberg Bay, and this one has researchers baffled. This same disoriented creature beached itself earlier, then was saved and released. But instead of heading into deep waters, it turned around and headed back to shore."

Kate said, "That whale's not disoriented. It knows what's out there."

The trio watched as someone handed the reporter a note. She glanced at it and continued. "Now we're going to take you live to another beaching fifty miles east, discovered earlier this morning."

The screen switched to a black female reporter walking alongside a beached sperm whale. Although dozens of people were collected along the shoreline, no one helped the creature, for it was clearly dead. News helicopters thumped in the background.

"Michelle Reiner, *Channel Eight News*, reporting to you live from Paradise Beach. Behind me is yet another beached sperm whale, but as you'll see in a moment, this one's a bit different." The camera followed Michelle as she waded to the opposite side of the enormous carcass where bystanders, knee deep in water, frantically snapped their cameras. When the news camera turned, Kate and Steven gasped. The screen filled with an enormous bite mark in the whale. Huge chunks of spilled blubber swayed with the tide.

"Look at the size of that bite mark!" Kate exclaimed.

Michelle continued. "I know what you're thinking, but relax. Researchers assure me that what looks like an enormous single bite mark is in fact the result of a number of sharks feeding from the same area." Sloshing closer, she pointed out smaller bites taken from inside the enormous wound.

John just smirked.

Michelle waded over to four long gashes beside the wound. "But what no one can explain are these deep, long tears through the whale's flank."

"I can," muttered John. "That would be where it missed."

Steven finally broke his silence. "Southwest . . . *aah*, the Agulhas. I should have known." He slid off his desk. "Follow me. We need to have a look at something."

~~~

Kate and John followed Steven into a vast exhibit room. Pedestals and platforms displayed skeletons of prehistoric South African marine life. Passing a twelve-foot sea turtle skeleton, they stopped in front of an enormous wall map of South Africa. Different colors indicated major currents.

Steven pulled a laser pen from his pocket and indicated a spot on the map. "Judging from the Motanza attack and the beachings, the pliosaur is clearly heading southwest. My guess would be that it's picked up the Agulhas, a warm, south-flowing current that flows between Madagascar and Mozambique and skirts along the coast of South Africa."

"What's so alluring about this particular current?" asked John.

"The creature is probably using it to help propel its tremendous bulk, conserving calories while looking for spots where upwelling occurs— steep embankments or any place producing plankton-rich waters that attract whales."

"Toward the Western Cape? Aren't there a lot of seal colonies in that area?" asked Kate. "Like around False Bay?"

"Yes, False Bay . . . or as the locals call it, the Ring of Death."

"Ring of Death." John repeated the words solemnly.

"Yes, charming, isn't it?" Steven traced the coast with his laser pen and circled the spot. "There's a rocky island in the center of the bay that houses sixty thousand fur seals. Surrounding the island, there's an area the seals have to pass through to swim back to shore. The area is so saturated with great whites, it's been labeled the Ring of Death. Right around the island, the elevation drops straight down to a depth of fifty feet. That's an ideal situation for a predator the size of pliosaur to move up close to its prey.

"You've probably seen the area on that TV documentary where the great whites soar through the air. The waters are so deep that during an attack, sharks can swim straight up from the bottom, reach full speed, and breach about six feet above the surface."

Steven's beam followed the coast and stopped on another area. "But before that, a little farther east, you have a real hot spot, the Dyer Island Channel. They even nicknamed it Shark Alley. That's also where they have the—" Steven's jaw dropped. "Oh no. The shark tours! They won't have a chance!"

"Shark tours?" John's mind reeled at the thought.

Kate matched Steven's expression. "Yes, it's a huge attraction. People fly in from all over the world for this. The tour operators chum the water for hours and then bring tourists out to watch them feed the sharks from the boat. But for some of those crazy tourists, that's not enough, they drop down in a cage right in the middle of a feeding frenzy—"

John cut in. "If the pliosaur's anywhere near there . . ." He turned to Steven and hurriedly shook his hand. "Steven, you've been tremendous, but we need to get to the chopper." Kate saluted Steven, and they were on their way.

Hurrying along the hallway, John said to Kate, "I'll call the Navy on the way. We don't have time to wait until they see the tooth. We've got to get these tours closed down immediately." The two bolted through the glass double doors and made for the jeep.

Chapter 22
STILL IN THE GAME

Kota slid his thumb to the edge of the driver's license, allowing him to see the small photograph of John Paxton more clearly. He looked over at the red X on Kolegwa's chest representing a sworn oath to kill his enemy, or take his own life if he fails. "Relax, you may still get a chance to fulfill your vow."

"You can find white man from that?" grunted Kolegwa in their native tongue.

"Yes. This can take me right to him!" Kota picked up the leather wallet from a table in the small hut. He slid out the corners of about a dozen business cards. "These will help too."

He turned to Kolegwa, eyes ablaze. "Remember the white holy man who came to the island and taught me their language, Afrikaans? The man who took me with him to Africa to learn their ways? You said it was a waste to learn outsiders' ways." He released a grim smile. "But now you will see. The chief's death will be avenged!" Kota raised the driver's license. "He thinks he'll stop Kuta Keb-la, but *I* will stop *him*!" He motioned to Kolegwa. "Come, there is little time to prepare."

Kolegwa followed Kota through the series of huts to the east corner of the village. They came to a guarded cave entrance. The guard quickly stepped aside . . . as did anyone in Kota's path.

Entering the cave, there was only darkness initially. Soon there was a hint of light and the increasing echo of the ocean. The passageway emptied into a breathtaking lagoon surrounded by a vast cavern. On the far side of the cavern, an opening looked out to the blue-green waters of the Indian Ocean.

The banks looked like a marine surplus store in the wake of a hurricane. The duo passed piles of clothing, life jackets, life rafts, and various small pleasure boats collected along the banks—all that remained of troubled seagoers who'd sought refuge on the island. Kota looked around contently. Clearly, Kuta Keb-la had dined well over the years.

Behind Kota and Kolegwa, villagers flooded into the entrance, watching with wild-eyed anticipation.

Kota paused at a wooden barrel. He decided to take one last look at his crate of souvenirs. He lifted the wooden top. Inside was a stack of life preservers adorned with the names of various ships—trophies they had collected over the years from fishing and whaling vessels that ventured too close to the island.

With great pride, he reminisced how they would paddle out toward the ship. Then, when they were close enough, the men would lie down in the bottom canoe and cover themselves with palm fronds. The only soul visible would be a small boy perched at the bow. He would hold up a pearl necklace and motion to the fishermen, as if he wanted to offer them a trade. It worked every time.

The greedy fishermen always waved the youth over, thinking they could take advantage of an ignorant native boy. And that was when they got the surprise. That was when their jaws dropped and their faces turned even whiter with fear. He recalled the look in their eyes when the tribesmen sprang up from the palm fronds with their spears in hand. The fishermen never had a chance. There was never more than a two-minute struggle. After the bodies were tossed overboard, they would burst a large hole into the hull and leave the ship to slowly find its way to the dark depths of the Indian Ocean.

Kota smiled with pride and closed the top of the barrel. *And the outsiders always wondered why this area has a bad reputation for ships being lost at sea. Yes, those were the good old days,* Kota thought . . . at least until he was a little older, and they sent him to school with the missionary. But that was good too. It gave Kota the tools he needed— knowledge of the outside world that no one else in the tribe possessed. Otherwise, he could have ended up with the intellect of Kolegwa. *Well, maybe not that bad.*

Heading farther along the bank, Kota passed two weather-beaten pleasure boats and stopped at a twenty-eight-foot naval patrol boat surrounded by tribesmen. A smear of blood crusted on the driver's seat evoked a smile from Kota. A look inside showed everything was loaded up: gas cans, life raft, and a suitcase of African rand bills.

Kota climbed aboard. *Now, what to wear?* He picked up a maroon sailing jacket that was already on the boat and tried it on. As Kolegwa started to board, Kota pointed to the pile of clothes and ordered in their native tongue, "First, find something that fits you. Can't have you walking around looking like an overgrown version of Shaka Zulu."

Kolegwa's brow wrinkled, not sure what that meant.

Kota watched as Kolegwa rambled through the pile of clothes. *It's a good thing I'm taking him with me,* he thought. *Otherwise, with the chief dead, he might try to empower himself while I'm gone. That is, if the imbecile doesn't follow through on his vow and take his own life.*

Kota turned his attention to the gas containers, then checked the boat's fuel gauge, and estimated there was more than enough for the trip. He looked through a briefcase filled with rand. Yes, they had everything they needed.

"What about this?" shouted Kolegwa.

Kota looked up and saw Kolegwa standing proudly in front of the pile of clothes. He wore a multicolored polyester shirt with every button strained to its limit and sleeves that stopped well above his wrist. His selection of lime-green pants fit in a similar manner, ending about five inches above his ankles. Kota smiled, "Nice choice. You're gonna drive those African women crazy. Come, let's go!"

Kolegwa turned to his family. He gave a heavyset woman and two little girls a hug, then climbed on board beside Kota. Kota smiled, took a skipper's hat from the driver's seat, and crowned Kolegwa. *"Aaah!* That's it. I knew something was missing."

Taking his place at the helm, Kota clapped his hands. Eight men, four to a side, hefted the vessel onto their shoulders. Carrying it pallbearer-style, they crossed the bank and waded into the lagoon until the waves reached the hull.

The engine roared to life, echoing through the cavern, muting the sound of the sea. Kota stood, facing the crowd along the banks. His machete thrust overhead, he shouted in their native tongue, "Prepare a pole at the base of the lagoon for the white man's head!"

The villagers sounded out in a victory cry as the boat disappeared into the glaring light at the opposite side of the cavern.

~~~

Kate zipped the jeep along a bumpy road as they entered Cape St. Francis. John had one hand on the giant tooth sprawled across his lap; the other held a cell phone.

"Okay, let me make sure I've got this straight," Lieutenant Vic Greeman's voice echoed through the phone. "You want me to close down the shark tours because of an eighteen-foot marine reptile heading their way?"

John raised his voice above the road noise. "I said *eighty!* Not eighteen, *eighty!* This creature is at least eighty feet long. The Motanza attack yesterday . . . that wasn't a whale; it was this same creature. Also, the beaching . . . the whales running aground in Jeffrey's Bay and Mossel Bay . . . it all proves the creature is headed southwest. That's why you have to close down the shark tours at Dyer Island immediately. Then we need to get some eyes in the air to find—"

Laughter erupted from the cell phone. *"Waaait* just a minute. I've got three of our choppers over Mazeppa Bay looking for survivors from the Motanza, and you want me to pull them to look for some eighty-foot reptile?" He assured John there was nothing to fear by adding, "Relax. I received a similar call several months ago. I'm sure you only saw a line of basking sharks feeding. They can look quite odd from the air, like one continuous creature."

John lowered the cell phone, baffled. He had not expected to be laughed at outright. He looked at Kate. "He's laughing. Says I probably saw a few basking sharks feeding in a line."

Kate motioned to John to hand over the phone. Clearly, he was getting nowhere fast, so he happily obliged. She raised her voice into the phone. "A basking shark doesn't have a mouth full of *nineteen-inch, razor-sharp teeth!* This is Kate Atkinson, and I have such a tooth in my possession. It has fresh gum tissue attached to the root, and it doesn't take a genius to know what that means. We'll show it to you."

Keeping one eye on the road, she continued, "If you don't close the shark tours this minute, you'll have a slaughter that'll make the Motanza attack look like a fish fry. And if this happens, I swear I'll take this tooth straight to the media—tell them how a certain Lieutenant Vic Greeman wouldn't cooperate. Don't worry . . . I'll make sure they spell your name right, *Lieutenant!*" She listened for a long moment. "Thanks, Lieutenant. Be there in an hour."

Kate clicked the cell phone off with a "that's how you do it" smile.

John shrugged. "Guess some things just need a woman's touch."

Kate swerved to avoid a pothole. "The lieutenant saw the Motanza footage, agrees that something's not quite right about it. Also, one of the tour operators is an old friend of his. Said he'll get them to take the day off, but he wants to see the tooth ASAP. Still, I don't think he completely believed me. He said we're wrong about the creature's length."

"We probably are," muttered John. "It's probably closer to a hundred." Kate wheeled around a corner, and they entered the airport parking lot.

~~~

After hanging up the telephone, Lieutenant Vic Greeman swung around in his chair and faced a Rolodex. He extracted a section of cards and placed them beside the phone. He plucked the first one from the stack. Above a shark's gaping jaws, it read "Shark Tours: Dive with Live Sharks." He reluctantly dialed the number. "The boys aren't gonna be happy about this."

After three rings, a deep, gravelly voice answered, "Shark Tours, wildest show in South Africa!"

"Drew, this is Vic Greeman."

"Vic, how you doing? Ready to drop down in a cage yet? Had a couple sixteen-footers yesterday you'd have liked. Hey, remember when you called earlier, asking if I've noticed any fluctuation in shark activity?"

"Yeah, why? Have you noticed an increase?" asked Vic.

"No," replied Drew. "Just the opposite. Earlier today, I went out to my usual spot and chummed for nearly three hours. Didn't see nothin'. Usually it doesn't take no more than twenty minutes before the first white shows up. Had to bring everyone back in and give 'em a refund. First time that's happened in over five years. It was like there wasn't a shark around for miles, like they'd all up and left the channel."

"But this isn't your prime season," Vic said. "Around this time of year, during the warmer months, don't the sharks usually disperse and start hunting for fish?"

"Yeah, but not like this."

Vic stared at the business card between his fingers. "Well, considering that the sharks seem to be on vacation, you might not mind my request so much."

~~~~

Drew Hensen hesitated in the doorway of his small, shack-like office at the edge of the Dyer Channel. Deep lines crisscrossing his sun-weathered face made him look older than a man of sixty-two. His purple tank top exposed lots of loose, leathery skin. He peered across the anxious tourists gathered on the dock. He opened his mouth, but the words didn't want to come out at first. He didn't want to say them, but he knew he had to.

"Sorry folks! I'm not gonna be able to take you out today!"

"Whaddya talking 'bout? I brought the kid out here to see a shaaaaak!" complained a man in his forties with a thick New York accent.

Beside him, a boy wearing a red t-shirt sporting a shark's gaping jaws whined, "Yeah, we came all the way from New York!"

The rest of the tourists chimed in, muttering their two cents of disappointment.

"People, it's not my decision." Drew raised his hands. "The Navy's closing me down for the rest of the day!"

The New Yorker quickly spoke for the crowd. "That's okay. There's plenty of ottah shark tours 'round here willing to take our money."

"Not today, they ain't!" replied Drew. "They're closing down everyone for the rest of the day. Not just me."

A man with long, sandy-blond hair spoke in a Swedish accent, "They can't do that. We have to leave tomorrow. Here . . . what if I give you an extra fifty?"

Drew shook his head and started refunding their money. "Sorry, I'd like to take you all out, but there's nothing I can do. The Navy's out there doing some kind of research and don't want anyone chummin' up the water. But it's only for today." Drew yanked back the money, and his eyes lit up. "Folks, tell ya what! If you buy your tickets right now for tomorrow's show, I'll give you a twenty-rand discount per ticket. How does that sound?"

The New Yorker grabbed his refund. "What do we look like, a bunch of suckaaahs? Come on, little Joey. We're outta heah!"

"We are too!" added the Swede, snatching his refund. The rest of the group followed suit, murmuring their disappointment all the way to the parking lot. Drew just stood on the dock, looking at each person's back while trying to get a handle on all the money that had just slipped through his greedy fingers. When the tally reached two thousand rand, he moaned. "Vic, you'd better have a really good reason for this."

After the dock emptied, Drew shouted back to his boat where a young man was mixing chum in a large barrel. "Charley, wrap it up best ya can. We won't be goin' out for the rest of the day. And you can go ahead and take off when you're finished."

Charley just waved a hand without questioning the order.

Drew turned to a loud screech in the parking lot. Behind the fleeing crowd, a sleek red Porsche skidded to a stop. On the car's side door, a magnetic sign read, "Dive with Live Sharks." A stocky man wearing shorts and a tight, red t-shirt shot out of the car and slammed the door in anger. He shouted to Drew, "Did they close you down too?"

"Better believe they did, Al! Just watched two thousand rand walk off the dock."

Al Whittal, an angler in his mid-fifties with receding gray hair, charged up the dock like a bull. "What's all of this nonsense about research that keeps us from going out and making a living? Vic sounded a little weird to me, like he was hiding something. All right, fess up old man. Did he tell you anything? Come on now . . . I know you and Vic go way back."

Drew paused. "Well . . ."

"Come on," Al said. "I know he told you something. I can see it in your beady eyes."

"Mentioned something about a creature."

"What kind of creature?"

Al pursued Drew as he walked farther out on the dock to his boat. Drew scratched his head, not sure he should say anything. *But this guy ain't gonna leave . . .* "He just said it was big and dangerous. Like the sharks we deal with every day aren't."

"Did he say how big?"

"No . . . just talked like our cages might not be able to protect us. I sensed there was more. But when I tried to get it out of him, he acted like he'd told me too much already." Drew stopped beside his boat.

"I'm not buying this research bit," said Al. "What do you think the real story is?"

Drew perched his foot on a piling beside his boat. "You tell me. All I know is the rest of the day is shot, and I've just lost two thousand rand!"

"Maybe not," Al said with a wicked grin. "Must be a great white . . . why else would he keep tight-lipped? A shark too big for our cages . . . you thinking what I'm thinking?"

Drew squinted back at him. "Could be a record-setter. Certainly make up for a day's lost wages. Imagine what the publicity would do for business." He turned to his boat. "Well, I'm already loaded."

Al slapped him on the back and laughed. "Don't have to tell me that—it's past noon, and I can smell it on ya!"

"I don't mean me, you skeeve. I'm talkin' about the boat," Drew grumbled. "Charley just finished making up a new batch of chum. Got plenty of bait fish too."

Al stepped onto the gunwale. "Then we're all set!"

Drew grabbed his shoulder. "Wait a minute. This is illegal, you know. Blue pointers are protected species. They could come down on us pretty hard if we get caught."

Al stepped aboard and laughed. "If I come back with a world-record catch, I'll be happy to pay a lousy fine. Just get your wrinkly butt in the boat."

~~~

John could feel his pulse pounding against the cool enamel of the giant tooth while he held it tightly in his lap. He looked down through the side window of the Aribus H135. His anticipation swelled as a series of tall mountains rose and dropped beneath them.

His mind raced, thinking about the lieutenant—how someone had finally listened and taken action. He glanced over at Kate. "So tell me about these shark tours. Do a lot of people participate?"

Kate nodded emphatically. "Oh yes! Every day tourists line up on the docks ready to go out. It's a big attraction. They're willing to wait for hours on a crowded deck just to get a glimpse of a great white . . . or as the locals call them, blue pointers."

Kate pulled up slightly on the cyclic control. "After the fishing industry dried up around the Dyer Channel, it didn't take the local fishermen long to realize they could make a lot more money as shark tour operators than they ever could as fishermen. I heard one tour operator claim that in six months he took out a thousand tourists on his boat alone—and that's not bad money at a hundred fifty dollars a head. Now, they say if you drive through the little town of Gans Bay, you'll find a handmade shark's cage in almost every yard. So if the lieutenant didn't stop them, you can bet there are at least a dozen boats full of tourists out there chumming the waters right now."

John gazed across the instrument cluster. Eventually, his eyes wandered back to Kate—across her khaki shorts, pausing on her long, toned legs as they worked the pedals. He realized this was becoming a habit with him, gazing at Kate. Just as she felt his eyes on her, he quickly looked back up to the instrument cluster. "How . . . how we looking on fuel? After stopping at the Navy, think we could make it to Gans Bay before dark? Have a look around before heading back?"

"Read my mind . . . oh, that's scary," Kate said with a gasp. "Now I'm starting to think like you!"

John looked through the window. "Could be hope for you yet."

Kate smiled, amused by his comeback. She glanced at the fuel gauge. "No problem on fuel. But visibility might be an issue. Aside from the darkness, the Western Cape can be quite foggy this time of year." She winked. "But you never know, we could get lucky."

John kept his eyes on the passing coastline.

~~~

As the main rotor slowed, John and Kate slid from the helicopter and stepped onto the Knysna Naval Base helipad. John grabbed the tooth, adrenaline pumping, eyes fixed on the naval base. Finally, they were getting somewhere.

Closing the pilot's door, Kate stopped cold. "Oh crap! That's not good." She kneeled beside the skid, eyeing a large, black puddle. "That's oil. Could be a line. I'd better check it out."

John knew there was no time for this. He said hastily while walking away, "I'll take the tooth to the lieutenant while you fix the chopper."

With a nod, Kate slid between the skids while John headed for the base. She paused while watching John walk away, tension written all over his posture. "Hey!" she shouted.

John stopped cold and looked back. He saw Kate smile from beneath the helicopter. "Relax!" she shouted. "It's all gonna be okay. I promise!" John stared at her warmly for a long moment. He appreciated her reassurance. A grateful nod, and he was on his way.

~~~

Lieutenant Vic Greeman's office was sterile, even by military standards. No jackets draped over chairs, no magazines, books, or papers in plain view. Nothing looked out of place with the exception of the giant, white monstrosity of a tooth sitting on his desk. Fluorescent light glistened off the enamel as Vic slowly picked it up.

"Yes, those rough moist areas along the root are where fresh gum tissue is still attached," assured John. "If you like, I can call Steven Jensen at the South African World Museum. He has seen the tooth and can verify it."

When the lieutenant finally looked up, his eyes told John that wouldn't be necessary.

"The shark tours . . . are they closed?"

Vic was still staring at the tooth in his hand, trying to come to terms with what it all meant. "Most of them."

Most?

The lieutenant seemed embarrassed, defensive. "There were some I . . . I couldn't reach. They didn't pick up. You have no idea how many—"

John couldn't believe his ears. "You mean someone could still be out there? Now?"

The lieutenant's eyes said yes.

John felt a rush of panic. "What are we sitting around here for?"

Chapter 23
ONE FOR THE RECORD BOOKS

Less than a mile outside the Dyer Island Channel, a small fishing boat was anchored beneath the evening sky. Trailing from the stern, a forty-yard streak of blood widened as it drifted toward the open ocean. Al took a break from slinging chum with a soup ladle and stood up to stretch his back. After peering in every direction, he said, "Well, it looks like everyone followed orders. Not a soul in sight."

"Yeah, everyone but us!" replied Drew while he struggled to work an enormous bait hook through a seven-pound section of tuna.

After hanging his soup ladle on the side of the drum, Al paused, looking at the water. "No. I take it back, looks like there's someone in the distance."

Drew nervously said, "Hope it's not the Navy. Can you tell what kind of boat it is? Can you see a cage?"

Al squinted. "Not yet, I can't tell."

Starting to panic, Drew dropped the bait hook to the deck. "Maybe we should hide everything. I could toss all of this overboard!"

Squinting at the small boat on the horizon, Al muttered, "I don't know, but the forty-yard streak of blood pointing to our stern might still look a little suspicious. Wait a minute, looks like a fishing boat. Think we're okay."

The small vessel drew nearer. Al wiped his chum-stained hands on the side of his pants and walked to the edge of the stern. He saw two figures standing at the bow of the approaching boat, a heavyset man with dark hair and a young boy. As the boat passed, the man rubbed his fingers from the bottom of his chin and outward in a rude gesture. A loud voice echoed from the boat in a thick New York accent, "Hey, you ka-ka-roach! I thought you was stayin' in today?"

Al looked back at Drew. "Another satisfied customer, huh?"

"Yeah, part of the two thousand rand that I lost today," replied Drew. "Figures Willie Strickland would be the one to take 'em out. That sucker's always undercutting me."

The small boat passed while the heavyset man held his hands on his hips, watching them until the boat went out of sight. "*Aaah*, don't mind them," said Al, walking back to the chum barrel. "Looks like they're just out cruising around. Come back over here, and let's see how far you can hurl this bait hook."

Drew reached down and picked up the bait, making sure the tuna was well into the hook. After checking to see that the hook was secured to the leader wire, Drew hoisted the bait overhead and swirled it around with all his strength. Gaining enough momentum for a good toss, he let it go with a loud moan. Forty-five feet out, the bait splashed into the bloodstained waters.

"Is that all you've got?" growled Al.

"That wasn't a bad toss!"

"Yeah, for an old woman with a severe case of arthritis maybe," replied Al with a laugh.

"Suppose you could do better?"

Al sat on the side of the boat and stared across the chum slick. "I can remember back at South Pier in the early '60s when even on a bad day I could easily clear a hundred twenty, hundred fifty feet, no problem."

"Well, this ain't the early '60s, and you're not a teenager anymore," grumbled Drew.

Al glanced at Drew and then looked back at the water. "Don't you mind that. I can still get it out there a good ways."

"Okay, Hercules. After I reel it back in, you can make the next toss." Drew sat back in his chair and started to harness himself in by buckling the straps.

Al looked over. "Gettin' ready a little early, ain't ya? Don't even have a hit yet."

"Hey, just want to make sure I'm ready."

"Well, the Durban Angler's Club would be ashamed of all that, those gismos!" He waved dramatically at the straps and the chair and Drew.

"Ashamed of what?" asked Drew as he buckled the last strap.

"All of this . . . being strapped into chairs and fishing from the boat, letting the boat maneuver back and forth, playing the shark for you. All of this technology takes the sport out of it. This boat fishing is for wimps."

Drew slowly turned the reel until the line tightened. "Oh yeah? So tell me how real men fish?"

Al stood up. "Durban! The early '60s on a little place called The Bluff," he bellowed.

Drew rolled his eyes and murmured, "Oh no. I guess I asked for it."

"There used to be a whaling company out there, and right beside it, a long breakwater called South Pier. The whaling company used to tow the dead whales right into the harbor. The place didn't smell like a bed of roses, but boy, did we pull some monsters out of there—some of 'em over a thousand pounds. Now, when I say 'pier,' this ain't no wooden structure with thick rails on the side to keep you from flying over. No sir, it was just a flat, two-thousand-foot-long, concrete breakwater."

Al paused for emphasis, then said, "Now we were real fishermen!" He walked closer to Drew's chair. "We used to fish right from the pier, where the shark had as much of a chance to pull you into the water as you had to pull the shark out." He slapped the back of the chair. "None of this pansy stuff with secured chairs or straps to hold you down. With the Durban Shark Anglers, it was just man against shark. The only things we used were a leather "Palm" to brake control the line as it left the reel, and a leather socket we used to call a "Bucket" strapped around our waist to hold the butt of the rod. Other than that, it was just a bamboo rod and a plain old wooden reel. That's all a real fisherman needs!

"We'd just ease down into a sitting position with the butt of the rod anchored into the bucket." Al crouched down, mimicking the stance. "Sometimes we'd play the shark for hours. It was backbreaking work, but when you landed half a ton of shark that way, you'd accomplished something. Your back and every muscle in your body would remind you of it for days. But after reeling the shark in, the battle wasn't over. You still had the problem of getting it up the rocks and onto the pier."

"How'd you ever manage that?" asked Drew.

Al stood up from his crouch and rested his hand on the back of Drew's chair. "Well, we'd usually bring the shark in close enough to get a rope around its neck, then everyone would slide it up onto the pier."

"Anyone ever get pulled in?"

"Yeah, a few times. I remember Jerry Madison one time had an eight-hundred-pounder on the line when it pulled him right off the pier. He landed in the water right beside one angry great white. He got out of the water so fast, I don't think he even got wet!"

Drew slowly turned the reel and grinned. "If you guys were really so tough, why didn't you just tie a couple of steaks to your legs and jump in there with a dive knife? Now that would be giving the shark a sporting chance: man against shark!"

"Yeah, yeah," replied Al. "You just sit there and tighten your straps."

~~~

Kate squirmed beneath her helicopter, straining to reach an open toolbox beside the skid. It was miserable and hot. She was in grease up to her elbows; the rest of her was covered in sweat. After a plane taxied by, she thought she heard a muffled ring from her cell phone in the cockpit. She listened for a moment, didn't hear it again, so she went back to work.

~~~

Shaking his head, John returned the lieutenant's satellite phone. "She's still not answering," he muttered, stepping from the naval Hummer and into the Dyer Channel parking lot. They made their way around a red Porsche and headed for the docks.

"Would have gotten here sooner in a chopper," Vic admitted, "but we're only a reserve base. The few units we have are still searching for survivors at the Motanza."

The lieutenant turned his attention to the docks. "Good. There's Rich Addison's boat. He's one I didn't reach." He squinted, approaching the dock. "Wait a minute."

They reached a small, shack-like office at the edge of the dock. "This is Drew's place," said the lieutenant. Passing the rickety building, John peered into a window. His eyes drifted across a huge set of shark jaws and various old photos of proud anglers standing next to enormous great whites strung up on the docks.

John's attention shifted to the window of the front door. Although the old wooden sign was barely visible behind the dusty glass, he could tell it read, "Closed." Checking the front door to make sure it was locked, they walked out farther on the dock. They passed the back corner of the office, and the lieutenant's eyes squeezed shut. "Drew, you old skate!" In Drew's boat slip, there was only shimmering water. "And I called him first," Vic muttered. "I knew I told him too much."

John heard footsteps approaching from behind. Someone spoke in a Swedish accent, "Are you looking for the man from the Shark Tours?"

He turned to face a tall man with long, sandy-blond hair. Beside him was an attractive, fair-skinned, blond woman.

"Yeah. Have you seen him?" asked the lieutenant.

"Yes, we came here earlier to take a tour, but he wouldn't take us out," replied the Swedish male. "He said the Navy closed him down for some type of research. But then after we left and walked around the docks for a while, we noticed his boat going out."

"Was there anyone else on board?" asked John.

"Just one other man. Big man!" replied the woman in her best English.

Vic squinted. "Are you sure that was it? Just the two of them?"

"Yes, just the two of them, we're certain," replied the Swede. "We took a good look. Thought he may have changed his mind about giving a tour today."

"Okay, thanks a lot," Vic said, walking away, John at his heels.

The Swede grabbed Vic by the arm, "Do you know how long the research is going to continue? Will we be able to take a tour tomorrow? That's our last day here, and we were really looking forward to—"

Vic yanked his arm back. "I don't know. You'll have to call tomorrow."

They headed farther out on the dock while the Swede looked on. John could hear him muttering to his wife as they walked away: "I knew we should have gone to Australia."

After walking out to the middle of the dock, the lieutenant stopped. John noticed him carefully surveying all the boats. On the dock across from them was a twenty-eight-foot fishing boat with part of its engine lying disassembled on the dock. Just in front of the fishing boat was a metallic-blue speedboat about eighteen feet long.

John's attention shifted to a loud clanking on another dock, where he saw a man banging a hammer on a homemade shark cage. Five yards past the cage, his eye stopped on a blond-haired boy in his early teens mopping the deck of an old fishing boat.

"Not much of a selection . . . guess that'll have to do," Vic muttered.

John didn't like the sound of this.

All of the sudden, Vic started jogging back through the parking lot and toward the other dock. John followed. "Hey, where are you going?"

As Vic approached the boy, he shouted, "Son, I'm gonna need to commandeer your boat."

The boy looked up, wiped his hair from his eyes. "Comma what?"

"I need to borrow your boat for a couple of hours."

John looked at Vic in disbelief. "What? Go out there? In this piece of—" he glanced at the boy. "No offense, kid."

The boy dropped the mop. "It is a piece of crap . . . my dad's. You can take it. Keep it, if you want. I'm tired of cleaning it anyway!"

The lieutenant boarded with a glance back at John. "How else do you plan to stop Drew? He's ignored my orders. Don't think he'll listen to me over the radio." He headed toward the helm. "Besides, it's not likely your creature ventured this far west already, assuming it's heading this way at all."

For a long moment John paused, his eyes fixed on the channel. *I sure hope he's right.* Either way he knew he didn't have a choice. If the creature was headed this way, they were the only ones who could reach Drew and his passenger in time.

Eventually, he stepped across to the gunwale. He glanced over at Vic. "Would you mind not calling it my creature?"

On board, John was confronted by a sense of unease. It was a strange, swelling fear. It was the kind of feeling that might stop someone before boarding a plane out of a sense of impending doom. He looked along the old wooden deck from bow to stern. The vessel appeared even smaller now that he was aboard.

Vic looked up at the boy. "How much fuel is in it?"

"Just filled it up, and there's an extra can by the stern," he replied, uncleating the bowline to help them shove off from the dock.

John noticed the bright surfboard logo on the boy's tee shirt. "Do you surf?"

"You know it, bro! Every chance I get!"

John glanced at all the shark cages in the nearby boats. "Not anywhere around here, I hope."

"No way, bro. I'm not that doff!"

John paused and gave another nervous glance across the water. "Just the same, do me a favor and keep it in for a couple of days, huh?"

"No problem. I'm grounded for the next week. Why else would I be out here mopping this old boat on a good surfing day like this?"

The engine fired, and Vic slowly pulled away from the dock. He shouted, "Tell your dad we'll be back in a couple hours!" The boy waved while the old fishing boat slowly headed toward the Dyer Island Channel.

~~~

Kate worked the stick as the helicopter finally lifted off. The thumping rotors were a welcome sound. She gazed across the instrument cluster and paused nervously on the oil pressure gauge. "Atta girl," she murmured to the chopper. "We're okay now, just needed to lick our wounds a bit."

The chopper veered off from the airport and headed for the coast.

CHAPTER 24

CATCH OF THE DAY

Al gazed out over the freshly chummed waters, while the sun dropped deeper into the horizon line. An eerie silence had settled over the channel. "Dusk . . . ideal feeding time. If it's out here, now's the time we'll see it!" said Al, watching for the slightest trace of whitewater.

Drew looked back from his chair while slowly reeling in the line. "Hey, you hear about the shark attack earlier today?"

"No! Where?" Al reached down to take another beer from the cooler beside Drew's chair.

"Somewhere around Keurboom, near Plettenberg Bay. Two surfers were hit by a blue pointer. Think one of 'em was killed."

"That's the first I've heard of it. But I can guess it was off one of those un-netted beaches."

"Believe it was."

Al looked out over the water. "If those buggers had seen half the things I've pulled from South Pier and these waters, they'd all move to the mountains and take up snowboarding."

Drew grinned from his chair. "Now that you mention it, I don't recall too many surfers taking shark tours."

Al shook his head. "Now, I guess in tomorrow's paper we'll be reading about some expert saying how this was just another case of mistaken identity. How the shark probably thought the surfer was a seal."

"Yeah, I heard that spiel before," said Drew. "How sharks supposedly don't have an appetite for humans. They say we have too much muscle and bone, and that sharks prefer the high-calorie fat of seals. That's why they claim most attack victims are let go."

"I still don't find too much comfort in the mistaken-identity theory," said Al, twisting the cap off his beer. "So the shark takes a bite out of you, then comes back, and offers to give you your leg back, saying, 'Sorry, mate, I thought you were a seal.' Maybe it's just me, but I don't feel any safer knowing that if I get bitten, it was by accident! And what about the instances where the shark did come back for a second bite? What does that do for the mistaken-identity theory?

"The number of attacks are also on the rise. Seems like every week you hear about another one on the news somewhere." Al took a sip from his beer. "But it ain't no surprise. I've been telling people this was gonna happen for years. World over, you've got all those long-liners out there with miles of nets raping the ocean for all she's worth. The sharks gotta come closer to shore to find food. All those scientists might be right; we might not be top choice on their menu. But if there ain't nothing else around, we'll do!"

"Ya got that right," said Drew. He turned the reel, drawing the bait in a little closer to the boat. "But on the other hand, I don't think the sharks should all be wiped out. After all, it is their ocean.

"Ya know sharks are important to the ocean's ecosystem. Like say, sharks eat seals and seals eat salmon. So killing all the sharks would mean the seal population would explode. Then all the extra seals would wipe out the salmon population." Drew slowly turned the reel. "Guess it's all some kind of delicate balance that we should be careful of."

Al laughed. "That's an interesting perspective coming from someone strapped into a chair, holding a line with a seven-pound chunk of tuna on it, in freshly chummed waters."

Suddenly, Drew's line stretched taunt. He pulled back on the rod. Al quickly turned around and looked at the water.

~~~

John and Vic continued to chug through the narrow channel as fast as the old fishing boat would take them. Off starboard was Dyer Island—a long, flat patch of sand with grassy interspaces and rocky outcrops. Its guano-coated rocks offered evidence of the thousands of jackass penguins, cormorants, and other seabirds that called the island home.

John gazed off port to Geyser Rock. Thousands of Cape fur seals lumbered along the rocky banks. Their gurgling calls filled the air as they all looked in the same direction. He did a double take on the seals' eerie behavior. *Are they randomly barking at the water or distressed by something they've seen?* Heading deeper into the channel, he noticed a small boat in the distance. With a glance down beside his feet, he saw a strap protruding from beneath the passenger's seat. He reached down and slid it out.

"Yes! Exactly what I need." After pulling the binoculars from the case, John carefully focused them on the boat ahead of them. He didn't see a shark's cage and could only count two or maybe three people on board.

"What have you got?" asked Vic. "Does it look like they're chumming?"

"No. It must just be a fishing boat coming back to the docks."

"Better stop them anyway; see if they've seen Drew's boat or anyone else who may have ignored my orders."

Vic pulled his boat alongside the fishing boat. A stout, dark-haired man shouted in a New York accent, "We ain't throwing any blood overboard or nothing like that. We're just out cruising around, seein' the sights. And where are all those people that are supposed to be out here doing research? I ain't seen no one except those two schmucks back there chummin' up the water! Looked to me like they was getting ready to do a little shaaaaak fishin' too!"

"How far back?" asked Vic.

"About a half mile or so," replied the heavyset man. "How come they get to come out here and drum up sharks? Ain't they supposed to be docked?"

"Yeah, how come they get to go out?" added a young boy, likely the man's son.

"They're not supposed to be out here and neither are you," replied Vic. He pointed to the captain. "And Willie, I know I called you earlier and told you to keep it docked. Now take it back in and leave it!"

"Okay, okay . . . we were on our way back anyway," replied Willy.

Vic pressed down the throttle and pulled away. Behind them, the man from New York yelled, "Go bust 'em!"

The boy joined in, shaking his fist in the air. "Yeah, go bust 'em!"

Vic maintained their course for about another quarter mile until they passed Geyser Rock and Dyer Island.

Looking over the side of the boat, John saw the water darken as they left the shallow channel. It felt as if his stomach dropped with the falling seafloor. The eerie feeling he got when he'd first stepped into the boat had steadily grown and was now almost unbearable. *Come on. Keep it together a little longer. We're just gonna get them and go back in,* John promised himself. He looked up and glanced across the surface. He noticed the silhouette of a small boat in the distance.

He picked up the binoculars to take a closer look. No shark's cage, but he saw a man seated in a chair while another scooped something from a barrel. Then he spotted the red trail leading from the boat's stern. *Well, at least it's just two of them on board, no tourists.*

John passed the binoculars to Vic. "That them?"

One hand on the wheel, Vic raised the binoculars. "Yep. That's Drew's boat." He slowly handed the binoculars back to John. "I'm kinda curious. Almost tempted to hang back and observe them from a distance; see if they come up with anything."

The lieutenant's lack of urgency did little for John's nerves. John grabbed him by the wrist and guided his hand back to the throttle. "Trust me. You saw the tooth. That's all you want to see."

The look in John's eyes had a sobering effect on Vic. "Okay, okay!"

They slowly headed for the distant vessel, proceeding just above idle speed.

~~~

"Looks like that little bull shark cleaned the hook pretty good. Pesky nibblers!" Al pressed the hook through another huge chunk of tuna. Swirling the bait overhead, he released it to the water. The bait splashed into the water about sixty feet away. "Okay, you minnows. Stay away from the bait this time!"

Tightening his grip on the rod, Drew looked up from his chair. "Hey, Hercules. That all you got? My toss was farther than that."

Al rubbed his shoulder. "Hell, that beat you by a good twenty yards. Besides, I ain't warmed up just yet."

Drew gazed off in the direction of Geyser Rock. "You figure that's why Vic thinks the shark's heading this way? That Cape fur seal population?"

"Oh yeah." Al walked back to the chum barrel. "How could it resist? Geyser Rock is like a neighborhood convenience store for sharks. Close to home, stocked with plenty of tasty items they love to eat, and open twenty-four hours a day. This area ain't called the great white capital of the world for nothing!" Then, as Al picked up the soup ladle, he paused. "Uh oh . . . looks like we've got company!"

Drew twisted around in his chair. "Doesn't look like a patrol boat. Looks more like a fishing boat; maybe someone's got the same idea as we do. What do you think we should do?"

Al hooked the soup ladle back onto the top of the barrel. "Just sit tight. We'll see what they want."

As the boat drew nearer, Drew's eyes widened. "Looks like a fishing boat, but he ain't dressed like no fisherman!" He dropped his rod onto the deck.

The lieutenant fought back a smile as Drew threw his rod away and tried to look innocent while strapped to the chair. Slowly, Vic pulled around in front of Drew's boat, then cut throttle about ten yards off their starboard.

Vic looked along the long chum slick leading to Drew's boat. "You gentlemen wouldn't be out here doing any shark fishing, would you?"

"No sir! Just came out here to dump our chum," replied Drew. "Didn't want to dump it too close to the docks . . . might bring in too many sharks!"

Vic laughed. "That's awfully considerate of you guys. What about that line you've got running into the water?"

Al spoke up. "That's just our beer. Got to keep 'em cool you know."

Vic looked at the thick line running from the rail into the water. "They must be awful heavy, judging from the gauge of wire you're using. Looks like that wire is strong enough to raise the Titanic!"

John watched, tense, finding no humor in the situation.

Vic continued his prodding. "And Drew, you must be expecting some rough weather, the way you're all strapped into that chair." He looked over at Al's chum-stained shirt, pointed, and said sternly, "That's enough, guys. You know you're not supposed to be out here. Let's go."

"But we didn't bring no tourists. It's just the two of us," pleaded Drew, his hands out to his sides.

Vic shook his head. "Pack it in. Let's go, guys."

Al and Drew shrugged in defeat. *Thank God,* thought John with a nervous glance around the water. Finally, they were heading back in. Drew reached down to undo the first strap of his harness, when suddenly his line stretched taut.

Vic laughed. "Don't look now, but it looks like your beer is making a run for it!"

Al's eyes sprang open when he saw the rod dancing toward the gunwale. "Drew, grab the rod!" he yelled. "You've got something!"

Straining against the straps, Drew leaned forward, reaching for the rod. It sat straight up, pinned against the gunwale six inches from his fingertips. Then, just before the rod shot over the rail, Al raced over and grabbed it. Getting a firm grip, he slowly pulled the rod back to Drew. "You got it?"

Drew braced his feet and the rod started to bend. "I've got it!" he shouted. "It feels like a monster!"

"Wind it in, wind it in!" yelled Al.

Drew dropped the rod forward, desperately winding to gain a few precious revolutions on his reel, then pulled back, using every muscle in his body. Suddenly, a splash of water jetted through the air from a swipe of a massive gray nose.

"Did you see that?" asked Al. "It's *huge*! You sure you're okay?"

Drew nodded, unable to speak as sweat beads streaked his face. Again, he dropped the rod down and wound the reel frantically.

Al slapped Drew's chair. "That's it, Drew. Bring it home, baby. This one's for the record books." Fifty feet out, another spray of water went flying through the air.

The lieutenant leaned against the rail, trying to get a glimpse of what was on the end of Drew's line. Apparently, his sense of duty or any thought of stopping them was overruled by sheer curiosity.

John's skin turned ice cold. He shouted across to Drew, "Cut the line. Cut it now!"

Drew pulled back with all his strength. The rod bent farther while his face turned a deeper shade of red.

Al pleaded, "Come on, Drew! Let me help. This is too much!"

"No way. I've got it!" grunted Drew, straining harder, holding his breath in one maximum effort.

Al stood up and for the first time got a good look as the creature on the end of the line. He took two slow steps back. "Drew . . . Drew! We were hoping for a record, but this thing's *huuuge*!"

Drew didn't acknowledge his presence. He just kept his eyes shut and pulled even harder, the rod now bent to its maximum.

And that's when the massive head burst from the surface, hitting the air with its mouth stretched open. With a tremendous crash, it hit the deck—the head of a great white shark, severed from behind the first gill slit.

Al stared down at the massive decapitation. Blood from the gaping wound gushed across his feet.

Drew looked over. "I've never seen that happen before!"

Al was completely dumbfounded.

"Show it to Vic," Drew said. "See what he makes of it!"

Al reached down, grabbed the cable protruding from the lifeless mouth, and wrapped it around his hand. Using every ounce of strength, he raised the three-foot wide head to the side rail. He shouted across to Vic, "Ever seen anything like this before?"

Stunned, John stepped back from the lieutenant. "Get out of here . . . now!"

John could only watch while Drew laughed from his chair, "Guess I pulled too hard. Didn't mean to yank its head off." It was all just a joke to the fishermen as Al strained to hold the huge decapitation high enough for everyone to see.

Then Al's knees buckled. The severed head fell to the deck as the tiny fishing boat began to rise from the water--a glistening white column appearing beneath it. Drew screamed from his chair. Like fireworks, loud crackling sounds rose with the boat. Planks from the deck were snapping like twigs.

John's view was a mass of white as he stared at a rising underbelly, fifteen feet wide. The great beast continued to rise from its straight-upward attack, water cascading from its body.

Massive paddle fins burst from the sea. Still, John was unable to comprehend the sheer size of the creature as the span of its paddle fins extended wider than the boat on which he stood.

John looked upward from the shadow of the towering beast. He watched Drew's boat rise forty feet above the water's surface, clutched within the pliosaur's jaws. The boat paused in midair. Its momentum catapulted Al upward another twenty feet. Chum thrown from the barrel painted a crimson streak across the deep blue sky.

John watched Al soar sixty feet overhead until he flew beyond his field of view. Still, he could hear Al's screams.

Then gravity seemed to finally take hold. The monster's upper body started falling, seemingly in slow motion, straight toward John and Vic and their old fishing boat, with Drew's crumbling boat still gripped in its jaws.

John glanced at Vic. Vic looked back at him. "It's real," Vic said, barely loud enough to be heard. At the last second, John dove to the left and Vic to the right. The massive reptile smashed through their boat, tearing it in half. Its head slapped the sea, the remains of Drew's boat spewing out across the water from the sides of its jaws.

A thunderous crash echoed around John as the great beast plunged beneath the surface in a streak of whitewater and bubbles. He rolled amid a cloud of debris, pulled by the powerful undertow created by the descending giant.

He tumbled, deeper and deeper.

Disoriented, John took a short breath but caught himself as saltwater burned through his sinuses. He desperately looked to his left, right, then below. He found the light from the surface and quickly swirled around. A bizarre object tumbled past him. He saw Drew's lifeless body somersaulting to the depths while still strapped into the chair. His right hand was caught under one of the straps as his left hand waved overhead. Trailing behind him was the severed head from the great white. The thick cable protruding from its jaws swirled like a ribbon in the wind.

John looked back toward the light and frantically swam through the debris. After what felt like near death under water, he burst through the surface, gasping. After several long breaths, his mind started to clear, though his head was pounding.

He looked around the surface for the source of the destruction but saw only scattered debris. Off to his left he heard something—a groaning. He spotted the lieutenant floating face down beside a sinking chum barrel. Reaching him, John threw an arm around his neck and pulled his face above the water. A red haze swirled below. For a split second, John thought it was his blood, then realized it came from Vic's torn pant leg.

He desperately examined the surface. *Now what?* His mind raced as fast as his pounding heart. He realized that in all the haste of getting out into the channel, neither of them had put on a life jacket. Past the sinking chum barrel, he spotted the large bait bin from their boat and backstroked for it as fast as he could tow the lieutenant. Reaching the four-foot, trough-like structure, he slowly crawled inside. Careful not to bring in too much water, he struggled to haul in the lieutenant. Vic slid in, and with a final groan, collapsed unconscious.

John lay half across the lieutenant, staring at the skies in horror. His breaths echoed in the tight confinement. He could see straight up through the top, but his view from the back and right side were blocked. To his left, a basketball-sized hole in the bin offered a look outside–if he dared. John slowly caught his breath, his head still pounding mercilessly.

He lifted his head and leaned over on one elbow. Three inches of bloody water slurred around the bottom of the bin. He glanced at Vic in the fading light. Beneath his torn open pant leg was a deep scrape that ran from his hip to his ankle. *From the creature?*

Trying to sit up more, the pain in John's head shot to his stomach, causing him to roll onto his side, vomiting up seawater. He then rolled onto his back, looking once again upward. The blue sky swirled then flushed white as he lost consciousness.

~~~

When he eventually came to, the throbbing pain in his head was so intense he realized it was probably what caused him to wake. He stared up at the clouds with no idea how long he had been out. The sky seemed darker, but he could not tell for sure how much time had elapsed. He leaned on his left elbow and looked through the hole in the side of the bin. Was it still around?

There was a splash about five yards behind him. John turned around and tried to see, but the side of the bin was too high. He waited, holding his breath.

Another splash—closer!

Something slammed into the fiberglass behind his head. Suddenly Al's face appeared in the hole as he banged his fist against the bin. "You gotta let me in. That thing's still out here. Let me in!"

Through the hole, John saw the water darken. He could hear Al frantically swim around to the opposite side of the bin—as if the bin could protect him from the inevitable. The enormous shadow drew nearer, transforming into gray, pebbled skin. John lay back and braced himself against the bottom of the bin.

Outside, Al's pleas intensified.

The bin tilted.

John saw Al's fingers curled over the top of the bin as he tried to tip it far enough to get inside. Water poured in through the hole; the bin tilted. John watched in motionless horror as Al's fingers slipped from the fiberglass. The bin fell back, righting itself on the surface.

Al splashed back into the water, screaming.

A deafening roar shook the bin.

Inside the small structure, John heard Al pounding and clawing against the wall behind his head. There was a hideous grinding. He could feel the vibration of the creature's stony skin sliding against the fiberglass. The grinding sound intensified until a sudden jolt brought Al's horrific screams to an end.

Eventually, the small tub-like structure began to settle. John's rapid breaths slowed and faded until he could hear the waves lapping against the bin. Lying against the lieutenant, he looked at the sky again. The pain in his head slowly returned after briefly being dulled from the horror. The clouds had grown darker. He lay still amidst the mixture of blood and water collected in the bottom of the bin with no perception of time. *Has it been five minutes or an hour? Is it gone?*

More time passed, and he felt the current taking over, pulling the small structure toward the open ocean. The waves were now more noticeable and slapped against the fiberglass in a strangely soothing rhythm. In total silence, John lay on the bottom of the bin. Although the blue sky had long since given way to complete darkness, he still didn't move a muscle.

~~~

Kate guided the helicopter through a darkening sky. Below, a blanket of fog hung over the Dyer Channel with only an occasional speck of black water appearing through the mist. Thousands of gray backs glistened in the haze. Tonight the occupants of Seal Island appeared to be lumbering on a cloud.

Banking right, she made another pass over the channel. "Okay, this time we'll take it a bit lower." Her frustration grew. "The dispatcher said they're out here," she muttered to herself. "Checks out; saw the naval Hummer in the parking lot. Okay, where are you guys?"

Descending, Kate's eyes grew wide. The rotor wash from the chopper blew back the fog to reveal a mass of boat debris strewn across the water. Hundreds of wood fragments glared in the light. She grabbed the mike on her headset. "God, no!"

~~~

Ten miles off the Dyer Island Channel, John continued to float helplessly with the current. He lay still against the unconscious lieutenant, wide-eyed, listening for the slightest sound. Outside the bin, there was nothing but darkness and fog.

Every bobble made him shudder. Every wave, every splash sounded like the creature's skin grinding against the fiberglass. Even the slightest shadow in the curling fog took on the form of the giant frill rising in the mist.

He dared another glance around at his surroundings. Was it his imagination or was the water level inside the bin rising? Minutes ago he could see his boot strings. Now they were barely visible, swirling beneath the red haze of water. He relaxed his neck and eased his head back against the lieutenant's shoulder. He hoped his belt he'd used as a tourniquet around Vic's thigh was doing the job. Was the man alive or dead? John had no idea. Either way, John was obsessed with keeping his forearm against Vic's cheek so that his face remained above the water. "No way," he whispered to the lieutenant. "No way am I gonna let you die. Not this time . . . not this time . . . ."

It was cold. Every muscle in his chest, shoulders, and arms ached from holding the same position for what seemed like hours. How long had he been adrift, and how far out? John closed his eyes. *Just a moment to relax.* But he refused to sleep. He feared the moment he drifted off his arm would stop supporting the lieutenant's face, drowning the man. He released a long breath in an attempt to calm his nerves. *That's it. Just stop thinking. Stop thinking—*

A shrill noise echoed through the bin. John nearly jumped out of his skin, scurrying back from the sound. He heard it again, and then it registered. He reached over the lieutenant's waist to his hip and felt the SAT phone which was ringing in his pocket.

"You gotta be kidding me!" Sloshing frantically, he managed to retrieve the phone, its buttons glowing in the night. He answered it. "Who? Kate?" He laughed weakly. "Am I still at the Dyer Channel?"

Chapter 25
SILENT WITNESS

No matter how many times John rubbed his eyes, they wouldn't adjust to the glaring lights in the Stanford Hospital lobby. His entire body ached. It was difficult to focus as he sat in a hard plastic chair. Even the floor seemed to sway like the current as the horrific images from the bait bin replayed in his mind. Worse yet, he could still hear the sounds—Al's heinous screams rising from the sea.

He took another sip from an electrolyte concoction. It seemed to ease the pounding in his head as he gazed blankly at his surroundings. Eventually, his mind drifted back to the pointless conversation he was having with the pair of officers seated across from him, Officers Berg and Branson. He didn't know which one was which and didn't care. With Vic in no condition to back his story, this was all a waste of time.

The heavier of the two had jowls like a bulldog. They shook as he fired another question. "When you said this thing hit your boat . . . are you sure you don't mean that you got distracted by what you saw in the water and then collided with the other vessel? And you're certain there was no fire or explosion?"

John rubbed his eyes. There's no way he could repeat the story again. "Guys, you're not buying my story, and I'm not gonna change it, so what do you say we call it a night?" Although it wasn't in his immediate possession, John still had his trump card, the tooth. "Besides," he smirked. "You"ll be more open-minded once you check the Dyer Channel parking lot and see what's in the front seat of Vic's Hummer."

The bulldog officer leaned back in his chair and gasped. "Yes, the tooth. I promise, we'll check it out in the morning." He shrugged at the other officer. "We've got his statement. We'll let the admiral handle the rest in the morning when he arrives."

"So, I'm free to go?"

The thin officer nodded, and with a wince, John rose from the chair.

~~~

Clicking on the light, John saw a heavy bag dangling from the ceiling. Beneath it sat a pair of cast iron dumbbells that would intimidate the average man. Beside a kitchenette was a ballet bar stretched across the wall. His eyes drifted up to a large photo of the jagged-tooth helicopter over a battlefield. *No doubt this is Kate's office*, he thought.

There was a shriek. The chimp bounded across a couch and raced over to John. Catching her with a groan, he set her down on the floor. "Crystal, hope your day went better than mine."

Kate followed closely behind him as she talked on her cell phone.

"Okay, Mom. I promise I'll keep you posted. And yes, I'll show you the tooth as soon as we get the chance." With that, Kate switched off her phone. She tossed her keys onto a counter in the kitchenette of the small airport office. "Well, Mom's up to speed."

She swung open the fridge. "And she agreed with me. You should have let them take a look at you when we were at the hospital. Men!" she spat. "No wonder women outlive them."

Ignoring Kate, John eased down onto the couch in front of a small TV. The thick cushions felt like heaven against his sore back. His thoughts were on the news. He needed to see if anything had been reported that could offer a hint at the pliosaur's movement.

He found the remote and clicked on the news while Kate slipped into the restroom. Channel surfing, he ran across an update on the Motanza. A photograph of a smiling young boy was on the screen. A female reporter said, "The Motanza Fishing Festival tragedy has just claimed its fifth life. One hour ago, fourteen-year-old Andrec Wells' body was found still tangled in the deep recesses of the enormous net . . ."

The photo hit John like a sledgehammer. He eased back into the couch, overcome with distress.

~~~

After a much-needed shower, Kate dried herself in the cramped restroom. She wiped the steam from a small mirror above the sink. Unfastening her hair, she let it fall down around her bare shoulders. "Aaah," she ran her fingers through her raven locks. "That's more like it, still a woman under all that mess."

Moments later, she emerged from the restroom, feeling refreshed and all the more stunning. She wore khaki shorts and a white shirt tied off at the waist. She knew she looked like a million dollars. *But John would be the last man to notice,* she thought wryly.

Entering the kitchenette, she motioned toward the restroom. "Your turn. Nothing personal, but you have spent half the night in a bait bin." Taking two water bottles from the fridge, she turned toward John and saw him staring blankly at the TV.

"Oh, no you don't. Don't start beating yourself up over all this. Remember the lieutenant. If it hadn't been for you fishing him out of the channel and fastening your belt around his leg, he wouldn't be alive."

"He's in a coma," John scoffed. "Even if he lives through the night, they don't know if he'll ever be more than a vegetable."

Kate sighed. "You're a 'glass is half empty' kinda mate, aren't you? At least all of this has gotten the Navy's attention. They may not have acted like they believed you at the hospital, but they know something's up. And you did manage an appointment with the admiral in the morning. And let's not forget the tooth. It was enough to make the lieutenant close the shark tours, so it'll be enough to convince the admiral. So for once, look at the bright side."

"Bright side!" John's despair turned to frustration. "Five people died at the Motanza, and two more in the Dyer Channel tonight, one man not five feet from me. I can still hear his screams . . . the kind of screams you never forget . . ."

Kate stared into John's eyes. For the first time, she felt the full weight of what he'd been through. "You're right," she said softly. "I'm sorry."

She eased down beside him on the couch. She leaned over gently until she was nestled against his shoulder. There was a long silence as she thought of ways to lighten the mood. When she finally spoke, her tone was more playful. "So, tell me John, what led you into this glorious field?"

"Medical school," John blurted absentmindedly.

"Medical school?"

"Well, to be more exact, *not* going to medical school."

Kate arced her eyebrows. "Ah, I see how that could narrow one's options."

John released a long breath. "Ever since I was a kid all I wanted to be was a doctor, maybe even a surgeon like my old man. One night during my second semester of pre-med, I was driving home for a long weekend. I was so full of myself—had just gotten engaged, all primed to be a doctor. There was nothing I couldn't do. It was late Friday night, and I was pretty much in the middle of nowhere, exhausted. Should have waited until morning, but it was no big deal. I could make the drive in my sleep . . . or so I thought.

"Coming into a corner, I woke up, and that's when I saw the light. I swerved, but it was too late. To avoid hitting me head-on, the motorcycle went over the curb.

"Pulling over, I ran through a field. No streetlights. It was so dark I didn't see the barbed wire fence the bike went through." He pointed to the scar on his left eyebrow. "That's where it caught me. I kept running through the tall grass, toward a terrible, high-pitched sound. When I got there all I saw was a vintage black BSA lying on its side with the throttle stuck, engine screaming."

"Vintage black BSA." Kate gasped. "The museum! This morning . . . wasn't that the same type of bike that was parked outside? The way you stared at it . . ."

"Pretty much," John said, the same distant look in his eye. "Twenty yards from the bike, I found the rider. Wasn't in too bad of shape other than the bleeding in his left thigh.

"It was a piece of cake. All I had to do was apply pressure where the femoral artery was severed until the ambulance arrived. At first, I was like a machine, focused . . . then something happened. The revving motorcycle shut off, and I could hear what the man was screaming. He had two little girls . . . begged me not to let him die. I don't know. It wasn't the blood that got to me, but it was like reality suddenly hit me: I was this guy's only hope. My hands wouldn't stop shaking."

John paused, staring blankly. "No one blamed me when he didn't make it. The doctors told me it was because the ambulance took too long to get there. Later, I was still at the hospital when I heard them break it to the family . . . the screams from his wife and children echoing through the halls . . . screams I'll never forget."

Kate rested a hand on his shoulder.

John shook his head. "Oh, there's more." He paused. "Later that night, at home I overheard Dad talking to Mom. He said that anyone with my training should have easily stopped the bleeding. If I hadn't panicked, the man would have lived.

"It seemed the local newspaper shared Pop's point of view. The next morning the headline read: Medical Student Fails Major Test. Both of my brothers went on to be surgeons. But after that night, I could never stomach the thought of being responsible for another life."

He shook his head with a disturbing smile. "But my lovely fiancée, Jenny, took it all in stride. Said she was still going to marry a doctor, it just wasn't going to be me. So, that's when it happened. That's when I got the revelation to be an archeologist."

He sank his head back into the couch. "Archeology . . . nice choice."

"But John, surely you don't feel responsible for all this?" Kate was puzzled. "That night on the island, you weren't the one who snuck into the lagoon," Kate reminded him. "It was Brad."

"Oh, but I knew," John said, "I knew. That night I couldn't bear the thought of coming back empty-handed. Redemption for my career, my pathetic life was on the other side of that wall. I knew if I told Brad the Rhidispians were in the lagoon, nothing would stop him. I would bring back something that would shock the world." He sighed, staring blankly. "And God knows I did."

"And now you feel like history's repeating itself," said Kate. "Like you went to that island and opened the proverbial Pandora's Box, and you can't close it."

"Thanks," muttered John.

Kate grew stern. "Look, your father was wrong then, and you're wrong now." She looked at him admiringly. His vulnerability warmed her heart. She eased her hand down on his knee and looked him dead in the eye. "Besides, in case you've forgotten, it was my mother who mounted the expedition," she said, flashing a warm smile. "You can't take all the credit."

~~~

Kate's comment almost made John smile. Without another sound, she had scooted down and curled up beside him. John gently rested his right hand on her shoulder. With his free hand, he picked up the remote and continued to search for anything that could be linked to the pliosaur.

~~~

Twenty-five miles South of Mossel Bay, Guy Peterson reeled in his line, calling it a night. He glanced across the stern of his thirty-two-foot fishing boat, wondering if he should go ashore or remain on the water until morning. Getting up from the chair, his fifty-eight-year-old back convinced him to drop anchor and stay out for the night. As he walked away from the stern, he saw something on the shimmering waters. An obscure black shape appeared out of the darkness.

Keeping one eye on the object, Guy walked to the helm, his curiosity piqued. Slowly he turned the boat around and decided to go investigate, see if he could figure out what he was looking at. As he drew closer, the outline became more visible—an old gray boat. He shined his flashlight across the weathered hull and shook his head. "Looks like an old naval patrol boat. Wonder how long it's been out here?"

He aimed the light over the gunwale. The beam revealed several gas cans lined up beside a deflated life raft. Smoke still rose from the burned-out engine. He again examined the boat from bow to stern and saw no one. "Looks like it's been abandoned . . . can't say I blame 'em."

After a glance around the surface, he reached across to pull the boat closer. "Well, even though it don't look like much, I should probably tow it—"

His jaw dropped when the life raft shot up. A flicker of light. Then the whistling sound of a machete blade.

~~~

Kota released the handle, letting the man fall back onto the deck with a thud. The shimmering machete blade protruded from his skull. Stepping across to the fishing boat, Kota stood over the body. He placed his foot on the man's throat and twisted the handle until he felt the blade release. A crimson streak crossed the shadowy deck.

Carefully, the two powerful figures slipped the body overboard with barely a splash. Kota leaned over the side, swished his machete beneath the water's surface, and withdrew a glistening clean blade. He looked back at Kolegwa and motioned him to get the gas cans loaded onto their new boat.

Kota walked to the helm and fired the engine. He and Kolegwa pushed off from the old patrol boat's hull. As they pulled away, the abandoned vessel slowly faded into the darkness.

Chapter 26
BIRD DOGS OF THE SEA

John sat on the corner of the couch, bleary-eyed but determined as he continued to flip through the channels. Kate was curled up beside him, fast asleep. He did his best to eat a braai, a South African delicacy similar to a barbecue sandwich which he'd found in the fridge. He had no appetite, but knew he needed his strength. He stopped on a station and leaned forward. The TV screen showed what appeared to be the tip of a whale's head gliding through the dark ocean waters.

A female voice spoke over the image on the screen. "There you have it, ladies and gentlemen: Captain Joseph Neman's Whale Cam! It's a camera attached to the back of a sperm whale, a clever way to hopefully capture the elusive giant squid on film."

This got John's full attention.

The image on screen switched to a female reporter standing on the deck of a research ship at night. She raised her hand to keep her long, brown hair from blowing in her face. Beside her was a distinguished man in his sixties with salt-and-pepper hair and a white moustache and goatee.

The reporter raised her microphone. "Beside me is one of the world's leading authorities on the giant squid, Dr. Joseph Neman, or as he is often referred to, Captain Nemo. I hope you don't mind me calling you that." She flashed a smile, teeth gleaming for the camera.

The captain ran his fingers down his signature purple squid tie and smiled. "No, don't mind at all; in fact, I've grown rather fond of it."

"Tell us a little more about your expedition." The reporter moved her microphone closer to the captain.

"Well, let me start by saying I think it's absurd that scientists know more about long-dead dinosaurs than the living giant squid that swim in the oceans of today. We know something about the habitats of dinosaurs and their biology, distribution, and even their reproduction, but we know none of these things about the giant squid.

"Other than a maimed, three-meter specimen off Chichi Island, scientists have had little luck filming this creature in its natural habitat. But we're searching for something more. Our quest is to discover a true living giant in excess of sixty feet. Now, for the first time in history, we think we have a good chance of filming this creature alive from the back of one of its known predators."

A gleam appeared in his eyes. "Try to imagine a creature with a very large, complex brain, tentacles the size of fire hoses, and eyes the size of hubcaps. Not to mention a beak-like mouth capable of cutting through steel cable.

"The giant squid is also a fierce warrior. This we have learned from the scars we've found on sperm whales over the years. So what we're looking for is nothing less than a true living sea monster!"

"Sea monster, huh?" John almost choked on his sandwich.

"How big do these creatures actually get?" asked the reporter.

"The largest giant squid ever measured was eighteen meters—that's fifty-nine and a half feet—and weighed one metric ton. However, the average size for these squid is somewhere between nineteen and forty-three feet, with the average weight being around one hundred ten to six hundred sixty pounds.

"Do marine biologists think they can grow much larger than the sixty-footer?"

"Oh yes," replied Nemo excitedly, now with big eyes and a smile on his weathered face. "That's what brings me to your area. Let me explain the course that we plan to take on our three-month journey. We began our expedition in New Zealand where most of the larger carcasses have been discovered. We'll continue around the southern tip of Argentina and search through the Atlantic until we reach the tip of South Africa, off the Cape area, where we should be by morning. Then we'll spend the remainder of our trip exploring the depths from the western to the eastern Indian Ocean."

The reporter asked, "So what exactly is the significance of the Western Cape that brings you all the way to the southern tip of Africa?"

Chewing his sandwich, John turned the volume up with the remote.

The captain leaned back against the ship's rail. "Well, that's where some of history's most interesting eyewitness accounts have occurred. One reliable source from the military reported a sighting of a squid the length of their ship, which was one hundred seventy-five feet long, making this giant squid nearly three times the size of the largest ever measured! The Indian Ocean has always been known for producing extraordinary specimens, and we're hoping this time it will live up to its reputation."

"When so many others have failed, Captain, what makes you so confident that you'll be able to film this elusive creature in its lair? What makes this expedition so different?" The reporter's face showed genuine interest, her eyes serious.

Neman nodded. "For starters, we will be using a submersible that runs much quieter and gives off less vibration than any of those used in the past. This should allow us to remain undetected by the creature's extrasensory organs. Also, we'll be using different lighting strategies than on previous expeditions. But if all of this doesn't catch the camera-shy squid, we're hoping that the Whale Cam will. As you saw on the earlier footage, it's exactly what it sounds like. We've attached a camera and a sonar device with suction cups to the back of a sperm whale."

"And why the sperm whale?" asked the reporter.

"Good question." Nemo raised a finger. "Analysis of sperm whale vomit shows that they are major consumers of giant squid. Obviously, whales know where to find their meals. So, we'll just follow them. Let the whales hunt them down for us, kind of like thirty-ton beagle hounds—bird dogs of the sea. As we speak, three whales mounted with cameras are swimming in the western Indian Ocean. Two of them are in a pod we've been following for weeks.

"Another thing unique to our expedition is that we're connected via satellite to classrooms around the world. This will enable students to watch live broadcasts from the back of our sperm whales as they search through the depths of the ocean. If we come up with even a glimpse of the giant squid embattled with one of our camera-equipped whales, it'll be one of the greatest accomplishments in the history of marine biology. And all of you will be able to see it within seconds!"

The reporter laughed congenially at his enthusiasm. "Well, that does sound exciting, to be able to view such an event live. How's the expedition going so far?"

The captain paused, as if thrown off by the question. "We've been having a little trouble with the transmitters on some of our underwater cameras for the last few weeks but hope to have it sorted out in the next day or so."

"We'll all be watching with great anticipation. Good luck, and thanks for having us on board."

John shook his head and took the last bite of his sandwich, "Now I've seen it all, a doctor calling himself Captain Nemo, chasing around the giant squid. And he thinks *he's* chasing a sea monster." He flipped off the TV, and the room went dark. He eased back in the couch and made another attempt at sleep.

~~~

From the main deck of the *Nauticus II*, Nemo watched the female reporter ascend the stairs leading to the ship's small helipad. His assistant, Nathan, a lanky man in his forties sporting a brown ponytail, walked up beside him. He looked perplexed. "Why did you tell her we've been having trouble with the transmitters? They've been working just fine."

Nemo looked him dead in the eye. "Well, it sounded better than 'we've spent nearly two months and three million dollars and haven't seen a tentacle longer than my arm.'"

"We do have that exceptional underwater volcano footage from last week," Nathan reminded him.

"Underwater volcano footage. Three million dollars . . . and all we have is some lava crawling across the ocean floor. That's pathetic. The world's expecting us to deliver a giant squid, and nothing less will do!"

"Well, maybe our luck will change when we reach the Indian Ocean."

"Couldn't get any worse," muttered Nemo as he watched the female reporter step into the helicopter. He gave her a forced smile and waved.

~~~

The small airport office was silent as John sat riveted to the news. His troubled mind wouldn't let him sleep. Kate remained snuggled up beside him on the couch, while the monkey snored lightly at his feet. Stirring, Kate stretched her arms and squinted up at him. "Turn that back off and get some rest. Remember, if anyone's to blame for this mess, it's my mother, and you can bet she's not missing sleep over it." With that, she rolled over and closed her eyes.

~~~

At two-thirty a.m., Professor Atkins' jeep rolled into the Dyer Channel parking lot. She weaved through a myriad of military vehicles until she found an out-of-the way spot in a corner of the lot. Popping the door, she slid from the driver's seat and into utter chaos. The parking lot was alive with flashing lights as men in Navy attire gathered near the docks. Thumping rotors echoed above while spotlights shot down from the sky, playing over the numerous patrol boats searching the channel.

Near a shack-like office at the edge of the docks, she saw a naval Hummer parked beside a red Porsche. The entire area around the vehicles was taped off like a crime scene. She proceeded toward the docks, for the most part unnoticed, with the exception of an occasional nod from a man in uniform. Every face she passed bore the same expression: confusion.

Chapter 27
NAUTICUS II

Thirty-five miles off Quoin Point, the *Nauticus II* lay at anchor. Captain Nemo stood alone at the side rail, gazing across a moonlit sea. His purple squid tie lifted with the night's breeze. Normally at three a.m., he would have been sleeping in his cabin. But tonight, he didn't bother to try to sleep, as thoughts of the expedition weighed heavily on his mind. He wondered if the Austins—a husband-and-wife marine biology team—really had good reason to leave the ship two weeks ago. Or was the alleged illness in the family just an excuse to get out of a hopeless expedition?

He looked down at the water. No longer did he see its glimmering surface as a source of wonder. Now it served as a cruel curtain that offered him only glimpses of something it would never truly reveal. Maybe his colleagues were right—he was attempting the impossible.

He closed his eyes and listened to the waves crashing against the ship's steel hull, a soothing sound that always calmed him. A familiar series of clanks echoed behind him, interrupting his quiet moment. A tall, thin figure emerged from the shadows of the stairwell and walked up to join him: Nathan. . .

"Who's watching the monitors?" the captain snapped.

"Freddie is." Nathan's tone was defensive. "I just came up to give my eyes a break. You can only look at those screens for so long."

The captain turned back around to face the water, his forearms resting on the side rail. "Well, don't leave him down there too long. Night before last I walked by and saw him slumped over the console, sound asleep. All four whales could have been in a death lock with a giant squid, and he would have slept right through it!" He lowered his head and gazed down the side of the ship. "But I guess with the way things have been going, he probably didn't miss much."

Nathan leaned against the rail. As always, his tone was upbeat. "Don't worry. I'm sure we'll have better luck now that we're in the Indian Ocean."

"I sure hope so," replied Nemo, his frustration obvious in his voice. "We've crossed two oceans, gone through nearly four million dollars, and only have the footage of that one squid from our fifth day back in New Zealand to show for it. And that squid was far from the giant we're looking for."

Nathan was quick to defend the project. "True, but the footage proved that the whales *can* find the squid! And now we've got another whale hooked up as of this morning. . . I know it's only a matter of time."

Nathan looked across the shimmering waters. "Any sign of that dolphin that's been following the ship?"

"Saw it a few minutes ago," grumbled Nemo.

"There it is," said Nathan as a glistening gray back broke the surface and disappeared. "See, that's a sign of good luck."

"I hope so. On top of everything else, I have the school representatives calling every day asking when I'll have something to show the kids. Like I can predict the future! All the money spent on that satellite and nothing to transmit."

"Well, hopefully the footage from the smaller squid we shot in New Zealand will keep the kids entertained for a while longer." Nemo slammed his fist against the rail. "But it's not an Architeuthis dux! Nothing less than a *giant squid* will—"

Wham! The captain was hit from behind, his right leg collapsing as he grabbed the side rail to keep from falling. Over his shoulder, he saw a taupe-colored dog streak by, chasing a chew toy. Sliding to a stop, the seventy-five-pound Weimaraner picked up the toy and vigorously shook it, as if killing its captured prey.

"Bad dog! Bad dog!" A voice echoed from the opposite side of the ship. A lanky thirteen-year-old boy with dark hair stepped out from behind a long stack of crates and approached them. "I'm sorry, Captain Nemo, it's really my fault. I didn't mean to throw it so close to you. I'll be more careful next time."

"*Next* time!" growled Nemo, his face turning a deeper shade of red. "I'm gonna give that dog swimming lessons if I see him on deck again, understand? Now get him out of my sight! And what are you doing up at this ungodly hour?"

Erick looked up through his thick glasses. "Okay, okay! I said I was sorry . . . I just took him out to pee. Come on Rex, let's go." As Erick walked away, Nemo grumbled to Nathan. "I can't believe he snuck that dog on board. I've been putting up with that beast for more than two months now. Last night I didn't think I was ever gonna go to sleep . . . cursed fleabag barked for hours."

"It's a big ship, Captain," replied Nathan. "Certainly there's enough room for the dog. And I really appreciate you letting Erick help out on the ship like this. He's always been fascinated with the ocean, and he's really a good little worker."

Rubbing the side of his thigh, Nemo looked over the rail. "Well, the boy spilled my supper all over the cabin last night as he was bringing it to me. But other than that, he does seem to try hard . . . that is, when I can find him."

"Well, thanks again. He's my only nephew, and my brother has been asking if I could bring Erick on an expedition with me as long as I can remember."

"All right," grumbled Nemo. "But that beast wasn't part of the deal."

"Why don't you turn in for the night? Some sleep will do you good," said Nathan, stepping away from the rail. "I'm going back to cover the monitors for a few more hours. I'll let you know if the whales find anything."

Nemo leaned back against the rail. "You go ahead. I'm going to stay on deck for a while, then I might call it a night."

After a nod, Nathan checked his watch and muttered on his way back to the stairwell, "Guess it's about time to go wake up Freddie!"

"What was that?" asked Nemo.

"Oh nothing," replied Nathan. "I just said it was time to relieve Freddie."

~~~

The small fishing boat pressed on through the night, plowing through the waves. Silently, Kota peered ahead through the windshield. His burning eyes locked on the endless sea. Beside him, Kolegwa again stood and stared off port. He nervously turned and examined their wake.

Kota knew what was on his mind. "You looking for Kuta-ke-blay?" he said in their native tongue.

Kolegwa nodded with one eye on the water.

"Do not fear," Kota pointed to the white tooth painted on his face. "As long as we bear Kuta-ke-blay's mark, we possess his power: the power to kill and never be destroyed."

Kolegwa felt the paint on his face. He looked at his white fingertips and nodded, reassured. After returning to his seat, he spoke up. "But how do we find evil one, the white devil who killed chief?"

"Worry not," replied Kota. "For the prophecy foretold that all who interfere will be delivered into our hands." The powerful tribesman glanced at the compass and held his course due north, in the direction of land.

A new predator had entered these waters.

Chapter 28
EVIDENCE

The early morning sun glared into the small airport office as John sat on the corner of the couch, a Navy business card between his fingers, cell phone at his ear. Kate waited in the kitchenette, listening anxiously.

He glanced at a wall clock. *It's past nine o'clock.* He couldn't believe the Navy hadn't already called him about the tooth.

Finally there was an answer on the line. "Officer Branson." The male voice was authoritative.

"Yes. This is John Paxton. You questioned me at the hospital last night, after the Dyer Channel incident. I wanted to discuss the tooth . . . the one in Lieutenant Greeman's Hummer."

"Oh yes, the giant pliosaur tooth!" said the officer loudly.

All right! John thought. *Now we're getting somewhere. We'll see who's crazy.*

"Yes . . . the giant pliosaur tooth," John repeated eagerly, but his heart sank at the officer's next words.

"What tooth?" Branson said flatly. "I had two of my men scour every inch of that vehicle, and they found nothing of the sort. I don't know what you're trying to do, but you'll have to take it up with Admiral Henderson. He has taken over the investigation. Hold, and I'll have the dispatcher connect you."

Click. John hung up the phone.

Kate said, "Something tells me that didn't go so well."

He stared at the phone in disbelief. "He said there's no tooth. His men searched the Hummer and didn't find anything. He was transferring me to the admiral, but I hung up. I have no idea what to tell him."

Kate stood and turned to the window. When she turned back around, the look of confusion left her face. "Mother!"

"What?"

"She's got it. I know it. Last night I thought she was rather inquisitive about the tooth. She knew we flew straight to the office after leaving the hospital. She knew that tooth was still at Dyer Channel!"

"Oh come on," John said doubtfully. "I think the Navy just doesn't want to admit it, like some kind of cover up. You know, to keep this out of the media."

Kate shook her head.

"Really?" John laughed. "So you think she would drive through the night, all the way to Dyer Channel, and steal the tooth from a military vehicle that's involved in an investigation?"

"Apparently you don't know my mother that well." Kate picked up the phone on a table beside the kitchenette.

~~~

Nathan sat alone in the surveillance cabin of the *Nauticus II*, staring at the monitors. It was early morning, and every passing minute made it harder to stay awake. Slowly his heavy eyelids won, closing completely, and he dozed. Moments later, a muscle spasm made him jump, causing him to wake. He rubbed his tired eyes. As his vision cleared, he looked along the four monitors, showing the whales' perspectives as they swam through the depths.

He heard footsteps. In the monitors' reflections, he saw the captain appear in the doorway. "Just checking to make sure you were awake."

"No worries, Captain. Bright-eyed as always!"

"How much time do we have until we transmit to the classrooms?"

Nathan glanced at his watch. "About three hours still."

After the captain disappeared through the doorway, Nathan turned back to the monitors. His eyes were drawn to monitor one. The water seemed lighter than the others. All of a sudden, the seafloor appeared on the screen, glimmering in the sunlight, growing brighter as the seabed slowly rose closer to the whale. This whale was heading for the shallows.

A quick sip from his water bottle, and Nathan scooted closer to the monitor. On screen, the waterline dropped below the camera, and he could see the distant shoreline. "Incredible," Nathan said, dumbfounded. "The whale's trying to beach itself."

~~~

Kate shook her head while dialing her mother from the phone on her desk. She pushed the button for speakerphone. "I can't believe she just took the tooth like that. What was she thinking?"

John leaned against the side of the desk. "You sure you don't want me to talk to her? Just stay calm. Try to reason with her . . . *calmly*."

The look in Kate's eyes told John she could handle it.

Two rings later, there was an answer. The steady hum of road noise in the background told them the professor was still in her jeep.

"Do you have the tooth?" Kate asked pointedly.

"Indeed I do."

"Mother! How dare you . . . you know it's the only hard evidence we have!"

"How's John doing? Is he feeling better?"

"He's doing fine other than the aneurism he had this morning when he found out the Navy didn't have the tooth. Mom, you can't just steal like that."

"Steal! I have every right to the tooth," said the professor in her usual unruffled tone. "I funded the expedition; therefore, everything acquired

on that expedition is my property. And I'm taking it to be carbon tested."
She chuckled. "Besides, you can't be naive enough to think the military
would actually return it to you."

"I'm not arguing your rights to the tooth," pleaded Kate. "I'm only
asking that you bring it back so we can use it as evidence when we talk
to the Navy. After that, you can do all the bloody testing you want. So,
for now, please return it, Mom, please. Lives are at stake!"

"No one is going to believe the authenticity of the tooth until it's
properly tested," countered the professor. "If you show it to them now,
they aren't going to take you seriously, not until they have it tested
themselves. And I'd rather keep it in my possession and oversee the
testing. Wouldn't you? Once this is completed, I'll be glad to bring it
back, and you will have all the evidence you need. Indisputable
evidence!"

"Indisputable evidence," John laughed, shaking his head. "That
tooth's as white as mine—it still has gum tissue attached. Its owner is
swimming off the coast as we speak!"

"I believe you, John, and Kate believes you, but no one else is going
to believe you until we get it tested. Trust me, the South African military
is not an open-minded lot. They'll most likely say the gum tissue is some
concoction you put on there yourself. But once tested, they'll be forced
to listen to you."

"How long will this take?" Kate asked.

"Normally, a few weeks. But I have some connections and can
probably have it done in a week."

"A week!" John slapped the table. "We don't have an hour. It's
already killed! Do you know what kind of damage that thing could do in
a week?"

"Look, I'm trying to help you two. I'm speeding up the process of
confirming your evidence." The professor's voice began to break up
from bad transmission. "I just can't risk having the . . . Navy or any . . .
take it." The phone crackled more. "I have to go now, the phone's . . .
signal. I'll contact . . . as . . . know something." The line went dead.

Clicking off the speakerphone, Kate looked at John with disbelief in
her eyes. "She's the most stubborn woman! I was going to ask if she
could just take a small section of the tooth for testing, but she hung up
before I had the chance."

John picked up the receiver. "Let me try to call her back."

He dialed once, then again. After a few seconds, he slammed the
receiver back down. "That's it. Now she's turned her phone off." He took
a long breath and looked down at the phone. "Well, I guess I'd better call
Admiral Henderson. But I have no idea what I'm gonna tell him."

~~~

While looking across the debris scattered along the coast of Geyser Rock, Admiral Henderson tried to piece things together. His stern, deep-set, gray eyes and tall stature made for an intimidating presence as he watched a pair of patrol boats dredge the Dyer Channel. In the distance, a dozen or so of his men scoured the waterline. He waded through the thousands of Cape fur seals crowding the rocky banks, their gurgling barks making it impossible to think.

The debris covered a half mile offshore, where most of it still lingered. The pieces were small, too small and too scattered. And that's what bothered him the most. Now that he was there, he could see clearly this was much more than a boating collision. The two vessels involved were virtually disintegrated.

Stepping closer to the water, he took his cell phone from his pocket. He pushed a button to take a call dispatched to him from his Simons Town office. "Admiral Henderson," he announced in a gravelly voice.

"Admiral, this is John Paxton."

The admiral cupped his right hand over his ear, trying to block out the barking of the seals. "Yes."

"I was the one who went out with Vic Greeman in the Dyer Channel last night after he closed the Shark Tours."

"Did you call in earlier yesterday from a fishing boat?" asked the Admiral. "Do you know a man named Libby Watson?"

"I do. What's he got to do with this?"

The admiral perked up. "That's what I thought. Now that you mention it, I think we did get a report on your creature earlier this morning on a beach near Natal."

"You did?" replied John in amazement.

"Yeah. It was chasing a bloody brontosaurus out of the water. Or was it a T-rex?"

"This isn't a joke!" pleaded John. "You have to believe me. A lot of lives depend on this."

"Look." Admiral Henderson gave a slight laugh. "I read the statement you gave the officers last night. And I heard you gave them quite the runaround this morning looking for some giant tooth." His voice grew stern. "Sir, I'm afraid the Navy doesn't have time for your games, and with all that happened yesterday, I think your joke is certainly in bad taste. Good day, sir."

"What do you mean, all that happened yester—"

The admiral had started to hang up, but paused. This Paxton character was the last person to see Vic before the incident. If he humored him long enough, he might get to the bottom of what happened. He returned the phone to his mouth.

"Two surfers were attacked early yesterday," said the Admiral. "One was fatal."

"Where?"

"Near Plettenberg Bay, a hot surf spot called the Keurbooms."

John quickly asked. "Where's Plettenberg Bay, in reference to Mazeppa Bay and Natal?"

"It's west. Way west," replied the Admiral, barely able to hear John's voice over the seals.

"What about in reference to Dyer Channel?"

"It would be just east of Dyer Channel, why?"

"Directly in its path . . ." John paused, then said with great emphasis, "Sir, with all due respect, I *assure you* this *same creature* is responsible for the attack at Keurboom. If you could talk to the surviving surfer, I'm sure he will be able to confirm what I'm about to tell you!"

"There was nothing unusual about the attack on the surfers," said the admiral abruptly. "Excuse me for sounding cold, but everyone knows there are large dangerous sharks out there. Those guys knew the risks when they decided to go out and surf off that un-netted beach."

"Admiral, I'm afraid this attack is far from normal. I have a tooth from the creature responsible; it measures nineteen inches long. And it's not a shark. I'm talking about a carnivorous marine reptile at least eighty feet in length!"

"Wait a minute," the admiral gave a slight laugh. "Now this is starting to make sense. You're the one that convinced Vic to close down the Shark Tours. That's why those guys have been calling me all morning asking if we were finished with our research."

"Yes. And there's evidence!"

"So, according to your statement, this creature is eighty feet long, and you have one of its teeth as evidence!" The admiral sounded amused. "And you're sure this tooth isn't just some kind of fossil, eh? It's real? With fresh gum tissue still attached?"

"Yes, and there's more evidence. The Motanza wasn't a whale; it was this creature. And the beaching . . . all the whales running aground in the last few days. Surely you can see that's more than a coincidence."

"I admit there have been an unusual amount of beachings. But that doesn't mean there's some prehistoric monster out there. Besides, if there were anything out there like what you're describing, the Sharks Board would have seen it. They patrol the beaches and monitor the barrier nets daily."

~~~

John stared down at the receiver. He could only imagine the admiral's expression. "Look. These attacks confirm that the creature is heading west, which would place Keurboom directly in its path yesterday morning. You don't have to take my word for it. You can talk to that surfer ... ask him what attacked him. There's not much time!" John heard the desperation in his own voice. "If you could just get a few of your choppers in the air, we could probably find this thing before it strikes again. Considering the creature's size, it shouldn't be difficult to spot from the air."

The admiral's tone grew more aggravated. "Every chopper I have is either here or searching for three fishermen still missing off Mazeppa Bay, and you want me to pull them to look for a dinosaur? That's justifiable? Besides, where is this tooth, your indisputable evidence?"

John paused, trying to choose his words carefully. "That's the part I was getting at. The reason your men couldn't find the tooth was ..." he hesitated, "because the person who mounted the expedition, which led to the discovery of the tooth, took it from the lieutenant's Hummer last night."

"So, someone stole this giant tooth ... from a guarded military vehicle?"

"No. Actually, they just borrowed the tooth for a while ... to get it carbon tested."

This shortened the admiral's fuse. "Look," he growled, "you already have half of my men out here at Dyer Island chasing their tails right now! I don't have time for whatever type of game you're trying to play here. Good day, Mr. Paxton!"

John hung up the phone and shook his head. "I knew that wasn't gonna fly."

Kate said sympathetically, "Didn't buy it, huh? Can't really blame the man. I'd have trouble believing you if I didn't know my *own mother* took it."

"Forget the admiral, forget the professor ... forget the tooth! I'm sick of all this." John shot up from the desk. "We've wasted half the morning playing phone tag. That's the last call I'm making."

"Well, what's the plan then?" Kate asked from in front of the TV. The playful chimp lay on the floor, entertaining herself with Kate's shoestrings.

"We're going to the hospital to find that surfer. He should be able to talk this morning, and you can bet someone from the police department or the Navy will be waiting to question him the second he wakes up. If we can get to the hospital and talk to whoever's questioning him, maybe the surfer will be able to back my story."

Kate clapped enthusiastically. "Bravo! I'm starting to realize why my mother hired you." She released her shoestrings from Crystal's grasp. "I'll go pull the truck around."

Chapter 29
EYEWITNESS

Staring over Nathan's shoulder in the ship's surveillance cabin, Captain Nemo anxiously watched the four monitors. The cameras appeared to be working properly atop the whales, with no technical malfunctions. Just a waiting game ... still. He glanced down at his watch: 9:35 a.m.

"Well, it looks like everything's in working order. If there's squid out there one of these guys ought to find it."

"Yeah, using four whales now will up our chances," replied Nathan. "And the picture is so clear—excellent reception."

"It ought to be. It's the best equipment money can buy. Now, if only we could get a glimpse of the squid, something to show the classrooms today other than a whale joyride through the Indian Ocean."

"Still scheduled to transmit to the schools at noon?"

"Yep, twelve o'clock sharp, so keep your eyes open. Surely one of these whales is hungry enough to hunt," said Nemo.

"Yeah, I'm starting to wonder if they're all dieting!"

Nemo frowned. With all of the pressure bearing down on him, he was in no mood for Nathan's wit. He squinted at the monitors. "Why do monitors two and three look so much lighter?"

"The whales in that pod have moved closer to the shallows. That's why the water's a little lighter."

The captain slapped Nathan lightly on the shoulders and sighed. "Well, that's about enough for me," he said. "I didn't get much sleep last night; think I'll try to take a short nap before we transmit. But if you see anything, let me know right away. Anything at all."

~~~

From the partially-opened back door of the surveillance room, Erick watched as Nemo exited the cabin through the main door on the opposite side. Seeing that the coast was clear, he slid the door open and walked in, his dog Rex closely following. Erick loved the humming sound of the equipment. With great fascination, he looked at the four monitors in front of Nathan, each of which showed a whale's point of view as it swam through the depths. He thought it was cool how the water displayed on the monitors bathed the room in a blue hue. Behind Nathan, he saw the four smaller monitors, each with a gridded screen and a red dot that marked each whale's position.

"You don't have to wait for him to leave," said Nathan, glancing over his shoulder at his nephew. "I don't think he minds if you come in and watch the monitors. Plus, the company actually helps me stay awake."

Erick shrugged and scooted up into a chair beside Nathan. "I don't know. I think he's kind of mad at me."

"Don't let him intimidate you. That's just his nature. I don't think he's aware of how he sounds when he talks to people sometimes."

"He doesn't really intimidate me. He just makes me nervous. And I don't think he likes Rex too much either!"

Nathan reached over and adjusted the tint on monitor two. Erick looked up from behind his thick glasses. "So how do you get the camera to stay on the whale's back?"

"We use suction cups."

"Does it hurt?"

"Never had any complaints!" replied Nathan with a smile.

Erick froze. Footsteps were heading toward the cabin. "I think Nemo's coming back. I'd better get Rex outta here. Time to go to my secret reading spot—the only place the captain can't find me. See ya!" He slid from the seat and bolted through the doorway. "Come on, boy!" Then just as Rex slipped through the doorway, Nemo entered the cabin through the door on the opposite side.

"Change your mind about the nap?" Nathan turned in his chair to face the captain.

"Naaah. Left my cholesterol medicine around here somewhere."

Nathan snatched a small bottle from the console. With a frown, he tossed it to Nemo. "You should really get off of this stuff. All it takes is the proper diet . . . If you like, I'll can make one up for you."

"Diet, smiet," grumbled Nemo on his way back to the doorway. "You just keep your eyes on that monitor."

~~~

Erick slowly walked to an area about midship. He could barely see the waves through the morning mist that still surrounded the huge vessel. He stopped where dozens of large cargo crates stacked three rows high were strapped to the starboard rail. Carefully, he climbed up the crates and scampered across their tops like a squirrel. He found an opening where several crates had been removed. He paused and steadied himself, knowing one wrong step from up here, and it was a thirty-foot drop to the water. He looked down at the haze-covered sea and snickered. "Mom would freak if she saw me doing this." He slowly climbed down into the six-foot-square opening with the ship's side rail at his back. Reaching the bottom of the small space, Erick said, "Come on, boy!" Rex darted through a narrow space between the crates to join him.

Erick made himself comfortable in the shadows. Using a crate as a backrest, he pulled a small flashlight from his pocket and backed it through a knothole just above his shoulder. After adjusting the flashlight until it was shining in just the right spot, he cracked his paperback and began to read.

Before turning to the next page, he took a deep breath and released it, savoring his surroundings. The salty air, the ocean breeze blowing through the side rail bending his pages, the sounds of the waves crashing against the hull—this was, without question, his favorite spot in the world.

After a few minutes, Rex pushed his chew toy toward Erick and began to whimper. The dog backed up and lowered his head in anticipation. "Not now!" Erick whispered. "Maybe a little later, after I finish this chapter." But Rex was persistent.

As the dog's whimpers grew louder, Erick glanced up from his book. "All right already! But keep it quiet!" He picked up the chew toy and hurled it over the crates toward the ship's stern. Rex disappeared through the narrow opening. Moments later, the panting dog returned with the chew toy in his mouth and dropped it beside Erick. Without taking his eyes from the book, Erick picked up the toy and gave it another toss in the same direction. Rex again darted through the small opening. But this time, more than a minute passed and the dog didn't return.

Suddenly, Rex began barking frantically. Erick dropped his book and climbed up to the top of the crates to see what the commotion was all about. *Nemo's gonna hear this!* His head rose above the top crate, and he could see Rex barking and jumping frantically. Then Erick spotted the chew toy with its triangle-shaped end caught on a control lever of the crane used to launch the mini-sub. The toy dangled tauntingly just out of the dog's reach.

"*Shhh!*" whispered Erick, leaning over the top of the crates. "If Nemo hears this he's gonna have us both walking the plank." The dog quieted for a moment as the sound of footsteps on metal came from the stairwell. "Rex, come!" Erick's tone was urgent. He climbed back to his secret hiding place behind the stack of crates, and Rex ran through the small crevice to join him. Turning off the flashlight, he said in a commanding tone, "Dead dog!" Rex immediately lay down on his side with one paw tucked over his nose, not making a sound.

"Good boy!" whispered Erick to the motionless dog. The footsteps drew closer then slowly passed.

~~~

Nemo paused near the stern and gazed off starboard. He spotted the dolphin playfully swimming; its glistening back disappearing and reappearing in the thick mist. "Some good luck sign," he muttered. "Since he's been following the ship, we haven't seen a thing."

He took out his pipe, put in a pinch of tobacco, and lit it, puffing on it a few times to get it going. The tip of the pipe glowed in the mist. Taking a long drag, he blew the smoke from the side of his mouth and leaned back against the metal base of the crane. Something cold and wet slithered across the back of his neck. He jumped forward in fright, spitting his pipe across the deck. When he turned around, he saw the saliva-drenched chew toy hanging from the lever.

"That cursed fleabag!!!" hollered Nemo as he grabbed the chew toy and hurled it over the rail with all his might. The spiraling toy disappeared into the mist and landed with a light splash about thirty yards out, near the dolphin.

Wiping the back of his neck with his sleeve, Nemo heard a second splash coming from the same direction—as if something of colossal size had burst from the surface and re-entered the water. He looked about, knowing the noise was much too loud to have come from a dolphin. As he walked toward the rail, a wave from the splash crashed against the hull. The port side dipped. Spray from the wave shot up in front of Nemo's face and fell across the deck in a fine mist. He steadied himself against the side rail. Squinting, he looked in the direction of the disturbance until long after the water settled.

"Hmm . . . wonder what happened to Nathan's good luck charm?"

The dolphin never returned.

~~~

John's heart pounded when they walked through Knysna General Hospital's double doors. He knew this could be his only chance to speak to a living eyewitness.

"I think we forgot something." Kate grimaced.

"What?"

"Before we left the office, I didn't take the chimp out to do her thing. How long do you think she can hold it?"

"Guess we'll find out." As they neared the receptionist at the end of the long hall, John said, "What's Ron's last name?"

"What?"

"Ron the surfer. What's his last name?"

"I don't know. I thought you knew," whispered Kate as they reached the front desk.

A young blonde in her early twenties glanced up at John and said into the telephone, "I have to go now. I'll call you later." Cradling the phone, she looked up at John with a smile. "Can I help you?"

John leaned against the desk, concern on his face. "Yes, we're here to see Ron, the surfer that was brought in yesterday from the shark attack." He lowered his head and rubbed his forehead. "We left as soon as the police called. We drove over ten hours just to get here."

"I'm sorry, but he's in critical condition. It's immediate family only."

Kate pointed to John. "But this is his brother. His *much older* brother."

"Please, I've got to see my little brother!" John said. "I was so upset that Kelly offered to drive me over here. She's such a good friend; she even left her only child at home alone to bring me here."

The young woman's eyebrows arced with concern. "Awww, it's too bad you weren't here a few minutes earlier. Your mother just left with your sister."

"Oh, that *is* a shame!" replied John. "The room number please?"

"Room four eighteen. Just take the elevator to the fourth floor and immediately turn right. It'll be near the end of the hall on your right-hand side."

"Thank you. You are *an angel*." John smiled warmly, and the receptionist did the same, twirling her long, blond hair with her finger.

Kate rolled her eyes, grabbed his wrist, and muttered, "Come on, Romeo."

Stepping off the elevator, they took a right and quickly walked down a long brightly lit hallway. As they approached the room, they saw an attractive young woman sitting on a bench just outside the door.

The tanned brunette stood up to greet them. "I'm Samantha. Are you friends of Ron?"

John reached out to shake her hand. "Yes . . . do you know Ron very well?"

"No, not really. I just met one of his friends the other day on the beach."

"Oh, well actually he's my brother," John said. "I was hoping to be able to speak to him alone."

"Oh, what a shame. Your mother was just here. She's such a nice lady."

"Yeah, the receptionist told me. But I'll see her and little sis later tonight at the house." John winked and reached for the doorknob, peeking first through the door's long, narrow window. He saw a thin black police officer standing behind the far side of the bed with a note pad. A nurse hovered close by with her back to the window.

The officer looked up from his pad and glanced at John.

"I don't think you can go in there yet!" Samantha said. "They just made me leave. The police are trying to question him about the attack."

John slowly let go of the doorknob and stepped away from the door. Kate sat next to Samantha. As casually as possible, John looked through the window, trying to read the officer's body language. He saw Ron in the bed, sitting up slightly with his midsection heavily bandaged.

Hearing a sniffle, John turned his attention to Samantha. He could see part of her bikini tan line beneath her low-neck t-shirt. "Were you there? Did you actually see it—the attack?"

The young woman looked down. "No, we arrived at the beach after he had already left for the hospital. All I saw was . . ." she leaned her head forward and tears rose in her eyes, "what was left of Dorian!"

John put a hand on Samantha's shoulder. He glanced at the window and saw Ron pointing to his stomach and shaking his head. He watched as the young man sat straight up in bed with his arms out to his sides as if arguing with the officer. The expression on the officer's face told John all he needed to know.

Then Ron fell back against the bed in obvious pain, his hands clutching the bandages below his ribs. The nurse pressed a button beside the bed. She stepped in front of the officer and motioned him to leave. Just as the officer opened the door, a doctor and two orderlies ran into the room. They quickly exited with Ron on a gurney.

Samantha stood up and started to cry hysterically. John approached the nurse as she closed the door. "What happened?"

"It looks like he got a little excited during the questioning and pulled some of his stitches loose. Don't worry. It's probably just superficial," replied the nurse. "I'm sure he'll be just fine."

John felt a tremendous sense of relief, but at the same time, ashamed of the fact that his concern was greater for the young man's story than his life.

He turned to Samantha and held her by the arm. "It's okay . . . it's okay. The nurse said he just pulled some of his stitches loose." But Samantha was inconsolable.

"She said he's going to be okay, Samantha. Why are you crying . . . what's wrong?" Kate asked, putting her arm around the girl's shoulders. Samantha sniffled, her long, brown hair sticking to the tears on her cheeks. "I know. It's just that I feel so guilty!"

She feels guilty, thought John. *Get in line!* "Why should you feel guilty? You couldn't have stopped what happened!"

"It's just that they were on the beach that day because of me. They were helping us shoot a commercial."

John held her hands. "You can't look at it that way. You're in no way responsible. Trust me on that one."

Kate tapped him on the shoulder. "Excuse me, but didn't you want to speak with the officer?"

He looked up just as the officer disappeared around the corner at the end of the hall.

Quickly excusing himself from the ladies, John raced down the hall.

He rounded the corner and lunged for the elevator just as the doors closed. Frantically, he tapped the button, but it was too late. Less than a minute later, he jumped into the next available elevator and pressed the button for the lobby. He watched the numbers atop the doors light up . . . four . . . three . . . The elevator stopped on the second floor.

The doors opened, revealing a stern-looking bulldog of a nurse. Stepping inside, she held the doors open for an elderly man in a hospital gown as he slowly rolled his IV in beside him. John watched impatiently as the man took steps so small, John could swear he wasn't moving at all. Once the journey ended, John quickly tapped the button for the doors to close.

Finally, the elevator reached the lobby, and John discretely inched his way in front of the nurse, preparing for a quick exit. Sensing John's strategy, the nurse put a thick arm in front of him and held the door open for the elderly man. John desperately looked over the shuffling man's shoulders, trying to see if the officer was still in the hallway.

Momentarily, the nurse lowered her arm to help the man with his IV, and John saw his shot. He sidestepped them both and made a break for the hallway. As his footsteps echoed around him, he didn't slow his momentum until he reached the reception desk. "Did the officer just pass this way?"

"Yes, he just went by about a minute ago," said the happy young blonde. "By the way, how's your broth—" Before she could finish the sentence, John was already through the double doors.

He scanned the parking lot, desperately searching for the police car. Then above a long row of hedges, he saw the roof of the officer's car slowly heading toward the road. With a quick burst of speed, John hurdled a three-foot-high section of shrubbery and landed in the parking lot, slapping his hands on the side of the police car.

The car skidded to a stop, and John ran around to the driver's side.

His gun half-drawn, the officer looked up at the strange man tapping on his window. The window slowly lowered, revealing the startled officer's eyes. "Sir, what is it?" said the officer. "Are you okay?"

Breathing hard, John spat out the words, "You were just in with the surfer . . ." He took another breath. "The one that was attacked by the shark . . . Officer . . ." John read the nametag. "Marimba?"

"Yes, I was with Ron. You're not another reporter, are you?" said the officer, putting his car back in gear as if ready to drive away.

John quickly shook his head. "No. Did he say anything about what really attacked him? What it looked like? Its size?"

The officer hit the brake and took the car out of gear. "He said it was enormous. But judging from the rest of his description, he's obviously still in shock."

John leaned his forearms on the door and shook his head. "No, he's not in shock. What he said was true. Especially about the creature's size. I know because I've seen it. What else did he say?"

Officer Marimba stared at John for a moment, as if sizing up his mental state, then reluctantly answered. "He said it was hideous, like some kind of dinosaur. Had teeth the size of his arm and came up beneath him like a missile with a mouth so big he could have stood up straight in it. And you're telling me there's something out there that fits this description?"

John nodded. "Yes, an extremely dangerous marine reptile. Larger than an adult sperm whale."

"And you've seen this creature?"

"Yes," replied John. "And a lot of other people are going to see it, too, unless we do something about it."

The officer paused, then said, "He also claimed that the deep scrapes across his abdomen were from this creature's skin. But the doctor said the scrapes were too deep to have come from the skin of a shark, and most likely came from a run-in with some coral." Officer Marimba eyed John warily. "Have you gone to anyone else with this?"

John took another deep breath and wiped his brow. "I've tried dealing with the Navy several times, but let's just say they don't quite believe me. I need proof. That's why I came here today. I was hoping that Ron would be able to help verify my story. I also have other proof—a fresh nineteen-inch tooth from this creature—but a colleague of mine has it at the moment, running tests on it to prove its authenticity."

The officer rubbed his chin. "I'm not saying I don't believe you . . . there's certainly something going on out of the ordinary out there. If it involves these waters, the place to go to would be the Shark Research Institute in Cape Town."

"How do you get there from here? About how far is it?"

Officer Marimba smiled. "Go ahead and jump in. I'll take you over there. I know the director personally. Besides, you need someone that was a witness to Ron's testimony, don't you?"

John's eyes flared with elation. "Great! Thank you, but, first I need to run back in and tell my friend to meet me there."

"Okay. I'll wait right here," replied the officer. John climbed through the hedge and ran back toward the lobby.

~~~

An ear-piercing scream echoed through the Bethelsdorp Elementary School hallway. A little dark-haired girl, still screaming, ran away from a pudgy boy and the thing he held in his right hand. The girl glanced back at the slithering, green object dangling from Tommy's fingers. They passed a group of students coming out of a classroom, and Tommy gave up chase when he spotted one of his friends. "Hey, Kev. Check it out!" Tommy held up a six-inch snake dangling by its tail.

"Where did you get that?" asked Kevin.

"Caught it this morning in the grass by the bushes behind the cafeteria. You know, the small patch that never gets mowed."

A gray haired man with a gray moustache stepped from a nearby doorway and glanced toward the boys.

"Well, you'd better put it away before Mr. Bensley sees it."

"Yeah, I know." Tommy slid the snake back inside a small mayonnaise jar with holes in the lid.

The dark-haired girl, Nancy, walked over to the two boys now that the fearsome serpent was back in its home.

"So, whatcha gonna do with it?" Kevin asked.

"I think I'll bring it to show and share," Tommy said. "Then I'll probably let it go back where I found it. So, what did you bring in for show and share today?"

Before Kevin could answer, Nancy butted in. "I brought in my butterfly collection! My daddy just picked up a swallowtail for me last week while he was away on business. Now I have more than two hundred butterflies in my collection. Mr. Bensley said it's one of the most impressive private collections he's ever seen!"

"I didn't ask you!" Tommy blurted.

Nancy stuck her nose in the air and asked, "Yeah, Kevin, what did you bring in . . . your stupid shark-tooth collection?" She laughed and turned away to join a group of her girlfriends as they walked by.

Tommy scowled. "Ooow, she makes me so mad! Thinks she's so hot because she always wins show and share. Just because her dad travels around the world on business and brings her back some stupid butterfly for her collection."

"But Mr. Bensley said show and share isn't a competition," said a boy listening nearby.

"Yeah, right," Tommy scoffed. "You see how she acts when her butterfly collection gets all the attention. She knows she blows everybody away. So, Kev, what did you bring in this time?"

For a moment, Kevin wondered if he was making a mistake. For the last two days he'd followed his older brother's advice and shown it to no one. He'd kept the enormous tooth hidden in his top dresser drawer ever since he found it by the whale carcass on the beach. But he couldn't resist another day, especially now, after the Keurboom attack on the surfers. Practically everyone in South Africa was talking about sharks.

"So, tell me already! What did you bring in this time? Is it in that bag you've been carrying around all morning?"

Kevin felt the long, spiked object pressing against the bottom of the plastic bag in his right hand and smiled. "Not telling. You'll have to wait and see."

Chapter 30
THE SHARK RESEARCH INSTITUTE

John felt his tension mounting as the patrol car pulled into the Shark Research Institute parking lot. "Here we are," Officer Marimba said, popping open his squeaky driver's-side door. John followed the officer to the entryway of the large office building, passing a fiberglass replica of a twenty-foot great white. John sensed he was finally in the right place. He reached for the glass front door. In its reflection, he saw Kate's truck pulling into the parking lot, so he waited for her to catch up.

Once in the lobby, Officer Marimba approached the reception desk while John and Kate studied the numerous shark photographs adorning the walls. Kate stopped in front of a black-and-white photograph of an enormous great white hanging by a noose. She read the caption underneath, "Twenty feet long and over four thousand pounds." She nudged John. "This guy could be used as bait for your creature."

"Would you mind not referring to it as 'my creature,'" John reminded her.

A blond-haired man in his mid-forties entered the room from a long hallway. He wore a light-blue shirt with the Shark Research Institute logo on its front pocket.

Officer Marimba shook his hand. "Tom, how've you been?" He turned to John and Kate. "This is Tom Hayman, director of the Shark Research Institute."

After giving them both a warm handshake, Tom asked, "So, what can I do for you?"

Officer Marimba looked at John, who nodded for him to start first. "Earlier this morning, I was at the hospital taking a statement from the young surfer that was attacked yesterday near Plettenberg Bay—the alleged shark attack. On the way out, I ran into John. He has a . . . rather unique story that I think may interest you."

With a deep breath, John thought, *Here I go again. I've repeated this story so many times I know it like my own social security number.* He started with the usual forewarning. "This may be a little hard to believe, but please hear me out. There is an extremely large marine reptile somewhere along the southern coastline. Now I'm not talking about a really big croc. This creature is somewhere in the eighty-foot range. And I didn't say eighteen. . . I said eighty!" John waited for a burst of laughter from Tom, but he was holding steady, arms crossed, one hand under his chin.

He's actually listening, John thought. *Now maybe we're getting somewhere. Thank youuuu, Officer Marimba!*

He went on to explain the various details about the creature, including the tooth which was currently being tested for authenticity. "You see," John said, "the tooth doesn't match up with any contemporary creature because it's from a . . ." he hesitated just a beat, "a prehistoric marine reptile. A pliosaur."

The director's face never flinched. He stared back at John for a moment, then said in an impassive tone, "Well, I guess that would certainly explain its size."

John stared at him in amazement. "So, that's it? You believe me . . . just like that? No dinosaur jokes . . . no smart comments—nothing!"

Unfazed, Tom continued. "First the Coelacanth, then a Megamouth, and now a pliosaur. With all the things I've seen come out of these waters, it wouldn't surprise me if Godzilla swam into False Bay and stepped ashore." Tom motioned for them to follow him down the hallway. "I'd like to have you take a look at something."

John laughed gleefully, grabbing Kate by the hands and pulling her into a bear hug. He high fived Officer Marimba, then the anxious trio followed Tom to the end of a long hallway. Pushing through a pair of stainless steel doors, John felt a chill from the temperature drop. The massive space was filled with various types of laboratory equipment. A faint scent of formaldehyde hung in the air. Following the director, they passed a female great white lying on a steel trough-like structure. The creature's underbelly was slit open. On a smaller table beside the large shark lay the lifeless bodies of six pups lined up in a row.

They then passed a woman in a white lab coat performing some type of autopsy on a juvenile great white. She reached deep into an incision in the creature's stomach and pulled out a hook. Then she examined a metallic tag just below the shark's dorsal fin.

Tom stopped. "What's that? Another hook?"

She held up the large steel hook. "And the tag matches the others."

The three guests looked around the large room and observed several people examining shark carcasses varying in size and species. "What happened to all these sharks?" John asked.

"Most of them were caught in the shark barrier nets we use to protect our more popular beaches," Tom explained. "Over fourteen thousand sharks are caught per year in the three hundred eighty-five nets we have along the southern coast. We patrol the nets daily, but unfortunately, about a thousand of them drown before we're able to set them free. Sad thing is that most of the species we pull from the nets aren't even dangerous. It's an ongoing battle, trying to protect the sharks and the swimmers. But so far, the nets seem to be the best solution."

Kate pointed to the woman who had just pulled the hook from the shark's stomach. "What's that all about? She just pulled a hook out of that great white. Aren't they a protected species?"

"That's another problem altogether," Tom said, looking down at the young shark. "Some of the local fishermen have been taking advantage of the gray area of the law. They take paying tourists out and let them 'hook a great white' and have the battle of a lifetime. When they reel the shark in, they put a tag on it and cut it loose with the hook still in its mouth. So now they aren't really shark hunting, they're just tagging and releasing—real scientific, huh? But what they may or may not realize is this can cause fatal trauma to the shark. Oftentimes, sharks swallow the hooks and receive internal injuries, like this juvenile that Lesley just examined."

"Is that what you wanted to show us?" Officer Marimba asked.

"Not hardly!" replied Tom with a slight grin. "Follow me back here. Watch your step when we get inside; sometimes it can get a little slippery." He led them over to an enormous cooler and unhooked the door handle. With a loud sucking hiss, the door pulled loose from the seal, and one by one, they stepped inside the cooler.

"Whoa!" Kate grabbed John by the arm as she slipped and almost fell to the ground. "You weren't kidding."

"No, I wasn't," Tom said. "A little spilled water in here, and it's ice. Are you okay?"

Kate nodded but kept a grip on John's arm. He patted her hand lightly in reassurance.

They continued to follow Tom along a three-foot-wide pathway between a series of wooden pallets containing dozens of frozen shark carcasses. Tom stepped off the path and walked across a few empty pallets. Frozen boards crackled and creaked beneath him with each step. He pointed to a few blood-spattered planks. "Watch out here again; it's slippery."

They all nodded an acknowledgement. A few yards farther in the cooler, and they stopped in front of a large storage area blocked off by a plastic-curtain barrier. Tom turned to face the group. "This just arrived on a truck earlier this morning. Some of our colleagues at the Natal Sharks Board discovered this a couple days ago near Paradise Beach. They didn't know what to make of it, so they sent it to us." Through the milky plastic, John could see the distorted outline of a huge white object with a dark center. Tom pulled the plastic back. Their jaws dropped.

In front of them was a twenty-foot cube of whale meat with what appeared to be an enormous bite taken out of its center.

Tom looked at John. "This look like the work of your creature?"

Kate immediately snickered as John mumbled, "Why does everyone call it my creature?"

They all moved in closer to the pale wall of flesh. "When you look at the area up close, you can see where some scavengers have fed from it. But there is no way a few scavenger sharks could account for this much tissue loss. Also, when you measure the entire radius of the wound, it's just too bloody symmetrical." Tom walked inside the giant bite mark and pointed to a series of deep, parallel incisions that ran vertically through the layers of blubber. "Looks like a massive rake ripped through the flesh. You can also see the areas between the smaller bite marks of the scavenger sharks, where the cut is deeper from the massive teeth."

"Unbelievable," Kate gasped. "Looks like the work of Jack the Ripper."

"Oh yes," Tom said, "a true calling card of pliosaur. Because of its long spiked teeth, it was known to be a sloppy eater. Over the years, we've examined a lot of whale carcasses. Nothing in today's oceans has inflicted a wound like this . . . until now."

Kate looked at the cavernous bite mark surrounding Tom. "How wide is the bite?"

Tom shook his head with a slight laugh. "It's over eight feet wide. But because of the condition it's in from the scavenger sharks, we weren't able to take any type of tooth count. So we don't know if the creature even had the whale all the way in its mouth."

Kate's eyebrows shot up. "You're saying that might not even be a full bite? Its mouth could even be bigger than that?"

"There is that possibility," Tom replied.

Officer Marimba muttered, "A mouth large enough for a full grown man to stand up in." He looked at John, who nodded knowingly.

Tom walked outside the bite mark to the undamaged flesh of the whale. "The size of the wound isn't the only thing unusual about this attack. The bite was taken from behind the whale's head. An angle of attack more consistent with a large pliosaur than a great white."

"What do you mean?" John asked, stepping closer.

"This attack was bold . . . it went for the throat. The rest of the whale was virtually undamaged. On a whale this size, white sharks would have gone for the tail first to disable it, then waited until it was dead to come back to feed from it. A much safer approach. This whale was nearly bitten in half at the throat! Tom's growing excitement reflected in his voice. He looked directly at John. "I knew there was something big out there! You haven't approached the media with this, have you?"

Without looking away from the jagged wound, John said, "I've only talked to a couple of people from the Navy, but didn't get very far."

Tom stepped away from the carcass. "Whom did you speak to?"

"The last person I spoke with was Admiral Henderson."

"That doesn't surprise me. He can be a little less than cooperative at times. But I'm afraid we're going to need his help. Especially when it comes to air power. Unfortunately, our resources are very limited at the moment. We only have two helicopters, and one of them is down. All our boats are functional, but considering what we're looking for, I don't think a boat is an option."

Kate pointed at Tom, grinning. She teased, "Now, I like him. This . . . this is a smart bloke!" She then wrinkled her nose and waved her hand in front of her face. "If it's all the same to you, gentlemen, do you mind if we take this somewhere where the air's a bit fresher?"

They all laughed appreciatively, the mood upbeat. Leading them back through the cooler, Tom said to John, "Let's try giving Admiral Henderson another call. Maybe two eyewitnesses and an eight-foot bite mark will be enough to get his attention."

~~~

Tom clicked on the speakerphone so everyone in the office could hear. John stood anxiously beside Tom while Kate and Officer Marimba sat across from them on the opposite side of the desk. "This is Tom Hayman with the Shark Research Institute. Could you put me through to Admiral Henderson, please?"

Once the admiral was on the line and pleasantries exchanged, Tom said, "I have a Mr. John Paxton here with me. Mr. Paxton said that he has already spoken to you about a tooth he's come across from an extremely dangerous marine reptile. A creature that he's personally seen firsthand."

"I know of him and this tooth," the admiral replied with caution.

"We also have a second eyewitness. I'm with Officer Marimba who has just taken a statement from a surfer who was attacked yesterday at Keurboom. And his description of the creature does match up rather well with Mr. Paxton's. In an interesting twist, I, too, have here at the institute likely evidence of this creature: a whale carcass containing an impressive bite mark. I would ask that you visit the institute immediately to take a look at the bite radius on this mark. Once you have seen this, I think you'll agree that it's time to start taking this matter seriously, and try to set up a plan to locate this creature."

The admiral cleared his throat. "Well, gentlemen, I'm afraid I'm going to need a little more than that. I'm not inclined to be taken by an eyewitness who is a friend of Libby Watson's and who made an appointment to show me the tooth but never showed up, claiming someone stole it."

"Sir, there is the second eyewitness who also confirmed the creature's description," Tom calmly reminded the admiral.

"Who?" mocked the admiral. "The surfer who the doctors say is in shock? And, Tom, this so-called bite mark . . . is it clean? Were you able to take a tooth count from it and accurately determine the creature's identity?"

Tom paused and looked at his guests, then sighed. "It wasn't quite clean enough to take a tooth count. But it's so symmetrical, it couldn't possibly—"

"Sorry, guys, but I have more urgent matters to tend to," said the admiral, promptly disconnecting the call.

Slowly, Tom clicked off the speakerphone then curiously turned to John. "Do you know Libby Watson?"

John shook his head. "Does everyone on the planet know this little man? I don't really *know* him, but I do owe the little guy my life. He pulled me out of the ocean the other day when my chopper went down. That's the only time I've ever met him."

Tom sat down in a chair behind his desk. "About a year ago we checked out a sighting of a hundred-foot sea serpent, called in by Libby. When we got out there, it turned out to be several basking sharks lined up in a row feeding. Apparently, he's led the Navy on a few wild-goose chases too. So the next time you talk to someone about an eighty-foot pliosaur, you might want to leave Libby's name out of it."

Suddenly, Officer Marimba's radio squawked. He looked at his watch and said, "Okay, I can be there in ten minutes," then quickly excused himself from the room.

After thanking the officer for his help, John leaned his hands against the desk. He looked at Tom. "So, what's the next step?"

Tom rose from his chair and pointed to a detailed map of South Africa on his wall. His finger rested on Cape Infante. "From the beachings and the attack on the surfers, we know the pliosaur is heading west. For starters, I think I'll take the chopper up and have a look around Cape Infante." His finger moved along the map as he spoke. "Then I'll continue farther along the Western Cape until I reach Gans Bay and the Dyer Island Channel, the most recent attack site. With any luck, the creature could still be here where it'll be more attracted to the fur seal colonies than any boats in the area. If I don't see it there, I'll continue to head west."

John looked at Kate who nodded. "Okay, sounds good," replied John, looking closer at the map. "Earlier, Steven Jensen with the Port Elizabeth World Museum mentioned that False Bay would be a good spot to check. He also thought that the Cape of Good Hope would be a good place to look in case the pliosaur headed farther out for larger prey."

"That's a good point," replied Tom. "The fur seals are quite agile. A creature this size could become frustrated trying to catch them and decide to go farther out for larger, slower prey." Tom glanced at his watch. "I'd better get moving. The Western Cape's a large area . . . I'll cover as much as we can before nightfall."

"What about my chopper?" Kate suggested.

John looked at her, wide-eyed with excitement. "Excellent! We can split up the area."

She smiled at his enthusiasm and said, "We'll drive back to the airport and get the chopper refueled."

"Also, we'll see if we can round up a couple barrels of chum," John said.

Kate continued, "We'll start farther east around Mossel Bay and work our way west until we reach the Dyer Channel. That way Tom can start just west of Dyer Island and follow the coast toward the Cape of Good Hope."

"That sounds good," Tom said, "we should be able to cover most of the Western Cape before nightfall."

As Tom made arrangements for flight, John motioned to Kate for them to take leave. As they walked toward the front doors of the institute, Kate looked over at John and said, "I've got one more question. What do we do if we find it?"

Chapter 31
TECHNICAL DIFFICULTIES

In the ship's surveillance room, Nathan had become fixated on monitor number one, virtually ignoring the other three at this point. He scooted to the edge of his chair. In his eighteen years of marine research, he had never seen a whale exhibit such bizarre behavior.

The door squeaked and slid open behind him. He didn't bother to look back. The heavy, deliberate footsteps and faint scent of pipe smoke told him it was the captain. The footsteps stopped behind his chair. Still, Nathan didn't take his eyes from monitor one, which indicated that this whale had become entangled in a shark barrier net near the shallows. For the last fifteen minutes, he had been watching a group of bystanders struggle to cut the net away from the tangled creature and push it into deeper water. Nathan glanced back. "Looks like this guy needs a compass!"

"What's that?" asked Nemo.

"The sperm whale on monitor one, trying to get untangled."

"You mean the whale still caught in the shark barrier net?"

"Same whale, different net. Folks cut him free from the first net, and then he swam out about seventy yards, made a U-turn, and swam back toward the beach. Now he's caught in another net not far from where they just released him. I've never seen anything like it. It's almost like he doesn't want to go back out to sea."

Nemo put his hand on the back of Nathan's chair. "Which whale is that? What's the location?"

Nathan glanced at the monitors used to track the whale's homing device and pointed at a dot. "That one's about four miles south of us, somewhere around Pearly Beach."

"Well, that whale certainly won't find any squid." Nemo scratched his chin, perplexed. "How much time do we have until we begin transmitting footage to the classrooms?"

"We're about twenty-five minutes away."

Short on optimism, Nemo grunted and paced the small room.

Nathan returned his attention to the other monitors. He focused on monitor three, where he saw the image jolt a bit. Then it twisted and turned as if freefalling to the depths. Then there was a poof of silt. Through the haze, he could see the light from the camera glaring off the rocky seabed.

"Great," Nathan sighed. "Looks like we lost another one."

"What's that?" said Nemo.

"Looks like whale three's transmitter and camera was just knocked off, my guess is by one of the juveniles playing."

"Well, you know the drill. How deep?"

"Not bad. Probably don't need to bother with the mini-sub. The pod's moved in near the shallows, only about a hundred feet." Nathan stood and stretched his back. "I'll run down and get it . . . the dive will loosen me up a bit."

The captain took a seat in front of the console. "Well, hop to it," he said. "I'll keep an eye on the monitors."

~~~

Through the window in Kate's airport office, John glanced at a small plane taxiing down the runway. He returned his attention to the TV. He took a sip of cold water, but no matter how much he drank, his mouth still felt like a desert. Was it exhaustion or his fraying nerves? Probably both. Every time he turned on the news, his mouth went dry at the thought of what he might hear next. Yet he *had* to keep watching. Knowledge of how this creature was moving was their only hope to stop it.

While Kate was in the restroom changing, he flipped channels and stopped when he saw a female reporter standing at the water's edge. *Uh oh, this doesn't look good.* He turned up the volume. The reporter was saying, "The Navy is still mystified by a boat that was discovered eight miles off Mossel Bay earlier this morning." The camera panned left, showing a gray boat being guided onto a trailer by two men in uniform. "To the Navy's surprise, the abandoned vessel turned out to be one of their own. After careful examination of the boat's weathered hull, they were able to discern the boat's ID number and discovered it had been missing for nearly twenty years.

"The vessel was last heard from while in pursuit of a boat allegedly transporting narcotics through the Indian Ocean. Traces of blood and cocaine residue found on the deck helped confirm the boat's involvement in a drug investigation. But no one can explain the whereabouts of the two naval officers who mysteriously disappeared nearly two decades ago."

Kate walked up behind John, tying off the bottom of her shirt. "Is that something about the pliosaur?"

John got up from the couch. "No, it's nothing. Just some old patrol boat that went missing suddenly showed up near Mossel Bay."

Kate shook her head as they walked toward the door. "Guess you never know what's gonna come outta these waters!"

When John reached for the door handle, there was a knock from outside. Opening the door, his jaw dropped. Professor Atkins stood before him holding a musician's flute case. The bags under her eyes indicated she hadn't slept much recently.

"Good morning, lad," said the little silver-haired woman.

"Mom!" said Kate.

"You came back!" gasped John.

They were both wide-eyed with astonishment. The old gal, on the other hand, was cool as a cucumber. "Of course, I came back."

John looked at the flute case. "Is that the—"

"Precisely, it is," she said loudly, and with a flourish, "the tooth! What are you so surprised about? I wasn't going to keep the bloody thing. When I saw the gum tissue on the specimen, I decided to test that first, which would only take a few hours." She winked. "And, of course, they found it to be reptilian . . . but not a match for any contemporary creature. No surprise to you and me, but I assure you it created quite a stir at the lab."

Opening the case, she slid out a bundled towel and unfolded it to reveal the enormous tooth. She pointed to where part of the root was covered in a clear plastic wrap. "You need to leave this on. Some of the gum tissue was starting to dry out and flake off. This sealed area has a solution in it that will keep the tissue moist." She handed him a manila folder. "These are the verification papers from the lab, complete with photos of the gum tissue and the appropriate lab numbers. This should be everything you need."

Momentarily speechless, John reached out and took the tooth as if it were a piece of priceless china. He looked at it for a long time, then up at the professor, and then to Kate who was wearing a scowl. "Still, Mother. I can't believe you took that—"

"No, no. We're all good here." John blurted. "And what timing! Professor, you're beautiful. After I show this to the proper authorities, I . . . I promise I'll have it right back to you. I swear . . . thanks a lot!"

The little woman looked at John, her eyes somber. "You go kill that bloody thing . . . then we'll really have something to study." With that, she turned and headed back to the parking lot without as much as a goodbye.

Placing the tooth on the couch, John scooped up Crystal. "Hey, one more thing," he said, catching up to the professor on the sidewalk. "We'll be gone for a while. Do you mind chimp-sitting until we get back?"

"That's some trade-off," smirked the professor. "I bring you back a priceless tooth, fully authenticated, and you give me a bloody monkey. Very well," she muttered, and headed off, guiding the chimp by the hand. Crystal blew a raspberry at John as they walked away.

Back in the office, John held the tooth like a newborn, nearly cradling it in his arms. "Wow. Guess the old girl had a change of heart."

"I think I know why," said Kate.

John turned to find Kate staring at the TV. "This was on the news last night. It's the surfer attack that took place yesterday," she turned up the volume so John could hear.

The reporter stood on the beach, moonlight reflecting off the waves crashing against the shoreline in the background. "An apparent shark attack leaves one man dead and another struggling for his life in the hospital." A photo of an attractive young man with shoulder-length, blond hair appeared on the screen.

"Dorian Anderson was born in Durban. This twenty-one-year-old South African native was schooled in Port Elizabeth, achieving public acclaim as a surfer. Placing in the top five in last year's Billabong Pro held at Jeffery's Bay, Dorian had proven himself as a world-class competitor with brilliant potential. He was also scheduled to continue his education at the University of Port Elizabeth with only one more semester to complete his bachelor's degree in marine biology. But earlier today, in the waters behind me, those dreams were tragically cut short."

As the reporter continued, Kate turned to John. "Dorian was the one surfing with Ron, the surfer we saw at the hospital. Dorian Anderson . . . I knew that name sounded familiar. Morene Anderson is one of Mom's colleagues, and Dorian was her son."

On the TV, John saw the camera turn and focus on the vast waters behind the reporter.

"Come on," he said, "we've got to go."

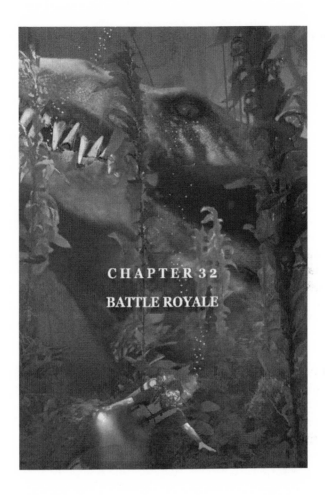

CHAPTER 32

BATTLE ROYALE

In full dive gear, Nathan treaded water beside the towering hull of the *Nauticus II*. The water felt cool and refreshing, a welcome relief from the endless hours he'd spent in the stale surveillance cabin. He lowered his dive mask. Through it, he could see the glistening backs of the whale pod about thirty yards out. He slipped the regulator into his mouth. A thumbs-up to Erick who was looking on from the starboard rail, and Nathan descended below the surface.

So close to them now, the whales seemed impossibly enormous in these live conditions. Like glowing serpents, streams of morning light slithered along their gray bodies. Their haunting moans echoed around him.

Descending beneath them now, Nathan turned his attention away from the sprawling giants overhead and focused on the seafloor. Off to his right was a kelp forest. A kick of his fins, and he dove beside the magnificent display of sea vegetation. The towering vines of seaweed and leaf-like blades swayed gently with the current. Another pump of his fins, and he examined the rocky seabed. And there it was, the flashing green light of the camera and transmitter laying at the edge of the kelp forest.

He reached the seafloor in a puff of silt. Picking up the homing device, he inspected the camera, slowly turning it in the haze. Other than a slight scratch on the lens, it appeared to be undamaged.

Then out of the corner of his eye, Nathan noticed a large plume of bubbles rise from the kelp forest. Gracefully, the silver froth floated up through the darkness toward the surface light, slowly dissipating before the whales. He followed the bubbles back down to their point of origin.

His blood ran cold.

Between the tall, waving kelp vines, he saw a set of enormous interlocked teeth and long jaws. Behind them, the kelp forest offered glimpses of an impossible length of gray, tiger-striped skin.

He dropped the camera to the seafloor as he ducked back, hiding behind the kelp. But the monster remained still, it's burning red eyes locked on the whale pod.

There was a series of clicking sounds from above. Near the surface, three bull sperm whales broke off from the pod. They drew closer and began to circle as if to investigate the enormous intruder.

Nathan watched the bulls move in closer. With every pass, the whales drew nearer. The water displaced from their massive bodies, making the kelp come alive.

Still, the pliosaur did not move.

Closer . . . and in the blink of an eye, the monster launched, using all four of its enormous paddle fins, latching its jaws onto the neck of the closest whale. Using its full weight, the pliosaur veered the whale around and released it toward the seafloor.

Nathan ducked as the whale barreled through the kelp, just missing him, and crashed into the seabed, shaking the seafloor. With a horrible moan, the creature twisted and rolled across the seabed in a huge cloud of sediment. Blood poured from its gaping wound.

Nathan felt a massive surge of water. He turned away from the whale writhing on the seafloor behind him. Through the haze, he saw the vast underbelly of the second whale flash overhead.

The pliosaur slowly rose from the towering vines of kelp. Vines tangled around a rear paddle fin were uprooted and rose with the beast. With the thrust of a front paddle fin, the monster pulled its head back as the second whale barreled by, just missing its pebbled skin.

Around Nathan, the seafloor fell dark as the pliosaur rose higher, blotting out the surface light. He could now see the creature's full form: the giant reptilian head, the four paddle fins that protruded out from an enormous tiger-striped body, slowly tapering down to a thick tail.

The colossal head methodically turned. Its front paddle fins swept out, ready for battle. Burning eyes searched for the whale.

The second whale appeared out of the gloom, picking up speed. As the whale closed, Nathan noticed the flashing green light on its back.

~~~

Inside the surveillance cabin, Nemo had both hands covering his mouth, stupefied, as he stared at the war being waged on monitor two. It showed the whale's perspective as it zeroed in on the pliosaur. The screen filled with the monster's spreading jaws. "This can't be happening!" gasped Nemo, flipping every switch on the console to make sure he was recording.

Back on the battle, the second whale barreled straight at the pliosaur.

Closer . . . And at the last second, the giant reptile twisted, avoiding the collision but still able to sink its barbaric teeth into the passing flank.

Captain Nemo nearly fainted.

~~~

In one of thousands of classrooms around the globe, a young teacher adjusted a TV set in front of her unruly third graders. She was pleasantly surprised when blue ocean water appeared on the screen. "Students, look now. We're getting a live transmission from the *Nauticus II*!" She pointed at a gray mass at the bottom of the screen. "Everyone look . . . see the top of the whale's head?" She stepped back, cocking her head to one side. "Hmmm. Why does it look like its spinning?"

Just then, a swath of blood washed over the whale's head and filled the screen.

Ooohs and aaahs spread through the classroom.

~~~

Inside the surveillance cabin, Nemo remained riveted to monitor two, watching the red cloud thicken on the screen. Then his eyes happened to drift down to the white light flashing beneath the monitor, and two words lit up: *Transmitting Live*.

He'd hit the wrong switch for recording. "Oh no! Can't have the kids seeing this." He quickly flipped the switch to off, holding his heart as he leaned heavily back in the chair. The flip of Captain Nemo's switch to OFF triggered thousands of disappointed moans in classrooms around the world.

~~~

Peering up from the seabed, Nathan saw the pliosaur deepen its grip on the second whale. The whale's enormous fluke kicked madly, but only managed to turn the interlocked beasts in a circle.

With a bellowing moan, the whale rolled. But the pliosaur, using its weight, rode the behemoth down toward the seafloor, its massive jaws closing, blood billowing like smoke from a chimney.

Nathan scurried back across the seafloor, trying to create some distance between himself and the fury.

The two giants slammed into the seabed, sending out a massive cloud of silt. The sperm whale squirmed madly. The monster's jaws twisted, sinking deeper. The blood cloud grew thicker. Nathan could barely see the pliosaur's head which was deep into the whale.

A horrible moan rose from the whale. The nearby kelp swayed crazily from its thrashing fluke. But the colossal jaws around the whale only sank deeper.

Deeper . . .

Finally, with a tremendous plume of blood, the whale's head dropped. Its rear section plopped in the opposite direction, still squirming. Blubber spilled, bathing the seafloor in an ivory gelatin.

The whale was completely bitten in half.

Through the red cloud, Nathan could just make out the pliosaur's nose rising. The jaws cracked open and unleashed a gurgling roar, expelling bubbles until the victorious beast completely disappeared behind a crimson haze.

But it wasn't over. The vast underbelly of the third whale soared overhead.

Nathan scurried across the seafloor. Disoriented and blinded by the bloody silt, he stumbled on, trying to distance himself from the titanic battle. Like tentacles, long vines of kelp reached through the silt, swirling around him. He was in the Kelp forest. He was going in the wrong direction. A swaying kelp vine nearly tore off his mask. Nathan sprung from the seafloor. Ducking and dodging his way through the tangle of vines, he made a break for the surface. He rose, swimming madly, but there seemed to be no end to the blood cloud.

Eventually, the haze began to thin out. He could finally see the hull of the ship about fifty feet above. Still, he couldn't resist a glance back at the battle.

The pliosaur slowly rose from the enormous red cloud. With a thrust of its forefins, the beast slowly turned around. Bloody blubber strung from its jaws.

The third sperm whale appeared even larger than the others. The massive whale veered around, its enormous fluke pumping, picking up speed.

Closing . . .

The monster locked eyes with the whale. All four paddle fins rose, ready for the third round.

The whale drew closer.

The pliosaur's head cocked back. Its jaws stretched open, and it unleashed a bellowing roar—a primal war cry, echoing through the sea.

Duly warned, the sperm whale quickly turned tail and headed in the opposite direction.

The pliosaur dropped its head, and with a thrust of all four paddle fins, lifted off like a dragon taking flight. The behemoth charged through the sea, every pump of its huge fins bringing it closer to the whale.

~~~

Nathan broke the waterline just in time to see the colossal splash as the pliosaur caught the whale. A giant paddle fin rose high, towering into the blue sky as the monster rolled over the whale, driving it beneath the waves.

Beyond the splash, Nathan saw the frightened whale pod dispersing, bumping one another, fleeing in every direction.

He made the short swim to the ship's stern in record time. He grabbed onto the ladder. Once his fins were out of the water, he collapsed onto the ladder, catching his breath. Slowly, he gained the strength to move.

The moment he set foot on deck, Erick appeared before him. The wide-eyed boy was pointing at the whale pod. "Did you see that? Some kind of dinosaur just hit a whale. You should have seen it!"

Nathan raised his mask, "You saw it?"

"Yeah, what was it?"

"You tell me," muttered Nathan as he plodded his way to the stairwell.

~~~

Barefoot and still in his wetsuit, Nathan burst into the surveillance cabin, dripping water. Nemo turned away from the monitors and locked eyes with his assistant. Their reeling minds couldn't find the words.

Nemo pointed at monitor two. "Was that . . . that what I think it was?"

Nathan dropped his hands to his knees, catching his breath. "It was enormous, Captain. Some kind of pliosaur . . . the size of a whale! Could you see it?"

Nemo gave a wide-eyed nod. "Saw it from the camera on whale two. Right as it charged the beast and got away. Then I lost the visual."

"Afraid whale two didn't get away. Trust me. I had a front row seat for the Battle Royale."

"Impossible," grumbled Nemo. "Whale two is still moving."

Nathan shook his head.

Dumbfounded, Nemo swiveled around to face the smaller monitors with gridded screens used to track the whales' positions. He pointed to the red dot on monitor two. "There's whale two. See, it's moved approximately fifty yards. It's just off starboard."

"I don't think so, sir. The last time I saw whale two, it was lying in TWO pieces on the seabed," Nathan said, his voice rising as he remembered the scene.

Nemo pointed to the red dot on the gridded monitor. "Well, this dead whale's doing better than thirty knots, son. See, it was here five minutes ago. Look how far it's moved."

Nathan approached the monitor to see for himself. There was no mistake. Unzipping his wetsuit, he said, "The creature must be carrying part of the carcass to a different area to feed."

"Not at that speed. It's carrying a full-grown sperm whale! Or at least half of one."

Perplexed, Nemo sat back in his chair. Then behind him, the second monitor on the wall crackled and came back on. It showed the blue ocean waters.

"Look at the video monitors," said Nathan. "The one showing the live feed from whale two is back on!" Nemo quickly turned around. Nathan added, "It is moving! You can see bubbles flowing across it."

"Mmm . . . I'm not so sure the whale's still moving," replied Nemo. "It could be the passing current making it look that way." Nemo again turned to the gridded monitors to check the whale's position. "It's still moving, all right . . . now it's off our starboard." Still trying to rationalize, he said, "There's a strong underwater current near here. Maybe part of the carcass dropped in the middle of it."

"I don't think so, sir."

"But how can it be? This makes no sense!" The image on screen shifted. A long, white object now covered part of the screen. Nathan squinted and he finally put it together. "That's it," he whispered. "Camera two is still moving . . . but it's not on the whale." He ran his finger along the object crossing the screen. "Do you see what I see?"

Nemo grumbled in the negative.

"Look closer. See that ridge, and those vertical scars?"

Nemo's lips slowly parted. Realization flared in his eyes, "Unbelievable . . . that's a tooth!" He stepped closer. "You're right! I don't believe it, but it has to be! The beast consumed the camera and homing device when it attacked the whale. That explains the movement."

Slowly, the captain stepped back from the monitor and sat down beside Nathan. They continued to watch as the creature's mouth closed, leaving only the glaring light from the camera reflecting from the insides of the interlocked teeth.

"Well, how long do you think that camera will hold up trapped in its jaw like that?" asked Nemo.

"I'm amazed it's still working at all. But I don't think it'll last much longer than the creature's next meal. Wow! Did you see that?" Nathan scooted closer to the monitor. "He's opening his mouth."

Again, the blue waters filled the monitor, framed by the edge of the white tooth. The water faded and a gray mass filled the screen. The image bobbled and turned to snow.

"What was all that gray?" asked Nemo.

Nathan looked at the gridded monitor to check the position of the homing device. His eyes slowly rose from the monitor. "Sir, I think it's our hull!"

Frantically, Nemo snatched the mike off the console. "Roger, tell Freddie I want him on the main deck, pronto! There's a rare … specimen off our starboard. We need to get it on film NOW!" Racking the mike, Nemo sprang from his chair. "I'm going up on deck to have a look."

The moment the captain reached the doorway he stopped, frozen in his tracks. "Did you feel that?"

Nathan looked down at the floor. "Like a vibration."

"Is that what I think it is?" asked Nemo without moving a muscle.

Nathan turned to the gridded monitors, his eyes locked on monitor two. "I think so, sir. It's right under the ship."

Another long scrape vibrated from the ship's hull.

Erick appeared in the doorway. "Is that the dinosaur? Is it gonna eat the ship?"

Suddenly, monitor two came back on. It showed the ship's gray hull beside the edge of the tooth. From the doorway, Nemo looked at the monitor and stepped back into the room. Erick came closer to Nathan, ever curious. "What's that gray thing on the monitor? Is it coming from one of the whale cameras?"

"The camera's in the pliosaur's mouth. Apparently it's running its jaws along our hull," explained Nathan. "Looks like he's trying to get a taste sample to see if we're suitable for consumption. Look, feel that! Every time the camera shakes you can feel the ship vibrate."

"Wow!" Erick sounded awestruck. "First you put a camera on a whale's back. And now you mounted one inside a dinosaur's mouth. Man, you guys are good."

They continued to watch the screen as the image shook every time the ship vibrated beneath their feet.

"Can it hurt the ship, scraping it like that?" asked Erick.

"No, I think it's just checking us out," said Nathan. "Once it realizes we're not a whale carcass, it'll probably—" And that's when the ship dipped port side. Nathan caught himself on the console. "Unbelievable!"

Erick and Nemo slowly came to their feet in the swaying room. "No, no way," Nemo said, bracing himself in the doorway. "That had to be a wave. We're a two-hundred-twenty-foot research ship! Not a canoe!"

"This isn't good, Captain. You saw it . . . the screen went out at exactly the same time," said Nathan. The moans of twisting metal echoed beneath their feet. The ship settled. Nemo froze behind Nathan's chair while everyone listened in silence.

Another long, scraping creak echoed from below.

"We've got to get a shot of this beast!" bellowed Nemo. He pointed at Erick. "Boy, make yourself useful and run up to the deck and help Freddie look for it. Now chivvy along!"

Nathan turned to protest, "No, Erick, stay away from the rail—"

But the enthusiastic boy was gone.

~~~

On the main deck, a thin man in his forties with slicked-back black hair, a thin moustache, and goatee leaned over the starboard rail. Craning his neck, Freddie stared straight down to where the hull met the waterline. After nearly losing his balance, he looked back to port side where Erick and his dog were standing. "See anything on that side?" he shouted.

"No!" yelled Erick. "How about you?"

"Nothing yet, but keep 'em peeled. It's gotta come out sooner or later." *Time to get ready*, thought Freddie. Pulling the camera up to his eye, he looked over the rail and adjusted the focus on the telescopic lens. Through the camera's eye, the glimmering wave tips softened then slowly became more defined as he continued to adjust the lens. Again, the blue waters softened, then with another twist of the lens became clear. But this time, the water was pitch black. Freddie tried to adjust the lens one more time, but the black water remained.

Realizing the problem wasn't with his camera, he took a look with the naked eye. Slowly, he lowered the camera. Directly below was a shadowy head beyond his comprehension. The massive nose pulled out farther from beneath the hull, and flickers of light revealed enormous interlocked teeth. A glowing red eye appeared. Freddie stood frozen for several seconds, resisting the temptation to step back from the rail.

The colossal head turned and rose to the surface. Instinctively, the camera rose back to Freddie's eye. Click! He snapped off a quick shot, then stepped back to get the entire head into frame. Click! He moved back farther. "Smile, baby! I don't know what you are, but you're the next cover of *National Geo—wooooah!*" The moment he touched the button, the enormous head lunged from the water, jaws swelling.

Whhham! The head slammed the hull just below the side rail. Unleashing a deafening roar, the massive creature dove. Water pulled in behind the descending bulk drew the ship to starboard, throwing Freddie back onto a large a crate. Splinters shot into his back, and his shirttail pushed up to his shoulders as he slid down the side of the crate. He hit the deck hard and slid face-first toward the side of the ship, camera extended out from his side in attempt to protect it. He stopped just as his head poked beneath the side rail. Breathing a sigh of relief, he gazed down the hull.

He got up from the deck and stared into the rocking water, but the great shadow had already vanished into the depths. He turned and saw the boy brushing himself off while walking toward him. "Did you get it?" shouted Erick.

Freddie pulled down his shirt, held up his camera, and gave a confident smile.

~~~

Inside the surveillance cabin, Nathan and Nemo recoiled from the shock. Neither of them uttered a sound, their expressions said it all. As the ship steadied, their attention slowly returned to the gridded monitor following the homing device. The red dot slowly moved north of the ship and disappeared.

"That's it. It's gone," grumbled Nemo.

Nathan nodded with relief. "Still, I'm not so sure," he added. "It's no longer in the vicinity of the ship, but I'm not sure how far it's gone."

"What do you mean?"

"The transmitter stopped sending a signal long before it went out of range. The creature was only a half mile from the ship when the signal stopped. It could just be a malfunction."

Nemo eased back against the doorframe. "Do you think it'll be back?"

"It's not likely," replied Nathan. "I don't believe it has much of an appetite for a steel hull." He glanced up at the console, at the large main monitors. Monitor two showed only snow. "Guess we can stop filming. There's no more feed coming from the camera." Nathan reached beneath monitor two and froze. The red light was off. "What happened?" He whipped around to face Nemo. "It's off! Someone turned it off!"

"What?" Nemo's complexion paled slightly as he began to realize . . .

Nathan pointed and talked and pointed again, animated, hands flying around his head for emphasis. "The switch to record the live feed from camera two. I left it on before I made the dive, but someone turned it off!"

Nemo's face then turned a deep shade of red. "You mean the feed coming from the whale when it charged the beast . . . that magnificent footage . . . none of it was . . ."

"No." Nathan gave a blank stare. "None of it was recorded."

"This isn't another one of your jokes?" warned Nemo. "You know I don't have a sense of humor."

"Sir, I wish I were joking."

Nemo's legs gave way. He slowly slid down the doorframe until he was seated in the doorway. His face buried in his hands in frustration. He'd been a mess with those switches, so panicked was he to get the scenes recorded but not transmit them to the schools. He'd meant to turn the recording switch on, but in his panic, must have inadvertently turned it off. The opportunity of a lifetime had just slipped through his fingers.

"Don't worry," assured Nathan. "I'm sure Freddie will come up with something."

Just then, Freddie appeared in the doorway. He looked down at Nemo slumped in the doorway. "What happened?"

Nemo's face rose from his hands. He could barely get the words out, stammering, "You got it . . . tell me you got . . . the shot!"

Freddie held up his camera. "They don't call me Ready Freddie for nothing."

Chapter 33
SIMON'S TOWN

John gazed through the side window, watching the helicopter's shadow pass the shoreline and sweep across blue-green waters of False Bay. He anxiously drummed his fingers on the leather flute case sprawled across his lap.

Kate glanced at the flute case. "I can only imagine the admiral's face when he gets a look at that. Still, I think this is a good call, taking the tooth straight to him instead of following Tom in the search. Now we can have the entire Navy searching too."

"Hopefully," John said, still concerned about the outcome of the impending meeting. "But it's odd that we haven't been able to reach Tom since we lifted off. Wonder why he's not answering his phone?"

Kate looked over. "Got me, but he was certainly eager to start the search. He could be over Dyer Channel as we speak."

"How far are we from the naval headquarters?" John asked.

Kate returned her gaze to the windshield. "It's just on the other side of the bay, about ten more miles up the Cape's coast. See that long, flat mountain in partial cloud cover? Simon's Town is not far from there, and that's where the naval headquarters is located."

"Good, I can't wait to have this chat with Admiral Henderson," said John as he patted the flute case for reassurance.

Just then, the helicopter vibrated slightly as if in rough winds. He looked at Kate, and she pointed out the window just as the sky broke into a roar. Seemingly from out of nowhere, a 109 Agusta LUH naval helicopter shot past them and followed the coastline in the opposite direction.

Kate said, "Must be still searching at Dire Channel."

John gazed into the distance toward Simon's Town. "In a few minutes they're going to find out what they're really searching for."

~~~

Tension mounted in the ship's video room while Captain Nemo, Nathan, and Erick watched Freddie anxiously plug his digital camera into the computer. "Okay, Freddie, it's all up to you," said Nemo, arms folded in front of him. "Let's see what you've got."

A voice came over the intercom. "Captain, can you pick up?"

Nemo keyed the mike. "Roger, I'm in the middle of something!"

"Captain, I'm getting dozens of calls from the school representatives. They're all asking about the sixty-second transmission that went out . . . the whale . . . Sir, they keep asking why the whale was bleeding. What am I supposed to tell them?"

"Tell them whatever!" barked Nemo. "Tell them it had hemorrhoids for all I care—just hold all my calls!"

"Aye aye, Captain."

Freddie squinted at Nathan. "Can whales get hemorrhoids?"

Racking the mike, Nemo returned his attention to the monitor. "Okay Freddie . . . show me why I pay you so much."

Freddie perked up. "Captain, you won't believe your eyes!" The photographer confidently clicked on the icon to open the first image.

The screen filled with what appeared to be dark water.

Nemo squinted. "That just looks like a close up of an oil spill!"

"Wait a minute, there's more," said Freddie. He quickly clicked on the second image. "At first it was so big, it filled the frame, so I backed up to pull the whole shadow into frame. Here." The second image appeared on the screen.

Nemo looked at the new image on the monitor, "Great. An oil spill from a distance."

Freddie nervously clicked on the third image. "Wait, there's one more!" The third photograph slowly appeared, and the screen filled with blurry clouds. Freddie looked back from his chair. His tone was defensive. "That's when it rocked the ship; it threw me back as I was taking the shot!"

"You're right," replied Nemo sarcastically. "I don't believe my eyes. Two oil slicks and some blurry clouds. Good job, Freddie!"

"Hey, it's not my fault! You should have seen the size of that thing!" pleaded Freddie. He clicked back onto the second image of shadowy water. "I mean it's there! That's the creature!"

Nemo stared blankly at the screen. He had the best ship and equipment money could buy. Still the greatest zoological find of all time had dropped into his lap, and he had nothing to show for it. What if the beast returned to the abyss never to be seen again? What if word got out that he'd missed it all? He would be known as the man whose negligence robbed the scientific world of its greatest find. His hands trembled in rage.

"All right," he said, barely able to contain his fury. "Nathan, get back to the surveillance room and keep an eye on the monitor. Let me know if the signal comes back on."

Nemo turned to Freddie. "You come on deck with me. We've got to find a way to lure this thing back to the ship. And this time we'll be ready for it, right?" Stepping toward the doorway, he looked down at Erick. "And you . . . just stay out of the way."

~~~

"There she is. Cape Town, the mother city of South Africa," Kate announced as the waters of False Bay terminated against the shoreline below. "And behind her, the world's most easily recognized mountain, Table Mountain. One long, flat table of rock shaped so perfectly, one would swear it was manmade. But, no sir, she's all God's work. On some days, the clouds even pour right across her top and form the perfect tablecloth." Kate glanced at John, eyes twinkling as she grinned. "You have to excuse me. Sometimes when I fly this way, I revert back to my chartering days."

Looking down, John saw enormous gray rocks protruding up from the white sands of Boulder Beach, while hundreds of black dots represented the resident colony of jackass penguins. Flying farther up the coast, he began to make out the silhouettes of ships anchored in Simon's Bay.

Slowly, the helicopter descended toward the small airport runway beside the Simon's Town Naval Headquarters. Through the window, John stared at a dozen or so naval patrol vessels that towered above the aqua-green waters of the bay. He was quick to notice that four of the ships were equipped with helicopters. *If I can just get the admiral on our side, we'll have all the air power we'll need . . . and fast,* he thought.

The moment the skids touched ground, John cracked the cabin door. Stepping out beneath the slow-moving blade, he shouted to Kate, "Keep it running. This won't take long!" He snatched the flute case from his seat and closed the door.

John jogged around to the front of the long, white building and slowed to a fast walk as he reached the double doors. Before stepping into the lobby, he held the door for a man leaving the building. The gray-haired man with a gray moustache nodded politely while passing.

Entering the lobby, John felt a surge of confidence as he headed for the reception area. Behind the desk, an attractive black woman frantically took a call while three other phone lines continued to blink. Putting another caller on hold, she looked up at John with a forced smile. "May I help you?"

John rested the case on the counter. "Yes, could you direct me to Admiral Henderson's office?"

"Is he expecting you?"

"Yeah, well, kind of. I'm a little late for an appointment. It's very important."

"I'm sorry, he's in a meeting right now and can't be disturbed. If you'd like to leave a message for him, I'll be sure that he receives it as soon as he's finished."

One of her phone lines began to beep from being on hold. When she looked down, John heard the admiral's voice coming from behind an office door nearby. He pulled the case from the counter and fast-walked to the hallway.

The receptionist sprang from her chair and cupped her hand over the receiver. "Sir! Sir, you can't go in there! Sir—"

John cracked the door open to make sure he had the right room. A guard rapidly approached him from behind. At the end of a long conference table, he saw the admiral standing with his back to a large picture window overlooking a busy naval yard. For once, John's mental picture of someone he had spoken to over the telephone was dead on. The admiral's face was as stern as he'd imagined. Gathered around the table were five other men, four of them in naval uniform. John opened the door wider and stepped in. To his surprise, he saw Tom Hayman from the Sharks Board among the group. *No wonder I couldn't reach him!* John's eye went back to the big window. Below, he could see a landing pad bristling with activity. Six 109 Agusta LUH naval helicopters were being prepped for lift off. Men in uniform hefted barrels into cargo doors. Two choppers had already taken to the air. He had definitely walked in on something. The entire naval yard and every face around the table had a sense of urgency.

"Sir! Who let you in here?" barked the admiral. A guard grabbed John's arm.

Tom quickly spoke up, "It's the gentlemen I was telling you about earlier . . . John Paxton!"

The admiral held his hand up and indicated for the guard to let go of John's arm.

"That will be all," he said to the guard, who retreated to the hallway. Without further introduction, John sat the flute case on the end of the long conference table, opposite the admiral. "Sir, I have something you need to see." He quickly unfastened the case, pulled out the bundled tooth, and unwrapped it from the towel. His face beamed with confidence and no small sense of relief. *Finally.*

There was a loud clank from the opposite end of the table. John looked up as the admiral slid a huge pliosaur tooth toward him like a disk on a shuffleboard court. When the tooth came to rest, the Admiral spoke matter-of-factly, "Mr. Bensley's fourth-grade class. Show-and-share day."

John slowly laid his tooth beside it. *I guess he believes me now*, he thought as he looked across the table expecting to hear a long-overdue apology. Instead, he found Admiral Henderson staring back at him with somber eyes. "Two more lives were lost yesterday morning."

There it was again—the dead, empty feeling in the pit of John's stomach. A rancid taste rose and mixed with the dryness in his mouth.

None of it seemed real anymore.

The admiral went on explaining the attack, but John couldn't hear the words. His mind was lost, trying to figure out what the total must be by now. *First the fishermen at the Motanza; the surfer near Jeffrey's Bay; then the two fishermen killed at Dyer Channel before his very own eyes—and now two more.* He steadied himself against the table. A moment later, the admiral's voice became audible, and John faded back into the conversation.

"Yesterday, Lieutenant Vic Greeman regained consciousness long enough to give a statement." The admiral paused for a moment. "Seems you two are lucky to be alive." His voice was different; gone was the sharp tone of certainty that John had heard over the telephone. "He confirmed the statement you gave at the hospital, about commandeering a boat in the Dire Channel to check on a couple of shark tour operators that he had ordered to stay docked. He confirmed the creature's size . . . everything that transpired." The admiral rubbed his forehead. "Vic was just taken off the intensive care list this morning. His leg was lacerated and badly broken, but fortunately the doctors were able to save it. As far as the other fishermen . . . as you may have guessed, their bodies haven't been recovered."

John slowly looked over at Tom and paused. His dry mouth struggled to get out the next question. "Have there been any other fatalities . . . that I'm not aware of?"

Tom dropped his head, unable to look John in the eye.

"There was a yacht," answered the admiral. "About three miles off the coast of Maputo, a young woman literally ran across the tip of a mast while skiing.

"Upon investigation, we found a thirty-eight-foot yacht lying on the seafloor beside the carcass of a whale shark. At first, we assumed the obvious. We thought it was a case where a ship had rammed a whale shark feeding too close to the surface. Upon further investigation, however, we found that the wound on the shark and the damage on the ship's hull didn't line up with this theory.

"The damage to the hull was very strange in a sense that it wasn't cracked or pushed in . . . it was just missing. Then we measured the hole in the vessel's hull and found it to be within eight inches of the bite radius found in a whale carcass at Paradise Beach. Coincidentally, the same carcass beside where the fourth-grader claimed to have found that tooth."

"What about the occupants?" John asked.

"The bodies of the couple that owned the yacht were never recovered. And that's the only other incident we are aware of at this time."

"What about all of the fishermen from the fishing festival?" John asked.

The admiral again rubbed his forehead and looked down at the pair of giant teeth in front of John. "That's unconfirmed. But yes, we think that was the creature also."

John felt his guilt turning to rage. He looked at all the men standing around the table in uniform. "Okay, men," he said, anger slowly building in him, "I would say we now have . . . *sufficient evidence! Yes?* So what are you going to do about it?"

The admiral looked somberly around the table and said, "That's what we were going over when you came in." He gestured out the picture window, where men were hustling to load barrels into the helicopters. "As we speak, a squadron of eight choppers is being deployed. They're loaded with barrels of chum, depth charges, everything we need.

"We'll be focusing on an area forty miles east and west of Dyer Channel, the last known attack site, and about three miles off the coast. As far as my men know, they are only looking for an exceptionally large marine creature."

John looked around the table in disbelief. "So, no one outside this room really knows what they're looking for?"

"No one other than our demolition team," answered the admiral.

"Don't you think you need to tell them?"

The admiral leaned his hands against the table. His face was tense. "I think it's safe to assume they'll know it when they see it. We can't risk word of this getting to the public; our worst enemy right now is the media. If they get word of an eighty-foot prehistoric marine reptile on the loose, we'll be trying to find the thing among hundreds if not thousands of boats, helicopters, or any other type of craft you can snap a picture from."

Tom nodded in agreement. "He's right, John. If the media gets hold of this, the amount of boats in the area will quadruple along with the pliosaur's feeding opportunities. This thing could go public at any time. All it'll take is someone in the right spot with a camera. We've got to get the creature today."

"All right then!" said the admiral. "What are we waiting for?"

As the men around John rose from the table, he picked up his tooth and started to pack it away. He paused, staring at the plastic covering over the root. *After all of the hell I went through to bring this back . . . I didn't even need it.*

Chapter 34
BAIT

Inside the surveillance cabin of the *Nauticus II*, Nathan carefully studied the small monitor with the gridded screen. Nemo entered the room, Freddie at his heels like a shadow. Glancing over Nathan's shoulder, Nemo said, "Before the signal comes back on, we need a way to lure the beast back. Otherwise, the signal is useless."

"But what do you plan to use for bait?" asked Freddie from the doorway.

The Captain turned to Freddie. "Go check the galley. See if there's any meat, fish, anything. Maybe roast beef, uncooked. We need blood, something to get its attention!"

With a nod, Freddie ran out the door. Nathan swiveled around in his chair. "I've got it! We could use the crane that launches the submersible. We could attach a bag of meat or whatever to the hook that normally connects to the submersible, then extend the boom over the side of the ship and lower the cable like a giant fishing pole. That way we can hold the bag about six feet above the water and get a shot of the pliosaur when it breaks the surface to get the bait. We could also attach something to the line above the bait bag. You know, to give it scale for the camera, like one of those empty six-foot crates we have on deck."

The Captain slapped Nathan's shoulder. "That's the smartest thing I've heard out of you in weeks. Yes. Yes, I like that, a shot of the creature with its head breaching the water. And I like the idea of using something for scale. That will certainly help the credibility of the photo." Nemo paused and stared into the doorway. "Now, if we could just find something to use for bait . . . with lots of blood. At that moment, Erick poked his head into the room followed by Rex. The boy's eyes shot open. Making eye contact with the Captain, Erick started back-stepping.

Nemo looked at the Weimaraner beside the boy, "What's your dog's name, son?"

"I'm sorry, sir!" Erick backed further. "I'll take him below."

Nemo kneeled down, his tone softer. "Oh no, son. It's okay. Bring him over here, and let's have a look at him."

With a puzzled expression, Erick said, "It's okay, boy. Go see the captain." He guided the dog closer.

Nemo reached out and rubbed the dog's silky coat. "My, what a beautiful dog you are. Oh, and a healthy dog, great muscle tone." Then a strange look came over his face, and he grabbed onto the dog's collar.

Nathan stood, waving his arms. "No, no . . . you can't do that! Not the boy's dog!"

Erick pulled back on the collar with all his strength, looking up at Nathan. "Can't do what?"

Nemo tightened his grip—not allowing Rex to budge. The startled dog whimpered in confusion as Erick's small fingers started to give way.

Nemo pulled the dog closer. "You'll understand when you're older, son. It's in the name of science."

Just as the captain gained complete control of the dog, Freddie entered the cabin holding his hands out. "The chef has eighty-five pounds of uncooked roast beef and about fifty pounds of salmon, but he won't let me touch it."

The captain stood up enraged, releasing his grip on the dog. "You tell that *cook* that if he doesn't give you all that meat right now, I'm going to use *him* for chum! And make sure you get every drop of blood!"

Nathan glanced at the doorway, making sure that Erick and Rex were long gone. "Were you really considering killing the boy's dog?"

Nemo looked back at him, his eyes wild. "See if you can find a clamp and some wire. That was a good idea, attaching something to the line for scale." He noticed Nathan still staring at him and muttered, "Naaah. I was just playing with the lad."

Nathan slowly looked away and returned his attention to the gridded monitor. The little red light suddenly came back on. They were tracking the monster.

~~~

Staring through Kate's windshield, John watched a squadron of eight Agusta 109 LUH helicopters gather over Pearly Beach. One by one, the light-gray craft fell into formation before the midday sun. *A beautiful sight*, John thought. Finally, he had the air power he needed. Still, the victims weighed heavily on his mind.

His eyes drifted to the flute case containing the tooth. So far no one had linked the deaths to him. *But that would soon change,* John thought. He recalled that fateful night twenty years ago, after the motorcycle accident. At first, no one blamed him. Then the media uncovered the evidence and showed everyone the truth. Overnight, his idyllic life as a medical student turned into a living hell. He raised his gaze back to the naval squadron. Yes, history was about to repeat itself. It was only a matter of time until all fingers pointed to him, *as they very well should. No, I can't go back and change the past,* John thought. *But I'm gonna stop this abomination.*

His earphones crackled. "Paxton, do you read?" said the gravelly voice.

"Go ahead, Admiral."

~~~

Inside the lead helicopter, Admiral Henderson stared intently at the water, determination in his eyes. He spoke into his headset, "Look, John, the Navy's perfectly capable of taking it from here. But if you feel you must help, you can tag along as a spotter. We'll first scour the Dyer Channel, for obvious reasons. Then the squadron will split—one group of four heading east, the other west. You can follow the west group.

"The lead chopper in each group is loaded with the depth charges. The other three and you will serve as spotters. Remember, fan out, but keep the search close to shore. The plan is to corner it before nightfall. Out!"

~~~

Falling into formation with the naval squadron, Kate adjusted her headset. "Well, you heard the plan. After we split at Dyer Channel, we follow the west group."

John raised a pair of binoculars. "I still don't like the sound of this. Following every attack and whale carcass, the pliosaur is clearly heading west. And still, the admiral's splitting up the squadron; having half of it head east. He should be focusing all of his efforts west of Dyer Channel."

"Guess he's playing it safe," Kate said, shrugging, "in case it changes directions." She eyed the lead chopper. "I still can't believe we had to pay off that guard to get depth charges. After saving Lieutenant Greeman's butt last night, you'd think they'd give us a crate."

John grinned as he peered through the binoculars. "Guess the military's kind of funny that way, about issuing explosive devices to civilians." He lowered the binoculars and gazed across the naval squadron. "I just hope the admiral knows what he's doing."

Chapter 35
THE SCENT

"All right!" Let's get that concoction in the water while the beast is still in the area!" shouted Nemo. He stood beside the control box of the enormous crane. Near the portside rail, Nathan struggled to tighten the clamp attaching a four-by-six-foot crate to the thick cable of the crane.

"Make sure you have the crate far enough from the bait bag so it won't get in the way," yelled Nemo.

Nathan stood up, screwdriver in hand. "Yeah, it's about seven feet above the bait bag. That ought to give the creature plenty of room to reach the bait without hitting the crate."

With a nod, Nemo pressed a button on the control panel. The crane's long metal boom rose higher from the deck to the whining sound of hydraulics. The cable grew taut. The wooden crate slowly lifted from the deck and swiveled through the air. Then the bloody bait bag rose from a large bucket, a red stream flowing from the bottom of the burlap sack.

Nemo brought the crane to a stop. The thick metal arm swayed slightly as it hung in the open air near the side rail. He called to Nathan, "Go to the surveillance room and see if it's still in the area. I don't want to put the bag overboard until we know the beast is close."

After Nathan went below deck, Nemo turned his attention to the ship's chef, who was chopping salmon into small pieces and dropping them into a plastic trash can. "This is not the way I usually prepare my salmon," muttered the small man in a French accent. He looked up at the bloody burlap sack, shaking his head. "And all of that beautiful beef . . . fish food. I hope you gentlemen don't mind eating bologna sandwiches for the rest of the expedition."

With rapid metal footsteps, Nathan emerged from the stairwell, his thumbs up. "Captain, we're in luck. The pliosaur is within a half mile of the ship."

"Okay, here we go!" yelled Nemo, and he pressed another button. With a whining hydraulic sound, the crane's arm swiveled sideways, pulling the sack over the ship's port side rail, a red stream trailing across the deck.

From the shadows of the stairwell, Erick looked up at the bloodstained sack dangling beneath the cable. He looked at Nathan. "Was he gonna do that to Rex?"

"No, he was just kidding," replied Nathan. "He has a very strange sense of humor. Just the same, you might want to keep Rex below for the rest of the expedition." Erick followed Nathan to the port rail where they watched the bloody sack lower toward the sea. Freddie anxiously waited with his camera. Nathan looked back toward midship and shouted to Nemo. "That's good. The bag's about eight feet above the surface."

"Why are you putting it so high above the water?" asked Erick.

"We want to make sure the sharks can't get to it. We're also hoping to get a shot of the creature with its head above the surface. That's why we have that crate attached to the cable, to give it scale, you know, for a size comparison. Come on, let's go see where the creature is on the monitor."

After Nathan and Erick disappeared into the stairwell, Nemo walked away from the crane. He joined Freddie at the port rail. "You ready this time?"

He repeated his mantra: "They don't call me 'Ready Freddie' for nothing." He grinned. "Hey, I've had two *National Geographic* covers, and after today it'll be three."

"Well, just make sure you have the lens cap off," muttered Nemo on his way to the stairwell.

Entering the surveillance cabin, Nemo saw Nathan and Erick hovering over the monitor, tracking the homing device. Nathan looked up. "Looks like the chum trail is working. The pliosaur is within two hundred yards of the ship, port side."

Nemo smiled then glanced at Erick. "Where's your dog?"

"I . . . I think he ran away," the boy replied nervously.

"Must be a pretty good swimmer," muttered Nemo. He looked back at the red dot on the monitor. "Which way did you say the creature was coming?"

"Port side." Nemo looked at Erick. "Run up on deck and tell Freddie the beast is about two hundred yards off port side—get a move on!"

Nathan continued to update. "Still coming . . . less than a hundred and fifty yards away."

The captain picked up a headset. Adjusting the microphone in front of his mouth, he headed for the doorway. "I'm going to check that bait bag. Put on your headset, and let me know every time that thing moves." Exiting the cabin, Nemo listened to Nathan's voice on the head set. "Testing . . . one . . . two . . . three . . ."

"Read you. Is it still within a hundred fifty yards?" asked Nemo, walking along the hallway.

"About one twenty-five and still closing."

Nemo reached the top of the stairwell and saw Freddie leaning over the side rail. The photographer glanced back in his direction then discretely reached down to check his lens cap.

"Any visual yet?" asked Nemo.

Freddie shook his head. "Not yet. You sure it's coming port side?"

"Still coming off port?" asked Nemo into the small microphone.

Nathan's voice crackled in his ears. "Should be coming straight at you."

Nemo jogged back to the control box of the crane and called back to Freddie, "Must be coming in deep. Keep 'em peeled. That's the only meat we have." Then Nemo pressed the green button on the box letting the cable out until the bloodstained sack dropped halfway into the water. Pressing another button, the crane's arm moved from side to side drawing the sack back and forth through the sea. A brown haze flowed through the burlap and trailed on the surface. He then raised the bait bag several feet above the water and paused it, the rectangular crate slowly twirling above. "Where's it now, Nathan?"

"It's slowed, sir. Seems to be hanging around . . . about a hundred, a hundred twenty-five yards off port."

"I've got something!" shouted Freddie. He squinted. "Wait, just a couple sharks."

Nemo ran to the side rail and looked over. He saw two great whites, maybe fourteen feet long, circling beneath the bag. One shark lunged from the surface, tearing a hole in the bottom of the sack leaving a string of beef hanging down through the tear.

"*Oh no you don't!*" Nemo raced back to the control box and quickly raised the sack another five feet.

"That's high enough . . . they can't reach it now," shouted Freddie.

Nemo walked back over and joined Freddie at the side rail. They watched as the two great whites began to swim in larger circles now that the bag was out of reach. One fin disappeared. Suddenly a gray head rose, bursting through the surface. The open mouth aimed at the bag with determination . . . until the great white lost its momentum, missing the sack and crashing into the sea with a tremendous splash.

"This is better than Sea World," said Freddie, snapping off a few shots with his camera.

Nemo growled into the microphone, "What's the location?"

"Sir, it's back to about a hundred seventy-five yards . . . no, wait . . . two hundred yards. Actually, it looks like it's heading in the opposite direction."

Nemo threw his hands up in frustration. He motioned to the chef to stop chumming. Then Nathan's voice returned over the headset. "That's it, sir. Now I've lost it on the monitor. The signal's gone."

Nemo lowered his head and said to Freddie, "Looks like it's going in the opposite direction." The captain stood motionless, gripping the side rail while gazing into the distance. Freddie lowered his camera and rubbed his eyes.

Erick ran up to them. "What happened?"

With an intimidating scowl, Nemo muttered, "It's gone. Looks like we didn't have enough *blood* in the water."

Erick quickly turned and walked away.

Freddie shook his head. "That's strange, the scent was strong enough to attract that pair of great whites." He looked over the side rail and noticed they were gone.

The chef put the plastic top on the chum barrel and made his way toward the stairwell. "I guess I'll go make you gentlemen some sandwiches. How does bologna sound, or would you prefer peanut butter and jelly?"

Ignoring the chef's sarcasm, Nemo walked to the opposite side of the ship. He gazed across the waters off starboard. While scanning the white caps, he murmured into his headset, "Any sign of it?"

His earphones crackled. "No, nothing. How 'bout up there?"

"Same, I'm afraid. All we got were a couple of great whites, and they left as soon as we stopped chumming and raised the bait bag."

Freddie walked over to join Nemo at the starboard rail. "Is he still getting a signal?"

"No, it's gone," said Nemo. "Probably got close enough to realize we were the ones that didn't taste too good earlier."

Freddie looked back to port side and pointed at the crane. "Well, you might want to bring in the bait bag. It's looking a little ragged on bottom, some of the beef's starting to drop out."

After reaching the crane control box, Nemo slowly raised the bait bag all the way up until the wooden crate touched the arm of the crane. Pressing another button, the massive arm slowly swung sideways, bringing the bloodstained sack even with the ship's portside rail. There he paused it. The bait bag swayed thirty feet above the water's surface. "That's close enough for now. I know the second I bring it on deck, Nathan will pick up a signal."

At that moment, he heard crates crashing on the opposite side of the ship. Nemo spun around and saw Freddie kick another crate out of his way while running toward starboard pointing his camera.

"Have you got it?" shouted Nemo.

After snapping a few more shots, Freddie stopped and lowered his camera. "Awww, it's only a dolphin."

Nathan appeared on deck just then and joined Nemo while Freddie jogged back over to port. "Shouldn't you be watching the monitor?" Nemo said.

"Don't worry, Erick's watching it. I left him my headset. He's asked me so many questions, he's as familiar with the equipment as I am."

Nemo leaned against the rail and looked out at the water. "We needed a stronger scent. We almost had it. It was so close—within a couple hundred yards."

Nathan joined the captain's gaze, staring out at the sea. A few moments later, Nathan spoke up. "I've got it! Maybe we could use the chum we have left for bait and try to catch a couple shark—"

Wham! The entire ship violently dipped to starboard.

Nemo looked up as the water's surface raced up to meet his face. He dropped down, hugging the side rail with both arms, water spewing around him. Beside him, unbound crates slid from the deck, crashing into the sea. The ship's momentum shifted in the opposite direction. The starboard side rose high. Clouds appeared in front of Nemo as the ship recoiled, dropping deep port side.

Again, the ship rebounded. The rail dropped forward, hurling toward the sea. Nemo held his breath. The wall of whitewater crashed through the rail and washed him back toward midship. He came to a stop lying on his back, coughing, just in front of the stairwell. The deck vibrated with a loud thud as the submersible toppled on its side, cracking the glass bubble on its nose.

In desperation, Nemo rolled into the stairwell. He grabbed the rail for stability as a loose crate rolled by, narrowly missing him. Before he could get a second hand on the rail, more water gushed into the stairwell and swept him down the stairs. Again, the ship counter-balanced, dropping toward the starboard, throwing him against the opposite wall of the stairwell.

The ship continued to list from side to side until it slowly steadied enough for Nemo to find his feet. He stepped back out onto the main deck. Rubbing his shoulder, he found Nathan in a similar state of confusion. "You okay?"

Without a response, Nathan walked over to the opposite side of the ship. His mouth open, wide eyes looking upward, fixated on the arm of the crane. Nemo turned around, joining Nathan's gaze. The crane was still swaying back and forth with its thick steel arm bent down, facing the water, a foot of severed cable extending from its end.

"It took the bait bag, crate . . . everything all the way up to the arm of the crane! That's got to be thirty-five feet above the surface!" said Nemo, gazing up in disbelief.

Nathan tapped him on the shoulder. "Wait till you take a look at this."

Nemo looked down and saw the mangled side rail bent down onto the deck. He slowly stepped closer. Looking over the bent railing, he saw a huge indentation that ran straight down the hull all the way to the waterline. Shiny metal glistened through a series of long, jagged parallel marks. Nemo walked around the section of bent railing and gasped. "Look at the size of that indentation and all those scrape marks. Its skin must have scraped the paint off!"

"Look at the top of the crane's arm," said Nathan. "The paint's been scraped off there too ... must have been from its nose." He looked around the deck and paused. "Wait a minute—wasn't Freddie over here?"

Pushing a loose crate aside, Nemo spotted a single hand gripping the bottom rail. He looked over and found Freddie. He was wide-eyed and shivering with his free hand clutching the strap of his camera. They quickly pulled him on deck. Still not a word came from his trembling lips. Carefully, they walked him over to midship and leaned him back against the outside wall of the stairwell. His fingers remained locked around the camera strap.

Nemo looked him dead in the eye. "Well, man, did you see it?" He shook him by the shoulders. "Can't you hear me? Did you see it?"

Freddie slowly raised the camera. "I . . . I got it. This time I got it!"

~~~

Huddled in the video cabin, everyone on board anxiously waited behind Freddie while he connected a cable into the computer to download the image from his camera. The second the file's icon appeared on the desktop, Freddie clicked on it.

"What's taking it so long?" asked Nemo in an impatient tone.

"It'll be up in a second, it's a huge file. Come on, baby . . . be there. Be there."

Freddie continued to chant until the screen flushed white. "*Yeeessss!*" Freddie screamed in victory as the enormous underbelly of the creature materialized on screen. At the top of the screen, was a hint of the gray, tiger-striped lower jaw, while just beneath the surface, a wide paddle fin stretched out of frame.

Nemo slapped Freddie on the back. "All right, man! It's just the underbelly, but at least it's something."

Freddie jumped up in excitement. "It was just a hunch I had while shooting that dolphin swimming toward the starboard. When it suddenly made a U-turn, I thought something must have scared it coming from the opposite direction. Then I recalled how quickly the two great whites disappeared from under the bait bag. It wasn't because we lifted it higher from the surface. No way. They sensed what was coming!

"So, I ran back to port. As soon as I got in position, I saw a huge dark shadow coming up fast. It was so big; it looked like the ocean floor was trying to surface! Just as I positioned the camera, an enormous gray blur flew out of the water, swallowed the bait bag, line, crate, and all. Its momentum carried it into the side of the ship just beside me. The impact felt like a bomb going off. And then all I could hear was its skin digging into the metal as the deck dropped from under my feet. Fortunately I was able to hook my arm on the side rail before I went over." Freddie was breathless with excitement and fear. Nemo seemed unfazed by Freddie's revelations and stared at the monitor. "Hmmm, now the only problem is, how are we going to lure it back to the ship? We're out of beef and only have a couple gallons of chum left."

"Wait a minute. You want to lure that thing back? We're lucky the ship's still afloat!" Nathan pointed at the computer screen, his finger shaking. "It looks big in the picture. You should have been down there when I saw it. You . . . you can't bring it back. We'll all be dead. Besides, we got the shot," said Nathan, slamming his fist on his thigh. "Captain, we don't need any more bait!"

"Yeah, I'm with Nathan," Freddie nodded. "The ship can't take another hit from that thing. The photo looks good to me. I vote we make port. Let's set up a press conference in Cape Town . . . or better yet, a bidding war for the photo."

Nemo shook his head. "It's not enough. I want underwater footage. I want to capture the creature alive, moving and swimming. The photo is a good start, but we need more. And not a word of this leaves this ship until we have the beast on film. Understood?" He smiled wickedly at Freddie. "Don't worry. There will be plenty of time for bidding wars."

"Captain, how are we supposed to get underwater footage?" asked Nathan. "You saw the condition of the sub and the crane. Besides, who in his right mind would go down there in a sub that size?"

Nemo shook his head. "I'm not talking about taking the sub down. What I'm planning on doing is using a few of the spare whale cameras. We can attach the suction cups to the hull of the ship. We could use a rope to lower someone down from the side rail with the rescue harness. Then, all they have to do is point the cameras at the bait bag from just below the surface. But we still need bait."

"Well, who's the lucky individual who gets to go down in the water and attach the cameras to the hull?" asked Freddie. "I'm not lining up for that job!"

Nemo looked around the cabin. "We'll worry about that after we figure out the bait problem."

Freddie noted, "If they're down there too long, they *will* be taking care of the bait problem."

"Don't give him any ideas," Nathan muttered. "Maybe it's time to do a little fishing. Simple. We could use the rest of the chum for bait. With any luck, we could probably land a couple of sharks large enough to do the job."

Nemo glanced toward the doorway. "A little dog catching might work better." He grinned menacingly.

Nathan stepped in front of the captain. "Look, how about a deal? I'll be the one to go down and set up the cameras if you'll just leave the boy's dog alone?"

Nemo looked at him in confusion. "But it's just a dog . . . we could get the boy another one."

"You never had any pets when you were a kid, did you?"

"Aw-right! Aw-right! Nemo groaned. I'll leave the boy's mutt alone . . . for now. You just take care of the cameras. But if we don't have any luck *fishing*, we'll revisit this topic."

Erick walked by and stopped in the doorway. Nemo gave him a snarl on his way out. After the captain was safely out of earshot, Erick looked up at Nathan and asked, "What were you guys talking about?"

"Nothing much . . . just fishing strategies."

Chapter 36
BLACK DECEMBER

Kate trailed the squadron of naval helicopters while John stared below at the glistening waters of Hermanus. With every passing minute, he felt a growing sense of unease. He couldn't shake the feeling that they'd missed something. "No, Admiral," John said into his headset, "I just think we're staying too tight to the coast. What if the creature is headed farther out?"

~~~

Inside the lead helicopter, Admiral Henderson gasped. "Look, John," he growled, "we don't have the air power to effectively cover a larger area. We must hold our course and try to corner it. I'm certain the beast will not venture past Cape Point."

John's voice crackled, "What's so significant about Cape Point?"

"That's where the warm waters of the Indian Ocean meet the cold Atlantic. It's an instant twenty-degree temperature drop, and I don't think the creature will find to its liking. Trust me," he said reassuringly, "this creature of yours is living in its final hours." He lowered his voice, "But listen, no matter what happens, we've got to keep a lid on this. The last thing I need is another Black December on my hands."

~~~

Inside Kate's helicopter, John shook his head. "I wish he wouldn't call it *my* creature." He lowered the binoculars. "But what was that part about Black December?"

Kate's eyebrows arced. "That was intense. Mom used to talk about it . . . she was young when it happened." Kate kept one eye on the water while trying to remember. "It was in Natal, December of '57. Six tourists were brutally attacked by great whites. One person was completely bitten in half."

"What did they do?"

"It was an all-out war on sharks. Spotter planes were hired to locate them from the sky. Rewards were offered for every kill. Hotel owners tried all kinds of nets to protect the beaches. Otherwise, they knew no one would ever set foot in the water again.

"Hundreds of sharks were slaughtered. Their carcasses were on the covers of all the local newspapers in an attempt to give the remaining tourist a sense of security. It was like the real life version of *Jaws*, except taken to a further extreme. They even brought in a naval frigate to drop depth charges to thin out the shark population. It was practically a war zone."

"So that's when they started using shark barrier nets?"

Kate nodded. "After Black December, they set up a special anti-shark organization. Back then it was called the Natal Anti-Shark Measures Board, designed to cut down on the number of sharks. But now they've turned their efforts toward protecting the sharks *and* the swimmers, a difficult task. They've set out nearly four hundred nets at forty-six different beaches. So far I'd say they've been quite successful."

Kate gazed down at the water. "But after all the years, the locals still remember Black December and wonder if the nets will be enough to keep it from ever happening again."

John's eyes drifted down to his watch. "I hate to mention this, but . . . do you know what today is?"

"I know," Kate said. "December second."

~~~

"First a bait cutter, then a chum slinger, and now a fisherman!" muttered the chef in a French accent from the stern of the *Nauticus II*. His left hand held a ball of string leading to the water.

"And a poor excuse for one at that!" said a voice from behind. The chef turned around and looked up at the towering figure of Captain Nemo standing with his hand on his hips. "And if no one catches anything soon, you'll be able to add dogcatcher to your long list of professions!"

On his way over to offer the chef some more bait fish, Nathan caught the last part of the conversation. He sat down the bucket of bait and said, "I know what we can do . . . why don't we try the radio and see if any fishing boats are in the area? We can offer to purchase their catch. We could just tell them we need the fish for research we're conducting."

"That might work," grumbled Nemo. "I'm sure there has to be someone out here having better luck than the cook here."

The chef looked back and said, "I don't see you doing any better!"

Nemo glared at the chef. "I haven't dropped a line yet, and I'm still tied with you."

~~~

With the sun sinking toward the horizon, Kate continued to head west, following the squadron of helicopters. John diligently searched the sea through binoculars.

But he couldn't shake the sense of hopelessness gnawing at his gut.

After a few moments, he lowered the binoculars. "I'm getting a bad feeling."

"I know," Kate said. "It's kind of like when you're on the freeway and think you missed your exit, but just keep driving." She glanced over. "Think we should go back?"

"We've been searching for four hours and haven't seen as much as a whale carcass. And that's Cape Point just ahead. There's no way the pliosaur moved this far since last night." John's frustration grew, "We missed it; I can feel it. All along, the admiral has had us searching too close to the coast—too shallow. The creature has headed farther out."

Kate worked the stick, banking the chopper into a turn. "I'll tell the admiral we're headed back for fuel. There's still time . . . we can look around the Dyer Channel, then work our way out before dark."

The chopper turned tail and headed east, following the coast.

~~~

From the ship's bridge, Nathan continued to make calls to any boats that may be on the same frequency. "This is the *Nauticus II*. We're a research vessel in need of some baitfish. We're trying to attract a rare species of marine life. We'll pay top dollar for anyone out there with a good catch. Hear that, anglers—top dollar for your catch. Any takers?"

"*Nauticus II*, this is *Jimbo's Baby*. I read you!"

"*Jimbo*, you have anything on board that can help us out? Over."

"Exactly what kind of fish you looking for? Over."

"Black marlin, sailfish, tuna, pretty much anything will work. Over."

"We're on our way out, haven't even dropped a line, but if you have a few hours, you can call us later. Over."

"Okay, thanks anyway. We'll let you know. Out."

After repeating the message half a dozen times, Nathan began to tire. He sat down to take a sip from his water bottle. He looked through every window on the bridge and still didn't see any other boats on the horizon. "Well, it sounded like a good idea at the time," he muttered.

~~~

Kate guided the Aribus H135 through a long, sweeping turn. Giving the binoculars a break, John scanned the waters below with the naked eye. After covering hundreds of miles of coastline, they were finally back at the Dyer Channel.

"Well, here we are!" Kate announced through her headset. "After searching all day. . . right back where we bloody started!"

As they moved into the channel, John could make out Geyser Rock, a brown, rocky island housing thousands of Cape fur seals. Across from it were the long flat sands of Dyer Island. The rocky outcrops and inland areas were speckled with thousands of cormorants, gulls, jackass penguins, and other marine bird species native to the island. In the background, silhouetted mountaintops rose majestically behind the small town of Gans Bay.

He was amazed at how much smaller the channel looked from the air rather than from the old fishing boat he and Vic had taken out. At a lower altitude, he could make out a stretch of boat debris collected on the rocky shoreline. It was surreal, John thought, starring at the same waters that almost claimed his life less than twenty-four hours ago.

"You're one lucky bugger!" Kate shook her head, looking at the debris.

John reached out to the radio switch on the console to connect with Tom, who was still with the squadron. It had been a couple hours, and there was still an outside chance that the Navy had come up with something. Switching frequencies, John paused, listening.

Kate veered the chopper around, "There's still a good bit of daylight left. . . . guess we'll take a look farther—"

John held up a finger, listening intently to his headset. Again, he listened to the ship's plea for bait.

He looked curiously at Kate, "Listen. There's something about that call. *Nauticus II* . . . I saw that ship on the news last night. They were researching the giant squid. Now they're making calls for bait fish to lure a rare species of marine life."

"I hate to break it to you, but a giant squid *is* a rare species of marine life," assured Kate. "They probably just ran out of bait. Squid do feed on fish."

"Thanks for the marine biology lesson," John said. "But if I were looking for bait for a giant squid, I would have said *'giant squid,'* not 'a rare species of marine life.' Just listen."

Kate listened in as the ship repeated its request for bait.

John gave a suspicious grin. "A funny feeling tells me they've seen something."

Kate's eyes lit up at the thought.

"Only one way to find out," John grinned and motioned Kate to patch him through. Kate flipped a switch on the instrument cluster, and John spoke into his headset, "*Nauticus II*, think we can help you out with the bait. What are your coordinates?" He looked at Kate. "Or where are you in reference to the Dyer Channel?"

He listened for a moment, then gave Kate an *I-knew-it* grin. "Eight miles south, straight out," he confirmed. "And what species of marine life are you trying to attract . . . reptilian, huh?" He again grinned at Kate. "Well, this *marine reptile* wouldn't happen to be about eighty feet long and sixty-five million years old, would it?"

~~~

From a white-knuckle grip, Nemo released the port side rail of the *Nauticus II*. He was beside himself. He swung his gaze from the setting sun and locked on Freddie. "A living pliosaur, I can't believe it! But it had to be . . . it's the only logical explanation. And this Paxton character has one of its teeth—all nineteen gorgeous inches worth." He looked at the camera dangling from Freddie's neck. "And we've got the only photograph of it." Nemo grabbed Freddie by the arm, looked him dead in the eye. "But I guarantee you, my friend . . . by sunrise, we'll have much more than that!"

Nemo's crooked smile faded when he saw Nathan appear on deck. "What do you think you're doing?"

"What?"

What are you doing topside? You should be making calls for bait!"

"But the man you talked to . . . Paxton. He's on the way with bait and chum."

"I know that," Nemo snarled, "but they had to refuel first. By the time they arrive, the pliosaur could be too far off to pick up a scent. Now get to it!"

~~~

From the bridge of the *Nauticus II*, Nathan continued to make calls for bait. With this Paxton character on the way with chum, he knew it was a complete waste of time. But there was no arguing with the captain. "I repeat, this is the *Nauticus II*. We're a research vessel in need of some baitfish. We're trying to attract a rare species of marine life. We'll pay top dollar for anyone out there with a good catch. Any takers?"

"*Nauticus II*, this is *Jimbo's Baby* again!"

"*Jimbo*, you having any luck today? Over."

"More than you, it sounds like. Just landed one drop-dead gorgeous black marlin! Over."

"Great! That'll work fine. Over!"

"Just give me your coordinates, and I'm on my way."

After relaying the ship's position Nathan sat down, content. He racked the mike and eased back, tempted to call it a day. But after thinking it over, he had no idea how long it would take *Jimbo* to reach the ship—he hadn't thought to ask where *Jimbo's Baby* was—so he decided to give it one more shot. The moment he picked up the mike, a voice came over the radio, breaking through the static. "Exactly what kind of creature you trying to attract?"

Nathan quickly keyed the mike. "Actually it's of the reptilian variety, so we're really not that picky. Any type of fish or even meat would be—" Nathan was interrupted by Freddie and Nemo entering the bridge, bickering.

"We can't go in for bait!" the captain raised his voice. "We've got to attract the beast while it's still in the area. We just can't risk leaving the area."

"But a creature that size needs a lot of food!" Freddie's tone was even louder. "That sixty-five-pound bag of beef was probably just enough to whet its appetite. Besides, we're not even getting a signal from the homing device any more. The pliosaur's probably miles away from here. We're going to need a strong scent to lure it back."

Nathan turned around. "Could you guys hold it down? I'm trying to remedy the problem now." He turned his attention back to the mike, just then realizing he still had the button pushed in. "Sorry about the shouting match in the background. So, do you think you can help us out?"

"What are your coordinates?" asked the unidentified voice.

After giving their position, Nathan asked, "So, what kind of bait do you have?"

The unidentified voice ignored the question. "You said reptilian . . . exactly what species?"

Nathan paused, as if thrown by the question. Then he keyed the mike. "I really don't have time to go into it. Do you have any bait on board or not? Over." No response.

Nathan stared curiously at the mike. He switched frequencies and began to repeat his call.

~~~

Fifteen miles east of the *Nauticus II*, a dark hand racked a mike. After glancing over at Kolegwa with a grim smile, Kota looked down at the compass. He turned the wheel and adjusted the small boat's course thirty degrees northwest.

~~~

Staring ahead through the helicopter's windshield, John saw the ocean appear beyond the trees. The sky grew darker. He was pumped, adrenalin racing as he spoke into his headset. "That's right, Admiral, apparently the pliosaur swallowed the transmitter when it attacked the whale. The signal is intermittent, but they still have the best chance to locate the creature." He listened for a moment. "Yes, we're headed to the *Nauticus II* now, loaded with chum. We'll relay you the coordinates the moment we pick up a signal. Out."

John lowered the mike on his headset and looked at Kate. "Admiral Henderson is up to speed, although he's not so optimistic. He says these transmitters weren't designed to be swallowed, questions how long the signal will last, or if the transmitter will even stay inside the creature."

Kate rolled her eyes. "Like he has the master plan. After flying around blindly with him all day, my money's on the transmitter."

John nodded his agreement as the treetops ended, and they soared out to sea.

~~~

Struggling, perspiration dripping from his forehead, Nathan slid the last section of black marlin into a burlap sack. Freddie stood and leaned back against a large crate on the ship's stern. "Whew! That was one big fish. Glad your calls for bait finally paid off." He wiped his brow, "Maybe now Nemo'll lighten up."

"Wouldn't count on it," grunted Nathan, tightening the clamp around the sack's end. He came to his feet beside Freddie. The two looked like they'd pulled a double shift in a slaughterhouse. Shirtless and slick with sweat, they were covered in blood up to their elbows.

Freddie took a whiff of himself. "Wow! I smell worse than that bait sack. I'd better get cleaned up before Nemo tries to affix my tucas to the crane."

After Freddie disappeared below deck, Nathan grabbed the long cable extending down from the crane. Guiding the cable toward the bait sack, he thought he heard something. It was a voice coming from starboard. Again, a faint voice echoed from beyond the rail. "Hello, over here! Over here!"

Nathan let go of the cable and curiously approached the rail. In front of the setting sun, he saw a small white boat about thirty yards out. Someone waved from the vessel. As the tiny fishing boat drew closer, Nathan could make out two people on board, both of them tall and black. The first man was clad in a maroon sailing jacket and khaki pants. The larger of the two looked like he'd dressed in the dark with his skintight, multicolored shirt and lime-green pants.

The boat continued to approach, and the man in the sailing jacket shouted, "We're low on fuel! We don't have enough to make it to shore. Can you help us out?"

Captain Nemo walked up behind Nathan. "What do we have here? Someone else bringing us bait?"

"No, I think they're low on fuel."

Nemo grumbled on his way back to the stairwell, "What do we look like, a filling station? Give them just enough to get to shore, and send them on their way!"

Nathan motioned the fishing boat back to the stern, toward the ladder. The man in the sailing jacket tossed up the bowline, and Nathan tied off the boat. Wiping his bloody hands on a towel, Nathan greeted the men as they stepped on deck.

"Thanks for letting us board," said the man in the maroon jacket, giving a firm handshake. In spite of his overpowering presence, his eyes expressed a gentle gratitude. "We were on our way back in, and . . . well, I guess we underestimated the amount of fuel we would need. Oh, pardon me, I forgot to introduce myself. I'm Kota and this is Kolegwa. So, do you think you could help us out?"

Nathan tossed them each a bottle of water from a cooler, then took one for himself. Kota nodded his appreciation as he looked curiously around the deck.

Young Erick walked up with his dog Rex at his side. Nathan introduced him to their new guests, then turned to Erick. "Could you go below and ask Freddie to bring up a couple of the five-gallon gas drums?"

The boy looked up through his thick glasses, "No problem. I can do it." He called to Rex, "Come on, boy!" They ran back to the stairwell.

When Nathan turned back to his guests, he found Kota wandering around the stern. The powerful figure approached the crane and looked down at the bloody burlap sack lying on the deck. "Looks like you're getting ready to do some pretty serious fishing."

"Yeah, we're out here conducting research on sharks. Studying the population, feeding habits, that type of thing," replied Nathan.

"Sharks, you say!" Kota smiled. He noticed the bent side rail and walked over to examine it closer. Kolegwa followed close behind. "My, my! What in the world did this?" Kota looked over the rail at the enormous indentation in the hull.

Nathan scrambled for words, then blurted out, "It was a ship . . . ah, we got tangled up when docking the other day and got rammed from the side. We were fortunate not to take on water." His tone sounded unconvincing, even to himself.

"And you left port with it that way? A bit risky, no?" asked Kota, eyes narrowing. "Guess that's what knocked over the mini-sub on the stern too, huh?"

After a couple minutes of silence, Nathan was relieved to see Erick back on deck, followed by Freddie carrying two gas cans.

After a long drink of water, Kota leaned back against the rail. The harmless look in his eyes that Nathan had first noticed was now gone, replaced by some smoldering sense of confidence. "So. Exactly what species of shark are you researching? Do you think you could show us around? I've always found sharks to be quite interesting." He paused, took another sip, then gave a smile—*a fairly wicked smile*, thought Nathan. Kota added, "But I'm even more fond of reptiles . . . especially the really large ones!"

Nearly choking on his water, Nathan said hastily, "I'd like to show you around, but I'm afraid we're running behind schedule. We've got a lot to finish up before dark. So, if you don't mind . . ."

Kota glared at him, well past the moment of politeness, then said, "Oh, sorry for the inconvenience. We also need to be on our way. Wouldn't want to, as they say, wear out our welcome."

Once escorted back to the stern, Kota and Kolegwa slowly descended the ladder. Kota looked over his shoulder and noticed the two gas cans already loaded on their boat. He looked up at Freddie. "Appreciate you loading them on board for us."

Freddie gave a friendly wave. He then whispered to Nathan, "Nemo told me to load those gas cans. Anything to get those two out of here."

Nathan untied the bowline and tossed it to Kolegwa. After pouring gas into the boat's fuel tank, Kota sat down at the helm and fired the engine. Then as the small fishing boat pulled away, Kota raised his hand and shouted back, "Good luck with your research. And be careful...dangers lurk everywhere in these waters, whether you can see them or not."

As the small boat drove away into the African sunset, Freddie looked at Nathan. "That was really strange."

"What do you mean? Their curiosity in what we're doing."

"No, not that," said Freddie. "When I loaded the gas cans onto their boat, I noticed about a half-dozen gas cans by the stern . . . and three of them were completely full."

Chapter 37
DEVIL'S CLAW

Peering over the mike on his headset, John studied the darkening horizon. "Kate, looks like we're running short on daylight. What's your ETA on the *Nauticus II?*"

Kate squinted at the instrument cluster. "About twenty minutes, tops."

John lowered his gaze through the passenger's side window, deep in thought. Now, with the Navy's cooperation and the assistance of the *Nauticus II,* he finally had the means to locate and destroy the beast. Staring into the inky blackness, a familiar tingling rose in the pit of his stomach. Was it the anticipation of having the pliosaur dead in his sights? Or a fateful warning signal that something was horribly wrong? *Relax,* he thought. *You overthink everything.* He eased his head back against the seat and let his eyes drift shut.

John felt something hit his leg. Kate again slapped him on the thigh and her voice rang in his headset. "John, wake up. I just received a call from the *Nauticus II.* They picked up a signal."

John wiped the sleep from his eyes. "Where?"

"About two miles west of us. Near a place called Devil's Claw. It's a local hotspot for whale watching."

Minutes later, John noticed a light in the distance. Soaring closer, a towering metal framework emerged from the mist. The light tower reached down to where a jagged mound of rock stood above the waves.

"We should be getting close," Kate said. She squinted at the windshield. "What's that? ... there, at two o'clock?"

"What do you mean, that rock?"

"No," Kate said. "That's what the locals call Devil's Claw. Taken many a ship to the deep sea floor. That's why they put that light on it." They drew closer. "Thought I saw something behind it."

Gliding over the rock, John saw something white contrasting against the dark, hazy sea. Kate hovered over the object, the searchlight cutting through the haze. Lowering altitude, the downdraft from the rotors swept back the fog to reveal the glistening flank of a sperm whale. Behind the lifeless eye was a colossal wound—and not a clean bite mark either. It looked like an enormous clawed hand had raked across the creature's flank. Long shards of bloody blubber spilled out from the deep incisions and drifted hideously on the waves.

Kate lowered altitude until they were ten feet above the whale.

John looked into the lifeless eye that seemed to be peering up at him. "We'd better call this in to the admiral. What are our coordinates?"

Kate glanced at the instrument cluster, but when she looked back to the whale, she froze. The muscles beneath its pale flesh rippled, and the huge fluke swept across the mist.

"It's still alive!" she gasped.

That's when it hit John: *this just happened.*

He swung his gaze frantically. Then looking thirty yards out from the whale, his heart all but stopped. He saw the tip of an enormous frill gliding above the fog, then he lost sight of it. "Get out of here!" he roared into his headset.

Before Kate could move the stick, the giant reptilian head burst from the sea—the canyon-like jaws spreading before the windshield.

Kate pulled up, and the creature missed the cockpit, but still there was a violent jolt. In falling, the spiked teeth snared the landing gear, hurling the helicopter straight toward the sea.

"I can't save this!" Kate shouted as the clouds turned into haze-covered waves. Another violent jolt and Kate buckled forward as white water crashed through the pilot's side door. John's vision filled with bubbles. He clung to his last breath as a coolness gushed over him. Through the windscreen, all he could make out was pebbled skin—the main rotor twirling and bending in the passing water. Plummeting deeper, there was a sense of release and the creature's back rolled away from the windscreen. But the craft kept tumbling toward the sea floor.

Crash! The helicopter hit something, sending the cockpit into a spin.

A bang—a loud shriek of metal and everything stopped. The craft was leaned toward the pilot's side. Just above John's head, a three-foot pocket of air was trapped in the bulbous windscreen. Gaining his senses, he un-clicked his seatbelt. In the dim light, he saw that Kate was unconscious. Her long hair swirled around her headset as bubbles trailed from her mouth. Unhooking Kate's seatbelt, John frantically pulled her lifeless body up until her face breached the air pocket. She regained consciousness, screaming and flailing her arms.

"Just breathe," John said, doing his best to restrain her. "That's it. Easy…easy." A few breaths and her eyes fluttered with life. "Where? Where are…?"

As the silt cleared, they saw that the chopper had come to rest at the bottom of some type of rock formation. Slowly, the sea floor materialized between the jagged columns of stone. "Tell me this is a nightmare." John nodded. "But I'm afraid we're wide awake."

"One more question. Does it know we're…?" The surface light disappeared and they both looked up. Just beyond a rotor blade, they found a gigantic lantern eye staring into the cockpit. At close range, the eye was almost hypnotic, like a giant red sapphire with the exception of the hideous black pupil in its center.

The red orb swiftly pulled away.

Kate screamed. The huge jaws swung down at them—opening and closing—grinding against the rocks. The horrible serpentine tongue slithered in the silt. A shower of rocks rolled down, pinging against the plexi bubble. The jaws closed and the head twisted from side to side, burrowing deeper.

Closer.

The interlocked teeth paused just above the rotor blade.

"I don't think it can get to us," John clung to Kate. Her breaths grew more shallow as if she was going into shock. "Take it easy," John whispered. "If it could reach us, it would have."

The duo now knelt in the passenger's seat so that their head and shoulders remained in the pocket of air. He could feel Kate shivering. John tried to hide it, but he was every bit as terrified as she was. How their paradox had changed, he thought. Only moments ago, he was so pumped to destroy the creature. Now, in the blink of an eye, he was fighting for sheer survival...his next breath.

"I'm sorry." Kate was frantic. "I shouldn't have taken us so low over the whale. I didn't know."

"Shh. It's no one's fault. But did you get the call off; the whale's coordinates to the Navy?"

"I didn't get the chance."

John looked around the windscreen. "It doesn't matter. There's not enough time to wait for them anyway." The air pocket seemed smaller. The oxygen was definitely being depleted faster than they were consuming it. *It's leaking out.*

The cockpit grew brighter and the surface light returned. "It's pulling away," Kate whispered with a glimmer of hope. Then, off to their left, the glowing red orb reappeared between two mounds of rock. It was looking for another way in. The eye then pulled away, replaced by passing gray-striped skin until it too was gone.

A moment later, the surface light again disappeared as the creature passed.

John glanced back to the flooded cargo bay. "Do you have any diving equipment aboard?"

"Yes." Kate's eyes brightened. "I have a tank, fins, and a mask. Oh, and a spear gun."

"Good." John slipped off his boots and dropped from the air pocket. Pushing off from the passenger's seat, he glided into the cargo bay. Apparently, most of the contents had been ejected through the open doorway on the way down. The crate of depth charges was gone. No air tank. All that remained of the dive gear was a single fin and the spear gun. One of the chum barrels remained strapped to the wall. Looking up, he saw a bundled life raft floating against the ceiling. He again glanced at the spear gun. *Right...like that would stop it.*

He hovered in the cargo bay's open doorway. From there, he had a clear view of how the helicopter was situated. The rock formation holding the craft was about forty feet above the sea floor. Further behind him was a ridge that dropped down another fifty yards or so to the deep sea floor, where he saw an old freighter lying on its side. About forty yards north of the chopper, he saw the Devil's Claw reaching up from the seabed like a giant stalagmite.

Swimming out from the doorway, he peered around a rock formation and there it was. The pliosaur was sitting on the sea floor about sixty yards away. Its red eyes were fixed on the helicopter as streams of surface light rolled across its gray, tiger-striped hide.

It's waiting us out.

A large great white glided up from the ravine. It caught sight of the monstrosity sprawled across the sea floor and darted off in the opposite direction. *I heard that,* thought John. Backing toward the chopper, he noticed the missing dive fin lying in the sand. Not far from the fin, there was a twinkling. Two of the depth charges were lying about half way between the craft and the creature.

John resurfaced in the air pocket.

"Did you find the dive tank?"

"No." John caught his breath. "And to try and swim out of here is certain death. We have to kill that thing."

"How?" Kate asked. "With what?"

"The depth charges may not be off the table," John said. "The creature is waiting on the sea floor about sixty yards out. Right between us and it are two of the depth charges." He took a breath, "If I can just lure the creature over them..."

"Lure it? How?"

"We still have one barrel of chum," John explained. "I can roll it down the embankment toward the depth charges. It's really rocky, should easily knock the lid off. The scent should draw the pliosaur right over them."

"How do you plan to detonate them? You can't bloody well push the button and run off."

"Your spear gun is still back there. If I get close enough to get a good shot, it should set one off."

"It should," Kate added. "Those aren't regular spears. They're tipped with bang-sticks."

"Bang-stick tips?"

"Yes, the shafts are tipped with 12 gauge shotgun shells, like a bang-stick. Had a close call with a shark one time, then got those buggers."

"Good," John said. "The depth charges are also in close enough proximity that if one detonates, they should both go off."

Kate gasped. "But if you miss. What happens then? You've seen how fast that thing can swim. You won't have a prayer."

John glanced around the dwindling air pocket. "Listen," he locked eyes with her. "If I miss, you make a break for the surface. The diversion might be enough for you to make it up to the top of Devil's Claw."

Kate's mouth fell open. "This is insane! You can't risk your life on one shot."

He gestured the rising water level. "We're out of options." Without giving Kate time for rebuttal, John dropped from the air pocket.

Swimming into the cargo bay, he unstrapped the barrel of chum from the wall and rolled it through the doorway. Outside the craft, he hoisted the barrel over a rocky ledge and down it went. Bouncing and tumbling over the rocks, the barrel hit the seabed and rolled to within thirty feet of the depth charges. *Perfect,* he thought. But not a drop of blood leaked out. The lid remained fully intact.

All the while, the monster did not move.

John resurfaced in the cockpit. "What's the deal with these lids?" he gasped. "The barrel bounced all the way down to the seabed and the lid never came off."

"They lock down. You have to flip the lever on each side."

"Good to know," John muttered. His heart fluttered when he saw that the air pocket had been reduced to about two feet deep. "Relax. There's still plan B." He winked and inhaled a deep breath.

What's plan…?" Kate's words faded as he dropped beneath the water. Gliding into the cargo bay, he snatched up the spear gun from the floor, noting that it was loaded with an additional spear attached to its underside.

He slipped down over the ledge of the rock formation, toward the sea floor. Staying low, John moved from one coral formation to another, doing his best to remain out of the pliosaur's view. Now that he was on the same level as the creature, it was nearly impossible to gauge its distance. He paused behind a large rock. At this close range, the beast looked absolutely enormous. The giant head tilted slightly and a cloud of bubbles rose from one of its nostrils. John ducked. He hoped that the monster wasn't aware of his presence. *At least not yet.*

Not quite close enough, thought John. He peered around the rock. The chum barrel was about twenty yards away, the closest depth charge not far behind it. He noticed some chum seeping through where the barrel's lid had been dented.

The giant's snout rose slightly. But the pliosaur did not move from the sea floor. A small stream of blood continued to rise from the barrel. But it wasn't enough to attract the creature. *Guess you're smarter than you look.*

Okay—just need to get a little closer, John thought. *Then I'll show myself and lure it right over the depth charges.* He spotted a large coral head within ten yards of the depth charges. *Perfect. From there I can't miss.*

Like a runner easing off of second base to steal third, John crept out from behind the rock, toward the coral head.

The giant's neck muscles tensed and the head turned. The eyes fixed on him. A quiver of excitement seemed to rush through the monster's body.

John froze. *Oh, crap.*

The muscles beside the neck rippled and the forefins jetted up from the sand. Cupping the water, the enormous paddle fins thrust backward, propelling the beast forward. And the realization struck John. The creature was always aware of his presence—it was just waiting for him to get closer.

At first, John remained perfectly still, staring at the charging behemoth like a deer in oncoming headlights. Then, doing his best to ignore the approaching giant, he steadied the spear gun on the depth charge. If he missed, he knew there would be no time to reload—there would be no time for anything.

The monster soared closer—swelling in size.

The hideous jaws fell agape.

Its shadow neared the depth charges.

John fired.

The spear streaked through the water and he dove behind the rock.

Kaboom! The first depth charge went off, igniting the other one simultaneously. An enormous eruption of rocks and sediment rose in front of the beast, sending it careening off course. The giant slammed into the seabed, it's head buckling back as its right forefin plowed into the sand, spraying up huge clouds of sediment.

John ducked as the shockwave spewed kelp and sediment over the rock. A beat later, he reluctantly stood. A spiraling cloud of blood was in place of the chum barrel. Like metallic snow, hundreds of dead fish twinkled on their way down to the sea floor. Beneath it all, he saw the leviathan lying still on the seabed.

~~~

Back inside the cockpit, Kate regained her balance after the helicopter jostled from the blast. More rocks and sediment splattered down onto the windscreen. She looked in the direction of the explosion tempted to cheer, but caught herself. Instead, she just waited, shivering in the cool water.

~~~

Hurrying back to the chopper in guarded victory, John froze. Amidst the falling plume of sediment, the horrible silhouette slowly rose from the sea floor. The pliosaur shook its head—clouds of silt shooting out from between its giant teeth. Rocks and dead fish rolled off its armor-plated back.

The head turned and its eyes locked on John. The monster dropped its head and pumped its fins furiously, crossing the sea floor.

Like a fleeing crayfish, John scurried back into the rock formation. He rose in the air pocket, startling Kate as he gasped madly for air. Kate grabbed him by the shoulders. "Well—is it?"

John finally caught his breath to answer. But he didn't need to. The surface light disappeared. Her will to survive finally broken, Kate just closed her eyes. "No!" John demanded. "Don't you give—" But his words were muted by the monster's fury.

This time the attacked was unrelenting.

The colossal head charged down between the rocks, snapping its jaws.

When it could move no further, the mouth closed and jolted forward, twisting and fighting for every inch. The creature paused and retreated, fading behind the silt.

The closed mouth, then again lunged toward the craft, bursting through the cloud of silt. Bubbles streamed from its nostrils.

The jaws opened slightly, nipping at the water. The beast roared in rage, sending a spray of bubbles around the cockpit. Some of the bubbles entered through the missing pilot's side door and rose into the air pocket. "Disgusting," Kate gasped. "You can smell its breath."

The jaws drew closer.

Closer!

Kate yelped.

This time, the teeth of the lower jaw hit the rotor blade and pressed it down to the windscreen. The billowing silt grew red with blood. The creature was thrashing its jaws so violently it had abraded its skin. And just that quickly, it stopped. The jaws closed and the interlocked teeth pulled away, fading behind the swirling red haze.

Then, as the silt cleared, they saw the eye peering down at them from a further distance. Shards of torn flesh hung down from its abraded skin.

The head rolled back and disappeared behind the rocks.

There was a moment of silence, and then *wham!* The chopper—the entire rock formation shook. More rocks pinged against the windscreen as the giant again slammed its head into the rock formation, as if trying to pry them loose.

Kate looked up. "If Plan B was to tick him off, I'd say you succeeded."

Another hit and the chopper jostled, slipping down in the rocks.

"It's going to knock down the entire rock formation, chopper and all!" Kate gasped.

"We have to divert its attention," John said.

"How?"

"I'm open to suggestions." John glanced back at the cargo bay. "I'm going to try something." With that, he dove into the back of the craft. Pushing a garbage bag aside, he spotted the bundled life raft pressed against the ceiling.

Wham! Another jolt shook the chopper. A shower of rocks and sediment fell down behind the open doorway.

He grabbed the raft and shoved it through the doorway, pulling the ripcord. A blast of bubbles, and the orange life raft unfolded. John swam just outside the cargo bay doorway, watching the raft race up toward the surface. All of the sudden, everything went dark as the snout and then the vast underbelly rose from behind the rock formation, soaring up from the seabed. Two pumps of its fins, and the monster was on the raft. Bubbles enveloped the beast's head as it chomped down on the raft, thrashing about like a dog shaking a chew toy.

The leviathan's attention eventually returned to the rock formation, the shredded raft hanging from its jaw. And then it seemed to register something else; the red haze falling around it. The beast was in a swath of blood from the whale it had left mortally wounded on the surface. Spreading its jaws, the creature snatched the whale from the surface and carried it down to the seabed. In a poof of bloody silt, the lifeless whale hit the sand and the monster settled down behind it. Through the scarlet haze, John could still see the lantern eyes peering in his direction.

John resurfaced in the air pocket. "It worked," Kate said. "I saw it go up and get the whale. We can swim for it." Panting, John shook his head. He barely had the heart to tell her. "It's not safe…it's still watching us."

Kate glanced at the windscreen only inches above her head, then at the water level at her neck. "No. No," she gasped. "We have to swim for it now!" Trembling, she looked around their tight confinement. "I can't die like this."

John's eyes darted, his mind spinning. There had to be another way out.

"Why didn't you bring the life raft in here and cut it open?" Kate pleaded. "We could have used the oxygen...a little more time."

"You can't breathe it," John said. "It's filled with gas, usually nitrogen and..." And then something occurred to him. "Where's the chopper's battery located?"

Kate glared at him. "I doubt you'll be able to jump start it."

"Where is it?" John demanded. "When batteries hit salt water, they..."

"It's in the aft avionics bay."

"Just show me!" John hollered.

Kate nodded. "Follow me," she said and dropped below the water. Gliding between the seats, she lead him to a compartment in the back of the cargo bay. Above it was a tear in the wall that looked out into the sea.

Swinging open the door, she quickly unscrewed a wing nut on the battery case, and lifted the plastic cover. Bubbles spewed everywhere, rising from the battery terminals and escaping through the hole in the side of the craft.

They swam back to the cockpit and surfaced in the air pocket. Kate gulped the air. "I get it. When the battery hits water, it somehow makes oxygen."

John explained. "The positive electrical charge hits salinity and the reaction creates oxygen. The other side, the negative terminal creates hydrogen."

"Yeah, that's what I said." Kate looked at the raising water level. "But how does it help us? We've got to get out of here."

He raised one of the plastic garbage bags from the cargo bay. "We're taking it with us." Kate glared at him with uncertainty. "This is feasible," John insisted. "I'll fill it with oxygen from the positive battery terminal. Then we'll breathe from it."

"Come on," Kate said. "That rubbish only works in the movies. Besides, the creature will still see us."

"It won't." John broke down his full plan. "The pliosaur is on the sea floor just south of the rock formation we're in. Devil's Claw is about forty yards north of us. If we exit from the north side and stay close to the seabed, we should be able to reach the base of Devil's Claw without being detected. Once we're on the north side of Devil's Claw, the mountain itself will block us from the creature's view. Then it's a straight shot up to the surface.

He could tell Kate had trouble focusing. Her eyes were glassy, confused.

"What if the creature comes up during this? We...we'll be in plain view."

"Try not to fixate on that," John said. The water level rose to her cheeks and Kate's lower lip started trembling. She looked around in panic. She was coming apart.

John knew she was on the verge of shutting down. For this to work, he had to get her to focus, or they were dead. He took a firm grip of her cold shoulders. "Listen Kate. Just focus on me. You've got this—right?" Kate gave a nod, but her eyes remained blank. John clicked the SAT phone onto her belt and handed her the reloaded spear gun.

"I'm going to fill the bag with air." He spoke loud and clear. "Then I'll give you the signal to follow me. But before you leave the air pocket, take several deep breaths. Right?" He searched her eyes for a trace of coherency.

She gave him a quick kiss on the cheek. John planted a long one square on her lips. He then held her face and looked her in the eye. "That won't be the last one...I promise."

A fire rose in Kate's eyes, and her face grew stern. "Well, what are we hanging around here for?"

A deep breath, and John dropped from the air pocket. Once back in the cargo area, he pushed the sack into the aft avionics bay and held it above the bubbles rising from the positive battery terminal. The bag grew taunt with air and he motioned for Kate to follow him.

The duo exited through the cargo bay doorway. Outside, and half-walking and swimming, they made their way through the towering rocks, to the north side of the helicopter. All the while, John kept a death grip on the bottom of the sack; their lifeline. Their last hope.

He noticed his feet getting light on the sand. *Oh crap.* Raising from the sea floor, he realized that he must have over-filled the bag with oxygen. Kate looked back and saw him. She lunged up to grab his foot. But he slipped away, taking flight like Marry Poppins. Just short of rising above the helicopter and into the creature's view, John loosened his grip on the bottom of the sack. A belch of bubbles from the bag and John dropped back down to the seabed.

Kate glared back at him and shook her head. She picked up the spear gun then continued to lead the way through the myriad of rocks.

Clear of the rock formation, they proceeded north across the sea floor. The mountainous Devil's Claw towered before them. They were now about twenty yards from the chopper and fully committed to the plan. John's forearms started to burn. But he kept both hands clamped around the sack, knowing that just one mistake; one slip and it was over. They would be forced to surface within the pliosaur's view.

Kate turned to him. The panic in her eyes told him she needed a breath. He nodded toward the bottom of the bag. Keeping a firm grip, he opened the bottom of the sack just enough for Kate to slip her face inside. The bag contracted and expanded three times, and Kate cautiously removed her face from the bag, her hair swirling with the current. Carefully, John raised the sack above his face and did the same.

The two shuffled across the rocky seabed, only stopping when necessary for a few precious breaths. A school of kob fish fled from their path. Were they scurrying off because of he and Kate's presence, or was something coming up behind them? Either way, John refused to look back. If the creature had already seen them, he knew there would be no point.

Passing an enormous coral head, they reached the base of Devil's Claw. Kate turned to him and her eyes shot open. This time, John knew she wasn't in need of air; she was looking up. She trained the spear gun on something behind him. Panic seized John's body and he dropped to the seabed, struggling to keep a firm grip on the sack. Rolling onto his back, he looked up to see the passing underbelly of a great white.

Seriously Kate—a shark! John rose to his knees in a cloud of silt. As the shark again sailed by, Kate took aim with the spear gun. And a thought crossed John's mind. He frantically strode toward Kate, shaking his head. He knew that if one of the exploding spear tips found its mark, it would surely alert the pliosaur. Kate's eyes flared with realization. She quickly nodded and lowered the spear gun. One more close pass, and the great white fluttered off and disappeared over the ledge to the deep sea floor. John glared at Kate and they carried on.

Finally, they were on the north side of Devil's Claw, and out of the monster's view. John looked up the mountainous rock to where it pierced the waters surface. *Now, it's just a one hundred foot swim straight up.* He nodded to Kate. His forearm muscles on fire, he opened the sack for Kate to take a final breath before the long ascent. This time, Kate kept her face inside the bag much longer. After about four or five rapid breaths, her breathing subsided. *That's it Kate, nice and easy,* John thought. *Don't panic. You're doing just fine.*

Steadying the sack, John had his own panic to contend with. His oxygen-starved lungs started burning more than his forearms. *Come on, Kate.* He needed a breath—and he needed it now. Kate finally drew her face from the sack, but in rising, her spear gun snared the plastic bag pulling it from John's right hand. The sack completely upended, its entire contents escaping in one large bubble.

John's eyes flared in horror. He could only watch as his only chance for survival drifted up toward the surface. Dropping the empty sack, he sprang up from a rock and swam like mad. Reaching the bubble, he pierced it with his head and inhaled until the bubble escaped.

On a partial breath, John made a mad dash for the surface. He ascended beside the rocky mountain, swimming and springing from one rock ledge to another. The air bubble just above him, Kate just beneath him. He stroked harder; his lungs were on fire. Still, the surface light seemed so far away. *Am I even half-way there?* Then just when he thought he couldn't make it something happened. The small breath he'd taken seemed to somehow sustain him. The minute amount of compressed air that he'd inhaled at the sea floor was now expanding in his lungs as he neared the surface.

The glimmering surface light grew nearer; about forty feet away.

Twenty feet...

Ten.

I've got this!

John broke the waterline gasping like mad in the pouring rain. Kate surfaced behind him and he pushed her up to the rock. Kate rolled onto the top of Devil's Claw. The rock was about thirty-five feet wide with the metal framework of the light tower protruding up from its center. John climbed up behind Kate. As she lay gasping before him, he said, "Told you we'd make it." He gulped a breath. "The creature didn't even see—"

The look on Kate's face told John he'd spoken too soon. He ducked just as the giant jaws slammed shut above him in a flair of lightning. The enormous surge of water from the rising beast washed them across the rock, plummeting toward the opposite side. John wedged his bare feet against a rock and latched onto Kate's arm just before she went over the ledge and back into the sea.

Pulling Kate back up securely onto the rock, John collapsed onto his knees, catching his breath in the rain. "Just a little too close." Kate ignored him; she was looking up—way up. Following her gaze, he saw the creature bursting from the sea—rising higher and higher until more than half of its body hung suspended above the waves.

"No," Kate whimpered. "It can't do that."

John's eyes turned back to the rock. He saw where the metal base of the light tower was embedded into the stone. "Hurry," he shouted. "Grab onto the frame of the light tower."

Scurrying across the slippery rock, the two latched onto the railing just as the colossus hit the sea, sending up a giant swell. "Hold on!" John shouted as a thirty-foot wall of water raced toward the rock. It exploded over the ledge, soaring high over their heads. Holding on with his legs and arms, John could hear and feel the metal tower bending and moaning beneath the weight of the massive swell.

After what seemed like an eternity spent under the gushing water, the huge wave finally passed. Slinging the wet hair from her eyes, Kate shouted, "It's trying to wash us back into the sea."

John swung his gaze to an explosion of water as the monster again erupted from the waves. Hurling its right forefin outward, the leviathan rolled in mid-air and crashed back into the sea right beside the rock.

This swell was even higher than the last one. Again, he fought to hang onto the metal frame until the rushing waters passed. After the second wave, John no longer had the will to look up. His only hope was to cling to the rail and his last breath.

Amid the swells, he searched for Kate, but could see little more than froth spraying between the railings. Eventually, the onslaught of pounding water stopped. The waves grew more shallow until he could again see the rock. The sounds of churning water faded and the sea settled around him.

Catching his breath, he saw Kate now sprawled on the rock with one arm loosely around the railing. *Thank God she's still there.* Releasing the rail, he slogged through the rain to help her. Kate tightened her grip and shouted, "Nooooo!"

John never saw it coming, but he heard it. A wall of white water slammed into his back, hurling him forward. Soaring beneath the water, he latched one hand onto a rail until the torrent broke his grip and sent him spinning across the rock. After the wave passed, John found himself lying flat on his back at the ledge of the rock. The open sea was just behind his head. Sitting up, he saw Kate panting beneath the frame.

And then everything went dark. John rolled away from the ledge as the massive head and neck rose, swaying above him. Missing John, the closed jaws slammed into the light tower. The top third of the tower collapsed, falling into the sea under the weight of the plunging head.

As the water retreated, John saw Kate shivering and clutching the fifteen feet of framework still embedded into the rock. He looked up. A remaining thirty-foot section of cable that was attached to the light was now dangling in the open air. He glanced down at the wet rock, then back up at the cable. "That's live." For a beat, the cable wavered in the air like a serpent under the spell of a snake charmer.

Then it started to fall.

John took off to catch the cable, knowing that if its live end hit the rocks, they were toast. Sliding to a stop, he caught the cable. Three feet from his hands, its severed end crackled and sparked in the rain.

"Oh, I've got a use for this," John shouted and pulled the cable taut. He ran to the edge of the rock, and as if on cue, the sea erupted before him. Seemingly in slow motion, the colossal head rose, turning in the pouring rain. Flairs of lightning danced off of its wet, jagged skin. The jaws stretched wider. John hurled the cable with all his might and dove onto the rock.

The jaws missed John.

The cable missed the jaws. But its crackling end fell, sliding down the pebbled throat in a shower of sparks until it hit the sea. The giant reeled back from the rock with a bellowing roar—the horrific sound transforming into bubbles as the jaws rolled back beneath the waves.

Kate ran to the edge of the rock and looked down, panting. "Did that kill it?"

John had his hands on his knees, catching his breath. "No," he said. "Probably just shook up it's senses a bit. But it might just keep it away."

Kate threw an arm around his neck and gave him a hard kiss on the cheek. "I'm definitely starting to see why my mother hired you. Just one question though?" she added. "What made you so sure that the electricity wouldn't crawl up the rock and zap your crazy tuchis?"

"Knew that the sea would diffuse the voltage…like a ground." He took a breath. "Just the same, we might want to back up a bit."

Then about thirty yards out, the giant head rushed up from the waves. John could feel the eyes lock on him as the beast stared at the rock for several seconds, and eventually rolled back into the surf. The tip of the jagged back breached the surface and grew steadily smaller as the leviathan headed further out to sea.

Kate put a hand on John's shoulder. "Don't worry," she said. "The *Nauticus II* can still track it. You'll get another chance." A beat later, she added. "You know, there is a bright spot in all this."

John stood fully in the torrential rain. "I *really* need to hear this."

"The transmitter inside the pliosaur . . . it's definitely working."

John just continued to stare out to sea until the distant shadow faded into the downpour.

~~~

Nemo headed down the stairwell, towards surveillance cabin of the *Nauticus II*. He was nearly out of his mind with anticipation. "I can't believe Paxton," growled Nemo. "He's forty-five minutes late."

Freddie tried to keep pace with the captain. "But we already have bait."

"But Paxton has the barrels of blood meal," Nemo said as his heels hammered the stairs. "We need that to lay down a strong scent."

"Maybe something happened," said Freddie.

"Maybe it did," Nemo muttered. "Maybe he alerted the Navy and they destroyed the beast. That's why he's not responding to our calls." They neared the doorway to the surveillance cabin. Stepping inside, he saw Nathan cradling the mike. Nathan turned to face them, his complexion was as flushed as if he'd seen a ghost.

"What is it?" grumbled the captain.

"That was Paxton . . ."

Nemo threw his hands out. "Well, is it a secret? Where is he?"

"Let's just say he has one hell of an excuse for being late."

~~~

From a hard bench seat in the cargo bay of the naval rescue helicopter, John handed Kate the SAT phone. "Thanks," she said. "Guess I'll call mother now…break the news to her."

"But you're okay," John said.

"Yes," Kate replied, punching numbers. "But her beloved tooth is still in the chopper at the sea floor. I barely have the heart to tell her."

"If she managed to retrieve it from a guarded military vehicle during a naval investigation, I'm sure she'll work out something." As the chopper took to the evening sky, John peered down through the doorway. Through the pouring rain, he saw the glistening summit of Devil's Claw growing smaller. Flickers of lightning reflected from the collapsed light tower as it leaned eerily into the sea. Waves crashing into the rocks sprayed up between the metal bars.

Lifting his gaze, John looked further out to sea to a pair of naval helicopters. As their beams of light scoured the darkening waters, he muttered to Kate, "You mentioned something about having another chopper."

Kate placed a hand on top of his. "Just maybe," she said, "the ship hasn't picked up another signal is because it's out of range. The creature is gone…headed back to whatever hell it came from."

John had no response. His eyes just remained fixed on the distant lights crawling over the evening sea.

~~~

Four hours later, and five miles southeast of Devil's Claw, Admiral Henderson peered down from the passenger's side window of the Agusta 109. After dispatching a chopper to pick up John and Kate, the lead helicopter and three others had scoured a twenty-mile radius around the creature's last known location. *Three hours and nothing.* They passed over the *Nauticus II*. Below, the spotlight played across the massive main deck and dropped back into the night sea. "If that cursed ship would just pick up another signal from the transmitter," he muttered.

Again, the pilot's voice rang in the admiral's headset. "What do you want to do, sir? Make one more pass before we head back in?" The admiral raised his gaze from a small boat below and nodded.

~~~

Kota looked up from the fishing boat's windshield to a roaring overhead. For a brief moment, the boat was bathed in a glaring light until the naval helicopter passed.

Awakened by the noise, Kolegwa rose angrily from the passenger's seat. "How long must we wait in this sea?" he blurted in his native tongue.

Kota grabbed him by the nape of the neck and turned his head toward the ship sprawled across the horizon. "Fool, can you not see it yet?" Kota snorted. Releasing the tribesman's throat, Kota studied the *Nauticus II.* "For it is as the prophecy foretold...all who interfere shall be delivered into our hands."

Kolegwa turned his attention to a second helicopter that approached from the west. "They try to stop Kuta Keb-la?"

As the naval helicopter's light played over the dark waters, Kota's lips curled into a wicked grin. "Nothing can stop Kuta Keb-la. For his reign has just begun."

Vengeance from the Deep - Book Two: Blood of the Necala is available from Amazon here.

ACKNOWLEDGMENTS

My special thanks to my editor Janet Fix for her keen eye, boundless energy, and enthusiasm for the project.

Also thanks to my friend Steve and his encouragement for this project from the very beginning, which helped push me through the challenging times.

Lastly, to my wife Danielle for her love and understanding, and for putting up with my endless hours on the computer and seeing to it that I managed to get some sleep throughout this process...and to my mom, the greatest mother on earth.

ABOUT RUSS ELLIOTT

Growing up in a small town near Lynchburg, Virginia, one of Russ's earliest memories is standing at the front of his first-grade class with his vast collection of dinosaur figures. One by one, he would explain in great detail the various characteristics of each creature to the class.

The seven-year-old's prehistoric presentation was so compelling that his teacher would then send him off to repeat it to every grade in the elementary school.

A move to Tampa, Florida, and nearly three decades later, Russ became an award-winning art director at a Palm Harbor advertising agency. Collecting over a dozen ADDY Awards for creative excellence (advertising's equivalent to the Grammy), Russ later became intrigued with fiction writing. An accomplished painter and sculptor, he found that writing offered something new. It was a medium that could be easily shared. A good sculpture, for example, could only be truly appreciated when viewed in person, where one could walk around it and experience it in its world of light and shadows—an experience that could not be captured in a photograph, therefore not easily shared. But writing offered him something more; it allowed him to sculpt an image in the reader's mind. Someone on the other side of the globe could read a scene and experience the images just as the artist had intended. Russ still considers himself a sculptor, though…only now, instead of clay and plaster, he uses words.

So nearly a decade ago, when one of the original "dinosaur kids" decided to pen his first set of novels, it was no surprise that his subject matter would be the greatest prehistoric predator that ever lived.

Other past and present hobbies include motocross and flat track racing, performance cars and competitive bodybuilding. In addition, Russ has two patents to his name. He created the art for his book covers and most of the images on his book's website:

www.VengeancefromtheDeep.com.

He now resides in Tampa, Florida, with his wife Danielle and his Doberman.

CHECK OUT OTHER GREAT DEEP SEA THRILLERS

MEGATOOTH
by Viktor Zarkov

When the death rate of sperm whales rises dramatically, a well-respected environmental activist puts together a ragtag team to hit the high seas to investigate the matter. They suspect that the deaths are due to poachers and they are all driven by a need for justice.

Elsewhere, an experimental government vessel is enhancing deep sea mining equipment. They see one of these dead whales up close and personal...and are fairly certain that it wasn't poachers that killed it.

Both of these teams are about to discover that poachers are the least of their worries. There is something hunting the whales...

Something big
Something prehistoric.
Something terrifying.
MEGATOOTH!

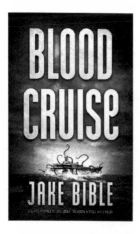

BLOOD CRUISE
by Jake Bible

Ben Clow's plans are set. Drop off kids, pick up girlfriend, head to the marina, and hop on best friend's cruiser for a weekend of fun at sea. But Ben's happy plans are about to be changed by a tentacled horror that lurks beneath the waves.

International crime lords! Deep cover black ops agents! A ravenous, bloodsucking monster! A storm of evil and danger conspire to turn Ben Clow's vacation from a fun ocean getaway into a nightmare of a Blood Cruise!

CHECK OUT OTHER GREAT
DEEP SEA THRILLERS

SEA RAPTOR
by John J. Rust

From terrorist hunter to monster hunter! Jack Rastun was a decorated U.S. Army Ranger, until an unfortunate incident forced him out of the service. He is soon hired by the Foundation for Undocumented Biological Investigation and given a new mission, to search for cryptids, creatures whose existence has not been proven by mainstream science. Teaming up with the daring and beautiful wildlife photographer Karen Thatcher, they must stop a sea monster's deadly rampage along the Jersey Shore. But that's not the only danger Rastun faces. A group of murderous animal smugglers also want the creature. Rastun must utilize every skill learned from years of fighting, otherwise, his first mission for the FUBI might very well be his last.

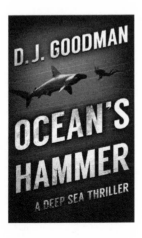

OCEAN'S HAMMER
by D.J. Goodman

Something strange is happening in the Sea of Cortez. Whales are beaching for no apparent reason and the local hammerhead shark population, previously believed to be fished to extinction, has suddenly reappeared. Marine biologists Maria Quintero and Kevin Hoyt have come to investigate with a television producer in tow, hoping to get footage that will land them a reality TV show. The plan is to have a stand-off against a notorious illegal shark-fishing captain and then go home.

Things are not going according to plan.

There is something new in the waters of the Sea of Cortez. Something smart. Something huge. Something that has its own plans for Quintero and Hoyt.

CHECK OUT OTHER GREAT DEEP SEA THRILLERS

THEY RISE
by Hunter Shea

Some call them ghost sharks, the oldest and strangest looking creatures in the sea.

Marine biologist Brad Whitley has studied chimaera fish all his life. He thought he knew everything about them. He was wrong. Warming ocean temperatures free legions of prehistoric chimaera fish from their methane ice suspended animation. Now, in a corner of the Bermuda Triangle, the ocean waters run red. The 400 million year old massive killing machines know no mercy, destroying everything in their path. It will take Whitley, his climatologist ex-wife and the entire US Navy to stop them in the bloodiest battle ever seen on the high seas.

SERPENTINE
by Barry Napier

Clarkton Lake is a picturesque vacation spot located in rural Virginia, great for fishing, skiing, and wasting summer days away.

But this summer, something is different. When butchered bodies are discovered in the water and along the muddy banks of Clarkton Lake, what starts out as a typical summer on the lake quickly turns into a nightmare.

This summer, something new lives in the lake...something that was born in the darkest depths of the ocean and accidentally brought to these typically peaceful waters.

It's getting bigger, it's getting smarter...and it's always hungry.

Made in the USA
Monee, IL
21 September 2020

43062428R00162